BRUMMIE ROAD

Ian Richards

January 2002

The King's gone, an this place'll never be the same.

Iss a cruel world what kills a mon fer dewin what he loves. Ay it? Iss a bloody cruel world what punishes ya fer bein a good mon. Fer bringin a lifetime a joy. Especially when theer's all sorts never done nuthin but hurt people. Ay that roit?

Thass why ah need ter see ya today. Ah need ter see ya here. Cos this is wheer it all started.

West Bromwich is a noisy town, a hard town, but today iss quiet. Shocked. The word spreads around: have yow heard abaht the King? Terrible news. Terrible. Because he was a good mon. Because he brought a lifetime a joy. Because he lived his life fer other people: his pranks an jokes, his smiles an songs, his goals up the Smethwick End an down the Brummie Road. He allwis celebrated wi the fans, allwis. Why? Because he loved us.

Because the King was human.

Ah'm human an all. Ah've med mistakes. Course I have. Thass why ah've asked yow here. Cos iss time ter set it straight. Iss time ter put things roit.

Look at that place: once it was nuthin but bare earth; a steep slope risin over an acre a hawthorn bushes. Bushes filled wi little brown song thrushes, the bird they call the throstle.

They built on that ground. They developed it. They threw up iron an brick, steel an concrete over the green land, gid it a new life, a new purpose.

An the people come, an the people med that place their own.

Ah was one a them people. An me time's nearly up. Ah went to the doctor a fortnight agew. The test results come back this week.

No, doe say nuthin. Let me finish. Ah need ter finish.

Me life's loike a jigsaw in front a me. Ah can see how the pieces fit together. How they shoulda fitted together. Iss a cruel world, an theer's all sorts never done nuthin but hurt people. The truth is that ah'm one a them.

Ah need ya ter listen. Please. Ah know ah doe deserve it, but ah've gorra tell someone. Ah've gorra tell someone how it all went wrong.

Am yow ready?

Part One

1964 – 1968

November 1964

– Am yow ready?

This is how it begins: in a terraced house, in an industrial town, in the heart of England. A sudden voice piercing the bathroom door; the hammering of knuckles on thin wood making Billy jump. He's been staring at his reflection in the mirror for so long that he's got lost in the trance of it. He isn't normally a lad for preening, not like Tommy and some of the proper mods, the real faces. But he's putting the effort in now. Today's the day. He's got to look the part.

The noisy interruption nearly makes him drop his precious bottle; as it is, he just manages to get a grip on the green glass before it slips through his fingers and smashes on the orange lino. He angles the mirror again to get his reflection just right, smooths down his tangled brown hair – sweeping his fingers across to give it a passable side-parting – and then starts fiddling with the top on the bottle.

– Billy! Ah know yome in theer. Come on!

Billy ignores him. Today's going to be the best day of his life – he decided that at 9.37 this morning – and he's not going to let Cartwright rush him, push him around or arse things up. Today's about growing up. Becoming a man.

Alright, fair enough; for the last three hours it's been the average Saturday. The best thing that's happened so far is Dad making him breakfast for the first time in weeks; burnt mushrooms on charred toast. But now it's one o'clock, and he's locked in the bathroom with a small green bottle. This is it. This is where the fun starts.

He unscrews the bottle-cap and has a sniff. He nearly retches. It's strong stuff; strong enough that he has to take a deep breath before pouring it out.

– Hurry up! What am ya playin at in theer, ya pie-can?

There. A little puddle of clear, watery liquid in his palm. Billy takes a more cautious sniff. It doesn't smell so bad from a distance.

The only problem now is working out what to do with it.

The label's no help. It says PERFUME FOR MEN – as if that's the most normal thing in the world – then follows up with a casual *Splash It All Over*. Splash it all over! Over where?

Christ on a bloody scooter.

A month or two back, he heard Tommy talking about how this stuff drives the girls wild. Tommy knows what he's on about. Two Cartwright brothers, and somehow Billy ended up mates with the wrong one. Born two or three years earlier, he'd have been old enough to knock around with Tom and the other mods, be one of the faces, dragging wenches round in his thrall. But five months past his fifteenth birthday, he's stuck with the lesser Cartwright brother for company. As if that point needs prodding home, there's a series of thuds at the bottom of the bathroom door as the most disappointing son of clan Cartwright starts rapping his toes against the pine.

– If yome *manipulatin* yerself, ah'm gunna tell the whole street! Yer nickname's gunna be Billy the Fiddler! Purrit back in yer pants an get yer arse out here!

He's the most annoying bugger in the free world, but Cartwright the Younger's got a point; time's ticking on. Billy's squirrelled away money from his paper round for weeks to put towards this; he's begged and borrowed from Dad, he's even dug out the odd tanner that's dropped behind the settee. It's now or never. He brings his cupped hand up to his face, and rubs the stuff into his cheeks; first the left, then the right. Then he lifts the bottle up over his head and shakes a good quarter of it into his hair and down his forehead, letting streams of it dribble down his jaw.

He puts the cap back on the bottle and places it on the wooden shelf by the mirror, next to a half-squeezed tube of Pepsodent. One last look in the mirror – his face is good and shiny with the perfume, and he reckons no wench in her right mind can say no to him – and he smooths out his collar, adjusts the knot of his black tie, checks the creases on his trousers, and flings open the battered bathroom door.

Cartwright's stood on the landing, hands in pockets. He's staring at Billy with eyes like a lobotomised dog.

– What the bloody hell have yow bin up tew? I thought ah'd atta ring the fire brigade an... hang on. Woss that smell?

– What smell?

Cartwright shakes his head. He's wearing that green fishtail parka he loves, the one Tommy passed on to him after outgrowing it, and the hood at the back shifts from side to side with the motion.

– Doe "what smell" me! Yow stink wuss than Tommy does! Yome wearin that soddin perfume, ay ya?

Billy can't keep the triumphant grin off his face.

– S'perfume fer men.

– Oh ar.

– It ay juss Tommy. All the mods am wearin it.

– Oh, course they am. But yow ay a mod, am ya?

– Nor am yow!

– I ay the one wearin perfume, though, matey.

A year or so ago – back when he'd never dreamed of calling himself a mod; when no-one was too cool to buy a Beatles 45, when girls were for staring at instead of fighting over – Billy started drawing a mark in the back of his maths book every time he had an argument like this with Cartwright. He filled the inside back cover in days, and filled the page facing it within a fortnight. Eventually the little black marks devoured his history and geography books too, until he gave up on the daily embuggerance of counting them. The arguments still happen, though. Arguing with Johnny Cartwright's like playing keepy-uppy with your football: there's no way to win, and no real point in doing it, but it doesn't half pass the time.

    – Yow gunna spend all day playin yer face at me, or am we off ter the match?

    – Awfully sorry, Yer Royal Poofness.

    – Piss off!

    – Hey, ya sure ya doe want ter stick some a yer mom's owd jewellery on, fore we gew?

    Bang. There it comes, crashing down like a lumphammer on Billy's chest. It smashes the breath right out of him. Cartwright realises a second too late what he's gone and said – Billy can see it on his face – but by that time, Billy already wants to run into the bathroom, grab that bloody bottle and smash it over the thick bastard's head. Right over his head.

    Cartwright holds his hands up, his face guilt-stamped.

    – Ah'm really sorry, mate. Honest. Ah never meant nuthin bad by that. Me stupid gob: iss allwis bin quicker than me brain, ay it?

    He smiles weakly, trying to ease his way off the hook. Billy can't believe the brass neck on him. Cartwright should know better than anyone not to mention mothers; not in Billy's house, not round Cartwright's, not anywhere. Why else did they become mates in the first place?

    – Look, ah'm a dickhead, ay I? Ah cor see fer the dick on me yed, ah cor. Look at it, floppin abaht!

    He's running up and down the narrow landing now, dangling his raised forearm from his face to mime the cock growing out of his empty skull. For a second, clowning around, it looks like he might trip up and plummet down the stairs, and that idea puts a smile back on Billy's face.

    The moment passes. Cartwright's safe and sound, and Billy's still smiling. Just about.

    – Does it tell ya which direction ter gew, that big prick on yer head?

    Cartwright's grinning now. He knows he's been forgiven. Just.

    – Ar, it guz all hard when I ask it the way. Here, look. COCK! TEK WE TER THE MATCH!

    Cartwright stiffens his arm, pointing it in a straight line from his forehead to the staircase. He goes charging off down the landing.

Friday nights are for music, Saturday afternoons for football. That's how it is; this week, every week.

The weekend starts here: Ready Steady Go on ATV of a Friday is the one hour Billy gets the TV to himself, with Dad off down the boozer pouring a gallon of mild down his neck. The thick glass screen with its array of plastic knobs and dials brings him all the sounds coming out of Liverpool, out of London, even over from America. In fact, Billy bought his first 45 – *Gonna Make Him Mine* by The Orchids – because he saw them play it on the programme.

Then Cartwright came round one Saturday, saw the record, spent the rest of the day calling him a poof and finally vowed to teach him the difference between good music and girly shite at all costs.

So along came the mod race; not as dangerous as the arms race or the space race, but just as bloody expensive. Tommy's wage packets from the repair shop were giving him enough (even after tax and union dues) to buy some of the really hip new black music from the States, and the most fashionable togs he could lay his hands on. As Tommy's little brother, Cartwright started to inherit the hand-me-downs and soul records and think he was God's gift. Whatever else they might have in common, Billy couldn't let him get away with that. These days, with only his paper round for income, and Dad struggling for steady work – struggling in general since what happened to Mom – he can't afford to get all the stylish clothes, so he has to concentrate on knowing his music inside out. It's the only way he can stay one step ahead of Cartwright.

He doesn't need a better reason.

In spite of the arguments and piss-takes, the mod race gives Billy something extra in common with Cartwright. Most of the lads round Dudley, Tipton and West Bromwich are into the rocker scene, and there's nothing like having some jumble-sale Jerry Lee Lewis calling them a pair of queers to encourage a bit of solidarity. At times like that, it doesn't even matter which of them looks the part. Fact is, neither of them has hopped on a scooter and powered off into Birmingham of a weekend to join the chrome flock zooming around the city's new road system. They've never gone down to Stourport – where the local rockers meet up – for a spot of aggro on the bridge, the chance to chuck a greaser in the Severn, rinse the Brylcreem out his quiff. At best, they're a cut above the pie-cans who spend Saturday nights jumping around dancefloors to the Joe Loss Orchestra.

Still, every weekend it's the same routine: football and music. But there's a missing ingredient, and Billy knows it; just one more thing that'll complete the picture, change his life for good.

Today, he's going to do something about it.

Today, he's going to ask her out.

– We'm gunna be late. Less gerra move on.

Cartwright traipses down the stairs with Billy behind him, their shoes leaving pale prints in the dust which covers the old wood. The floorboards creak with every step. Weak sunlight shines through the small glass pane above the front door, teasing dull colours out of the podged rug in the hall.

– Come on then, Perfume Boy, fore we miss the bus.

– Aroit, aroit! Christ on a scooter!

– Doe keep sayin that, Billy. It gets on me nerves.

– Ar. Ah know it does.

Billy takes his overcoat down off the hook on the wall, and feels around the inside pocket for the team card in there, before thrusting his arms into the warm wool.

– Ah'll juss let Dad know we'm off. Gew on out if ya want.

Billy opens the door to the front room cautiously as Cartwright slips out into the street, and a wave of heat billows out to meet the sudden cold from outside. There must be a weekend's worth of coal piled into the grate, glowing angrily. The room's a furnace; the curtains are drawn, and the only light is the flickering greyness of Grandstand on the telly.

Dad's in his armchair. Of course he is. These days, he only seems to get out of it to cobble a makeshift meal together or head down the George for a few jars. He's wearing a pair of old grey trousers and a white vest, his head slumped to one side, sweat on his skin.

Billy eases his body into the oven-like room.

– We'm gewin up the match, Dad.

– Who'm they playin?

– Um… ah cor remember.

They're playing Blackpool, but Billy doesn't feel like saying so. It'll set Dad off talking about the '48 cup final, and how footballers nowadays can't hold a candle to the lads that played back then. A few years back, Billy would have listened patiently to a speech like that, and might even have accepted Dad's opinion that modern football players are useless, society's going to the dogs and Billy's entire generation are a bunch of ungrateful little bastards. He'd have believed that stuff back in the days when he used to go to the Hawthorns with Dad rather than

~ 13 ~

Cartwright. But those days are gone; long gone. It's been two years now since Billy first decided to go with Cartwright. The Saturday that Billy told Dad he was off to the match with a mate that week, Dad just nodded his head and said he'd leave it for this week.

Ever since, from one Saturday to the next, it's been the armchair, a bottle of mild and Grandstand.

– Doe forget yer scarf.

Billy's blue and white scarf's already wrapped around his neck. He pulls it a bit tighter. It gives his hands something to do.

– Ta-ra then, Dad.

He nips out through the door, feeling the warmth ebb from his bones with every step.

The bus stop's halfway down the hill, just where the road dips away to a steeper slope and the view to the south-east opens up: houses snaking across the landscape in dark brick rows, sooty fingers of smoke rising from chimney-pots, melting away into charcoal clouds. The chimney-stacks of the factories are tall against the horizon, like scoring pegs in a domino board. While they wait for the bus, Billy picks out the Hawthorns floodlights in the sprawl, dwarfed by the pillars of industry all around them.

A few minutes pass before the number 74 roars over the crest of the hill, a cream and dark blue double-decker with the West Bromwich Corporation logo painted below the bottom deck windows and an advert for Cammies & Cadman barbershop pasted up above them. Cartwright and Billy both stick their arms out, and as the bus slows, the conductor leans out the back, his navy blue uniform well-starched. He looks the pair of them up and down.

– The Hawthorns?

Billy nods, and Cartwright gives the conductor the thumbs-up. The vehicle comes to a halt, engine humming.

– Hop on, lads. Yome in good company today.

There are boys all along the top deck, blue and white scarves pressed to the windows, shouting *COME ON YOU BAGGIES* against the cold glass. Billy grins, grabs the icy metal pole to hoist himself on board, and fishes in his pocket for the shilling fare. Cartwright boards behind him. They head up the curling steps to the smoky den of the upper deck, and plonk themselves in the seats up front. Billy moves himself up by the window, while Cartwright puts his legs up and rests his polished shoes on the faded NO SPITTING sign.

The gears grind down below, and with a lurch, the 74 pulls away down the hill.

– Gorr'enny fags?
– Ar.
– What ya got?
– Packet a Park Drives.
– Can I ha one?
– Nah.
– Gew on.
– Nah.
– Come on, Cartwright. Doe be a rotter. Ah borrered yow that Parade magazine. The one wi Eve Eden in the middle pages.
– It was much appreciated.
– An I ay had it back, neither.
– No. Well. Ah'm pursuin summat special wi Miss Eden, ay I. We'm seein one another hexclusively now, we am.
– Juss gi us a smoke, ya selfish bastard!
– Aroit then! Jesus! Ah'm just a fountain a tobacker, me, ay I?
Cartwright holds a Parker out for Billy, and pulls a match from a little box of Swans. He lights his own smoke first – Cartwright down to the bloody ground – and after some match-to-mouth manoeuvring, manages to spark Billy's up too. The bus trundles its way into West Bromwich – the Black Lake gas tanks on the horizon a sure sign they're getting close – and Billy blows a grey cloud onto the window to cover the houses, factories and shops in an extra layer of mist. The cigarette does its job, calming the storm in his belly. They're a proper man's smokes, Parkers. Miles better than those doo-dahs with filters on the ends; saft little things like that will do for women and kids, but on a matchday, you need something to really get you going.
He puffs away quietly for a while, having a good cough every now and then, and it's nice to have a bit of peace from Cartwright's babble, even though the rest of the lads on the top deck are shouting their heads off. Every few minutes the bus stops, and a fresh set of boys pile on, heading straight upstairs, filling the spaces around Billy and Cartwright. There are plenty of insults flying around – Billy sticks two fingers up at this one lad asking why he stinks like a French brothel – and a fair bit of yelling right at the back of the deck, but no one giving out any serious grief. All the stuff that lads normally fight over – mods versus rockers, different towns and streets against each other – gets shelved of a Saturday as soon as the blue and white scarf goes round your neck.

One kid's got a little tranny – a Regency from the look of it – which he tunes into Radio Luxembourg for a bit of music, and within a minute, with Ray Davies's voice crackling through the speaker, there's a singalong on the go. They sing about wanting to be with a girl in the daytime. They sing about wanting to be with a girl all of the time. Billy joins in, shivering as he belts out the words. He wonders if any of the other lads have got a special girl in their mind as they sing it. They must do; you have to if you're going to sing it with proper feeling.

He's thinking about that bus stop near the ground. He's thinking about her.

Cartwright joins in between lungfuls of smoke, while Billy stubs out his fag in the O of the NO SPITTING sign. He glances at Cartwright before they hit the chorus, and they're both grinning.

Saturday afternoon. Football and music. Nothing beats it.

There's something so simple, so instinctive, so satisfying about being able to get together with other people in one place and sing, dance, clap your hands to a beat. A scruffy lad in specs sitting on the back seat jumps up as the guitar solo wails out of the little transistor set and starts spinning round in the aisle, stamping his shiny black shoes against the hard deck, strutting like Chuck Berry towards the front. Billy watches over his shoulder, laughing so hard that it sets him off coughing all over again, spicing his tongue with the taste of Park Drives.

The bus zooms on through Dartmouth Square, past Broadhead's and the clock on the right, with the newspaper seller perched in his wheelchair just beneath it, and then they're onto the Birmingham Road, past the old garages, with Dartmouth Park on the left; seeing that wide stretch of green gets Billy going, knowing they're so close to the ground. The vehicle slows down as it reaches their stop. The conductor pipes up from down below.

– Birmingham Road! All off fer the Hawthorns!

The rush for the stairs is mad, so many shoes drumming against the floor all at once, and the conductor has to shift quickly to dodge the stampede. Scarves whirl and flail in the tight space, and Billy gets a mouthful of wool more than once on his way out, but after a minute or two of jostling – and a few headshakes and curses from the conductor – they're all off the bus and out into the open air.

The noise of the matchday crowd's a welcome chaos in Billy's ears as they step onto the pavement opposite the ground, just by the transport café. There are hundreds, thousands shuffling along the Birmingham Road through sparse traffic, the flood swelled by folks coming along Halfords Lane from the Hawthorns Halt railway station, a colourful mix of blokes wearing hats and flat caps, and eager kids with necks hugged by their homemade blue and white scarves. No one can get hold of navy blue wool for love nor money, so an army of mothers have done their best with whatever they can find. No two scarves are exactly alike. They vary in pattern, length and colour, knitted over a few days to last for years, and each one's a personal treasure; its warming touch a reminder of the hands that crafted it. Billy reaches up and tightens his own again, feeling the holes forming between the loops.

Lively voices clamour all around, accents as subtly distinct from one another as shades of blue wool: they've come from all over the Black Country, on the buses, on the trains, on foot, and a lucky few in cars: from Dudley and Brierley Hill, Oldbury and Cradley Heath, Tipton and Wednesbury, Rowley Regis, Smethwick, Blackheath, West Bromwich itself. And from Birmingham too: from Bearwood, Ladywood, Hockley, Perry Barr, Handsworth. It's a sudden rush of life at the heart of the nation.

Billy moves into the stream of people on the pavement, with Cartwright just behind. A couple of mounted policemen ahead sit perched above the crowd – one on a bay horse, the other on a nervous grey which twitches its ears and tosses its head – and move slowly against the tide. Billy feels a sudden sharp pain in his elbow, and turns to see a small lad on his left spinning an old rattle a bit too enthusiastically. His dad, a tall bloke in a grey mac and flat cap, is holding his hand tightly. He looks across at Billy.

– Did he catch yow wi that rattle, mate? Matthew! Leave it till we'm in the ground!

– Iss aroit, mate. Is it his fust time?

The bloke nods, and Billy looks down at Matthew's face. His nose is running and his eyes are wide, half-excited, half-terrified beneath his bobble-hat. Billy grins, and leans down to whisper to the little lad.

– Doe worry! Yow'll love it, bab!

Matthew's dad claps Billy on the back with a smile and a shout – *hey, we'll demolish em today, mucka!* – and takes his son off across the road towards the Halfords Lane Stand.

And Billy looks up at the Hawthorns, at the round barrel roof over the stand on the Birmingham Road. The iron and the brick, the steel and the concrete he first saw ten years ago, holding his dad's hand and spinning a rattle of his own.

Half-excited and half-terrified. But there was nothing for him to be afraid of inside those four stands. It's the rest of the world which is a huge, deafening, cruel place. Not here. This is where Billy comes to be away from everything else, just for a couple of hours.

His refuge.

– Am we dewin the usual?

– Ar, may as well.

They traipse round the corner of the Woodman pub to the Handsworth Side, skirting round the gates for adult supporters and heading for the juniors' queue, along with every other fifteen and sixteen-year-old. All you have to do is stoop an inch or two lower and put on a squeaky voice to pass for fourteen, and you're in for half-whack. Cartwright fiddles to get the wrapper off a Mint Cracknel bar as they bend their knees and walk through the gate. Billy nods to the ticket bloke sitting behind his metal grille.

– Gewin ter the match am we, sir?

He says the same thing week in, week out. Every time Billy feels like answering *no, we'm off ter Dudley Zoo, mate*. But the fella always says it with a smile, so Billy does his best to give him a polite reply as he hands over his four bob.

– Ar, juss the one please.

The grasshopper-clacking of the turnstile shepherds him on into the stand, and he's hit by the sudden smell of pipesmoke as he makes his way down the rows of brightly painted wooden seats towards the terraces below. The littluns are down the front, perched on the concrete wall by the touchline with their rattles whirring; a couple of bobbies stand on the pitch in front of them in their thick black uniforms, having a laugh and a joke; the older blokes sit on the garish rows above, holding packets of ready-rubbed shag like personal mascots. Here and there in the pre-match chatter, round Lancashire vowels stand out from the Black Country lilt where little knots of Blackpool fans are mingling with Albion supporters. Billy carries on down the steps to the terraced section of the stand, with Cartwright behind him.

They get a decent spot about a third of the way up the terrace, just to the right of the halfway line, with plenty of space all around; the only other soul in spitting distance is a middle-aged fella in a raincoat to their left. He's wearing a little cardboard hat which says JIMMY HAGAN FOR PRIME MINISTER in blue and white letters – they were free in a local paper before the election last month – and cradling a pipe between gloved fingers. He turns and nods hello at Billy, as Cartwright starts making odd noises next to him.

– Mmmmhh.

– Ya what?

– Hhhmhh.

– Wish yow'd gi that bloomin Mint Cracknel a rest. What am ya tryin to say?

– Ah juss cut me tongue open on the mint.

– Serves ya bloody right. Why'd ya buy it? Iss broken glass in a sweet wrapper, that stuff.

– Iss tradition though, ay it? We allwis win when I have a bar a Mint Cracknel comin inter the ground.

– No we doe! Ya did it back in September, an we lost two on the bounce!

– Ar, but thass onny cos ah took the wrapper off wrong. Theer's a trick tew it. Ya need ter peel it without tearin fer it ter work. See, ah managed it at the Wolves match, an what happened? We won 5-1.

– An that onny happened because yow took a wrapper off a chocolate bar a bit funny.

– Not juss cos a that. Ah did wear me special socks an all.

– Hang abaht; what's gewin on up theer?

To their right, there's movement and noise in the stand that backs onto the Birmingham Road. It's a dwarf compared to the Handsworth Side – just a few dozen rows of terraces separated halfway up by a walkway – but in its lower section, near the pitch, Billy can make out a group causing some kind of disturbance. All around the ground, heads turn to see what's happening.

It's difficult to hear at first, above the rattle-whirring from the kids down by the touchline and the chatter of the adults. But the noise grows. And grows.

Clapping. Shouting. A familiar rhythm – The Routers' song *Let's Go*, the one which gets played on Radio Luxembourg all the time – except the crowd gathered behind the goal have changed the two words after the quickfire claps:

> *Clap, clap, clap-clap-clap, clap-clap-clap-clap–*
> *WEST BROM!*
> *Clap, clap, clap-clap-clap, clap-clap-clap-clap–*
> *WEST BROM!*

Cartwright stares.

– Iss a choir. Christ almighty, iss a bloody Kop choir!

For once, Cartwright's spot on. It's a bloody Kop choir.

A home end.

People singing. People chanting. Not at a concert, not at a Saturday night dance, not at a church service: at a *football match*.

– Cartwright, mate, we've gorra get up theer. Cartwright?

Billy turns round to discover that Cartwright isn't even standing next to him anymore. He's off, tearing away like a madman for the north side of the ground, tripping over his own shoes.

– Oh, Christ on a scooter! Wait fer me!

Billy takes off after him, racing straight over to that stunted stand on the Birmingham Road.

It's a short and shallow climb up the bank of railway sleepers at the back of the northern stand, and they aren't the only ones making it. Dozens of lads their age and older are rushing up the makeshift steps, the soles of their shoes drumming a beat against the wood better than anything on Top of the Pops. The singing, shouting, and chanting swell as they near the top, cascading over the lip of the terraces and out onto the wet Hawthorns pitch.

Billy reaches the face of the stand a couple of seconds before Cartwright, who's puffing and wheezing a few steps below him. It's odd seeing the ground from a different angle, but that's nothing compared to seeing and hearing the choir close-up for the first time: it's madness down on the lower terrace, new arrivals jostling to find space among the press of bodies so that they can join in with the songs. Every word of every chant the choir belts out sends a pale cloud of breath to hang over their heads, creating a low-level fog beneath the girders and stanchions of the roof. Angry glances go around some of the older heads on the upper terrace, exasperated remarks like *iss gerrin loike a bloody circus in here*, and the usual *kids today*, but as soon as a new song begins, all the dissent gets drowned out. They race down the steps, and it only takes a few moments for Cartwright to reach Billy's shoulder, coughing and spluttering, just as the choir start up again.

AL-BI-ON, AL-BI-ON, AL-BI-ON!

Billy remembers seeing newsreels of the last World Cup at the cinema a couple of years back, with all these South Americans clapping and shouting *BRA-SIL* as Pele and Garrincha lifted the trophy. It all seemed so foreign, so exotic; nobody in England would have made an exhibition of themselves like that. If you wanted to make some noise at a match in Britain, you spun your rattle, you shouted encouragement to your favourite player, you cheered when your team found the net. Music had no place in football.

But in the last couple of months, he's heard about Everton fans singing their team's name during matches, and Bristol Rovers supporters singing *Goodnight Irene* from the stands, and the Spion Kop at Anfield bellowing out that Pacemakers song, the one which was in Carousel. Music's slowly leaking from Friday nights into Saturday afternoons. It's happening all over the country.

It's happening here: at the Albion, up the Birmingham Road End. A generation raised to a rock and roll beat, bringing their sound onto the terraces.

– Amazin, ay it?

Billy glances across at Cartwright and sees a face flushed with cold, excitement, exertion. He's grinning like a maniac.

AL-BI-ON, AL-BI-ON, AL-BI-ON!

They push into the crowd, picking the gaps between blokes to work their way down the packed terrace into the thick of the choir. Once they're about half a dozen rows down, the crush of fans takes them and carries them along in its currents. The press of bodies forces the breath out of Billy, squeezes his ribs till he's sure they'll crack like twigs, and it takes a few seconds to get a gasp of air back in, like coming up to the surface after a dip down the swimming baths. He manages to find his feet again a few steps up from a crush barrier, sandwiched between two bigger lads, with Cartwright just behind him. One of the big lads turns round as Billy jostles his arm.

He's a year or two older than them, with a Ringo Starr haircut and a set of teeth more crooked than Dudley Castle. He shakes their hands as if they're his oldest pals.

– Aroit lads, ah'm Bricey. How's yer singin?

– Um… iss okay, ah spose.

– Hey, woss that smell?

Billy feels his face go hot.

– Iss nuthin.

Cartwright jerks a thumb at him.

– He's wearin perfume.

Bricey stares at Billy for a few heartbeats, then shakes his head in disbelief.

– Well, as long as ya mek some cowin noise, mate, no one'll care what ya gerrup tew in yer spare time.

– No! No! Iss perfume fer men! It ay nuthin funny! Iss fer *men*! Cartwright, ah'm gunna kill ya!

Billy's drowned out by a voice further back up the terrace yelling a command to the whole choir.

– Lads, we'm dewin *Oh When The Stripes*! New boys, foller our lead! *Gi it some ommer!*

Their view of the pitch is suddenly framed by hundreds of arms in the air, hands clapping a simple rhythm, and voices all around them launching into a new number. Cartwright and Billy mime along for the first couple of lines, clapping their hands with all the others, until they pick up the words.

OH WHEN THE STRIPES! GEW MARCHIN IN! OH WHEN THE STRIPES, GEW, MARCH-IN IN!

Within the space of a minute, they're hollering their lungs out as if they've been doing it for years.

AH WANT TER BEEE IN THAT NUMBER, WHEN THE STRIPES, GEW, MARCH-IN IN!

Halfway through the second verse, the team runs out onto the field, with the tannoy playing the usual old scratched Sousa recording, *Stars and Stripes Forever*. Bobby Cram's bouncing the ball on the pitch in front of him; Clive Clark rolls his socks down to let the Blackpool full-backs see his pale shins – the cuts and bruises he got off the Sheffield Wednesday defence last Saturday have healed just in time to be replaced with a crop of new ones – and in the centre circle, Bobby Hope runs his hands down the blue and white stripes on the front of his shirt. Tony Waiters, the Blackpool keeper, runs towards their stand their brand new home end – and takes up his position in goal as the song fades away into a round of applause that echoes the traffic driving down the Birmingham Road behind them. The junior sports reporters from the newspapers park their arses on the grass just shy of the byline, pull their notepads out of their coats and lick the tips of their pens. In the centre circle, the referee leans over, draws up his black socks until their white tops perch just below his knees, and then takes a tuppence from his pocket.

Graham Williams shakes hands with Jimmy Armfield, Blackpool's captain, and the referee tosses the coin.

It's a frustrating match – they often are for Albion, these days – but that doesn't even matter. For the first time since he started coming to the football, the experience of being in the crowd is more important to Billy than what happens on the pitch. The songs and chants flood the air constantly, with the chatter of old rattles laying down a rhythm, and this section of the ground becomes theirs, all theirs.

It takes a quarter of an hour for the flood of recruits into the Brummie Road choir to dwindle, and by that point Albion are already 1-0 up. They've taken over a whole corner of the stand, two or three hundred of them, and in response to their enthusiasm, the team launch a series of energetic attacks on the goal in front of them right from kick-off. After eight minutes, Clark plays the ball out to Jeff Astle who's moved into a right-wing position, and Astle thumps a cross into the box which John Kaye heads past Waiters into the net.

For a moment they're stunned. And then all hell breaks loose. Everyone at the back of the choir leans forward on tiptoes, putting their weight on the shoulders of the lads in front, and as those lads lean forward too it sets off a domino-chain surge down the terraces, everyone being shoved forward in a stampede down the steps toward the little concrete wall at the bottom of the stand, cheering and waving their arms in the air. Kaye turns to the stand and grins at them all before returning to the Albion half, and that's enough to set them off all over again.

AL-BI-ON, AL-BI-ON, AL-BI-ON!

It's nearly 2-0 within a minute, as Astle plays in Bobby Hope, and Hope chips a ball up which Clark heads just wide of the post. They sing all the louder, and to cries of *GEW ON SAMMY* and *YOW SHOW EM*, the biggest lad in the choir even climbs up onto a crush barrier, balancing his feet on it and grabbing hold of one of the pillars supporting the roof. Swinging off the pillar, Sammy uses his free arm to conduct the rest of them below. They're packed in tight, holding their precious blue and white scarves in the air during the songs until their arms ache and hands go numb. As Clark skims the top of the crossbar with another chance, one lad pulls fistfuls of shredded newspaper from his pockets and throws it into the air to rain down over their heads. Between songs, they laugh and joke with one another and shout encouragement to the players, standing on tiptoes to get an extra inch's view over the heads in front, leaning forward again and getting carried by the surge whenever the team has a sniff of goal, cosseted by the warmth of other bodies and heady Bovril reek of the stand.

Inevitably, Cartwright stops singing every few minutes to shout out a few of his typically disastrous predictions about the match.

– Look, Geoff Carter's through on goal! He's gunna score! HE'S GORRA SCORE!

– Armfield's tackled him, Cartwright.

– S'aroit. We've got a corner. Kaye'll nod this un right in. Juss watch.

Billy watches through a curtain of drizzle as Kaye meets the corner and volleys it over the bar.

– Look, we'm all over this lot. We'll ha that second goal soon, juss watch.

Bricey and the other choir members around them, who've got less experience of Cartwright – and haven't built up the same threshold of patience with him that Billy's perfected – don't react well to this commentary. It takes about half an hour before Bricey finally has a word.

– Will yow shurrup about the match? Yome a bloody Jonah, yow am.

– Nah. Me name's Cartwright. Any road, Bobby Cram's gunna score from this free-kick. Juss watch.

– He's gone an spooned it, look. Yome a Jonah. A bloody curse.

– Keep the faith! This one's a home win all the way. Got two points writ all over it.

– Shurrup an sing, Jonah, ya saft bastard.

In the second half, they watch as all of Albion's early vigour comes back to haunt them, and so many energy-starved legs seem to sink into the turf. They watch as Gerry Howshall and Terry Simpson, their wing-halves, fall deeper and deeper to try and contain the Blackpool wide men; the entire team drops back with them to defend the goal in front of the Birmingham Road End, desperately protecting their 1-0 lead. They watch and they sing, hoping to coax that last bit of fight from the players. They work their way through all the songs they can think of, all the ones the choir leaders like Sammy and Steve decide on, as Graham Oates crosses for Blackpool, Ray Charnley heads it into the Albion goalmouth, and Graham Rowe equalises.

They go through their repertoire all over again as Albion force their heavy legs forward to try and retake the lead, only for Chippy Clark to shoot agonisingly over the bar. When Alan Ball tucks home a close-range shot from a corner to put Blackpool 2-1 up, they switch to the songs they all know from the pop charts, the ones they've watched on Ready Steady Go the last few Friday nights and heard on Radio Luxembourg whenever they've tuned in. As Ball scores again four minutes from time to seal a 3-1 win for Blackpool, they're lost in a non-stop medley of the Drifters, Manfred Mann, the Kinks, Gerry and the Pacemakers, the Dave Clark Five, Wayne Fontana and the Mindbenders, the Zombies, the Hollies and the Animals.

The referee blows the full-time whistle during the second verse of *Oh Pretty Woman*, and with their shredded voices, Billy and Cartwright and the rest of the choir cheer the team's efforts over the last couple of hours. And to Billy's surprise, the players turn towards the Birmingham Road stand, and with smiles on their tired faces, applaud them back.

Bricey turns to the pair of them as the crowd starts the slow process of filing out, and croaks to them with what's left of his voice.

– Two weeks' time. Arsenal match.

Cartwright stares dumbly at him.

– Yam dewin this again?

Bricey laughs.

– Mate, we'm gunna do it as long as it teks. We'll do it till we *win*.

Night's approaching the way it always does around this time of year; swept in on a tide of mist and chimney-smoke, with a chill which scorches the lungs. And the day's still not done; in all the excitement of the match and the new Brummie Road choir, it almost slipped Billy's mind that there's something else to do today. Something far more important than football.

It's time to go and see her.

With the musical roar of the terraces still ringing in his head and fans trudging home all around – grumbling into the dusk with scarves pulled tight, ripping useless pools coupons into confetti – he stands next to Cartwright on the street, alongside the row of buses parked at the back of the stand, the dusk perfumed with the stink of diesel.

Cartwright points a thumb towards the Halfords Lane.

– Ya comin inter the club shop?

Billy shakes his head.

– Nah mate, ah'll atta leave ya to it. Got summat ter do. Ah'll see ya on Monday though, aroit?

Cartwright groans.

– Oh, not this again. Not the bus stop. Ya must be jokin. Will ya juss give up?

– Ah juss want ter see if her's theer.

– An if her is, what then? It ay like yow'll say nuthin to her. Ya never do. Three whole bloomin months of standin at that bus stop wi her, every other Saturday, an yow ay said a single word.

– Ah'm waitin fer the right time, ay I? Ya cor rush things like this.

– Cor rush things? Three bloody months! We'll be livin on the moon by the time ya get round ter sayin "hello".

– Oh, shut yer arse an gi yer mouth a chance.

Billy turns away and starts walking. Cartwright calls after him.

– Good luck! Gi her one fer me in fifteen years, eh?

At first he thinks she isn't there. When he catches a glimpse of the bus stop through the fine mist of sleet and the matchday crowd, he can't see her amongst the figures huddled around the metal sign. His stomach feels crushed, like some big centre-half's stuck an elbow in. He's run halfway to Smethwick just to get there on time, same as he's been doing since the summer, and she's not even there.

And then a flicker of movement from near the wall. The twitch of an umbrella. She *is* there, hidden by the branches of the trees that hang over the wall. He can just about make out her face, her curly brown hair masked by the dying leaves clinging to the nearest tree. A sense of purpose rushes straight through him again, and he stops to check that everything's set for the final push. He's a bit wet, but that isn't the end of the world. The rain hasn't washed off his Brut, which is a plus point. Fair enough, the smell of beer, fag smoke and Bovril that's clung to him since he set foot inside the Hawthorns pretty much swamps the posh stuff, but he'll just have to make do. He takes a deep breath, and gets ready to make his move.

There's a grinding roar behind him. The bus pulls past, indicates to turn into the stop. The queue at the stop starts to file on board. She takes her brolly down, shakes the drops of rain from it, and with a flick of her curly hair, steps onto the bus. Billy closes his eyes.

Next time. There's always next time.

January 1965

– Hold still, me wench.

– Aaaagh!

– Ah said hold still.

– It hurts!

– It hurts cos ya keep wrigglin abaht. Yam loike a snake wi a bellyache. Now juss keep yer head down an we'll try again.

– Aaaagh!

– Oh, hell's teeth.

Kath sighs and lifts the steaming iron back up. From her awkward vantage point, bent double over the ironing board with her head resting against its flat top, Judy looks up at her next door neighbour.

– Yam pullin me hair out!

Kath shakes her head, smooths down her plain white Crimplene shift with her free hand, and then tucks her own hair – haloed by the dim, shadeless lightbulb hanging above – behind her ear. Judy watches her, noting every movement, every detail, until she's sure she can copy them herself later on. If she can be a bit more like Kath – just a bit – that'll be a start.

It isn't just that Kath's a year older, out of school with a decent job in the typists' pool down at the Beechman Works. Or that she's a wiz on her sewing machine, always knocking up something dead stylish to wear. It's not even that Kath always seems to have one gorgeous lad or another calling for her, as if there's some official government waiting list that boys sign up to for getting used and discarded by her. It's the smaller things, too. Take Kath's hair; it's *straight* hair. Hair that shines with the warm glow of a hot stove-hob.

Hair that isn't all bloody curly. Kath's never had curly hair. Horrible, horrible curly hair which won't straighten no matter what you do with it.

Kath raises her eyebrows.

– Well, ah'll tell ya what, if ya doe want me ter get rid a the curls...

– No, yow've gorra get rid of em! Ya promised!

– Aroit. So hold still...

Judy shifts her weight from one foot to the other and closes her eyes. She hears the sizzle as Kath spits on the iron, and opens one eye again, her nerves dancing a jig.

– Yam sure that iron ay too hot?

– Shurrup yer moanin, ya saft cow.

Kath plunges the iron down onto the board, presses hard onto Judy's chestnut curls, and Judy sniffs at the sudden Bonfire Night smell.

– Be careful, Kath! Fer the love a God, be careful!

– Doe put me off, missis, yow'll gerrit scorched.

The iron hisses and steams, tugging at Judy's scalp and covering her cheek in warm condensation, but as Kath's pale, freckled hand pushes the iron inch by inch down the length of her hair, the awkward kinks obey, forming a thin brown mat on the ironing board. Kath chirps away as she works.

– Come on then, tell me a bit more abaht im.

– Ah've already towd ya evrythin.

– Ya dae hardly tell me nuthin! Ya juss said yow'd bin asked out at the bus stop off some fella!

Judy blushes, partly from the steam, partly from the memory.

– Well, thass what happened, ay it? He was waitin fer the bus lass week, an ah sid im watchin me. He'd juss come out the football, had his scarf on an evrythin. He was a bit quiet at fust, loike.

In fact, the lad stood there grinning at her for about five minutes without saying anything. She started to worry about him; she'd read an article in a magazine last week all about sex attackers – blokes who creep about in raincoats with nothing on underneath! – and she was already expecting the worst of the chap staring at her with his hands in his pockets. By the time he stepped forward to speak to her, Judy was holding her furled umbrella like a cricket bat, ready to repel the pervert by any means necessary. But instead, he asked her – a bit sheepishly – if she wanted to go to the pictures in town next Saturday.

She looked him up and down. On reflection, once you got the idea of him being a depraved sex-fiend out of your mind, he didn't seem a bad type. Worth spending a quiet Saturday evening with, at the very least.

– So thass what happened. Excitin, eh? Careful, yome gunna scorch me!

– Stop yer werritin. We'm nearly done now, any road; e yam, turn yer head over an ah'll do the other side. So, what film am ya gewin ter see?

– Doe know. Spose we'll wait an see woss on.

– Maybe ya can tek im ter the recordin booth afterward, pledge yer love fer eternity?

– Gerrout of it!

Round the corner from George's Cinema is a little place where, for a couple of bob, you can go inside a booth and have your voice put onto a record. On a quiet afternoon last summer, Judy and Kath went in there and recorded themselves singing Dusty's *I Only Want To Be With You*, hopelessly out of key with each other and bursting into fits of giggles at every other line. Judy's still got the record; she plays it more often than Dusty's version. Not that she'd ever admit that to Kath.

– An... we'm done! Look at ya! Yome a diffrent girl!

– How do ah look?

– Ya look fab. Honest.

– Really?

– Dead swish, me wench! Yow'll knock im out!

Judy lets out an uncertain breath, and picks up her hand-mirror to study the results. Her hair feels strange, its normal volume crushed, plunging straight down to her shoulders where it scalds the skin under her cardigan. It's still fresh and clean with that Linco smell, since she washed it in the sink a couple of hours ago. But for once it really does look stylish; proper look-again hair, just like you'd see on the girls in *Honey*. Kath's still smiling by the ironing board, her arms folded.

– Well? Woss the verdict, me darlin?

Judy checks her cardie and the hemline of her skirt, tugging it down around her knees a bit more. It all looks good. For the first time in a long time, everything looks good.

– Thanks, Kath. Really. Iss unbelievable.

To her surprise, Kath hugs her quickly and tightly, then lets go and gives her the thumbs-up.

– Knock im dead!

With the January sun rusting over the Remembrance Gardens, her bus winds its way through the Saturday evening traffic into the centre of town. He's at the bus stop already; she can see him through the grimy window, lank hair being flicked by the wind, hands in his pockets, still looking nervous.

She gets out of her seat carefully – the sharp metal frame around the padding can catch your skirt and rip it wide open if you're not careful – pulls her handbag onto her shoulder, thanks the conductor and hops down onto the pavement before the bus has even fully stopped.

– Aroit?

He grins.

– Aroit, Judy.

– Call me Jude. Me friends allwis do.

– Ar, fair enough, Jude.

– An what do yower mates call yow?

He smiles, and shrugs his shoulders. It makes the hood of his parka shake.

– Ter be honest, most people juss call me Cartwright.

*

Getting ready for the date's been a bit tricky for Cartwright, who's had to put up with more than his fair share of grief from Lover Boy. He only went round Billy's house to borrow some of his trendy perfume, and the whole thing turned into a Nuremberg trial.

– Yow. Am. A. Rotten. Bastard.

Billy was sitting in the living room in an almighty sulk, Grandstand playing out the half-time scores on the telly. Albion were away at Stoke, and Cartwright wasn't betting on the result being good. Despite the best efforts of the Brummie Road choir following them both home and away, they haven't won a match since October. It was difficult to tell which Billy was more miserable about: Cartwright's romantic night out, or Albion's dire fortunes.

– Oh, come on Bill. Her seems like a good girl. An yow had plenty a chance to mek yer move, dae ya?

– I ay talkin about it wi yow, Jonah. Yome a traitor.

Cartwright sighed.

– Doe call me Jonah, ya know ah doe like it. An gerroff yer high horse an all, iss shittin evrywheer. Look, ah went up the bus stop lass week, ah sid her, an I asked her out. It ay against the law, mucka.

– Traitor.

– The world a women's like a buffet, ay it. Fust come fust served. Ya cor juss hang around fer months an months till all thass left's the sausage rolls. Yow've gorra get stuck in. Which is what ah'll be dewin tonight, by the way.

– Ah'm gunna kill yow.

Right after saying that, Billy moaned, a horrible noise from the back of his throat which made Cartwright take a step back. For a second he thought Billy was about to keel over and drop dead on the thin brown carpet. He could already hear the coroner's words ringing round his skull: *apparently it was a broken heart, your honour. His best friend stole the girl he loved. A terrible, terrible tragedy.*

Then he looked at the grey, crackling TV screen. The Albion half-time score had come up. They were losing again. Billy had put his face in his hands.

Cartwright thought about sitting down next to him and trying to cheer him up. Alright, what he'd done was a bit rotten, but at the end of the day, there were plenty more fish in the canal. And what was it Tommy said when they were out fishing? Most fish swam downstream, but salmon fought against the current to get upstream, because they were different. They didn't even swim like your average fish, Tommy reckoned; they were dogged and vibrant in the water. Cartwright had always liked that. He sat down on the settee and rested his hand on Billy's shoulder.

– Ya see, Bill, ah'm a vibrant salmon.

Billy took his hands away from his face.

– Yome definitely summat. Salmon ay the word ah'd choose, though.

– Doe ya see what ah'm sayin? Ya cor float downstream all yer life. Ya need to gew out an fight fer the things ya want.

– Am ya sayin that ter mek me feel better, or yerself?

Cartwright opened his mouth, and then closed it without replying. He had the feeling it wasn't the type of question you were supposed to answer, even if you wanted to.

He was saved from having to say anything more by Billy's dad getting back from his brief visit to the pub and barging in through the back door. With his cheeks red from a combination of the cold and a couple of pints of M&B's finest, and his greying hair blown into a crazed tangle by the wind, he marched into the living room like some mad professor about to announce the discovery of life on the moon.

Instead, he dumped his frame in the armchair and bellowed at them.

– Right, yow pair, tek yer horrible music an saft clothes somewheer else.

Cartwright and Billy got up and shuffled obediently out into the hallway. Cartwright sighed.

– Look mate, ah doe want no hard feelins here or nought like that.

– Oh, right? Why'd ya come round then, if yow ay here ter rub it in?

– Ah juss wanted ter lend a bit a that perfume off ya. Heard it drives the wenches wild, loike.

Billy narrowed his eyes, and for a second it looked like he might throw a punch. His fists were clenched down by his sides, jaw tense, mouth pressed tightly enough that the cluster of red spots around each corner had turned white. Cartwright got ready to defend himself. He didn't want to have to lamp his best mate – not round his house, at any rate – but he was buggered if he'd back down. Winners didn't back down.

Luckily, he didn't have to. Billy just about managed to open his mouth and spit out a response.

– Upstairs. Bathroom. Top shelf.

Cartwright raced up the stairs as fast as his winklepickers could carry him, found the ornate bottle in the bathroom, and splashed a bit of the fragrance onto his skin. Then he breezed back down to the hallway, where Billy was leaning with his back against the wall, hands in his pockets, staring down at his shoes.

– Cheers fer the smelly stuff, pal.

Billy didn't answer, and didn't look up. Cartwright shrugged. That was fair enough, he reckoned. Sometimes, when you were swimming upstream, you just had to leave the other fish behind.

He didn't bother saying goodbye.

And now, looking at Judy at the bus stop, he reckons he's done the right thing. She isn't one of those girls you watch for on the beach at the seaside, the proper dolly birds who can knock you out with an idle glance, but all the same, there's a lot to like about her. She looks a bit like Cathy McGowan, with nice fleshy cheeks and brown hair which was curly last week, but now falls straight down to her shoulders, with a short fringe tickling at her eyebrows. There are far worse things you could spend a Saturday looking at. The final scores on Grandstand, for a start.

– What am ya smilin at?

Judy asks the question with a smile of her own, and Cartwright realises he's had a smirk on his face for the last half a minute.

– Oh, nuthin. Juss thinkin abaht a mate a mine. Am yow hungry, loike?

– Yeah, a bit.

– If ya want, we can grab some food fore gewin ter the flicks.

He's feeling pretty flush, Cartwright, having finally persuaded Tommy to lend him a few bob for the evening. Tom's just got his pay packet for the month, so he's not short, and he lobbed a fistful of coins at Cartwright with a shout of *e yam then, sod off an leave us in peace!* It isn't much, but just enough to play the gent and pay Judy's way. As long as she doesn't go getting grand ideas.

She nods her head, as if reading his mind.

– Aroit then. Which cinema am we gewin to?

– King's. Theer's a decent chippy juss round the corner.

Up go Judy's eyebrows.

– Hm.

– Is that aroit?

– Fine.

– Well, wheer'd ya usually gew?

– Me an me friend Kath usually g'ter George's, on Paradise Street.

– God, not the Bughouse.

– Ar, iss aroit theer. Sixpence fer a seat, an a free mallet tew hit the fleas with.

Cartwright grins.

– Well, we'll call tonight a treat then, eh?

He just can't keep that smile off his face. Bollocks to Billy. There's no better feeling than sauntering into town along the Golden Mile, a few bob in his pocket and a girl by his side. Singing your heart out on the Brummie Road terraces comes close – it takes you away from the crushing weight of everything for an hour or two – but this is the real thing, this is what men were made to do of a Saturday. For all the times he's told Billy and the other lads that he gets his fair share of skirt, it hasn't really happened as often as it should. Unless you count those frantic fumblings behind the school gym with Iris Duckhouse, which tend to be less a wet dream, more a wet nightmare.

The last of the high street shoppers flood by on either side; little flocks of middle-aged women wrapped up warm against the chill, headscarves flapping in the breeze, clutching their buys for the day but still stopping to peer into the shadows of one window or another. There are more cars on the road than usual – there always seem to be, these days – and a few annoyed cyclists ring their bells and shout as a baker's van whizzes past and rocks them in its slipstream. When they reach the first junction, Cartwright slaps a hand against the black and white pole which supports the traffic lights, looking up at the buildings of the Golden Mile towering on either side. It's a grand old high street, running from Carter's Green right down to Dartmouth Park; at the far end, it links up with the Birmingham Road about half a mile from the Hawthorns, and that phantom line beyond which separates the Black Country from the city of Birmingham. This is the spot. This is his sacred place.

– What am ya dewin?

Judy's watching him, and he realises that he's still rubbing the chilled metal of the traffic light. He smiles.

– Evryone's got theyselves a special place in the world, doe ya reckon?

She stares at him as if he's just asked her to recite the times tables in Hebrew. He thinks carefully. She might not be the brightest of bulbs. Best take it slow.

– Ya know, somewheer ya can gew an feel at peace, no matter how bad things get. This is it, fer me. This is wheer ah come.

– West Bromwich high street?

She's still wearing that multiplication face, only now it looks like she's trying to do the sums in Swahili.

– Course! Wheer else? Ya got evrythin ya need in the world roit here!

He sweeps an arm around. From here they can see K & J, the Midland Electricity Board, Martin's Bank, St Michael's Church, the Ladybird Shop. Where the high street joins Lodge Road further on down, there's the town hall and Millichip's solicitors; the Gala baths and the hospital, which sends a shudder running through Cartwright every time, bringing back memories flavoured with cock-a-leekie soup and semolina pudding from his two month spell there as a nipper. Then there's Hill & Long furniture, Bodenham's with all its posh frocks in the window, Marks & Sparks, Woolies, Burton's, Belcher the butchers with its tile mosaics of cattle on the walls and a jar of suck on the counter to hand out to kids, and the billiard hall. Everything you need.

– But it ay as good as the Bull Ring, is it?

Judy's got him pinned with those eyes, those keen and colourful eyes, and it takes him a few heartbeats to realise that she's talking absolute shit.

– The Bull Ring? What the bloody hell's the Bull Ring got ter do wi it?

– Lot more shops theer, fer starters. An iss all indoors! Theer's escalators, air-conditionin, the whole lot. Dead modern, it is.

– What pie-can wants ter do all they shoppin indoors? Thass what high streets am med fer. Atmosphere. When Albion won the cup in '54, they paraded the trophy roit down here, an the whole town turned out ter see em an cheer em home. An open-top bus, police on white osses, the lot. It was the best day ever. Ah banged me head on a lamppost.

– Ya did what?

– Theer was a lamppost roit here, wheer this traffic light is now. Ah was up on me dad's shoulders. As the bus went past ah tried ter lean over an shout ter Ronnie Allen so he'd gi me a wave, an ah cracked me bonce roit inter the bloody thing.

– Oh.

– Doe worry, it dae do no damage. Lucky, though; if ah'd nutted it a bit harder, ah coulda growed up ter be a roit saft bugger.

– God forbid.

– But doe ya see? Thass why this is me special place. That FA Cup was the onny thing the Albion have won all me life, an it brought the entire town together roit in this spot. Ya cor do that in no shoppin centre. The high street's what we've all got in common. This is West Bromwich. An iss beautiful.

He shouts those last words over the growl of the 74 speeding past; in the nick of time, Cartwright spots the bus ploughing through a huge

~ 34 ~

puddle of rainwater and jumps back to dodge the tidal wave. He runs his hands down his parka to make sure he missed the worst of it. Then he realises Judy's glaring at him. Dripping, bedraggled, drenched Judy.

– Ah doe care how beautiful it is. Ah want ter be indoors. Ah want ter be indoors NOW.

*

The chip shop's an oasis of warmth away from the sharp, stinging cold of the high street. Her belly hollow, her body numb from her wet coat, Judy's never been so glad to open a door and smell those first scents of oil and grease. Cartwright follows her in, clinking coins in his hand, and Judy watches him nod to the broad-chested, stubble-jawed bloke working the fryer.

– Doe worry, Jude, ah'm buyin. Fish an chips twice please, mate!

She's got a few bob in her purse and thinks about offering to go halves – it'd be the modern thing to do – but then her heavy, wet coat sends another shiver through her. No. Her money's better off where it is.

After handing three bob over to the man behind the counter, Cartwright turns to her again, an awkward, lopsided smile on his face.

– Really sorry abaht yer coot gerrin soaked. Am ya feelin aroit?

– Ah'm cold.

– Well, a fish supper'll warm ya. An we can allwis get them wet clothes off ya in the cinema, eh?

Judy glares at him. The only thing stopping her from marching straight back to the bus stop and going right home in a huff is how much she's been looking forward to tonight. How long she's waited. Nothing's going to spoil it now; she's determined to get back later tonight and tell Kath that it was a magical evening, even if she has to sit next to the world's biggest idiot for another two hours to accomplish it.

The food isn't long in coming. The fryer hands them two fish suppers wrapped in yesterday's *Express & Star*, and they leave the shop and head round towards the King's. It may not be the most romantic meal in history, but to Judy it's a slice of paradise, wolfing down steaming chunks of food that leave her fingers bright with grease in the streetlight. It could be the warmth from the cod and chips, or it could be the gentle burning of the electric lamps painting the high street a prettier colour, but either way, she doesn't feel as lousy as she did before eating. She even feels contented enough to try another chat with Cartwright.

– What d'yer mom and dad do?

– Ay sid me dad since ah was six, bab. That time we went ter see the Albion cup final parade, that's me last real memory of im. Done a

~ 35 ~

runner, he did. He was allwis in an out a trouble. Me mom lasted another couple a years, but her lungs wor no good. Her died when ah was eight.

– Jesus. Ah'm sorry.

– Nought ter be sorry fer, me love. Ah live wi me nan an me brother Tommy, iss all the family ah need. Evryone's gorra learn ter stand on their own sooner or later.

– Ya must have loads a mates an all, though?

– Nah. Well… theer's Billy. Ah usually see him of a Satdee. We gew up the Albion together. Have done fer a couple a years. His mom got killed in a car accident a winter or two back; ah spose thass why we become pals in the fust place. We'm the bloody Dead Moms Club, me an Bill.

– Ah shouldn'ta brung it up.

– No, iss fine. Ah doe mind talkin abaht it. Ah've had a long time ter get used ter the situation. Iss Billy what struggles wi it. Acts loike he's been cheated out a summat; as if God went an took his mom away out a spite. He cor accept it: folks die. Sooner ya get used tew it, the happier yow'll be.

Judy nods, but she's not sure whether she agrees. Being upset about your mother dying seems pretty natural. When she was little, she always used to cry over Dad butchering one of the pigs the family kept in the back yard; losing her mom seems unthinkable next to that. Still, she can't help looking at Cartwright in a different light. It can't have been easy for him. She moves her body a little closer to his; just staving off the cold.

– Any road, bad luck ter be talkin abaht all this, missis. Ya g'ter the pictures offen?

– Ar, ah gew wi Kath evry now an then. Thass me next door neighbour. Well… her's me best friend, ah spose.

Cartwright coughs as a lump of fish goes down the wrong way, and thumps his chest for a few seconds.

– Woss the best film ya seen?

– Ah loiked Ben Hur.

– Ugh. Too bloody long.

– Well, ah loiked Lawrence of Arabia an all.

– Christ. Too much sand, not enough happnin.

– An Spartacus was aroit.

– Now yam talkin! Spartacus was a good un. All got a bit saft at the end, mind.

– A bit saft?

– Ar, well. When they all stood up an started shoutin out "ah'm Spartacus", it took some believin. Yow'd think they'd keep they gobs shut an save their own skins, loike.

– They was stickin up fer one another! Showin solidarity!

"Solidarity" is a word Judy's dad uses a lot, especially when he's talking about work. It isn't a word she thought she'd ever have to use on a date, but the evening's throwing up its fair share of surprises already.

– Bloody stupid, all the same. Why get yerself killed over someone else? Yow atta look after yerself, ya do. Thass the way things am. Sometimes yow atta swim upstream.

Judy picks a hair-thin sliver of bone from her fish, and flicks it into the wet gutter.

– Sounds loike selfishness ter me. What abaht loyalty? Yow've gorra stick by yer friends, ay ya?

Cartwright doesn't answer straight away, so she looks across at him. He's stopped walking, just staring ahead of him with a mouth full of chips that he's stopped chewing, as if his jaw's frozen.

– Am yow aroit? Have ah said summat wrong?

He gulps the chips down quickly and scratches his chin.

– Nah, ah'm fine. Iss juss that… well, theer's a time an a place fer friends, ay tha?

*

They turn onto St Michael's Street. With his mind cantering off like a runaway pony, Cartwright has to jump quickly to dodge a blue Morris which zooms round the corner suddenly, motoring along the street at breakneck speed (or at least, what passes for breakneck speed with a Morris). The driver paps his horn angrily, and after waiting a few moments, Cartwright sticks two fingers up at the car, although he does it as quickly and quietly as he can in case the Morris driver sees it in his little round wing-mirror. Swimming upstream's all well and good, but if you end up getting lamped in front of your girl, you may as well climb out of the bloody river and squelch your way home.

It's a short walk to the King's. The steamy smell of jacket potatoes seeps into the night from a vendor's cart across the road, and up ahead, the stout block of the cinema peeks from behind the 220 bus as it pulls away from the stop. Cartwright pushes the heavy wooden door and holds it open for Judy, welcoming heat engulfing them again as they enter the foyer. He's timed it perfectly; they're early enough that the queue at the ticket booth isn't too long, and they're in with a chance of getting back row seats. It's a little something to thank his lucky stars for as they join the line, the soles of their shoes peeling off the carpet with a quiet ripping noise at every step.

It takes a couple of minutes of patient shuffling to reach the booth, where a woman with heavy make-up and skin more creased than a ten bob note is clutching tickets between her yellowing fingers. Cartwright steps up to the glass and does a V for victory sign.

– Two fer James Bond.

She stares at him through her thick-rimmed glasses, and corrects him in a taut voice.

– Two fer James Bond, *please*.

– Ar, yeah. Please.

– Circle or stalls?

– Stalls. At the back, please.

The ticket-woman gives him a long look. Cartwright studies the wall. The old trout can stare at him as long as she likes; she probably went up the back row herself enough times in her day. Although from the look of her, it was in the days when every single film starred a bloke with a top hat and a twirly moustache tying some saft wench to a train track.

Finally, she thrusts two slips of paper at him, and croaks again through her tar-clogged throat.

– D'ya want any raffle tickets wi them?

– Woss the prize?

– A poster a Napoleon Solo off the telly.

– I ay really that bothered abaht TV, love.

Judy leans round and chips in.

– Ooh, ah like The Mon From Uncle!

– Ar, gew on then love, we'll ha two tickets fer the raffle an all, then.

The coins are dwindling away in his pocket, and he winces at the extra cost, but hands the money over anyway. It's worth it: things are going well. No time to start playing the Scotsman with his cash. He takes the raffle stubs off the woman in the booth, and turning towards the auditorium, gives Judy her ticket. Their hands touch, and linger together for a second.

Things are going very well.

The raffle's held just before the house lights go down, with the crimson curtains still drawn across the screen. Their number comes right out, the very first ticket, and Cartwright bounds down the aisle to the manager with a huge grin, and shakes his hand. It must be a sign.

– Ta fer this, mate! Great stroke a luck!

The manager smiles back, his chubby features shining under the lights, and answers quietly.

– Tell ya the truth, son, we onny sold fower tickets. Yow bought two on em.

– Oh, roit. Still, yam dewin me a big favour here! Ah wo forget it!

He takes the glossy print of Napoleon Solo off the manager, gives the ice-cream girl a wink – she's always been a saucy one, her – and heads back up the auditorium to his seat in the shadow of the balcony up above. Nipping into the back row again, with a few apologies to the kissing couples he has to brush past, he spots Judy giving him two thumbs up and plonks himself back down next to her with a real sense of triumph. The lights come down, the curtains slide apart, and the Pearl & Dean advertising reel flickers into life as Cartwright hands the poster to her. She whispers her thanks.

– Iss a good picture, ay it?

They lean closer to one another to study it in the light from the screen. Napoleon Solo's standing in a grey suit and tie, hair side-parted, holding a pistol, giving the camera a smile. It's a debonaire smile set in a bright, healthy orange face. He has to fight back the mad urge to smile back. As the forthcoming attractions reel ends and the main feature starts to roll, Judy puts the poster back on her lap, and Cartwright casually drapes his arm over her shoulders, the wool of her cardigan warm to the touch. He feels her stiffen slightly at first, then relax. And through the usual hazy shroud of cigarette smoke, the film starts.

Within ten minutes, Bond's already broken into a warehouse, blown up a load of drugs, snogged a belly dancer then used her as a human shield, and electrocuted some bloke. Cartwright can't believe it. He had a definite plan for how to kick things off: wait for a quiet bit in the film, grab the all-important first kiss, maybe explore the hemline of that skirt a bit, and be upstairs outside before you could say *shaken, not stirred*. But if Bond carries on at this rate for a whole two hours, he's not even going to get a look-in.

Still, as the opening credits come up and Shirley Bassey starts belting her lungs out, he manages to turn his attention away from the screen and towards Judy. He leans across the arm of his seat, and she turns her head to face him. The dim light illuminates her eyes, bright beneath dark lashes, and her soft, inviting mouth, and he's suddenly, painfully aware of the almighty storker developing in his trousers. She moves herself towards him, and Cartwright reaches for her, and closes his eyes.

And suddenly it's there behind his eyelids. Billy. Sat next to him on that old sofa in his living room, with his face in his hands. Cartwright's stomach lurches and he opens his eyes again, pulling away from Judy. She's got her own eyes closed, waiting for him to make his move. He's heart's going like a piston. He leans forward a second time – this time he can almost taste her lips – but Christ on a bloody scooter, there's Billy again. Billy's sat right in the seat where Judy should be, saying *yome a traitor, yow am, Jonah.*

He jerks back again as if he's been electrocuted, sitting bolt upright in his chair. Judy tugs at his sleeve and whispers.

– Am yow aroit?

He stares at the golden glow of the screen, feeling sweat cover him like a second skin.

– Ar, ah'm fine.

From the corner of his eye, he can see her still watching him. She sounded hurt when she asked him if he was okay, but he doesn't know what he can say to her. He can't even look at her for fear that Mr Misery will put in another appearance; maybe crying his eyes out into his Albion scarf this time, left alone in his house with a half-mental dad and a broken heart. Cartwright feels sick. You're not supposed to start thinking about your best mate when you've got a storker. It's not normal.

His guts clench suddenly as the terrible, devastating thought occurs that he might be one of *them*. He barely realises that he's whispering to himself: *no, no, no, no.* Anything but that. He'd rather be dead.

Through the tobacco fog inside the cinema, he watches Bond smack some blonde's arse up on the screen. That's the way to do it! Confident. Assured. In control. *Come here and kish me. Now off you go, shweetheart.* But he isn't Bond, and he isn't in control.

Cartwright sits and watches the film, feeling more miserable than he has for a long time.

*

Judy sits and watches the film, feeling more miserable than she has for a long time. They were so close to kissing, so close, and she felt so ready for it. In spite of getting a bit soaked earlier on, she's had a good night, and she felt a quiet thrill in her stomach when Cartwright put his arm around her as the film started. For months and months – it really does feel like forever – she's had to put up with Kath wittering on about the dates she goes on, all the lads who are after her, while Judy nods and smiles, asks all the right questions and gasps and giggles in all the right places. Through it all, she wondered when it would be her turn. She wondered when she'd have chance to make Kath feel a bit of that gnawing envy. If that could ever happen.

And then the moment came: she lost herself in it, and as she leaned towards him he opened his eyes, and the look on his face was terrible. He was revolted by her. She could see it so clearly. He won't even look at her now.

So that's it. She isn't good enough. No matter how much time she spends with the sewing machine, altering her clothes to keep up with the latest fashions, or how much time she spends in front of the mirror with her make-up, and trying so hard not to put on more weight, or even how long she spends with her head on the ironing board getting rid of those horrible curls, it'll never be enough. Kath's the one the lads want. Always has been, and always will be.

Judy focuses her attention on the screen and does her best to follow the film, as a last effort to get some enjoyment out of the night. To be fair, it's a good picture: there are gunfights and car chases, and whenever she sneaks a glance at Cartwright he seems captivated by it too, although he still looks a bit sick. His expression hits new depths of dismay about halfway through, when James Bond gets captured and tied to a table made of gold.

– Woss he dewin theer?

Judy nudges him.

– Shhh.

– Oh my God. Wheer's that laser gewin? OH BLOODY HELL, WHEER'S IT GEWIN?

A bloke in the row in front turns round.

– Will yow pipe down, mate?

– Pipe down? A fella's abaht ter get unmanned up theer!

– Shhh. He'll find a way out, wo he?

– Oh Jesus, that doe look good. Thass gunna mek his eyes water, tharris.

– Shhh!

A weak torch-beam washes over their row as the usher tries to find the source of the noise. Thankfully, Cartwright has the sense to keep his mouth shut, although in the torchlight he still doesn't look well. After a fruitless search, the usher switches the torch off and moves back to his perch at the back of the auditorium.

As Bond bluffs his way out of being lasered, Judy wonders if Cartwright might say something else. She clings to the hope that she might feel his arm around her shoulders again in the darkness; that there might be a second chance, that this time it will all be alright. But minute by minute, that hope's being ground into dust.

She closes her eyes against the salty sting needling them, and runs her fingers through her hair until it begins to twist and curl again. And slowly, she realises that her left arm's going numb.

Cartwright's never been so glad to see a film finish. It was pretty exciting – at times it was almost good enough to make him forget about his own problems – but as soon as Bond started seducing Pussy Galore, there he was again, sneaking a look at Judy and still imagining Billy sitting next to him in the darkness of the back row. When the film finally winds down and the pictures on the screen fade – sparking the usual rush for the exits all around as folks try to get out before the national anthem comes on – he takes a deep, relieved breath.

They're too late to make it out before the opening chords of God Save The Queen. Half of the stalls have already emptied, and the aisle's clogged with folks scurrying away from the screen. The ones who haven't made it to the door in time groan as the music begins, and with a chorus of sighs they dutifully turn back to face the screen and murmur along. Cartwright stands up, along with Judy and everyone else still stuck inside, and makes the usual token effort to observe custom.

– Lah, lah, lah, laaaah-lah QUEEN; lah, lah, lah, laaaaah-lah QUEEN...

As he sings, his ears pick up a noise just next to him. Judy isn't singing along; in fact, it sounds more like she's sobbing. He turns to look at her again: she's got her hand cupped over her mouth, and he realises with a jolt that there really are tears in her eyes. And then they make eye contact, and before he can say a word, Judy pushes past him and runs for the exit.

There are gasps from the people in the aisle, and Cartwright himself isn't sure how to react. No one likes having to sing the national anthem at the end of the film, but it always happens, and running out of the auditorium while it's playing is about the worst thing you can do. It's right up there with queue-jumping. And anyway, who gets so emotional over God Save The Queen that they burst into tears halfway through the first verse?

So Cartwright's surprised to find himself fleeing towards the exit in pursuit seconds later, to further outrage from everyone else in the cinema, enduring the shouts of *bloody kids!* and *no respect!* and *should be ashamed of yourselves!* until he reaches the door and passes into the quiet foyer. He glances down to the far end, where the outer door's just swinging shut, and sprints towards it with his heart going faster than a drum roll, feet pounding the sticky floor.

She's sitting on the steps. Cartwright pulls the door open, takes an icy breath and calls her.

– Jude!

– Gew away!

Her shoulders are shaking. He walks down the steps, sits next to her and puts a hand on her arm. She tries to shake it off; she's breathing in loud gasps. That sound scares the shit out of him; he remembers his mom making the same kind of noises towards the end.

– Woss the matter, love?

Gasp.

– Panic attack. Ah get em all the time.

Gasp.

– Panic attack? Bloody hell. Is theer anythin ah can do?

Gasp.

– Ya could piss off an leave me be.

Gasp.

– Come on, ah cor do that. Look at me. Breathe deep an hold it in. Just for a few seconds. An a few more. Now… breathe out.

– If ya doe loike me, why bother hangin around?

– What d'ya mean, "if ah doe loike ya"? Course ah loike ya! Ah doe gew around buyin fish suppers fer folk ah cor stond, me wench. Breathe in. Hold it theer… an breathe out.

She turns toward him, and he's relieved to see the tears are gone, although her face is flushed, her eyes a bit puffy. But for all that, she's as good to look at as she was when he first saw her. He slides his hand down her arm and wraps it around her freezing fingers.

– Come on, ya must know ah loike ya! Ah really, really loike ya. Yam beautiful.

He puts his other hand on the gentle slope of her waist, clear even through the thick layers of clothing. And he moves his face down towards the clouds of breath coming from her mouth – she's breathing faster and faster again now – and this time there's no one inside his head, no one there except her, and there's no mistaking the excitement in his gut. There's nothing wrong with him; at last, everything's absolutely clear in his mind, and he know what he's got to do.

He breathes deeply, puts his arms around her, pulls her close and kisses her cheek, relishing the touch of her chilled skin on his lips.

*

Judy digs her hands into the folds of his parka jacket as he brushes his mouth over her cheek, and wonders whether to laugh or to start crying again. Somehow, she feels like doing both. The anxiety's still tearing at her, making her heart skip and her stomach freeze. It's been at least a year

~ 43 ~

since she last had an attack like this, and even longer since it happened in public. A humiliating end to a horrible night.

After the kiss – if you can call it that – she looks at Cartwright's pale face, shining with sweat, and the expression of disgust she saw in the cinema's been replaced by an odd look of regret.

– Jude, yam a fantastic girl. An the lad who gets yow will be the luckiest bastard alive. But it shouldn't be me. Ah shouldn't have asked yow out. It was wrong.

Her stomach tightens.

– So ya doe loike me, then.

Cartwright grins.

– Oh, it ay that, missis. Ah loike ya plenty, ah do. An if ah'd sid ya fust, that wouldn't be a problem. But ah cor swim upstream all me life. Mates am mates. Yow was right abaht that, earlier on. Ya should allwis put friends fust.

– Ya what?

– Listen: ya know that bus stop wheer we met last Satdee? Theer's a lad who waits theer evry week, same as yow do. He'll be theer next week, an all. Ya cor miss him, honest. He looks loike Gerry out a The Pacemakers. Onny a bit dopier. An wi a blue an white scarf on. Jude, ah want ya ter do all three on us a favour, an ask him out next week.

– Ask out some lad ah've never met. Roit. Thass a brilliant way a givin me the elbow.

– That ay what ah'm dewin. Honest. Juss trust me an gi Billy a chance.

– Billy?

– Ar. Remember ah towd ya abaht im earlier? He's a good lad: ah reckon yow'll mek a great pair. But doe say it was me who towd ya to do it. He wouldn't like that, the saft ayputh. Let him think ya chose him over me.

Judy pulls away from Cartwright's embrace, and rubs her eyes. It's been a horrible, horrible night, and being treated like the present in a game of pass the parcel is the last straw.

– Me bus is on the way. Ah'm off home.

– Look, Jude, please. Yow deserve Billy, an he deserves yow. Do it fer me. After all, ah did win ya that Napoleon Solo poster.

– Ah left that inside.

– Oh well. Get Billy ter win ya another un next week, eh?

The 54 comes down the street. Judy stands up and sticks her arm out to flag it down.

– Ah'll gi it a think.

– Woss that mean?

– It means ah'll gi it a think. Look, ta fer buyin me dinner. An fer the film an that.

The bus slows, stops, and the conductor waves her on board. She fiddles with the change in her purse, pays the fare, and then turns to look at Cartwright on the pavement. He's almost lost in the last wave of people coming out of the cinema. She holds onto the pole as the bus pulls away, watches him watch her until the bus rounds the corner, and he shouts one last thing down the street. Then the conductor – a tall West Indian chap with a gentle voice – says *if you'd like to take a seat madam*, and ushers her forward.

She rests her tired head against the window, watching the Golden Mile zip by through the dirty glass. And Cartwright's voice echoes around her head: *next Saturday*.

April 1965

Kath Riordan's late. Again.

It's not her fault. She always tries to be on time, wherever she's going, but with so many things to get done, her best never beats the chime of the clock. She's used to bustling into work, straightening her blouse and skirt with a quick *sorry Mr Barrett* (which, if he's in arm's reach, Mr Barrett answers by pinching her backside as she passes, bringing a wince and a flush to her cheeks). But even outside of work, she's hopeless. No one who knows Kath ever bothers trying to meet her at the time they've arranged, except Judy, who for some reason has just never learned. Kath knows every time she rolls up half an hour late to meet Jude, she'll get the full act off her: tapping foot, folded arms, knowing glare. It's always the same.

Because she has to look good before she leaves the house, and that takes time. Jesus wept, if only people knew just how much time it takes, hunched over her little round mirror in the bedroom. First the make-up, taking special care with her eyes, putting her Miners mascara block and eyeliner to good use, with a touch of blue shadow and then some foundation on her lips to make those dark eyes stand out all the more. Then she has to get the right outfit. Shift or two-piece dress? Boots or heels? Old-fashioned stockings or new, trendy tights? Sometimes she wishes she could just take Judy's approach, which has always looked more or less like putting on the first thing which falls out of the wardrobe in the morning.

But for all the time she'd save, it still wouldn't work. Because she has to look good. If you look good then you feel good, and if you feel good then you can forget for a few hours that you're the only daughter of an immigrant labourer, stuck working in a typing pool with a horrible, lecherous boss who's forever perfuming the back of your neck with his whisky breath.

So when Kath hops off the 113 into the Saturday sunshine, she's well aware that she should have been here nearly an hour ago. Rushing to get her feet on the kerb, she nearly knocks the conductor off the bus.

– Oh God! Jaysus! Ah'm sorry!

The red-faced conductor looks like he's about to give her an earful, so she smiles and flutters her eyelashes a bit. The conductor forces a sickly smile, and even waves goodbye to her as the bus pulls away.

Kath puts a palm to her forehead to feel the warmth there. The sun isn't all that hot, but it might be enough to brown her pale skin a bit; she's determined to be the first girl in the office with a tan this year, if only to put one over on all the show-offs going over to Jersey and Guernsey for Easter. Last summer, on the Isle of Wight, Carol Parker poured olive oil over herself to give the sun a helping hand, and came back with a hide like a lobster. Everyone gushed when she walked through the door: *Carol, yow look amazin! Ya lucky thing! Yome ever so Continental, missis!* Carol milked the compliments, although she didn't smile much, as it made her face peel.

Kath hasn't bothered with olive oil. However tempted she is to make sure the sun does its job, she also wants to look as stylish as she can, and that inner voice she relies on for fashion instinct screams at her that looking the height of style would be a bit tricky if she was strolling about town dripping with yellow goo.

She isn't actually sure what the plan is yet; it's a surprise, according to Judy. They're meeting up on Jed Mon's Bonk, the hill that runs up to the power station, and as she's even more late than usual, she has to check round quickly to get her bearings. To her left, ten or fifteen paces from the bus stop, a gully cleaves through the parallel rows of houses. It's right where Judy told her.

She hurries into the narrow passageway, her feet rattling on the cobbles, glad she's had the sense to wear her Mary Quant boots with the flat soles, even though they don't look as nice with the shift as her white slingbacks. There are blackened bricks to either side of her, the house-rows like a charred string of bangers fresh off the stove. She reaches the centre of the gully, where the back yards open up in a long stretch of washing lines on both left and right, each line strung from kitchen to outhouse, and weighed down with damp clothes airing in the spring sun. The songbirds perched on the garden walls scatter as she passes, shooed by her echoing footsteps. On the corner, she can hear the chatter from the back yard of the Gunsmiths Arms; the back gate's open, the cobblestones carpeted with feathers, and dozens of caged pigeons outside the pub are being auctioned in time for the new racing season. And as the alleyway ends ahead of her, she catches her first glimpse of Jed Mon's Bonk.

Sometimes, doing her makeup in that little round mirror at home, she still catches a glimpse of a quiet little Irish girl getting ready for her first day at school in England. A bookish lass who preferred shuffling pieces round a chess board to pop music or fashion mags, with no friends except for the curly-haired girl next door whose accent she could barely understand. It took ages for her own tongue to master the slopes and curves of the Black Country dialect until she could pass herself off as a native, as if she'd spent her whole life in these orphan towns on Birmingham's doorstep. But every so often, it catches her out, makes her feel foreign again. There are times when the Black Country can make anyone feel like an outsider.

Once, leaning over the wall of their back yard, Judy's da told Kath that the Devil lived up Brierley Hill. He said the Black Country was Satan's kingdom on earth. There was nowhere else in the world that he felt so at home as among the fires of the foundries, the dark smoke from the factories, the air filled with sulphur and soot, the ground packed with limestone and coal. And when folk flooded into the area hunting for work – Welshmen, Scotsmen, Irishmen, men from every single county of England – the Devil took each of them up on the hill and plunged them into the ground until their heads were submerged, making them breathe and swallow the powder-black Staffordshire soil until they were near death, before pulling them back out. When they emerged, each was a Black Country man: his old language and speech were forgotten, replaced by the words of the factories and mines, the foundries and kilns. Each man had sold his body to the masters of industry; whatever spirit he had left belonged to the Devil alone.

At the time, Kath didn't learn anything from that story except that Judy's da was an awful gobshite. But the tale itches at her mind all the same, every now and then.

The patchy green slope in front of her stretches up for about thirty yards to a low wall, with a newer metal fence running behind it marking the boundary of the power station. The grass is ragged where kids have scrambled up and down it over the years. She reaches the bottom of the hill in time to hear a shout, and squinting up against the sun's hot flare, she sees the hefty shape of a young man falling arse over tit down the bank towards her.

Judy promised her a surprise. And here it is.

*

– So. What would yow do?

– Onny five minutes ter live, ya say?

– Ar. Sky's full a Russian missiles. H-bombs, A-bombs, the bloody lot. An hard rain's a-gunna fall.

– Well thass a saft question, ay it? Ah'd spend evry second wi the girl ah love.

– Oh, fer Christ's sake. Trust yow ter gew an waste yer last five minutes on the planet.

Cartwright rattles disgust from his throat and rests his back against the wonky old wall behind him. It sheds a few stone crumbs every time he touches it, and he's reluctant to put his full weight against it, but right now he needs all the support he can get. He looks up at the power lines tracing a dark track above as the lovebirds kiss again. The cables stretch from the power plant two hundred yards behind them, over their sun-soaked spot on top of Jed Mon's Bonk, and down into the streets below. On the other side of the power station, a train clacks down the freight line from Baggeridge Colliery, some driver putting in overtime, hauling the week's wagons of coal. In the middle of that racket, the birds are giving it their best effort up above. Poor bastards are probably wondering when they'll get a bit of peace and quiet.

Cartwright doesn't care a threepenny bit about the birds, mind. There are far, far bigger problems afoot. Billy's the least of them: his best mate turning into a saucer-eyed ninny because he's had a girlfriend for three whole months is a breeze to deal with. But work? What a cast-iron bloody nightmare.

Because turning sixteen a fortnight ago meant more than just a few pints and a couple of frames of snooker down the club – although that's exactly what the pair of them ended up doing, after Cartwright finally prised Billy away from his one true love for an evening. For Cartwright, happy birthday sweet sixteen meant leaving school the very same day and getting himself a job. Earning his keep. Tommy's played the man of the house for long enough.

Besides, he's lucky, not having to stay and sit the County Certificate exam like Billy is, and Judy down at the girls' school. Why bother? All you get from it is a piece of paper saying you know your letters and your numbers. You don't need an exam to tell you that. As long as you can order a pint of M&B down the boozer and count out two bob to pay for it then you're sorted for life, and you can insert the County Certificate into the orifice of your choice.

But the day after his birthday, when he woke up with a rancid mouth, hairy throat and golf ball eyes, the reality of it bubbled up in his stomach along with the night's yeasty leftovers. School was done with. No more History, or Games, or Woodwork. No more canings. No more exploratory voyages with his hand inside Iris Duckhouse's blouse behind the gym. Instead of Tommy banging on his door to get him up out of bed and off to the bus, he fetched his bike from the shed, and with a heavy gut, he cycled round all the factories and works asking after vacancies.

And bloody hell, were there vacancies.

Tool room fitter-turners. Jig and tool makers. Centre lathe operators. Hydraulic press operators. Press brake operators. Drillers. Millers. Grinders. Punchers. Fettlers. Diecasters. Machine moulders. Core makers. Hand flame and profile gas cutters. Automotive fitters. Electric welders. Pneumatic rivetters. Sheet metal workers. Mine car erectors. There were jobs in nearly every place he went, positions crying out to be filled. They were giving work to blacks and Indians and all sorts, fresh off the boat. But just out of school, with no experience save for having made a half-decent set of shelves in Woodwork once, he got nothing but *sorry sunshine*, and *maybe next year, eh?*

It was two or three days before someone took pity on him. At FBG Bolts & Rivets down Oldbury way, the foreman on the shop floor ushered him into the offices, where a fella with a beer gut, thick-rimmed NHS specs and a painfully obvious toupee shook his hand and asked him a few questions. *How owd am ya? Wheer d'ya g'ter skewel? What classes d'ya tek?* And finally, amazingly: *When can ya start werk?*

He was so chuffed, he told the gaffer he could start right off, there and then. His new boss, Mr Ashfield – known as "Wiggy" to everyone stood out of earshot of him – smiled and patted him on the back before wandering over to the corner of the office, picking up a broom, and thrusting it into Cartwright's hand. *Best get crackin, then. Floor out theer's a fuckin disgrace.*

And that's it. Five days a week brushing shit off the factory floor. Five days a week hunching over and scratching those thick bristles over cold stone until his back feels brittle as plastic, until he's sure his spine will never straighten again. It's beyond basic, and the ribbing he gets off the other blokes is rotten (*yow can come an taych mar missis how ter swayp!* and *cor they find no coloureds ter do that job, mate?*). Course, it's money in his pocket, and there are perks to go with it, like the canteen wenches giving him a free plate of chips and mushy peas of a lunchtime (Elsie usually gives him a wink to go with it too, the randy old cow). But there's no getting over the disappointment: *this* is work. This is what he's spent sixteen years getting ready for. Scrub scrub scrub, brush brush brush, with a complimentary bollocking whenever he stops to lean on the broom for five minutes' rest. And Wiggy enjoys dishing out those bollockings. When he gets going, he's like a hose switched on full blast with no sod holding on to it, spraying curses in an endless stream over every poor bastard in the room.

The one saving grace in the whole embuggering situation is that Billy doesn't know he's only a broom boy at the factory; for the last few weeks, Cartwright's been letting him think that he's manufacturing nuts and bolts like a dynamo, and he's on the fast track to a management position.

He clears his throat and resumes that role like a professional.

– God, look at yow pair a schoolkids.

Billy and Judy glance across the yard at him in unison, their tangle of tongues finally over. Billy huffs.

– Jonah, yow onny left school five weeks agew.

– Ar, but ah'm a proper workin mon now, ay I?

– So ya keep tellin us.

– I atta comport meself wi the dignity befittin me position, ay it. Unloike some folks. Look at the state on ya! Ya look loike John Wayne had an accident down the Dulux works.

That isn't a lie: Billy looks a right plank. He's excelled himself. He's wearing a cowboy hat with Albion rosettes pinned to it (God alone knows where he's dug it up from), and while he's been tucking into his leading lady, it's been knocked skewiff on his head. They've got the makeshift banner laid on the slope between them. It's a length of blue cloth – one of the old curtains from Billy's living room – with thick white brushstrokes on the top spelling WBA, and below that, BRUMMIE ROAD END. It's mounted on a couple of old broom handles from work that Cartwright's supplied, although obviously he's skipped over telling them that those same lengths of wood are responsible for all the blisters and callouses that have flowered on his palms recently.

Course, he didn't get a look-in on making the banner itself; Billy and Judy did that bit together. Same as pretty much everything else they've done for the last three months. Three long months of being a third bloody wheel, with a job that most immigrants would turn their nose up at. It's almost enough to make you wish for a bit of nuclear annihilation.

– Any road, Jude, how abaht yerself?

– Mm?

– Five minutes till all them Russian bombs come droppin. What d'ya do wi the time?

– Iss a bit of a morbid thing ter be thinkin abaht, ay it, Jonah?

– Morbid or not, bab, iss gunnew happen. Sooner or later, loike. Some saft bastard somewheer'll say the wrong thing, or shoot at the wrong bloke, an then that'll be it fer us. Flash, bang, wallop. What a picture.

She sits upright, arching her back in a way which makes it abundantly clear he's about to have an argument on his hands.

– Or not. What if we say summat? We say enough's enough? Tek yer A-bombs an yer H-bombs an stick em roit up yer silo?

– Yow've been listnin ter too much Donovan, missis. Wanna stick ter The Beatles, ya do. Ya doe catch Paul McCartney or John Lennon rattlin on abaht this "peace" business.

Billy puts his arm around Judy's shoulder; of course, it wouldn't be a proper argument without him diving to his sweetheart's rescue.

– Ah reckon her's right. Theer cor be a war, not a proper nuclear one. It'd destroy the Albion, an evrythin. Even the Commies wouldn't do that.

– Oh, Albion'll be the Russians' fust target, mate. They ay never forgid us fer beatin they Red Army team in that friendly back in '57. Ya remember the one? Under the floodlights? They was 5-1 up at half-time, an we ommered em 6-5 after Davy Burnside did his ball-jugglin in the centre circle. They wo never forget that, ah'm tellin ya. They've got all the bombs aimed fer the Hawthorns roit now, they have.

– Bollocks have they!

– Eve a destruction, Bill. Eve a destruction.

– Seriously, Jonah. It wo happen. It cor happen.

– Fer the love a Christ, will yow stop callin me Jonah? Ah doe allwis predict stuff wrong.

– Yow ay exackly got the best track record, though, have ya?

– Well, ah'll be right abaht the nuclear war, yow see if I ay. An ah'm gunna spend me last five minutes on earth standin roit in front a yow pair, sayin "ah bloody towd ya so".

If they've heard him, they take no notice. They turn back to face each other, and with hopeless smiles stretched across their faces, lean in to lock mouths again. Cartwright looks back up at the sky, straining his eyes in the hope that he might see a few dozen bombs hurtling down. Instead, the wobbly wall propping him up gives a lurch, and his shoes slip on the loose soil beneath the soles.

Cartwright loses his footing and tumbles.

The fall's confusing. His vision's a blur of blue and green, the colours going in a circle so quickly that they become a jumbled mess, and he feels like he's getting a full-on kicking, with his arms, elbows and ribs getting knocked hard in quick succession. He reaches the bottom of the slope grazed and breathless, flat on his back. Then he opens his eyes to find himself lying at the feet of a gorgeous girl, with a sudden, unexpected and astonishing view all the way up the length of her legs into the depths of her skirt.

Just like him, the day's looking up.

*

– Oh my God! What happened? Is he aroit?

– Iss difficult ter tell from up here, Jude.

– Who's that standin over im?

– Iss difficult ter tell from up here, Jude.

– Is that Kath?

– Iss difficult ter... ah tell ya what, love, shall we gew on down an see?

~ 53 ~

Judy gathers as many of their things together as she can, and sets off down the slope. Billy grabs the rest and follows her. Like he's been following her for the last three months. Devotion isn't the word. He doubts there's a dog in the world that'd follow its master half as far as he'd follow Jude.

At first it was terrifying. A paralysing fear; a saw that sliced gradually through his nerves. The kind of gut-shredding feeling you got watching Albion try to defend a one-goal lead. The knowledge that there was everything to lose; that it could all fall to bits with the slightest wrong move. Fear of an atomic war was nothing compared to that terror which Billy got each and every time he walked up to the bus stop to try and speak to Judy, for all those months that he watched her from such a painful distance. So many efforts, and so many failures, he lost count.

But on that snowy January evening when he came out of the Brummie Road End, having watched Albion notch up their first win in months against Tottenham – an absolute peach from Bobby Cram in the first half, then a tap-in by Chippy Clark in the second to seal the points – she was there again, at the bus stop. And this time, he was shocked to realise she was the one watching him. They made eye contact, and she smiled. An actual, honest-to-God smile.

It took him a full five minutes to convince himself it was really true, that he wasn't fooling himself, but she really was shooting surreptitious glances his way, and giving him little grins. It was almost as if she was waiting there specially for him. But he was rooted to the spot. He knew he was going to blow it all again. He could well have blown it all again, if she hadn't breezed right on up to him, introduced herself, and started chatting away as if they did this every day.

He was gobsmacked; it had only been a week since Cartwright took her to the pictures (a week in which Billy had refused to even speak to the treacherous bastard), and panic started gnawing at his belly again. He was suddenly aware of his fragrant Bovril breath, and his hair sticking through the holes in his woolly hat at all angles. But in spite of his nerves, his meaty mouth and his catastrophic headgear, he somehow managed a smile, and decided to try a bit of small talk.

– D'ya come here offen, then?

– Iss a bus stop.

– Yeah. But, ah mean, iss a good un, ay it?

– Ah spose it is. Ah've never really thought abaht it that much. Iss a bus stop.

– Yow've got all the trees here, an…

– Am yow gunna chunter on abaht the bus stop all day, or am ya gunnew ask me out?

– Ask… ask ya out? Out wheer?
– Oh, bloody Nora. Try the pictures.
– Roit.
– Ask me, then!
– D'ya wanna g'ter the pictures wi me?
– Ah'd love tew.
– Will the Bughouse be aroit?
– No. We'm gewin ter the King's.
– Oh, okay. Fair enough. Woss on?
– Atta see, wo we? They've got a nice raffle theer, though. An ah'd love a poster a Napoleon Solo.

That day, he learned that sometimes things happen against all odds. The Albion defence keeping Jimmy Greaves quiet for a whole ninety minutes. The girl of your dreams picking you over your sleazy worm of a best mate. There's no explaining it; these things are just meant to happen.

The days passed, and then the weeks, and then the months, and he got to know her even better, and the fear just got smaller and smaller. He got used to her taste in music – Jude loves all these folk singers with things to say about the world, and once you get over the fact that you can't really dance to any of their songs, it isn't bad listening. In turn, she tried some of Billy's favourite mod records – not just The Who and The Kinks, but some of the newer sounds, the black music from America – and she seemed to enjoyed them. Or if she didn't, then at least she was too busy kissing him to moan.

He started speaking to Cartwright again, eventually. It's too good an opportunity to pass up, the chance to rub the arrogant bugger's face in it. She's an absolute cracker, is Jude, and she picked him. Him. He'll never let Cartwright forget that, if he lives to be a hundred. Fair play to the daft bastard, he seems to take it in his stride, keeps his mouth buttoned whenever Billy gets a couple of digs in at him, but still, that doesn't let him off the hook. Billy's determined to keep the fun going as long as he can. It's no more than the slimy little sod deserves.

Oddly enough, Judy still seems to get on alright with Cartwright. Neither of them have told Billy exactly what happened on their first and only date; Jude just promises that she was never even the slightest bit interested in Cartwright. If she says so, that's enough. She'd never lie. He's almost certain she'd never lie.

– Billy, hurry up! He might need an ambulance!

Judy's voice pulls him out of his daydream, but gazing at her face is nearly enough to send him straight back into another. For the first time in a couple of years – for the first time since losing Mom – he really feels

~ 55 ~

like things are going to work out alright for him. The world's never been a perfect place; not for him, it hasn't. But maybe this is as close to perfection as it's meant to get.

It was terrifying at first. Of course it was. But as Billy follows Judy down the slope to where Cartwright's lying prone on the ground, the only fear left in him is what he'd ever do without her.

*

– Kath! That yow, me wench? Hang on, we'm comin down!

Judy scurries down the bank, careful to pick her steps carefully, trying her best – like she always does – to keep her feet in a changing world.

It's not just assassinations and space walks. It's not just foreign wars and civil rights. Changes are happening around the Black Country, too: all the old bomb sites she grew up around are being filled in, and the local councils are taking a wrecking ball to the slums the Luftwaffe missed, putting up their brand new towers in the sky, like something from a science-fiction flick. In Birmingham they're busy building the city of the future: gigantic roads everywhere, ready for the good times ahead when everyone, even the poorest of folks, will own their own car; entire streets and shopping centres forged from bright new concrete. They're even rebuilding New Street Station under the ground!

She can't think of anything more exciting.

If everything around her can change so much in such a short space of time, then the rest of the world can change too. It's so obvious. Bob says so, and Joan. Even Donovan, and Tom Paxton, and Phil Ochs, and Buffy Sainte Marie, and all the other folkies she's picked up scratchy recordings of in the concrete bunker record shops in central Birmingham. At the Jug o' Punch Club down Digbeth Civic Hall on a Thursday night, you can hear the Ian Campbell Folk Group singing Ewan MacColl covers, Jon Raven performing old industrial songs of the Black Country, and a lad from Acocks Green called Jasper who always sings funny topical songs. Everyone on the scene is committed to stopping a war before it starts, ending the poison of racialism, giving a helping hand and a say in the world to all people. Soon there'll be a fair chance for everyone in life, no matter what they look like, where they come from or who their parents are.

Panic attacks are a thing of the past, now there's such a bright future ahead. Billy's part of that future: she's played him all of her Dylan and Baez records, and quite a few of the other political folkies, and he seems to like them. He still prefers his mod stuff, obviously, even though most of that's just empty pop crap with nothing to say about the world. It's

~ 56 ~

fine. So what if he seems to spend more time worrying about West Bromwich Albion than the deteriorating political situation in Rhodesia? You can't change a fella overnight. Things like that come with time, patience, and a lot of dedicated pestering.

That's why she's agreed to go along and watch the football today. Maybe she can get Billy along to one of the anti-Vietnam marches in a month or two. Maybe. She's invited Kath to the match as well so she won't be bored stiff on her own. Talking to Kath about politics is like discussing beachwear with an Eskimo, but they can always catch up on the latest gossip, like they used to of a Friday night before Judy met Bill. Whenever they chat now – finding spare minutes here and there to slip into each other's houses and have a good natter – it all feels so different. These days, it isn't just Judy hanging on Kath's every word anymore, living her life through her friend's scrapes and exploits. She's finally got a life of her own to brag about, and sometimes it really feels like Kath's a touch green about it all.

That in mind, is there any harm in introducing her to Cartwright? He's a nice lad. More or less. And she had a lovely night out with him back in January! More or less.

She reaches the bottom of the slope with Billy beside her. It is Kath standing over Cartwright: they can see her clearly. And it looks like they're already getting along just grand.

*

Kath looks down at the figure lying at her feet. His eyes are out on stalks; she takes a quick step back and flattens her skirt around her legs before speaking.

– Am yow aroit, mate?

He smiles and props his head up with one hand, elbow resting against the stubbly turf.

– Ah was dewin quite nicely juss then, ta.

He pauses for a few seconds, an uncertain look replacing that confident smile, and then clears his throat.

– So... what'll yow do when the Russians annihilate us?

– Sorry?

– Yow've got five minutes ter live. How d'ya spend it?

Kath blinks.

– Ya mean after ah've finished queuing ter use the loo?

He laughs – maybe a bit too hard, given it isn't the best joke she's ever come out with – and opens his mouth to answer, but a couple of arriving figures cut him off. It's Judy, with Billy close in tow.

– Jonah, thank God yam aroit! We thought ya was a goner up theer! Any road, ya must a met Kath at least. Her lives next door ter me. Her's me best friend!

The useless lump in the parka smiles again.

– Oh, we was gerrin well-acquainted, ar.

– Kath, this is Jonah.

– No, not Jonah. Cartwright. Johnny Cartwright.

Kath frowns down at the lad on the floor.

– How come they call ya Jonah?

– They doe. They call me Cartwright.

– Well, ah spose iss nice ter meet ya, Jonah.

He reaches up with his right hand, and for a horrible second she isn't sure whether he's offering a handshake or trying to get his fingers where they definitely don't belong. Before he can manage either, Billy jumps in.

– Any road, Jonah, shift yer arse, eh? Ya cor lie abaht all afternoon. We've gorra match ter get tew.

– Doe get tellin me ter shift! Ah've been ready an hour, now! Iss yow an Jude ah bin waitin fer! Jesus, it comes ter summat, it does. A workin mon bein ordered abaht by schoolkids.

So he's got a job. Kath's used to being the only one with any money whenever she's out with Jude and Billy. For the first time, she finds herself giving the freak at her feet a second glance.

– Oh? Wheer d'ya work?

Jonah – or Cartwright, whichever he really goes by – sits up with bright eyes as soon as she speaks.

– Ah'm down at FBG Bolts & Rivets. Trainin me up fer a management job, they am.

Kath stares at the lad coolly, carefully.

– Management? Seriously? Ay yow a bit young fer that?

His cheeks flush. He fidgets a bit, adjusting the collar of his Fred Perry shirt.

– Doe let me youthful looks fool ya, missis! Ah'm a wise owd head, me. Trust me; as soon as they interviewed me down the factory, they knew ah was they mon. Ah took ter the job loike a dog ter water.

– Ya mean a duck ter water.

– No, a dog. A dog ter water.

Billy interrupts.

– Jonah, her's roit. How many dogs have yow sid bobbin down the cut recently? Iss a *duck* ter water.

– No it ay! Yow watch, on an hot day, all the dogs, they dive roit inter ponds an lakes an gew splashin abaht. They love it! They tek tew it loike a dog ter water!

Kath watches Billy roll his eyes and shrug his shoulders with the same expression that she tends to pull when Judy starts on about some hot new political cause.

– Roit, have it yower way. Ya took ter the job loike a drownin poodle.

– Oi! Doe yow talk tew a workin mon loike that!

– Oh, shurrup yer chunterin an gi us hand wi this, will ya?

Him and Judy are hoisting up the banner they've made for the match, grasping a broom handle each and trying to get the sign vaguely vertical. The wind's catching the sheet and making it difficult to hold. Cartwright dashes to give Billy a hand, and for a few heartbeats Kath watches the pair of them grapple with the broom; each lad looks more like they want to snatch it off the other one than help each other get it upright. The realisation dawns on her, sudden but sure, that Cartwright's the lad who Judy went on a date with that one night in January; the one she wouldn't talk about for days afterward, and even then only in abrupt, evasive answers. This is the mystery man who she insisted was an absolute dream fella, but who she dumped for Billy within a week. Pretty odd for Jude to invite him along on her afternoon with Billy. And to invite her along too.

Unless.

Wouldn't it be just like Judy to try and set her up with some stray?

– Kath! Can ya spare an hand, love?

With Cartwright and Billy manhandling one side of the banner, Judy's struggling with her own end. She's a meddling little cow, that one. Kath's happy enough on her own; she's had plenty of lads take her out in the last couple of years; enough that her mam saw fit to start lecturing her about personal morality and the evils of artificial contraception. Also enough that she's learned to enjoy a bit of personal freedom in her life. Why should love and sex be things to fret about? There are years ahead to find a good bloke, to think about building a life for herself. The typing pool at work's full of women who used to be girls just like Jude: so eager to find themselves a fella to settle down with and raise a kid or two that they forgot about the bit that should have come in between; their youth.

But Judy's heart's in the right place. It's what you have to remember with her. Billy's the same; Kath's never seen a pair so suited to one another, in all their doe-eyed glory. It wouldn't do any harm to keep her happy. Go through the motions.

She takes the strain of the banner off Judy for a second, and with a bit of wrestling, they manage to get the thing upright and steady. It'll have to come straight back down when the bus comes, but for now, that doesn't matter. The important thing is that they're here, they're together, and they're having fun. And in that difficult pose they set off through the alley, smiles and giggles, as a sudden shout and clatter in the yard of the Gunsmiths Arms sends a storm of pigeons flapping over their heads and into the bright spring sky.

*

Kath's either a devil or an angel. Cartwright's never believed in either before, but when he looked into the heavens above her hemline, he had what could only be described as a spiritual experience. Not the kind of spiritual experience which makes you take a vow of celibacy, either.

Twenty minutes on the bus to the Hawthorns – a ride which seems to last an hour – puts him in thrall. He can't look away. While Billy and Judy do their usual Mills & Boon act, he studies the celestial vision opposite him as closely as he can. Ruler-straight, shoulder-length amber hair; a pale freckled face with bright green eyes, a chest that isn't as pronounced as Jude's but goes well with her slender figure. Even as the usual crowd of lads pile on and head for the top deck singing *WE'VE GORRA TICKET TER ROID*, it barely distracts him from Kath.

Until she opens her mouth. Then she pesters Cartwright for details about his job to the point where he starts to lose the will to breathe. She wants to know everything about what he does down at the factory, what kind of training he's being put through for this "management position" of his, and what responsibilities they'll be giving him. He has to think sharp to keep the answers coming. And when he drags his attention away from knotting tongues with Judy, Billy keeps giving him funny glances, looking like he might just be starting to suss things out.

As if all that isn't bad enough, Tommy's waiting for him on the Birmingham Road as they get off the bus, leaning against a wall with his black jacket slung over his shoulder, idly flipping a ha'penny up and snatching it out of the air with barely a glance as supporters bustle by on their way to the ground. His busy blue eyes scan the matchday crowd, flicking from one person to another, forever on the lookout for one thing or another; only Tommy ever knows what. He's doing his best to look cool. And annoyingly, he's managing it. Like he always does.

– Aroit, little Johnny?

Cartwright shrugs.

– How do, Tommy.

His brother stops flicking the ha'penny for a few seconds to sweep his hand across his blond hair, checking the rough parting down the side. Cartwright finds himself lifting his hand to do the same, and then puts his arm back down, annoyed at himself. He shouldn't be copying Tommy; not anymore. Not now he's paying his own way in the world.

There's a sudden pain in his ribs; Kath's standing beside him, nudging him insistently.

– Ay ya gunna introduce me, Jonah?

– Oh, bloody hell. Aroit. This is me brother. Tommy.

– Nice ter meet ya, Tommy. Ah'm Kath.

Cartwright watches his brother glance Kath up and down. He looks lost for words. Cartwright can't even remember the last time that happened.

– Yow a friend a little Johnny's, then?

– Juss met im today.

– Well, doe worry. Ah know what he's loike, but trust me, it doe run in the family.

Kath giggles at that, a bit too much for Cartwright's liking. He feels his cheeks flush. He shouldn't let Tommy yank his chain, he knows it, but there's a big difference between knowing something and heeding it. A bloody big difference.

– Nah, me wench, Tommy couldn't live up to mar standards. He ay got the career prospects ah've got, fer starters.

There's a moment, a wonderful moment in Cartwright's mind when he reckons that he's just landed a killer blow to shut his brother up once and for all. He's watching closely for the look of surprise on Tommy's face, the telltale expression that shows he's been taken down a peg or two. That expression never comes.

Instead, in a heartbeat, Cartwright suddenly remembers that Tommy knows exactly what he does for a living. There are no secrets in their house; no tall tales of being on the fast track to the boardroom would ever have survived Cartwright coming home from his first day in his filthy overalls. With the horror that comes with knowing he's been caught in a lie, Cartwright braces himself, sees Tommy smile, and waits for reality to collapse on him.

– Nah, thass roit.

Tommy says the words quietly, humbly. For a precious second, Cartwright thinks he's off the hook. Tommy's going to be a gent and keep his mouth shut! After all, that's what brothers are for!

– Why would ah wanna piss abaht earnin twenty quid a week when ah could be sweepin shit up loike yow fer a few bob at the end a the day?

Oh no. No, no, no.

– What was that, Tommy? Summat abaht sweepin up?

A few seconds ago Billy was busy pointing out the matchday sights and sounds to Judy, but his ears have pricked right up now. Cartwright wants to tell him to shut up, but he finds that he can't even look him in the face.

Tommy doesn't have that problem.

– Aroit, Billy. Ah loike the hat, mate! Ah was just talkin about little Johnny pushin a brush abaht a factory fer a livin. Loike a little housewife, he is, keepin the place spick an span. Still, it keeps him out a trouble, eh?

– Sweepin up? Thass his job? His whole job? He ay weldin, or brazin, or castin, or mekkin bearins, or foilin papers, or runnin round the place wi a bowler hat an a briefcase? He juss tickles the floor wi a *broom*?

The eyes are on Cartwright. The accusing eyes. He wishes the Birmingham Road would swallow him up.

– Is that what he's bin tellin ya? Johnny, yome a funny bastard, yow am!

A bloke walks up carrying a hot dog in each hand, both of them slathered in marigold-yellow mustard. Tommy's best mate, Dodd the Mod; a rough bastard in smart clothes who'll happily pat you on the back or break your nose, depending on how he feels at the time.

– Cheers, Doddy! Hey, yow'll never guess what? Me dopey little brother's onny bin tellin all his mates he's gunna be runnin his own factory in twelve months or so!

Grinding his teeth until he's sure the enamel will splinter and crack in his mouth, Cartwright interrupts.

– Is theer summat ya wanted ter see me abaht, Tom?

Tommy takes his hot dog off Dodd the Mod and then licks some stray mustard off his fingertips.

– Rent money, ya little pillock.

– Roit then.

Cartwright steps up close to hand a few coins over. As he presses the cash into his brother's palm, he grabs Tommy's hand as tight as he can, squeezing so hard he's sure something will give with a crunch.

– Ah wo forget this, Tommy. Ah swear ter God.

Tommy says nothing, but he's got a smirk on his face as Cartwright lets go of his hand and steps away. Pocketing the hard-earned change Cartwright's given him, he nods to Kath.

– Stay cool, missis.

Kath's fiddling with her necklace, a little bronze cross. She won't stop staring at Tommy.

– Nice ter meet ya!

Tommy clicks his fingers and points the index one at Billy and Judy, gun-like.

– Tek care, lovebirds.

– Ar, see ya later, Tom!

He leaves, and Cartwright turns to face the others. His face is hot, but he keeps his expression calm, neutral. He's buggered if he's going to lose whatever dignity's left in him. Judy's avoiding his eyes, staring down at her boots. When he finds the courage in his gut to look at Kath, she's taking a bigger interest in her nails than in him. Only Billy's prepared to make eye contact with him, and he's got a grin the size of Czechoslovakia across his face. He's not going to let this drop. With a nauseous lurch in his belly, Cartwright realises that this has made Billy's year.

– So.

He stares at the three of them until they all return his gaze. He tilts his chin up.

– Anyone fancy gewin to the match wi a lousy floor-scrubber, then?

*

The queue for the turnstiles is longer than usual, and they shuffle forward like a line of grannies on pension day. As Judy witters to Kath about her plans for leaving school, Billy adjusts his cowboy hat, tucks the homemade banner down by his leg, and then leans over to Cartwright.

– Iss aroit, Jonah. Iss fine. So ya med up all that stuff abaht becomin a managin director a the company by this time next year! T'ay the end a the world. No need ter be embarrassed.

– Honest?

– Course.

Judy squeezes Billy's elbow, and he turns to look into those perfect eyes for the millionth time.

– Theer's a bloke sellin programmes, Bill!

– Ar, theer usually is.

– D'ya want one?

– Yeah, gew on. Actually, while yam at it, ya can get one fer the Great Pretender here an all.

He jerks a thumb towards Cartwright, who smiles weakly at the joke, and waits till Judy's out of earshot before answering.

– Ah'll smosh yow one in a minute if yow ay careful, Bill.

The Black Country's finest broom boy manages to grind that sentence out from between his teeth, keeping a crazed grin on his face at the same time. With a glossy layer of sweat on his brow, he's starting to look like a ventriloquist's dummy.

– Now, now. Imagine what a mess yow'd mek. All that blood yow'd atta sweep up.

– Aroit. So ah've started at the bottom, ay I? Well, we'll juss wait an see what ah'm dewin in a year's time, eh? Cos ah tell yow here an now, mucka, ah'm gunna mek summat a mar life. I ay gewin down me owd man's road. Ah'll show yow. Tek mar word.

The words tumble off Cartwright's tongue with such anger and passion that for the first time in ages, Billy feels really bad about having a go at him. He's just about to back down and apologise when Judy gets back with the programmes she's bought. Cartwright forks over a sixpence for his, while Billy angles his head down next to Judy's so they can glance over theirs together, and he can bask in the clean smell of Sunsilk on her hair.

He can sense the tension in Cartwright, and he decides not to push his luck too much with him. After all, it'll only be a few weeks until he has to go out and look for work himself, and who knows what he might end up doing? Passing the County Certificate might give him a leg up, but then again, it may not be worth the paper it's printed on. It's no use bragging to your rivals that you've won this week if you go and get thumped 5-0 the next. It's time for him to lay off Cartwright. At least until he knows for sure that he's not going to be pushing a broom around a factory himself next month.

The queue snakes its way into the gates, the usual line of scarf-wearing men and boys, with a woman here or there holding her husband's or boyfriend's hand. Billy's walked through the turnstiles more times than he can remember with Dad, and a fair number with Cartwright after that. But today will be the first time he's taken Judy through, and Kath too.

It hits him now, for the first time: he's got to take care of people he loves. He's got to be a man. Responsibility. It's not just a word being thrown around by teachers anymore; it's in his life, and it's biting at his thoughts. From now on, it's always going to be there.

When you're little, you've got your old man to keep you safe at the match; then you get older, and your mates look out for you instead. All you've got to worry about is whether the Albion can score, whether the defence can hold on, whether they can get two points out of the game. But now it's up to him to make sure the girls are alright on the terraces. Judy's hand's soft and warm in his own, and suddenly he imagines that it's the hand of an imaginary son; his own little lad coming along to the match for the first time. He remembers bumping into a bloke bringing his own kid here for the first time back in the autumn, shepherding the lad through the crowd with his old rattle whirring. He could never do that, surely. Could he?

It's not like he's got to worry about it any time soon. He hasn't even been to bed with Judy yet; last month he admitted to her that he's never done it before (even Cartwright doesn't know that; the dim bastard still believes that story about Billy shagging a milkmaid on holiday in Cornwall eighteen months ago) and she told him she hasn't either. It's not all bad news: they've found some pretty enjoyable ways of keeping each other company in the meantime, but they're going to wait a little while before going that extra step. And that's fine. When you love someone as much as he loves Jude, that's absolutely fine.

The queue shuffles forward. When they reach the gate, Billy puts two red-brown ten bob notes onto the counter for the ticket man, paying for both him and Jude. He's buying adult tickets nowadays, and for the first time, that feels right. He takes his four shillings change and pushes through the turnstile; following him, Judy somehow manages to get her legs caught between two of the revolving bars, and he has to turn and help her wrestle on through.

Responsibility. It's a man's job. But he reckons he might just be up to it after all.

*

Judy's never felt so small. She's not really sure what she expected the inside of a football stadium to look like – she imagined something a bit like an open-air circus with seats or benches, some kind of amphitheatre around the pitch – but she's confronted with a totally foreign sight as she follows Billy onto the terraces.

The Brummie Road End's a choppy sea of heads and hands, population swelled by six months of notoriety as the first proper home end in the West Midlands. There are so many people; there are too many people, swaying with and against one another, and above them – if you turn your back on the pitch and look right up towards the daylight shining under the roof at the back of the stand – there are enough flags and banners to put a medieval army to shame. Most are handpainted signs, spelling BAGGIES, THROSTLES or WEST BROM in haphazard print. Some banners have got people's names on them, and although she doesn't know half of the Albion players from Adam, Judy at least recognises names like "Kaye", "Clark" and "Astle" from Billy harping on about them.

Other Brummie Roaders who don't want to show up empty-handed have brought along Union Jacks to wave. Some hold their scarves over their heads, some wave their bobble hats or caps, some still twirl wooden rattles like she's seen fans do in newsreels. A few yards away, behind a crush barrier, three lads are holding up tiles of slate, one in each hand, spelling A–L–B–I–N–O. She tries to shout to the boy on the right-hand side that he's got his letters mixed up, but he can't hear her over the noise from the rest of the stand.

Billy nudges her, and points to the banner under his arm. She takes hold of one handle, and together they unfurl it to display their handiwork: WBA. BRUMMIE ROAD END.

Just like that, they blend in with the rest of the madhouse.

There's a small swell of panic rolling through Judy's chest at being pressed in among so many people, and she works hard to keep it under control, the way the doctor's told her. There must be twenty or thirty thousand inside the stadium, a pulsing mass of people, stamping, clapping, cheering from the terraced stands on all four sides of the pitch. Billy points at the stand behind the opposite goal and tells her it's called the Smethwick End. To their left, running the length of the touchline, the Handsworth Side (but Billy says everyone's calling it the Rainbow Stand now, because of the gaily-painted seats in its upper tier). And to their right, the Halfords Lane Stand, with wooden frontage and letters of the alphabet all along the pitchside.

They're standing near the front of the terraces, among the kids and younger teenagers who perch on the concrete wall by the pitch, their legs straddling the stone. A chubby police constable whose uniform looks at least a size too small keeps pacing the byline, casting annoyed glances into the crowd every now and then. The teams come out and the songs begin, making Judy jump at the noise.

AL-BI-ON, AL-BI-ON, AL-BI-ON!

She finds the programme more interesting than what's happening on the pitch. There are advertisements on almost every page, some from local companies posting vacancies or shifting goods, while others scream about all the fun things you can blow your wages on of a weekend. The fun! The friendship! The *excitement* of ten-pin bowling! Discover the exotic world on your doorstep! Visit West Bromwich's very first Chinese restaurant!

Even this place which has cradled generations and survived world wars is marching into the space age. Hemmed in on terraces which have felt thousands of feet down the decades, she wonders for the first time what effect this exciting race for progress is going to have on ordinary people. On her.

– Billy!

– Ar?

– D'yow ever wonder wheer yow'll be in the future? Loike, in 1970?

He clasps his hands together around the handle of their banner and ponders it.

– Up the Brummie Road, most loikely.

– What about 1980?

– Up the Brummie Road, most loikely.

– 1990?

– Tough one. Up the Brummie Road, most loikely.

– The year *2000*?

– Up the Brummie Road. Except we'll all be hoverin over the terraces in our space-suits by then. An the ball's gunna be jet-powered.

– Roit. How will the players run after a jet-powered ball?

– Oh, the players'll be robots, bab.

He leans over and squeezes her waist with one free hand. The choir starts up behind them, ribbing the policeman pacing the byline.

WHO'S THAT COPPER WI THE HELMET ON?
DIXON! DIXON!
WHO'S THAT COPPER WI THE HELMET ON?
DIXON OF DOCK GREEN!
ON THE BEAT ALL DAY
ON THE WIFE ALL NOIT
WHO'S THAT COPPER WI THE HELMET ON?
DIXON OF DOCK GREEN!

The chubby policeman looks even angrier, and starts pointing at faces in the crowd to warn them, but the players are ready to start the game, the Brummie Roaders are shouting and singing, and right now, Judy doubts whether the whole West Midlands Constabulary could shut them up.

*

The game's ten minutes old, and Kath can't take her eyes off it. The action. The movement. It's as if there's a free-flowing chess match going on right in front of her. She's always thought she was well rid of the timid teacher's pet she used to be – that brainy girl forever getting picked on at school needed to grow up, and that's exactly what she did – but it's that old side of her which is so excited, so captivated by what she's seeing on the pitch.

She mentions to Cartwright that it reminds her of chess, as much to break the ice as anything. It was really cruel, the way his brother went and embarrassed him. He's a good-looking lad, that Tommy, but still. There was no need for it. She leans over, cups her hand around his ear and yells over the choir behind them, and even then, Cartwright struggles to hear her. She repeats herself, and he doesn't seem impressed.

– What am yow on about?

– Chess. Look at yer man, theer. The one near the goal, on the right side.

Cartwright smirks, and leans over to cup her ear and shout his reply.

– He's a full-back. His name's Bobby Cram.

– He's a castle.

– He's a what?

– A castle. A rook. When the blue an whites have got the ball…

– They'm called the Albion, missis, not "the blue an whites".

– When the blue an whites have got the ball, he runs up the pitch on the right. When they lose the ball, he runs back, and then moves across ter protect the goal from enemy attacks. Allwis up, down, an across. He's a castle.

– He must be Dudley Castle, then. Seen better days, loike.

– An that fella up near the front. Keeps runnin diagonally; sometimes towards the corner of the pitch, sometimes towards the red team's goal. Allwis diagonal attacks.

– Tony Brown.

– Well, Tony Brown's yer bishop. An yer man in the middle, doe gew up too far, stays back ter support the attack.

– Gerry Howshall.

– He's a pawn.

– But when Howshall reaches the other end a the pitch, he doe turn into a queen, does he?

Kath ignores him. She's starting to realise it's often the best thing to do.

– Our boys, the blue an whites – the Albion – they try ter find gaps between the red players tew attack. But why do they gi em so much space when the red side have got the ball? Ya never gi folk space on a chess board; ya need ter hem em in, trap em so they mek mistakes.

Cartwright looks like he's got absolutely no idea what she's on about. He's forming that expression Mr Barrett always puts on at work when she makes a suggestion he doesn't quite understand. It's the kind of expression that precedes a pat on the back (or the arse), and a comment of *good girl*. Kath soldiers on before Cartwright can do either.

– They shouldn't gi em room ter run wi the ball. They shouldn't even gi em room ter pass the ball. They should run at em, pressure em, force em back. Same as when yam closin in fer checkmate in chess. OI! YOW, THEER! GERRIN AN TEK THE BALL OFF IM!

Cartwright laughs in a way that sounds more than a little forced.

– Nah. That wouldn't work.

– Why not?

– Cos they'm footballers, not bloody marathon runners. Can ya imagine how far they'd atta run evry match if they was chargin the other team down evry time they lost the ball? They'd be knackered. Yow'd atta scrape em up off the pitch at full time. No one can run that much. Not after a Friday night piss-up an a big Satdee lunch.

– So, stop the players drinkin an stuffin emselves before a matchday.

– Jesus Christ, woman! Next yow'll want em ter gi up smokin!

Cartwright shakes his head in disgust at the thought, and as if to ward off evil spirits, pulls a Parker from the pack in his pocket and sticks it between his lips. He offers one to Kath. She shakes her head. Ciggies do your skin no good, and even in the shade of the Brummie Road End's roof, she's got high hopes for that springtime tan. A cold breeze tickles at her leg, and looking down, she realises she's laddered her right stocking by the knee, which'll mean forking out three and eleven for a new pair. But as the Albion rush forward, and catch a sudden gap in the other team's line, she doesn't even care.

*

Cartwright's sucking the glowing fag down to his fingertips as Albion score their first. When the players press forward with the ball, the noise up the Brummie Road grows, and when the ball hits the back of the net, the surge begins. It starts way up the back, like always, everyone on tiptoe leaning on the shoulders of the lads in front, and cascades right down to where Cartwright's standing with Kath.

– Quick, gimme yer arm!

– Ya what?

– Yer arm!

He manages to loop his arm around Kath's just as the surge hits them and pushes them down towards the wall at the front. He laces his fingers with hers as Jeff Astle wheels away to celebrate his goal.

It's a well-deserved lead, and all the signs up and down the Brummie Road with Astle's name written on are high in the air, being waved back and forth. Up above, near the back, standing on a crush barrier again to lead the choir, Sammy gets the heart of the stand going, and Cartwright joins in as the chant ripples down to the front.

WE YELL! WE YELL!
AN WHEN WE YELL WE YELL LIKE HELL
AND THIS IS WHAT WE YELL:
ONE, TWO, THREE, FOUR,
THREE, TWO, ONE, FOUR
WHO FOR?
WHEREFORE?
WHO THE HELL ARE WE FOR?
A-L-B-I-O-N
AL-BI-ON!
AL-BI-ON!
AL-BI-ON!

When they get to the "Al-bi-on" bit, Kath even starts chanting along. She doesn't half have a good voice. Almost without thinking about it, he tightens his grip on her hand. And she squeezes back. He's sure he feels it, just for a second, that gentle pressure around his fingers. All of a sudden, it doesn't seem to matter about Tommy humiliating him, about Billy winding him up. Nothing seems to matter.

He doesn't even know why he lets them get on his nerves so much in the first place. Actually, come to think of it, that's not true; he *does* know. He never had much of a head for schoolwork, and he doesn't even have any natural talents; he's alright at kicking a ball about in the park, and he's alright at making a few trick shots on the snooker table, but nothing more. When you take all of that away, what have you got left? Nothing but pride. Pride in being yourself, pride in surviving all the shit that life's thrown at you, and still coming back for more. It's not easy to stand around smiling while your brother (the lad who once ran crying to your nan because he pissed his pants in church) and your best mate (the idiot who actually expects you to believe that he once knobbed a milkmaid in Cornwall) trample that pride into the ground.

But the feel of Kath's hand, the thrilling touch of her skin; it's worth all the pride in him and more.

The first chant gives way to a second, the whole crowd roaring to the tune of *The Battle Hymn Of The Republic*:

WHEER WAS THE GOALIE WHEN THE BALL WAS IN THE
NET?

WHEER WAS THE GOALIE WHEN THE BALL WAS IN THE NET?
WHEER WAS THE GOALIE WHEN THE BALL WAS IN THE NET?
HE WAS HANGING ROUND THE GOALPOST WI HIS BALLS AROUND HIS NECK!

This time, Kath's singing even before he is. As they chant together, her hand slips out of his. As subtly as he can, Cartwright tries to find it again, but it's gone.

*

Full time. A 1-0 Albion win. A jubilant crowd pouring out of the Brummie Road End.

Billy spots two familiar faces as they wander out: a man and a young lad. It takes a minute to place where he's seen them before; way back in the autumn, he spoke to them before the lad's first time at the match. The kid's not carrying a rattle anymore, but he's still wearing a bobble hat in spite of the warm sun overhead.

– Aroit theer, mate! Has he enjoyed his fust season, then?

The dad looks up, surprised, and squints at Billy to see if he can recognise him. After a few seconds' scrutiny he still looks none the wiser, but answers anyway.

– Ar! He's gone football mad, ay ya, Matthew?

Matthew puts one small fingertip in his mouth and gently chews on it in reply. At Billy's side, Judy's fiddling with her handbag, pulling her new Kodak Brownie out.

– We ay gorr'enny photos of ourselves yet! Would ya mind tekkin some pictures of us, Mr…

– Oh, ah'm Bob. Bob Freeman. Ar, gi us yer camera, love. How d'ya work it?

– Iss dead easy. This wheel ter wind it on, this button to work the shutter.

They huddle together down the road from the ground, all smiles and giggles as Mr Freeman winds the camera's film and puts his eye to the viewing lens. Slowly, with Matthew clinging on to his trouser leg and gawping at the scene, he starts to take pictures.

Click. Billy with his hands on Judy's neck, pretending to throttle her; Judy laughing hysterically and swinging her handbag at Billy's head.

Click. Cartwright and Billy with an arm around each other's shoulders, both sticking a thumb up for the camera.

Click. Judy sniggering, her hair blown over her face, with Kath kissing her left cheek and Billy kissing her right.

Click. The four of them: Kath on the left with her dress hitched up her legs to make the hem short, like the new skirts; Cartwright beside her, gazing at her with an enigmatic smirk; Billy and Judy to the right, arm in arm, sticking their tongues out.

Mr Freeman hands the camera back to Judy.

– Hope they turn out aroit, darlin. Tek care. Matthew, come on! We'd best get home fore yer mom comes huntin after us!

Judy tucks the Kodak away. It'll be a few weeks before she gets the film developed, but when she does, she'll get copies done for Billy, Cartwright and Kath. These pictures will be like a memento shared between the four of them. She's sure the future's going to be wonderful, but all the same, days like today race by far too quickly.

– Guys; d'ya promise we'll stick by each other? Us fower? In the future, loike?

Cartwright shrugs.

– Depends on all them Russian missiles ah spose, missis.

Kath laughs and puts a hand over her heart.

– Oh, ah'll allwis be with ya, sweetheart. Without me, who'd sort yer clothes an yer curly hair out?

Billy nods cautiously, and raises an eyebrow as he puts on a ridiculous Hollywood voice.

– We'll always have the Brummie Road, sweetheart.

Judy rolls her eyes.

– Seriously, though. No matter what happens, we'll allwis be mates, the fower of us. Till death do us part. Promise?

Faces straight, they all nod dutifully. Judy smiles in the sunshine. Whatever the years ahead bring, she's sure everything will work out well. When you've got friends you can rely on, nothing can stand in your way.

She's certain of it.

April 1966

Jonah motors down the narrow roads of the estate like a man on the run, pushing the second-hand scooter for all it's worth – all twenty pounds, nine shillings and sixpence – feeling the wind scour his eyes and ears of the morning's graft and fill his lungs with precious life. His new job at the foundry's better than sweeping bloody floors, and it puts a few more bob in his pocket, lets him save up for the odd treat, but charging furnaces is hard and hot work, and walking out into the fresh air at the end of each day is like being reborn.

The strong gusts and the slipstream rattle the World Cup Willie keyring dangling from the Lambretta's right-hand mirror and whip his Republic of South Vietnam flag, mounted on the back, into a flapping frenzy. He wobbles a bit going round the corner, swayed by a devastating combination of the westerly gale and the twelve bottles of Double Diamond he put away down the boozer last night. In the process, he comes within a whisker of mowing down the Co-op delivery lad on his bicycle, and has just enough time to swear at the kid before pulling to a halt outside the house and puncturing the engine's snarl with a belch that tastes of Woodbines. The night's revelries are doing their best to force their way back up his throat, and it takes a second or two to swallow them back down before putting the kickstand down and climbing off. It may be his first ride, but he's chuffed at how fast he's getting the hang of the Lambretta. Not quite like a dog to water, but close enough that he already feels right at home with the 50cc engine revving between his knees.

He glances along the terraced row and picks out Judy's house a few doors down. The front door's open, and Jonah spots Judy's mom hunched over outside, scrubbing the doorstep. Her sleeves are rolled, and he can see one of her pale forearms scarred from burns; Judy mentioned once that she got those in the war. He doesn't know the whole story, but Jonah reckons she deserves some respect all the same. After all, it isn't her fault her daughter's grown up such a bossy little cow.

– Aroit, Mrs Fletcher!

The kneeling woman squints up at him, a few strands of greying brown hair slipping from under her headscarf.

– Ah. Mornin, Jonah.

Twelve months ago he'd have moaned at being called Jonah, but he doesn't even blink at it anymore. The name's stuck like plaster. Who was *Cartwright*, really, at the end of the day? Just a yampy little lad who worried about things that didn't concern him, and always let his ego get the better of him; he's best left in the past. But Jonah, now; Jonah's a young man with a future.

– Is Jude abaht, missis?

A shrug. The tight grey curls that have escaped her scarf shake with her scouring.

– Her might be lookin after Billy.

– Lookin after im?

Mrs Fletcher doesn't get chance to explain any further. Billy's better half – love of his life for fifteen torrid months – appears in the doorway, eyes narrowed, arms folded.

– Yooooou evil little shit!

– Judy! Language!

– Sorry, Mom. But in mar defence, he is an evil little shit.

– Jude, yow wor brought up ter use words loike that!

– Oh, gi it a rest, Mom. Yow've sid the state of our Bill. Iss the least he deserves.

Jonah eyes Jude warily. It's hard to believe she's the same girl he took to the pictures one cold night the winter before last. That shy, plump, likeable lass has been brutally bludgeoned to death by Moody Judy: a tempestuous seventeen-year-old permanently angry over some terrible wrong that's happening somewhere or other in the world and determined to share that anger with everyone around her. She's even taken to loafing about some weekends with university students in Birmingham, trying to "expand her horizons". Fat chance. As far as Jonah's concerned, there's no way anyone can expand anything in Birmingham these days without running into a bloody great ring road.

Still, that does him no good here and now. Confronted with Moody Judy in full sulk, Jonah decides a smile's called for. His charming smile. The kind of smile which gets him places at the odd Saturday night dance, which sometimes results in a lucky few minutes by a secluded factory wall, or the thrill of sneaking in the back door of his house with company. The kind of smile which might even win Kath over sometime soon. Fingers crossed.

– Ah'm here ter pick Billy up fer the match, me wench.

– He's in the bath.

Judy's mom scrubs away by his feet. Jonah realises he's standing on her clean step, and shifts his square-toes back onto the pavement.

– Well, is he nearly done?

– Done? Oh, ah reckon he's done enough. Done bloody plenty, he has.

Jonah breathes deeply and tries to stay calm. Sometimes he thinks Judy sets out to wind him up these days – like she wants him out of Billy's life altogether, so she can be left to warp the poor sod's mind – but he won't give her the satisfaction of getting all het up. He forces another grin.

– How long's he bin in theer?

Judy makes a theatrical show of casting her eyes up to the ceiling and counting.

– Oh, it'd be abaht… twelve hours.

– Twelve hours?! Has he hit an iceberg or summat?

Jonah squeezes past Judy into the hallway and starts up the stairs before she calls him down.

– No. Not the new bath. The owd un.

Jonah turns.

– The one out in the back yard?

– Correct, my dear Holmes.

– Well, what the bloody hell's he dewin out theer?

– Thinkin abaht what he's done, if he's woke up. Or what yow done tew im. Either way, I ay speakin tew im. Ya can gew out theer yerself.

Another deep breath. Jonah exhales this one slowly between his teeth, and thanks a god he doesn't particularly believe in for saving him from hearing stuff like this seven days a week. It's crossed his mind now and then, in the past year, how different things could have been if he'd stuck to his guns over Judy when he first asked her out. If he hadn't persuaded her to start seeing Billy instead. Would he have put up with fifteen months of strops like this?

Not bloody likely.

That's the best thing about Kath. It's not just that she's such a looker; she doesn't spend every waking hour moaning at you about the state of the world, either. In the twelve months he's spent getting to know her – all the times he's taken her to Albion matches, stood up the Brummie Road with her – he's come to feel like she's different. Being around Kath isn't anything like going out and pulling a bit of skirt on the town of a weekend; it's more than just wanting to park the pink bus for a night. She talks a lot of sense about stuff – especially football – and he enjoys listening to her. He loves making her laugh, too, telling silly jokes and doing impressions of Billy and Judy. It feels a bit saft to say it about a wench, but she's like a mate to him.

But how do you ask out one of your mates? For all that Jonah's used to chatting up the dolly birds of a Saturday night, he's never actually thought about going steady with one before, and he's definitely never struck up any meaningful friendships with any of them. The most he's ever given them on a Sunday morning is a quick breakfast, a cup of tea, and a promise-filled walk to the front door before his nan wakes up and starts hollering at him. He'd ask Billy for a bit of advice, except that he'd never live it down. And the idea of asking Judy for advice makes him sweat harder than any foundry furnace.

– What am ya waitin fer?

He pushes past her, walks down the hallway to the kitchen, his shoes clopping on the floor's red quarry tiles, and opens the back door.

The rusting iron tub's propped up on bricks in the small yard at the back of the house, and Billy's squeezed into its narrow girth, both arms hanging over the sides, his knees squashed up by his chest. He's still wearing his glad rags from last night: feet in shined shoes propped against the tub's dirty rim, black drainpipes – the ones Judy picked out for him at Burton's last month to match his tie – feathered by blossom that's blown off the tree by the house and scattered across the yard. His odd resting position's hitched his trouser legs up, exposing his pale matchstick calves. His head's lolling back, mouth wide open to the sky, as if the clouds will open up and pour water right down his gullet. To top it all, there's a rank odour around him that the strong wind can't quite carry away; ambling over, Jonah glimpses the lake of regurgitated beer that's flooded down Billy's shirt during the night, pooling in his lap and in the base of the tub around him. It's stained the white material an earthy shade of brown on its journey, and in places it's even collected in the shirt's folds, forming little vomit fjords which ripple briskly in the breeze.

– He showed up at midnight, more or less. Spent a quarter of an hour knockin on Kath's front door, till he realised it was the wrong house.

Judy's stood in the doorway behind Jonah, cupping her hand over her nose and mouth, her face sour at the smell.

– Then he woke me mom and dad up bangin on our door. Fell inter the hallway singin *Pretty Flamingo*.

– Thass a proper shame, tharris. Still, at least he dae embarrass hisself too bad, eh?

– Then he was sick on me dad.

Jonah scratches his head.

– Thass a gesture a respect in some countries, bab. Iss all the rage. Ya cor gew nowheer fer folk spewin on one another. Yer owd man should feel honoured that Billy chose im ter chuck up over.

– Am yow fishin fer a smack? This is yower fault!

– *Mar* fault? How's that? We onny went out fer a few swift halves.

– Swift halves? Christ almighty! Half gallons? Half barrels?

– Missis, it ay against the law tew have a few jars the night
befower the big match. Or it wor lass time ah checked. Iss still a free
country, ay it? Ya cor change that, however many Chairman Mao books
ya stick yer nose in.

– Woss that sposed ter mean?

It isn't really supposed to mean anything. He doesn't have a
problem with Judy being all political; with her dad being a shop steward, it
makes sense for her to follow in his footsteps. Still, she can be such an
annoying little do-gooder with it at times. With a raging hangover, the
words just slip out.

– Nuthin. Forget it.

She folds her arms. Never a good sign.

– Ah've had enough a yow. An im. Ah want the pair on ya out.
Five minutes.

She storms back inside and slams the door. Behind him, a
plaintive groan.

– Jonah, is that yow?

Billy's eyes – two craters of puffy indigo – have opened a slit. His
voice is a parched croak. His chin's shiny with puke.

– Ar, iss me. Am yow aroit?

Billy winces.

– I think ah'm sittin in sick.

– More rollin in it than sittin in it, mucka. Come on, up ya get.

– If ah'm gunna die, cor ah juss do it here?

– Yow ay jed juss yet. Ah doe fancy our chances if yer better half
comes back out again, mind. Her's in a choppin mood.

– Can you gi us an hand?

– Look, kidda, doe tek this the wrong way. But ya smell a bit
ronk. Ah reckon yow need a bath.

He manages to keep a straight face as he's saying it, something
he's quite pleased about. He's still busy keeping that straight face when
Billy breathes out calmly and lunges at him suddenly with a wild right
hook. The punch doesn't come anywhere near him – Jonah doesn't even
need to dodge it – but the swing has enough momentum to rock the
bathtub, tilting it off its supporting bricks, and rolling it all the way over, to
Billy's hapless alarm.

– BALLS!

– Am yow aroit, our Bill?

The bath's capsized, upside down, vomit and all. Billy's cocooned
underneath it with just one arm sticking out, trapped by the heavy rim. He
answers with all the dignity he's still got left, his voice echoing out from

the rusty tomb with the muffled sound of someone talking down a bad telephone line.

– Ah'm fine. Ya mind gerrin this tub off me?

– Depends. Am ya gunnew hit me after?

A few seconds pause.

– Probly not.

– Aroit then. Ah trust ya, pal.

With that tentative peace accord in place, Jonah lifts the tub – the bloody heavy tub – off the ground, and as it clanks back into an upright position, he takes Billy's hand and helps him up. He realises a bit too late that Billy's hand is as plastered in stomach juice as the rest of him, but he doesn't mention it. Mates are mates. Jonah decided that a long time ago, and he's sticking to it. He wipes his palm clean on a handy geranium leaf while Billy finds his feet.

– Ta.

– Thass what ah'm here fer. Well. No it ay. Ah'm here ter gi ya a lift, ay I?

– I ay sure ah'm fit fer the match, pal.

– Not fit fer the League Cup final? Ah've been waitin twelve bloody years fer today, mate. Twelve years juss ter see Albion win another cup! An ah took the afternoon off specially ter come an sort yow out. Thass fower hours' wages ah wo be gerrin.

– Ya shoulda took the day off in advance, loike me, eh?

– Oh, ar. Then ah coulda spent lass night pourin pints down me neck as if they was dandelion & burdocks. Fuckin hell, the state on ya!

Jonah stands to one side to let Billy into the house, but Judy's mom rushes over and shoos him back out.

– Doe come in wearin that lot, Bill! Ah've brought some of our Roy's clothes down fer ya. They should fit. He was a rake-thin little bastard in his day an all.

From the dark depths of the house they hear the voice of Judy, who's lurking within earshot.

– Mom! Language!

– No, iss yow what has ter watch yer language, madam. Ah'm yer mother. Ah fought a war. Ah can say what ah loike. Now, Billy; am yow sure yow've got evrythin up out on ya? Yow ay gunna do no more up-chuckin? Me husband wouldn't loike it if ya sicked up over the clothes he used ter wear. It wouldn't bother me, ya know, but he reckons he's gunna squeeze back into em any day now.

– Ah think ah'm aroit now, Mrs Fletcher. Thanks.

Jonah perches on the wall of the empty pig-sty out back while Billy changes into a pair of brown trousers, a white shirt and patterned V-neck jumper.

– Looks bostin, that does. Dead smart. Get yerself a flat cap, yow'll be all set, mate.

– Piss off.

– Yow'll wanna watch it up the Brummie Road wearin that lot. Some a the owd uns ull think they'm back in the Blitz. They'll be watchin the sky fer bombers.

For once, Billy takes the barb with a smile.

– Ar, well. Onny Bomber they'll see is out on the pitch. Our Tony, bombin forward ter score against the cockneys, eh?

– Oh, so yam in the mood ter watch the match after all? Good thing ah brung me scooter round then, ay it?

– Ya bought it? Ya finally bought it?

– Popped round Dodd's house roit after work. Iss parked outside, marra.

For the first time since Jonah arrived, Billy starts to look like a living human being again.

– Come on then. Ah've gorra see this.

Before they can make it to the front door, Judy corners them one last time. She points an index finger at the tip of Billy's nose. His bloodshot eyes swivel towards one another to focus on it. Her voice is like a glede under a door – what Jonah's come to think of as her Dalek voice, after those saft robots on the telly – and she wags the fingertip with every syllable.

– Yow. Me. Conversation. Later.

Jonah jumps in before Billy can spoil the moment by saying something spineless, wagging his own finger through the air in exaggerated chops.

– Gunna. Be. A. Bloody. Long. Conversation. If. Ya. Talk. Loike. That. Ay. It?

Judy whirls round and stomps off up the stairs, her boots thumping the thin carpet. Billy groans.

– Oh, thass brilliant, Jonah. Her was already in a mood; *now* look what her's loike.

Jonah smiles to himself as he opens the door to reveal the sun shining on his pride and joy out front.

– Yam welcome, mate.

*

Billy shields his eyes against the vicious stabbing of the sunlight, and studies the lime green Lambretta parked by the kerb. Jonah's fussing over it already, like a mother getting her son ready for the nit-nurse, dabbing away imaginary specks of dirt with his shirtsleeve.

– So. What d'ya reckon? Marks out a ten?

Billy puts on his best Janice Nicholls voice.

– Ah'll gi it foive.

– Out a ten?! Yome loffin.

– Gorra gi ya the marks fer effort, ay I?

Jonah laughs out loud and shakes his head; Billy grins too – the first time he's managed it since waking up. The moped's an impressive machine, well worthy of Billy's grudging respect, and Jonah knows it.

– Woss that?

– Woss what?

– That flag, theer.

– Republic a South Vietnam, bab.

– Ya cor fly that. Iss wrong.

– Wrong? How come?

– Yow ay sposed ter support South Vietnam. They'm on the same side as the American warmongers.

– Mate, the onny monger round here's yow. The Yanks am dewin the roit thing! Someone's gorra gi the Chinese a kickin, ay they?

– They ay fightin the Chinese.

– Well, who am they fightin?

– Doe know. T'ay the Chinese, though. Ya need tew ask Jude abaht the ins an outs of it all.

– Ah'd rather poke me eyes out wi a salad fork. Balls ter the flag; d'ya fancy a lift or not?

– Is it safe?

– Onny one way ter find out, ay tha? Come on, Tonto. Saddle up.

Jonah swings his leg over the moped with a Lone Ranger flourish. Billy shakes his aching head, and reluctantly mounts the Lambretta behind Jonah.

– Yow've gorra put yer arms round me, ay ya!

– Oh Jesus. People am gunna see us, Jonah. It doe look roit.

– An yow'd rather em see ya gew flyin off the back? Look, no one's gunna mind; iss scientifically proved that poofs cor ride scooters.

– When was that proved?

– A few years back. They did experiments. All scientific, loike. It was on the news an that. Shurrup yer moanin an gi us an hug.

~ 80 ~

With a disgusted sigh, Billy gingerly puts his arms round Jonah's waist. There's a hollow gurgling from his belly, and he hopes the ride isn't going to upset his stomach again. Jonah starts the engine.

– Hi-hooooo, scooter!

The exhaust hums. Jonah guns the motor and steers them out into the street, the sun high over a town pinning its hopes on a young man named Tony Brown.

*

Like most supporters, they didn't take to the idea of this new League Cup competition at first; why bother with a tu'penny-ha'penny trophy, some minor midweek distraction from proper football?

And then Albion drew Walsall at home in the second round.

Forty-one thousand people packed the Hawthorns to see the first competitive fixture between the two neighbouring clubs in sixty-five years, and those forty-one thousand watched Albion march to a 3-1 victory through a Stan Bennett own goal, and a brace from the twenty-year-old inside-forward Anthony Brown.

Tony Brown, who'd joined Albion as a schoolboy five years ago.

Tony Brown, who'd waited on the fringes of the first team until his chance came.

Tony Brown, who could find the back of the net from eighteen yards out with his eyes closed.

But watching an Albion youngster come of age was just the icing on the cake that night. They fell in love with the League Cup, too. Evenings under the floodlights brought a whole new colour to football: the way the artificial illumination painted the turf a vivid shade of green, and highlighted the stripes of navy blue on the Albion shirts till they glowed against the white. It would never match the grand old FA Cup, but from the minute Billy and Jonah left the Brummie Road that night, they were already making their plans for the next round.

That came three weeks later, at Elland Road. Enveloped in a pall of fag smoke on the Scratching Shed's crumbling terraces, Billy and Jonah and the rest of the travelling fans watched Albion put four past a weakened Leeds United to reach the cup's fourth round. Johnny Kaye, Chippy Clark and Jeff Astle provided three of the goals, but it was Tony Brown inspiring all of their cheers and their chants again, scoring for the second round in a row. A player from their generation, firing the club into the future. A symbol of the new Albion.

The lad they were calling Bomber.

In front of thirty thousand at the Hawthorns the next month, Bomber scored for the third consecutive round in a 6-1 rout of Coventry City, and the Brummie Road spent the second half taunting Coventry boss Jimmy Hill, who'd been bragging to the media that his star striker Bobby Gould would be Albion's downfall. By that point, Billy wasn't sure the cup run could get any more enjoyable.

And then Albion were drawn against Villa in the quarter-finals.

The Sunday morning queue for tickets stretched all the way around the ground and off down Halfords Lane towards Smethwick. Four miles of sooty brick and backstreets separated West Bromwich Albion from Aston Villa, and the divide between Birmingham and the Black Country ran dark and deep through those four miles. Either side of that boundary were different accents, different slang. Different industries, different streets. A hundred years ago, Birmingham slogger gangs had tried pushing their criminal influence over that boundary, and been fought to a standstill by the men of West Bromwich. For nearly a century since, men in claret shirts and men in blue and white stripes had pulled in the crowds as the age-old struggle between the Black Country and Birmingham continued on a football pitch, year after year.

Cup derbies are something unusual. Something special. On that freezing November night, Villa managed a goal through the ever-prolific Tony Hateley, but Johnny Kaye bagged a brace for Albion, and in front of a crowd spilling off the terraces, with thousands locked outside the ground, Bomber Brown added another goal to his increasing cup tally.

Villa were out, and Albion through to face Third Division Peterborough in the semi-finals. The underdogs fought hard, but Albion triumphed 2-1 at the Hawthorns in the first leg – Tony Brown claiming one of those goals – and 4-2 at London Road in the second, with Bomber grabbing a hat-trick this time.

Albion were through to their first cup final since 1954. No Wembley trip this time round; the FA insisted on two legs, one home, one away. The second leg was at the Hawthorns on the 23rd of March, but first, Albion had to face West Ham at the Boleyn Ground. They had to deal with Martin Peters, Geoff Hurst, Bobby Moore.

They had to go to London.

And they had to make sure each of them got the day off work. Last summer, Billy had got himself a job as a machinist at British Crankshafts Ltd in Warley, not long after Jonah had started at the foundry. After perusing a medical dictionary for an hour in the library, Billy decided he was going to have tonsillitis for the day, while Jonah inventively plumped for diphtheria. Then came the discussion, held down the boozer seven days beforehand, of whether to fork out the money for the train or get a lift on one of the Throstle Club coaches. But there was a third option. Whenever Jonah was around, there was always a third option.

– Itch-oikin?

– Ar. Itch it all the way down ter London. Doe cost we a penny ter thumb a ride, it doe. An it'll be a voyage-a-whatchacallit. Discovery. Adventure. Findin the heart of England.

– Itch-oikin.

– Ar.

– Jonah. Doe tek this the wrong way, loike, but ah'd rather have it off wi Barbara Castle than gew itch-oikin ter London wi yow.

Jonah's eyes brightened under his sandy fringe as he saw another tack to take.

– Ya might be able ter do both! Ah tell ya, theer's all these women drivers on the road nowadays. They cor steer the cars ter save they life, but ah bet they wouldn't say no tew a couple a strappin young lads showin em the ropes.

– *Both* on us?

– Well, we could work out a system. Ah'll see ter the fust wench that gis us a ride, yow ha the second. An so on, loike. Odd numbers fer me, even numbers fer yow.

Billy mulled this over for a few seconds before an important consideration wormed its way into his mind.

– I have got a girlfriend, Jonah.

– Well her ay comin, is her?

– No, but all the same, it wouldn't be roit, would it? Morally roit, ah mean.

– Woss morals got ter do wi it? Iss onny a bit of how's-yer-father. Ah doe remember anythin in the Bible abaht that bein wrong.

– "Thou shalt not commit adultery."

– Ar. Adultery. When yam married. It doe say "thou shalt not roger some tart in a Cortina on yer day off." Any road, why am ya so fussed abaht what Judy might think? D'ya reckon her's all sweetness and innocence at some of these student parties her guz tew?

Billy's mouth relaxed into an O as those words burrowed into his mind and took root.

– But... her onny guz ter them parties fer intellectual reasons!

– Is that what they'm callin it nowadays? Ar, I expect they do a lot of bonin up wi each other. Givin them intellects a good seein-tew.

– Ah doe believe it. Her wouldn't do nuthin loike that.

– Oh, it ay her fault. Iss human nature, mate. All abaht impulse. An my impulses reckon we should itch-oik ter London fer the West Ham match an attend ter the fair damsels a the motorways en route.

~ 83 ~

Three pints later Billy was coming round to the idea, but even then, his resolve nearly crumbled at the crucial moment. Jonah was just speculating how many girls they could feasibly knob in a six-hour round trip when Billy spotted Judy walking into the club over Jonah's shoulder, and switched subjects with seconds to spare.

– So basically, thass why it doe mek economic sense fer us ter join the Common Market at this point in time.

– What am yow on abaht the Common bloody Market for all of a sudd… oh bollocks. Aroit, Jude!

– How do, Jude! We'm gewin ter London next week, bab. Itch-oikin theer.

Judy narrowed her eyes. Billy coughed.

– Well, we might g'ter London or we might not. We ay decided fer certain yet.

Judy put her hands on her hips. Billy scratched his head.

– Actually, we'm probly not gewin ter London. Just a saft thought, loike.

Jonah nearly choked on his pint.

– What d'ya mean, we ay gewin? Course we am!

Jonah's spluttering was interrupted by the landlord striding up to their table, a concerned expression carved into his face.

– Aroit petal, sorry ter bother ya; iss juss that wenches ay allowed in the bar, loike. Yam welcome ter gew an sit in the lounge if ya want.

Billy and Jonah both craned their necks slowly to look at Jude, who'd narrowed her eyes at the landlord. Out came the Dalek voice.

– I. Am. Trying. To. Talk. To. My. Boyfriend.

The landlord wiped his hands on his apron and tried again.

– Well, yome welcome ter talk tew im in the lounge, flower.

– Thanks fer the suggestion, *flower*. But as it happens, ah'm happy talkin tew im here, *petal*. Now, could ya scoot off an leave us in peace?

The landlord stared blankly at her. He didn't look like the type of bloke who heard the word "no" very often, and he was floundering in uncharted waters.

– We've got cushions in the lounge, an all. Brand new cushions! Really comfy. All special fer the ladies, loike!

– Well if iss so bloody comfy, *yow* gew an sit in the soddin lounge!

The landlord's mouth dropped open, and he retreated to the bar muttering about society going to the dogs, with wenches coming into pubs and cussing like navvies. Jonah shook his head and mentally marked off another pub they wouldn't be welcome in anymore. Billy had one last go at arguing his corner.

– Look, me love, iss the cup final fust leg in London. A big match. Maybe the biggest ever! An really, when ya think abaht it, it ay no diffrent tew all them student parties yome allwis at, is it?

– Ya mean when ah meet up wi me friends ter discuss the struggle fer peace an equal roits? I ay sure how a football match is even slightly loike that.

– Is that really all ya do when yam theer? *Discuss* stuff?

– Course it is. Why? What else d'ya think ah'd be dewin?

– Well, Jonah reckons that ya might be havin a bit of… AARGH, bloody hell, Jonah! Cor ya pick yer pint up without spillin it over me?

– Me hand slipped.

Judy shook her head.

– Look, the pair on ya can do whatever ya loike. Stay here an get pissed. Gew itch-oikin ter London. Doe spare a thought fer me, whatever ya do.

She turned on her heel and walked out. Jonah grinned.

– Well, theer ya gew! If that ay permission, ah doe know what is!

The big day came, and they started out in high spirits. After catching the 74 into Birmingham – giving the Hawthorns a massive cheer as they passed it – they managed to hop on a bus to Sheldon, disembarking on the A45 which stretched out of the city's suburbs and into the south-eastern countryside.

– Here we am, our Bill. This is wheer it starts. Get ready fer an adventure! An remember: ah'm shaggin the odd numbers.

– So, we juss stick our thumbs out?

– Ar. Wait fer a car ter come, an let yer thumb do the talkin. It'll onny tek a minute or two.

Three quarters of an hour. A full three quarters of an hour sat on the kerb, taking it in turns to hold aching arms out to passing cars with thumbs extended, before a sorry-looking Austin 1100 pulled over for them.

Jonah was practically hopping from one foot to the other with expectation, so it came as an unpleasant surprise to peer through the dirty windscreen and realise that the driver's seat wasn't occupied by a tasty blonde with a mountainous bosom, but a middle-aged vicar with untameable nostril-hair. The greying clergyman leaned over the passenger seat and laboriously wound down the window.

– What's your destination, chaps?

– We'm off ter London!

– I'm afraid I'm only going as far as Rugby. Is that of any use?

After a brief roadside consultation, Billy and Jonah agreed that they could set aside the disappointment of failing to make a sexual conquest in order to get thirty miles closer to their destination, and avoid another numb-arsed forty-five minutes on a kerb in Sheldon.

It was the first disappointment, but far from the last. Not only did the vicar not have any kind of car radio – he found the wireless "distracting" – but he also liked to pass the time by singing. As they chugged their way into the Warwickshire countryside, he launched into an unprompted repertoire of his favourite hymns from Sunday service, warbling away about God until the windows seemed to rattle. Halfway through *The Lord's My Shepherd*, he urged them to sing along, and they politely declined. They might be members of a choir, but they didn't mean they sang bloody hymns; Billy shuddered at the very idea of the Brummie Road End singing a rhythmless dirge like *The Lord's My Shepherd*.

The vicar dropped them off on the Dunchurch Highway within spitting distance of Rugby, and faced with a bit of a wait, they decided to kill a quarter of an hour by each putting a knot in one end of their scarf, and then using them to hit one another. Billy was busy whirling his round his head like a lasso when Jonah spotted a Bedford lorry bearing down on them, and stuck his thumb out just in time to catch the driver's attention.

It was carrying a load of electrical components from Wigan down to Luton. And like their first ride, they were devastated to find that it wasn't being driven by an impossibly-proportioned nymphomaniac; this time, their travelling companion was a glum Lancastrian driver called Arthur, with thick black specs and a cap wedged tight over his thinning grey hair. He was passing through Rugby to get onto the M1.

– You ever been on motorway before, lads?

They shook their heads. They'd both seen news clips of the huge transport artery, but that didn't prepare them for the experience of coming up the slip road, accelerating to a faster speed than they'd ever known in a car before, and suddenly rocketing out onto a still river of white lines and grey tarmac. In seconds, the motorway swelled and filled the whole arc of the windscreen: six lanes, mostly empty, divided across two carriageways with a narrow grassy reservation, and miles of steel crash barrier. The few other vehicles – a loose scattering of rattling cars and lonely lorries – didn't surge ahead of them or fall behind, but stayed together in a cluster for mile after mile, until it felt like none were even travelling to a destination anymore, but had become lost, suspended permanently in some endless void between distant cities.

Arthur was listening to a dreary sermon of gardening tips on the Home Service; it took half an hour of murderous persuasion before he agreed to let them switch to Radio Caroline, and then another twenty minutes to actually tune in to the pirate station. Billy, wedged in the middle of the cab between Jonah and the driver, spent that time with his head between his knees, ear pressed to the radio like a safe-cracker, his fingers adjusting the dial in minute increments every second or two. Just when he'd exhausted all of his reserves of patience, having drawn nothing but wild signals and the occasional American crooner from the airwaves, he got a tantalising hint of Mick Jagger's voice, lost in the crackle. One more adjustment, and they had the whole motorway rocking with the new Stones single.

It lasted ten seconds.

The Bedford whizzed under an immense concrete flyover, and with a maddening burst of static, the Stones were gone. When they emerged on the other side, the signal had evaporated into the cement. They sat in silence the rest of the way to Luton, where Arthur dropped them off, and it promptly started to rain.

– Doe worry, Bill. We'm nearly theer now, mate. An the next driver's gunna be a wench, an all. Bound to be. Law of averages. Proper stunner, ah'm tellin ya.

– Jonah. Has it occurred ter ya that beautiful women might not juss drive up an down the motorway lookin fer sex?

– Why not? If ah was a beautiful woman, thass what ah'd do.

– Oh Jesus. Ah'll pretend ah never heard that sentence.

– Woss the matter?

– Ah'm itch-oikin ter London wi Norman fuckin Bates. Thass the matter.

It took one more lift. This time they were picked up by a student called Keith, who had longer hair than they'd ever seen on a lad before – to the extent that Jonah briefly got his hopes up when he saw it through the windscreen, before realising the depressing truth – and then finally, they were there. London. Like a birthday present bought by a desperate relative, dreary in its normality after the expectations they'd built up in their minds. By the time they got lost for the fifth time, tried to ask for directions – and got ignored – and found themselves in a wet backstreet tripping over drunken tramps, the drizzle-drenched capital city was the last place on earth they wanted to be.

Still, things started to look up as they converged on the East End, linking up with small groups of other Albion fans on their way to Upton Park. The story quickly spread amongst the other supporters that Billy and Jonah had hitched their way down south, and suddenly they were hailed as heroes, patted on the back by the other touring Brummie Roaders and travelling Baggies. Of course, Jonah did his best to ruin their newfound status by chuntering about how West Ham were doomed. Bomber had scored nine goals in the cup so far – nine! – and he was bound to take the Hammers apart! Billy listened quietly, trying to remember the last time one of Jonah's predictions had actually come true. He made it all the way to the Boleyn Ground without thinking of a single one.

Inside, around five hundred Albion lads had nabbed a stretch of the terraces behind the goal. Before they could even get a song going, they were getting charged by a load of West Ham boys, and that was the start of fifteen or twenty minutes' argy-bargy up and down the terraces. The team line-ups were announced – the Cockneys pausing from their latest terrace charge to boo the name of Johnny Byrne, their goal-starved centre forward – and then, under the flare of the floodlights, kick-off.

Albion spent the first half building a solid wall of striped shirts in front of their goal. It was a cup final and an awayday all rolled into one, but the early excitement vanished gradually as Albion frustrated West Ham's attacks, playing four men in defence instead of the usual three. Before long, the pushing and shoving in the stand was more interesting than what was happening on the pitch. There was nothing malicious in the ruckus; it was just teenage fans mobbing together, charging in one mass towards opposition supporters in the same stand, and then the opposition pushing their way back. A handy diversion when the match wasn't living up to expectations; after all, as long as no one was starting fights, what harm could it do?

Then the breakthrough: an hour into the game, with a no-score draw on the cards, Albion counter-attacked with Chippy Clark up the left wing; Clark put a cross in for Jeff Astle, back in the side for the first time after three months out, and Astle smashed a first-time shot low past Jim Standen into the West Ham net. The travelling Brummie Roaders stopped their terrace charge and struck up a chorus to the tune of The Troggs' *Give It To Me*.

GIVE IT TEW ASTLE! GIVE IT TEW ASTLE!
HE WILL SCORE! HE WILL SCORE!

Just over ten minutes later, disaster. A throw-in in the Albion half. Bobby Moore threw the ball to Brian Dear, and got a short pass straight back. And then Moore volleyed the ball high into the box, over the heads of Geoff Hurst and Johnny Byrne, over the heads of Graham Williams and Danny Campbell, right over Ray Potter, bouncing off the far post into the corner of the Albion goal to make it 1-1. And the storm of West Ham attacks carried on for another twenty minutes, the London side looking for a winning goal, and Albion struggling to hang on.

With thirty seconds of injury time left, just when it looked like they'd done enough to see the game out, Dennis Burnett put a low cross into the penalty area, Johnny Byrne flattened Ray Potter in the six-yard-box, and then stabbed home a West Ham winner. The referee blew time within seconds of Albion kicking off again.

Two hundred miles they'd hitchhiked to watch a 2-1 defeat, and two hundred miles they were going to hitchhike to get back again. This time in darkness and rain, with the misery of an unlucky defeat dogging every step.

Escaping the East End was a wretched walk to the Underground with crowing West Ham fans all around, and even more gloating to suffer on the bright red tube train when they got on. The only thing worse than losing to a late goal is having it happen in a cup final, and the knowledge that they'd have another match to try and put it right was no comfort.

They hitched a lift to Hemel Hempstead through a torrential downpour and got dropped on the M1 slip road in the pissing rain. After standing around like planks for ten minutes, shivering and trying in vain to flag down cars accelerating up towards the motorway, they decided to try their luck walking up the hard shoulder with their thumbs out.

It worked; a car did stop for them a quarter of an hour later. Unfortunately, the flashing blue light on the roof suggested they weren't getting a goodwill lift. The PC in the passenger seat wound down his window.

– Evening, lads. Off for a little walk, are we?

– Tryin tew itch a lift home, constable.

– You know it's against the law to be doing that on the motorway, don'tcha? Eh?

– Well, ya could allwis tek us home yerselves. Then we wouldn't be breakin the law.

– We've better things to do than drive to bloody Birmingham tonight, sunshine.

– We doe come from Birmingham. We'm from the Black Country.

– What's the difference, eh?

– Well. Iss further away, fer starters.

– Look, we'll take you as far as the next service station. Then you're on your own. And stay off the hard shoulder, you soft bahsterds.

The next service station was at Toddington. Billy had never even heard of Toddington. It sounded like the kind of place where blokes grew prize-winning artichokes, and kindly old ladies solved brutal murders committed in the cricket pavilion. However, all he could see was a squat little pre-fab restaurant, an enormous concrete pedestrian bridge over the motorway, and the enveloping darkness of the trees and fields beyond. The police dropped them in the car park and advised them to find somewhere warm to sleep if they couldn't hitch a lift within the next hour or so.

– Oh, brill. This is juss fab, ay it? Thanks a fuckin bunch, Jonah. Ah gorra be at work in the mornin.

– Look. Bound ter be loads a cars passin through here, ah bet.

– All driven by busty blonde stunners in swimsuits, ah spose? Jonah, ah've had enough. Ah doe know how yow allwis manage ter do it, but this is one fer the all-time list of occasions when ah shoulda run a bloody mile as soon as yow opened yer gob. "Itch-oik ter London an back". Ah must be saft. Talk abaht pickin the key ter Box Thirteen.

– E yam, look over theer! Far side a the car park! A coach!

– Many women coach drivers abaht nowadays, am tha?

– Quick, the driver's abaht ter get in! We might be able ter jump on! Run fer it!

They sprinted across the deserted car park, jumping puddles and weaving round the odd road cone, and made it to the coach just as the driver – a burly bloke in a donkey jacket – started climbing on board. Jonah shouted through the open door between gasps of breath.

– Oi, mate! Any chance of a lift?

The driver sat down, turned to look at them through the door, and to their surprise, addressed them in a broad Black Country accent.

– What am ya dewin in a service station car park this time a night?

Billy answered first.

– We'm itch-oikin home, mate.

– Ay dewin a good job of it, am ya? Sound loike ya come from a civilised part a the world, at least. How come yam down here?

– Went down ter London ter watch the cowin Albion lose. Useless bastards.

– Is that roit?

The smile on the driver's face spread wider.

– Yow'd best hop on, then.

They stepped onto the coach, and turned to face the passengers tucked away in their seats, obscured by a haze of cigarette smoke. There were a few heads poking out into the aisle, hands clutching bottles of beer, bemused faces checking what the delay was in aid of. Faces that seemed oddly familiar.

The coach driver barked at them to sit down. Billy found an empty seat halfway down the bus, next to a man in a suit who was busy looking out of the window. Jonah took one just across the aisle.

– Smoke, son?

The fella next to him was holding out a packet of Players. Quality fags, at least to Billy's Woodbine-hardened throat.

– Oh, ta!

– Yer welcome. Look like you've had a rough day.

The inquisitive Scottish accent made Billy turn as he was putting the cigarette to his lips, and in the clumsy half-light of the coach's interior, he was surprised by how much his neighbour looked like Albion's inside-forward, Bobby Hope.

He looked across the aisle to where Jonah was sitting by a bloke who looked strangely like the Albion goalkeeper, Ray Potter. Jonah was staring back at him, eyes wide in the gloom. There were a few chuckles from the back seat, and Billy twisted round to see more doppelgangers in the fog; one telling a long, rambling joke who looked a bit like Jeff Astle, and another listening raptly who bore more than a slight resemblance to Tony Brown.

Billy was tempted to put it down to the stress of a long day, maybe exacerbated by having stood out in the freezing cold rain on the hard shoulder of the M1 for longer than any man would deem sane. Even in years to come, he'd struggle to ever fully accept that the hour-long journey up the motorway with the Albion team ever really happened. Not because it was unusual to see the team out and about – they're always warmly welcomed in the pubs around the ground, and most own houses in West Bromwich on streets filled with folks who pay to watch them play every Saturday – but the idea that they'd miraculously happened on the team bus idling in Toddington service station was too peculiar by far.

No one would ever believe the story they told, and some who heard it even suggested that the last leg of Billy and Jonah's odyssey to London and back was an event so traumatic that they concocted that ridiculous tale and convinced themselves it was the truth. But no matter how much scorn and disbelief came Billy's way, he clung on to the memory of stepping off that coach outside the Hawthorns just after midnight, shaking hands with all of the players, and asking them in the dusky glow of the headlights whether they fancied their chances in the second leg.

We'll see, said the bloke who looked uncannily like Tony Brown. *We'll see.*

*

There are thirty-two thousand inside the ground, but it feels like more. Much more. Up the Brummie Road, it seems as if there are that many crammed onto the newly-extended terrace alone. There have been matches at the Hawthorns down the years which have pulled far bigger crowds – FA Cup ties, games against local rivals – matches which have had all four stands teeming with bodies, and folks clambering up the floodlights to watch the action. Tonight, no one goes to those lengths. But tonight, everyone wants to be standing up the Birmingham Road End. Tonight, the Brummie Road comes of age.

Tonight, the banners are everywhere; scarves are held aloft from the minute each new arrival takes their spot on the terraces. Tonight, there are folks in costumes even odder than Billy's 1940s hand-me-downs (which have only grown more bizarre as an ensemble since some anonymous donor pushed a red, white and blue butcher's hat onto his head on his way through the turnstiles). Tonight, there are blokes and kids coming up the Brummie Road for the very first time, leaving behind the diminutive Halfords Lane Stand, the colourful Rainbow Stand, the distant Smethwick End. And they're singing. Everyone's in full voice long before kick off, wanting to stake their claim as part of the choir, to be able to brag about this in years to come. Not just about being at the Hawthorns for Albion's first cup final in twelve years; that's not enough anymore.

They need to be a part of the Brummie Road End.

WE'M GEWIN UP THE BRUMMIE ROAD, TER SEE THE HAGAN ACES!

Jonah's shivering, although the press of bodies all around is more than enough to keep him warm. It's the first home match all season that Kath hasn't come to. When he parked the scooter over by Bradford's Bakery (and Billy finally let go of him and jumped off the Lambretta as if the seat was electrified), he expected to see her waiting there. It's where they always meet, where they've met for every home match since last April. While Judy's stayed away from the Hawthorns since that first visit, Kath always loves coming here. Of course, Jonah knows the real reason she keeps coming along is to be with him; up on the Brummie Road terraces with their arms linked, singing and shouting till their lungs are hollow and throats brittle, their bodies pushed together by the crush, surging back and forth with every Albion attack, but safe and happy in each other's company. That must be the reason. He doesn't tell her that, obviously. He doesn't tell anyone that. But why else would she keep coming back, week after week? After all, it's not as if wenches are really interested in football.

– Gerrin a bit cramped now, eh?

Billy offers the observation just as the folks around them shuffle up closer, and more bodies are packed onto the terrace. A scattered cheer goes up behind them, rippling out across the face of the stand, followed by the pompous razz of a brass instrument; the Trumpet Bloke's turned up. He only ever comes to evening matches – he must play in some kind of jazz band on Saturdays – and as usual, he's brought his instrument with him to play a souped up version of *Oh When The Stripes*. After a few moments of raucous anticipation from the crowd, he starts playing the jaunty tune, and everyone sings along as the team line-ups are announced.

The match starts; the songs don't stop, and nor do the team. Johnny Kaye is a whirlwind, running tirelessly, attacking the West Ham goal in front of the Smethwick End with a fury and dragging Bobby Moore hopelessly in his wake. After just nine minutes, he pounces on a stray ball inside the Hammers penalty area, swivelling on the penalty spot and smashing a half-volley into the top corner. It levels the score on aggregate, and ignites the swaying masses all around Jonah.

JOHNNY KAYE – ENGLAND!
JOHNNY KAYE – ENGLAND!

Minutes later, Tony Brown picks up the ball in the Albion half, and there's an immediate rush of excitement for the man of the hour; Bomber feeds a pass through to Jeff Astle in the centre circle, who dribbles to the edge of the penalty area before laying it off to Kaye on the right flank. Kaye puts in the cross, only for Astle to volley agonisingly over the bar from six yards out.

Still, before twenty minutes have passed, Johnny Byrne tries to head the ball back to Standen in the West Ham goal, and Bomber nips in to nod it right over Standen's head, making it 3-2 to Albion on aggregate. He's scored in every round of the League Cup – the first player ever to do that in any cup competition – and as the Brummie Road is still chanting *TONY! TONY!* Chippy Clark adds another with a diving header on the half-hour.

EASY! EASY! EASY! EASY!

There have been tough times for Albion in the last few years. Football's like that. Life's like that. Sometimes it's difficult to cling to even the leanest shred of hope for the future when the weeks take on a treadmill monotony, and glimpses of glory are few and far between. But when your fortunes change, how quickly everything looks exciting and new all over again. For the Brummie Road – the entire teeming, singing, laughing, crying home end – that moment comes when Graham Williams pops up to drive the ball in from a full twenty-five yards out. They switch

from singing players' names to the name of the manager – *HAGAN!*
HAGAN! – and in the clenched fists of triumph, and the fiercely-hoisted
scarves, and the smiles of personal satisfaction, there's a ripple of
realisation running along the terraces that this night is all theirs.

At half-time, Jonah joins the queue at the roofless block of toilets
down the back of the stand with hundreds of other blokes. They shuffle
across the tiled floor, along the length of the urinal, and as he pisses out a
bladder of beer, with clouds of steam billowing into the cold night air,
Jonah looks up at the stars and thanks the universe for letting him be here,
now.

West Ham find their feet in the second half, but they only manage
one consolation goal through Martin Peters; the aggregate result at full-
time is 5-3 to Albion. They welcome the whistle with breathless ecstasy,
so many shredded voices croaking approval. The team traipse up to the
directors' box in the Halfords Lane Stand, and lift the League Cup to a
storm of applause, with supporters blanketing the pitch under the bright
artificial lights.

GREATEST ALBION
GREATEST ALBION
WE'LL SUPPORT YOU EVERMORE
WE'LL SUPPORT YOU EVERMORE

And Jonah means every word more than anything he's ever uttered
before. This is the most incredible thing he's seen in his whole life. It's a
cup win; the first trophy the club have won since he was five. As Billy
stands at his side, holding his Union Jack butcher's hat in the air and
bellowing to the sky, he tries to think to himself how he'll describe all of
this to Kath when he next sees her.

And that thought's enough to send a sudden nervous cramp
through his belly, as he wonders what could possibly have happened to
stop Kath from being here with him.

*

As the streetlights flicker down the Golden Mile, the taxi swings
round the corner past the homely glow of The Goose, bears down the street
past Dickens Sports, and comes to a halt outside the Adelphi. Kath opens
the door and swings her legs out, and after paying the driver, Tommy
scrambles after her, dead sharp in his hired suit. On the pavement, they're
surrounded by West Indian folks their age and older, dressed just as smart
as Tommy – it might even be their Sunday best some are wearing,

complete with pork-pie hats on the heads of the fellas – and a handful of white boys and their lasses, mods and modettes. It's all smiles and chit-chat in spite of the cold air, and a black girl admiring Kath's outfit stops to ask how much it cost in a sweet, lilting accent. It's a black and white striped courtelle dress with long sleeves, and a pretty modest hemline just above her knees; she loved it from the minute she saw it on the rack in C&A. The assistant told her that the material's called courtelle because "yow courtelle whether iss wool or nylon"; it's exactly the kind of modern thing which should impress Tommy.

At least, she hopes so.

She wasn't sure about coming at first, when Tommy asked her along. The Adelphi's got a bit of a reputation. At the Gala you never get much trouble, but at the Adelphi, things tend to be on edge. Sure enough, there's a smattering of lads, white boys, hanging round the fringes inside, giving each other the evil eye. They don't seem to mind the Jamaicans; it's all local trouble, quarrels between different streets and estates, lads from Hill Top and Bird End and Golds Green settling scores. The quick, angry scuffles start early, their exact break-out points in the hall always marked by sudden migration; a surge of bystanders moving away from the violence, and lads looking for trouble rushing towards it. They die off as quickly as they start, most of them. Sometimes the boys exhaust themselves with the quick flurries of punches, and walk away breathing hard with their chins high. Occasionally one flattens another, leaving him on his back in a pool of beer and blood. At least one fight gets broken up by a black man separating two white kids; Kath doesn't catch what he says to them, but they both meekly shake his hand, smile, and toddle off like lambs.

– Y'aroit, missis? Havin fun?

She looks over at Tommy, who's got a glass of whisky in his hand, staring at her with a vague smile. She's usually confident when she's out with a lad; she lets them feel like they're in control, like she's following their lead, but when push comes to shove, it's always their job to impress her. Never the other way round.

Tonight, for the first time, she feels like the tables have been turned on her.

- Iss a bit slow on the dancefloor, ay it? No one's botherin wi the music.

Tommy laughs.

– Gi it time. They'll be up theer soon. Trust me.

Kath nods, but she's starting to feel a bit disappointed with the whole night. She's missing the cup final for this. She's been to the Hawthorns for every home match all season – she likes spending time with

Billy, and especially Jonah, who's got a way of catching her off-guard and making her laugh which not many people can do – but above that, watching the Albion has become part of her life. After another abysmal week at work, you go through every emotion on the terraces on Saturday, and even if the result's a bad one, it still cleans all the rotten stuff out of your mind for a while. Learning the strengths and weaknesses of all the players, finding your favourite – she loves Bobby Hope, who can stand in the centre of the pitch and launch long pinpoint passes in any direction – and having some pride in your town; all these simple things become so important in that place.

She's always struggled to feel at home in the Black Country, but somehow, she instantly feels at home up the Brummie Road.

She's still wondering how the team are getting on against West Ham when the music changes. The DJ's been playing soul numbers all night, but at ten o'clock, he switches to spinning Jamaican 45s. A strong bassline thumps through the floor, an offbeat kicks in, and a thrilled horde rushes for the dancefloor. Tommy squeezes her arm, flaps his fingers in a quick *come on* motion, and pulls her along with him.

She's never seen dancing like it. It seems like all the West Indians in the whole place – who've been idly tapping their feet or clicking their fingers to the American soul songs – have poured into the middle of the room under the dusty old chandelier and suddenly lost every bone in their bodies. When Kath was taught the gospels as a little girl, she used to imagine people possessed by demons jerking and twisting the same way the black dancers are now. It's absolutely mad, but there's an infectious repetition to the dance, and it fits the music perfectly.

The songs themselves are odd. Some are raunchy numbers with words you'd never get away with on the radio, and yet some sound as if they're written about the Bible. It's during one of these ones – as she listens to the Jamaican singer list the Ten Commandments in time to the offbeat rhythm – that Tommy leans over and shouts in her ear that it's called *scar music*. That doesn't sound right. She must have misheard him. Nothing this hypnotic, exciting and beautiful could have such an ugly name.

But it doesn't matter what it's called. What matters is getting out all of those grotty feelings from the week, getting them out quickly, and that means copying how the coloured folks dance. It's tricky at first, not what Kath's used to – although Tommy and Dodd and all the other mods seem to know it pretty well – but she learns within the space of a few songs how to loosen her limbs, sway her body on the downbeat and move her feet on the offbeat. She beats the soles of her Mary Quants to the dancefloor with the rhythm, and wonders how many shoes have stamped this same floor down the years to The Beatles, Buddy Holly, Glenn Miller, how many have traced graceful foxtrots or stuttered a Charleston. Her whole heart syncopates, and as the blood pumps through her body, she laughs with the simple joy of living. It's so easy to lose that feeling. It's so easy to let yourself be weighed down and eventually crushed by work, by home life, to give in to the creeping despair that flutters at the fringes of your mind, until you're crying into your pillow at night and hoping the new day will never come.

Life's about distracting yourself from the threat of that despair, about filling the void. She sees Judy do it with her politics, and Carol at work do it with her little games of one-upmanship. She sees her ma do it with religion. She sees Billy and Jonah do it with music and football. Kath's done it so many different ways, but they only ever fill that emptiness in her for a little while. Just a little while.

But dancing, now. Moving her body, burning all the energy and tension in her muscles, floods her head with such happiness that she'd carry on for hours if she could. As it is, she manages about forty minutes on the dancefloor, and by the time the upbeat numbers are done, she's nearly fit to flop down in a heap. The DJ spins a slower song – still Jamaican, still formed around that strange offbeat, but without the frantic tempo of the *scar music* – and Tommy leans in to put his arm around her and support her weight. She doesn't mind. She doesn't mind at all. As he kisses her, Kath relaxes and enjoys the taste of his tongue, the feeling of his arms around her waist, his fingers running down her spine. Life's a long, hard struggle, but not right now. Here and now, everything is as good as it comes.

*

There's a knock at the front door. Judy puts down her book – she hasn't been paying attention to it anyway – walks into the hallway, opens the door. Billy steps forward and throws his arms around her, squeezing tightly.

– We did it!

He kisses her forehead.

– 4-1! 5-3 on aggregate! We won the cup, Jude! We won the League Cup!

– Good. Ah'm pleased.

– Is Kath next door? Her wor at the match, her's missed evrythin!

– No. Kath's out. Look, we need ter chat.

– Course we do! A performance loike that, ah could talk fer hours abaht it! Ya shoulda sid Tony Brown, he was…

– No, Bill. We doe need ter chat abaht the football. Not this time.

Judy works hard to keep her voice level, to keep from losing her temper or getting upset. She's amazed that he doesn't see what's going on, even now. It's as if he walks around from day to day hearing and seeing everything that goes on around him, but none of it registers. He's got all the awareness of a kitten tied up in a sack. If it doesn't have a direct bearing on football or the price of a pint, he doesn't want to know.

– It ay workin, is it?

– What? Is the boiler on the blink again?

– Billy. Listen ter me. I ay sure...

So much to say, but Jesus, the words aren't coming. How do you tell someone that all of the fun, the fun of those early days, just seems to have disappeared? How do you tell them that you still like them – they're a good person, and everything – but that liking them isn't the same as loving them? How do you tell them that they drive you absolutely barmy sometimes, and lately it just seems to be happening more and more? How do you tell them that these days, whenever you daydream about the future, they have no place in those fantasies?

How do you tell someone all of that without breaking them for good?

– I ay sure we'm roit fer one another, Billy.

Judy's been avoiding eye contact with Billy during the conversation, looking down at her shoes, up at the ceiling. Now she forces herself to watch him as the words sink home. It's her punishment, her penance. She watches as all the joy from tonight's football game drains out of him, the void quickly filled with shock and disbelief. His mouth hangs open as he realises exactly what she means.

She hopes he won't cry. If there's one thing that could break her resolve completely and make her take it all back, it's that. She already feels guilty about doing this here and now, but she couldn't leave it any longer. Not after last night. If she leaves it till tomorrow, she might lose her bottle altogether, and then they'll just carry on in the same old rut; Judy trying desperately to stake a place in the great wide world, to make some kind of impact on things which matter here and now, in 1966, in the space age, while Billy's world carries on triangulating around the pub, the snooker hall and the Hawthorns. That can't happen. There's no way.

He catches enough breath to ask a short question.

– Someone else?

– No. Never.

It's not a lie. Not really. She's never actually done anything with that lad at the anti-war meetings; she enjoys sitting with him and spending time with him at the protests, and she even catches herself thinking about him every now and then. But nothing else. Her conscience is clear on that.

– But ah love ya, Jude. Ya know that. Ah'll do whatever it teks. Please. This is such a mistake! Cor ya see?

Does Kath ever have this difficulty brushing off any of the boys she's gone out with down the years? Has she ever stayed with one long enough to get emotionally attached? To fall in love? It's been painfully obvious for months that Jonah's infatuated with her, but she never seems to pay him any attention outside of Saturday afternoons. Maybe ignorance really is bliss.

– Ah know, Bill. An I hope we can stay friends. Ah really do. But it cor be nuthin more than that.

They stand in silence for a long time. First, Billy takes off his hat – an odd-looking plastic thing in red, white and blue – and holds it to his chest like someone paying his respects to the dead. Then he turns round, and shuffles back into the hallway. He turns round to face her one last time.

– Is it aroit if ah drop yer dad's clothes back another time, then? Onny, ah'll need summat ter wear home. Iss a bit cold out.

Judy presses a hand to her mouth, and nods. Billy nods back. And then he's gone.

The house is quiet, but for the echo of the door closing.

*

The night's piercing cold, a proper March chill which seeps through layers of clothing and right into your bones, but Jonah barely notices. He feels as warm and dizzy as if he'd downed ten pints, even though he hasn't touched a drop since last night. He weaves the scooter home through the endless tangle of buses heading away from the ground, and into the quieter roads of West Bromwich's outlying council estates. It takes twenty minutes or so to reach his nan's house, and he steers the Lambretta to the pavement, kills the engine and climbs off. In the misty light of the streetlamps, he sees a girl standing on the corner at the end of the street facing away from him. He recognises the figure, and realises it's Kath. He starts walking towards her, whistling *The Sun Ain't Gonna Shine Anymore*. He's just about to call out to her, when another figure joins her on the corner. He recognises the silhouette. The pork-pie hat, the dapper suit.

He stops. Stands still. Watches as the two of them kiss.

He feels calm as he turns his back and walks back down the street. His legs have started to shake a bit, but after a couple of hours standing on the terraces, that's only natural. He lets himself into the house quietly so as not to wake Nan up, picking out the floorboards he knows won't creak like a kid avoiding cracks in the pavement. He still feels serene as he lets himself into his bedroom in the dark, smelling the dust in the air and the damp in the corner by the window. It's only when he lies down on his rickety old bed that the anger finally begins to fill him, growing unstoppably as he hears the door downstairs minutes later, and the pair of them giggling their way up the stairs.

Jonah closes his eyes and lets fury cradle him to sleep.

July 1966

Matthew's sitting so close to the telly that his eyes are going funny. He closes them tight, letting the light from the screen burn green patterns behind his eyelids. He wants to remember it all, keep it tucked up tight in his mind.

He opens his eyes. The dots behind the glass buzz quietly, fizzing out light like Dad's blowtorch sprays sparks, and he watches them carefully, putting his melting Aztec bar to one side. The marching band in their big fluffy hats have finished tramping up and down the field, the Queen's come out and shaken hands with everyone, and now the two men in the middle – Mr Horacio Troche and Mr Bobby Moore – swap flags with each other, with men all around them taking pictures, and the referee – Mr Istvan Zsolt of Hungary – puts the ball on the centre spot ready for kick-off. This is it. This is the World Cup. He's spent so long waiting for it, hearing everyone talk about it at school, hearing Dad talk about it at home, hearing Robert Dougall and Kenneth Kendall talk about it on the news, lying awake at night holding his breath for it.

It's going to be a load of shit.

He says that as often as he can now, ever since he overheard Dad telling Mr Sawyer down the butcher's that England have been a right load of shit since Alf Ramsey started tinkering with them. He asked what it meant, and Mr Sawyer went red in the face – redder than usual – and Dad leaned down and explained it was a grown-up way of saying they were really special. Matthew loves learning new words. He's seven and a half now; almost a grown-up himself, so he reckons it's best to act the part. It's quite exciting, and deep down he reckons that being a grown-up must be a right load of shit too.

The match starts. It's disappointing at first; it isn't like watching proper football, not like being at a match down the Albion, sitting on the white concrete wall down the bottom of the Birmingham Road End. All the colour's missing, and without colour, football loses its life. Some of the group matches – the ones with Argentina and Spain and West Germany – are being played a few miles away at Villa Park, but Dad says they aren't allowed to go and watch them, because if they do then there'll be no food on the table. That means Matthew has to watch it all on telly or listen to the wireless. Still, it's not so bad when you get used to it. In a way, the novelty alone makes it fun; after all, apart from cup final day, when else can you sit and watch live football on television?

The front door opens, and Matthew hears a chorus of banging and shouts out in the street. Then there's a hefty wooden *clunk* as the door closes again, muffling all the noises outside. Dad's back from the tobacconist's. Matthew usually likes to go along too; he's not allowed inside, but he enjoys standing in the doorway and smelling the aromas that seep out, reading the little notices posted behind the glass, each one a tale of a missing pet or a good lodger in search of a bedsit. Dad walks into the front room and peers out through the window. Matthew turns his back on the telly – England have got the ball in midfield, but they can't find a way through the solid wall of the Uruguay back line – and he kneels on the chair to look outside with Dad. There's a dark blue van out in the street; two men in overalls are lifting furniture out of it.

– They've took the house next door.

Behind Matthew, Kenneth Wolstenholme raises his voice as Perez shoots just wide for Uruguay. From the TV set, Matthew can hear the tinny sound of their supporters inside Wembley chanting *OOH, OOH, OOH-ROO-GWAI*.

– That bloody lettin agent. He said he wouldn't let any a that lot move in here. Not on this street. Lyin bastard.

Matthew rests his chin on the windowsill. On the telly, Mr Wolstenholme comments that Uruguay are sensibly playing at a slow pace on the tiring Wembley turf.

– See, this is juss the start. They'll invite the whole world in, now. Juss watch.

Matthew stays quiet. Surely the point of the World Cup is to invite the whole world in? In Birmingham they've put signs up in different languages, and even made a big football out of flowers in Victoria Square! But Dad doesn't seem happy about any of that. He looks out of the window for a little while longer, then shakes his head and stomps off with his weekend supply of Woodbines.

Matthew settles down to watch the rest of the match, but as England win one corner after another and still don't score, he gets distracted by Dad rattling about the house. The clock ticks down, the white shirts pushing up the pitch still can't break through the grey line of Uruguayans, and Dad spots the council's letting agent outside and goes out to have a word with him. Dad always seems to enjoy having a word with people he disagrees with, pushing his face really close to theirs and talking quietly so they have to listen carefully, then shouting when they least expect it. He does that to the letting agent, suddenly bellowing *YOW PROMISED YOW WOULDN'T LET ANY OF EM ON THIS STREET* right at his nose, and the letting agent shakes his head and says *they've gorra live somewheer, ay they*? And then Mr Istvan Zsolt of Hungary blows the full time whistle on a goalless draw at Wembley, and Matthew goes out into the back yard to kick his ball, the proper old casey which Dad found up on the factory roof last year, against the wall of the house.

First he's Roger Hunt, then he's Jimmy Greaves. He practises hitting the same brick in the wall each time with his right foot and then his left, the normal routine. It's dead tough, but he's getting better; he almost always hits the spot with his right, and with his left he can do it about once every five or six times. He's Nobby Stiles, and then he's Tony Brown. Matthew can spend hours doing this, especially when the days are long and the evenings are light and warm, and he doesn't always notice the sun going down. He's being Gordon Banks, kicking the ball high up the wall and then catching it, when one kick sends the ball spinning to the left; he throws out an arm to push it wide, and realises too late that it's going to fly right over the fence. He watches as the ball sails out of sight into next door's yard.

There are a couple of old housebricks down the end of the yard. Matthew carries them over to the fence, puts one on top of the other, and then uses them as a step up to peer next door. He gets his chin over the top of the fence, clutching the wooden slats tight in his hands, and spots the ball over by the storm drain on the far side of the yard. It's getting dark, and he can't see any lights on at the back of the house.

Matthew wonders whether to go and knock on the front door of the house and ask for his ball back. It's what he always used to do when Mr Evans lived there. But now there are new neighbours. And Dad doesn't like them. If Dad doesn't like them, then Matthew can't like them either. They might not even let him have his ball back. It's his only one – it's the best football ever – and if he loses it then it's gone for good. With his heart drumming, he hoists himself up to sit on top of the fence, swings his legs over the top, and drops down into the neighbours' yard.

He runs over to the drain, snatches the ball up, tucks it under his arm, and runs back to the fence. Then he realises, too late, that without a step on this side, he can't climb back over. He's not tall enough. He's starting to panic when a voice addresses him calmly from the back door of the house.

– Hello.

Matthew turns round slowly. There's a man standing in the doorway. He's got a big black beard, and there's a cloth wrapped around the top of his head like all the women inside the hairdresser's have. His eyes and his face are dark, a bit like the Uruguay players on telly. The man smiles.

Matthew doesn't say anything. He squints against the setting sun, watching the Cloth Man carefully. You're not supposed to talk to men you don't know. They can kidnap you and lock you away forever, so you never see your mom ever again. And Dad doesn't like the Cloth Man. He doesn't want him living next door. Matthew doesn't know why, but he knows that Dad's never wrong.

– Can you speak, young man? Do you understand me?

His accent's a bit strange, but Matthew can tell what he's saying. And in spite of everything – in spite of the danger of being kidnapped and locked away forever – he thinks of a question, and he decides he has to ask it.

– D'yow come from Uruguay, mate?

The Cloth Man bends forward, and Matthew thinks he's going to be sick – Matthew was sick after dinner just the other week, sat in front of the telly during *Softly Softly* and puking up all his fishfingers and chips into a bucket which Dad fetched from outside – but instead, the Cloth Man just bellows out a string of laughs.

– No, no! I'm Punjabi! You've heard of India, haven't you? But of course, you've been watching football this afternoon. Did England win?

He pronounces the last word *vin*, like the German soldiers in all the films.

– It was a draw. Nil nil.

– All that effort and no one scored a bloody goal? Ha! Do you think they'll win this Jules Rimet cup, then?

– Course they will! They'm a load of shit!

– I see. That's… a very convincing argument. I'll tell you what; keep practising with your ball and maybe you'll be playing for England soon, eh?

– Ah'm gunna play fer Albion fust. Loike Tony Brown, an Jeff Astle.

– Then I wish you all the best. When you score the winning goal at Wembley Stadium, I hope you remember that it was Parama Singh who told you to practise!

Matthew nods.

– Ah will. Mr Singh?

– Yes?

– Have ya got any bricks ah can stand on ter climb over the fence?

Mr Singh smiles.

– If you introduce yourself, then you can come through the house and use the front door, like a gentleman.

– Oh. Ah'm Matthew. Matthew Freeman.

– Then welcome in, Matthew.

They walk through the house, which is filled with boxes and sheets from the removal van, and Matthew walks out through the front door and waves goodbye to Mr Singh. Then he turns and sees Dad sitting on the doorstep of their house, smoking a Woodbine. Matthew bounces the ball on the ground as he walks back into the house, feeling Dad's eyes follow him all the way inside.

*

The World Cup's ten days old, the brief summer heat has been washed away in a blanket of drizzle, and in the centre of Birmingham, Billy's dying.

As deaths go, it isn't the most enjoyable. He's covered from head to foot in sores and lesions, breathing his last in an isolation ward at the Queen Elizabeth Hospital in Edgbaston. That alone would be bad enough, but worse still is the knowledge that it's all Jonah's fault. Everything that's ever gone wrong in Billy's life is Jonah's fault, and now his death's going to be Jonah's fault too. At this point, Billy's accepted that if there's an afterlife, it'll only be a matter of time before Jonah pokes his head round the door and fucks that up too. Within an hour, he'll have deflowered the Virgin Mary, used the Holy Spirit to make a martini, and flogged the pearly gates to some heavenly tatter.

It began at Villa Park. Nothing good ever begins at Villa Park. It was a mistake to venture into the dark streets of Witton in the first place, but Jonah had got them tickets to watch the group match between Argentina and West Germany, nestled away in the steep Holte End with a legion of German supporters. Albion fans have invaded enemy territory before, but this was the first time they'd ever been alongside the real enemy. The Krauts. The Hun. Jerry. Fritz. They'd grown up hearing nothing else from their parents and the local cinema screens but stories of what the bastard Germans were like. Even though Billy was only born in 1949, he felt like he'd lived through the war a thousand times over. Everyone knew what the Luftwaffe had done to the Midlands, to every part of England with industry to destroy; you could see it on every derelict street, every rubble-filled patch of wasteland, every old crater pooling with rainwater. He half-expected they were going to get bayoneted the minute they were overheard talking English. Either that, or they'd be frogmarched through the nearest exit to sit out the rest of the World Cup in sunny Colditz.

In actual fact, as soon as the German blokes standing around him realised he was English, they couldn't get enough of talking to him. He got chatting to a chirpy bloke called Werner who came from Essen, and who spent the first half pointing out all the strengths of the West German team to Billy: Beckenbauer's knack for dictating the pace of the game, Seeler's aerial ability and lethal right foot, Haller's incredible finesse on

~ 105 ~

the ball in spite of his lumbering size. Werner reckoned that West Germany were in with a really good chance of winning their second World Cup, repeating the Miracle of Bern back in 1954. Billy told him about Albion winning their first trophy since '54 in March, but then remembered that had happened on the same night that Judy dumped him, and immediately started to feel miserable again.

He'd done his best to put her out of his head altogether in the last three or four months, but his best was never quite good enough. In that time, he'd found out just how cruel the human mind can really be. Even in the happiest of moments – times when he felt that life away from Judy wasn't so bad at all – his own thoughts would suddenly ambush him, hit him with a wonderful memory of her, of the two of them; laughing down their old bus stop, cuddling in the cinema, the tender awkwardness of lying beside one another after their first time in bed together. Then his mind would follow up with the fatal uppercut of picturing her with some faceless bastard, some posh student or trendy radical. Her new fella. The two of them laughing together, laughing at all of her funny stories about her useless ex-boyfriend. Pathetic little Billy, always out of his depth.

He didn't know if there was a new lad or not. He hadn't spoken to her since March, not properly. He still saw Kath – who was going steady with Jonah's brother these days – up the Brummie Road End every now and then, and she commiserated with him and promised him things would get better. But she didn't try and pretend that Billy had any hope of getting back together with Judy. That door was closed, locked, bolted.

By the middle of the second half, he was so deep in self-pity that he barely noticed Argentina's number 12, Rafael Albrecht, smash into Willi Schulz with a savage body-check. While Werner and the other Germans filling the Holte End booed and jeered, the Bulgarian referee spent a full five minutes trying to explain to Albrecht that he was being sent off, relying on hand gestures to try and get the point across. It played out like a lovers' tiff. As Albrecht was finally led off the field by two Argentinian trainers, Jonah decided that this break in play was the best possible moment to share his pressing news.

– Ya know Pete Price? That lad ah lend records off sometimes?

– Ar, ah know. What abaht im?

– He's got smallpox.

– He's got *what*?

– Smallpox. Went on holiday to Morocco lass month. Apparently iss all the rage down theer. They cor get enough a the stuff, spread it round wheerever they can. Any road, turns out he brought some back as a souvenir. He's in hospital wi it now.

– Bloody hell! Is he aroit?

– What, apart from havin smallpox? Ar, he couldn't be better.

– Hold yer foot up. Why am ya tellin me this?

– No reason.

Billy turned back to the pitch, where Hottges was preparing to chip a free kick into the penalty box. Jonah cleared his throat.

– Onny, yow might ha smallpox an all.

– Ah might ha *what*?

– Smallpox. See, ah went round ter Pete's house after he got back from his hols, before he got his symptoms. Wanted ter gi im back his Move LP. Load a rubbish, it is. Never gunna mek it anywheer near the charts.

– The smallpox, Jonah. Get ter the bit abaht the fuckin smallpox.

– Ar, well. When his skin turned nasty, an the doctors diagnosed im, he had ter name evryone he'd come inter contact with. An ah was one of em. Ah've had ter gew an get meself vaccinated. Just as a precaution, loike. But evryone ah've bin in contact with needs ter gerrit done an all.

– Jonah, fer fuck's sake! Theer's abaht fifty thousand people in contact wi ya roit now! An they come from all over the world! D'yow actually understand what could happen here? Ya mighta started a pandemic! Yam abaht ter destroy the world!

– Am ah bollocks.

– Well, yam abaht ter destroy the Villa, at least!

– Oh, a bit a smallpox wo hurt em. Might liven the place up, actually.

Billy felt the sweat suddenly covering his skin. His stomach was churning. He didn't know the symptoms of smallpox, but he definitely didn't feel right at all. How long had he spent around Jonah already today? Two hours? Three? Argentina and West Germany carried on kicking lumps out of each other on the pitch, but Billy couldn't care less anymore. He couldn't wait for the ref to blow the final whistle. When full-time finally came, he left Jonah standing on the Holte End terraces with the Teutonic hordes and rushed for the exit, pushing past disgruntled Brummies and Germans alike. After a sleepless night, he raced to the doctor for an inoculation. It was already too late.

Two days later, he found the first sore on his leg. Within twelve hours of that, they'd spread across nearly every inch of his skin. Three hours later, he was in hospital, quarantined from the world, from everyone he'd ever known or loved.

The first couple of days are the worst. They take all the clothes he's been wearing off him, telling him they have to destroy them in case they've been contaminated. Losing an old jacket and jeans isn't so bad – they aren't exactly the height of fashion in the first place – but worse than that, they take his Albion scarf, the one Mom knitted for him, which he wore to the match. It's threadbare, but he's taken care of it all these years, knowing there'll be no replacement. That scarf means more than any photograph of her. A picture reminds you what someone looked like, but it's flat, nothing more than an icon; a handmade gift carries memories and emotions like a carpet gathers dust. Wrapping the scarf around his neck always reminds Billy of the Saturday she first surprised him with it, the morning when he gobbled his boiled egg so fast he nearly choked, just so him and Dad could catch the 74 down to the ground and he could show off his Albion colours, prove himself a real supporter. During his first night on the ward, Billy lies awake for hours with a lump in his throat, wondering again how things so precious can vanish so quickly.

Being in isolation is a special kind of torture; hours of solitude he spends singing songs to himself just so he can hear something, check he hasn't gone deaf and dumb. Then, after the second day, Billy asks one of the two nurses who brings him meals – the younger one – if he can have a radio. He says it in the weakest, croakiest voice he can manage, hoping it might sway things for him. Her nose and mouth are hidden behind a blue mask, and she says nothing; he reckons his luck's out. But the next day, she brings him breakfast with a surprise: her own Super Six tranny – a bright red one about the size of a housebrick, though lighter to hold, and new enough that it still has a shine about it – and with it, he's got a whole world of football to look forward to.

He follows every single match of the tournament through the little speaker, the clipped tones of Brian Moore and Maurice Edelston bringing him matches from Wembley, Goodison Park, Hillsborough, Ayresome Park, Old Trafford. With the radio inches from his ear, and his illness sometimes putting him into fitful dozes, he lives in a world of grass, boots and leather, his only companions Pele, Eusebio, Franz Beckenbauer, Lev Yashin, Bobby Moore. On his mind's towering terraces, with a capacity crowd hollering around him, he watches Pak Doo-Ik chalk up a historic win for North Korea over Italy, and Hungary channel the spirit of past heroes to put the much-fancied Brazil to the sword. He cheers until the walls echo when Bobby Charlton scores a thumping goal from outside the penalty area to get England off the mark against Mexico, and taps his palm against the bedsheets in mute applause when Pele bows out of the tournament through injury. And as the days crawl by like insects in the sun, England stride imperiously through the rounds, with talk on the airwaves of them meeting the Soviet Union in the final, or maybe even the increasingly impressive West Germany.

As long as Billy's concentrating on the football, he doesn't have to think about anything. That is, until the day the nurse brings him another surprise with his breakfast.

His sores have been itching since he woke up, but he can't scratch them – he's already taken off a couple on his neck and let out a stream of blood and pus – so the best way to ease the discomfort is to rub the pillow over his face, get a little bit of friction. He's just in the middle of a good hard pillowing when he opens his eyes and realises with a jolt that the nurse is waiting at his bedside with a tray.

– Yow aroit, Mr Collier?

– Oh. Aroit, Sue. Ar, ah'm fine. Juss... never mind. What is it?

– A girl come in ter see ya. We couldn't let her in, ya know. Iss the rules. Her did bring ya a package, though.

Billy takes the tray, with a bowl of oatmeal and a box. He puts the food to one side and opens the first flap of the box. A haphazardly folded sheet of paper falls out, and he opens it up. His stomach clenches as he recognises the wobbly, lopsided handwriting, a short note written in a hurry.

Billy -

I've made you something special. You've needed one for a long time now. I hope you'll find a use for it, and that I'll see you again soon. I mean that. Don't let the bastards grind you down.

Always your friend,

- Jude

He reads it through, then goes back to the beginning and reads it through again. Only then does he open the box fully, and tilt it upside down to let the contents fall onto the sterile blanket.

The nurse leans forward.

– Oh, thass a lovely scarf!

He picks up the striped scarf, letting it rest gently over his palms; it's almost exactly like his old one, but thicker in its weave and slightly longer, too. Looking at the colours, he realises there's another difference: the blue stripes in the scarf are a proper shade of navy, same as the Albion shirt. In twelve years of going to matches, Billy's never known anyone find real navy blue wool for their scarf. She's either traipsed round every shop in a hundred mile radius, or spent a small fortune, or both. Billy looks up at the nurse.

– Can ya tek a note back out fer me?

– Fraid not, me love. Anythin yow touch'll be contaminated. We cor risk an epidemic.

– What if ah wear gloves?

– Yam still breathin on the paper.

– If I hold me breath while ah'm writin?

– Sweetheart, yow've got smallpox. Even ah shouldn't be in here wi ya, but someone has ter feed ya, ya poor sod.

A vacuum forms inside Billy's chest. He holds his new scarf tight to his chest and sinks down into the tight bedsheets.

– It'll be aroit, bab. Tell ya what; if her comes in again, ah'll tell her ya said thanks. An when ya get better, ya can sweep her off her feet, eh?

Billy can tell the nurse is smiling behind her mask, trying to be reassuring, but her eyes give her away. He realises suddenly, horribly, that she's not expecting him to leave this bed alive.

– Ah'll stick the wireless on fer ya, shall I? Ah think England am playin this afternoon. Bit of football should cheer ya up, eh?

Billy closes his eyes as the commentator reads out the England and Argentina teams for the quarter-final at Wembley, bitter in the knowledge that football's kept him going for so long, but only realising now – now it's too late – that there should have been far more to life than this.

*

– God, this stuff's horrible. Could ya pour us a bit more?

– Steady on, missis. I ay carryin ya home.

– Lazy cow. T'ay loike iss far away. Theer, thass enough.

Judy puts the half-empty Babycham bottle down next to the brandy after topping Kath's glass up. She picks up her own glass, and clinks it against Kath's.

– Cheers.

Judy takes a sip, and the combination of brandy and bubbly sends a burning fizz right down her throat.

– Yam roit. It is horrible.

– Ah'll finish it if yow doe want it.

– Yam the most considerate friend ah've ever had. How would I ever ha coped without yow as a neighbour?

– Yow'd ha turned out a curly-haired, angry little madam wi no fashion sense. Lucky ah was here.

– So, what am we toastin tew? Peace an equal roits?

– Pffff. Sounds loike a borin world, that.

~ 110 ~

– Kath!

– Doe "Kath" me. Tew happiness. How's that? When ya finally find it, never lerrit gew.

– I ay bloody happy, though, am I?

– Yow'll be fine, missis. Ya need ter work out exactly what ya want in life, an gew roit after it. Thass what ah'm dewin.

– All loved up, am we? How long's it gunna last this time, then? Ya musta set yerself a new record already.

Kath barks a startled laugh, and slaps Judy's arm playfully.

– Cheeky cow!

Judy smiles, a bit embarrassed. The brandy and Babycham's making her light-headed, and she's not really sure where that last remark came from. She takes another gulp and moves on.

– Ah know what ah want. Iss gerrin it thass the problem.

– What d'ya want?

– A fair world? An end ter war? People ter treat one another decent fer a change? A society wheer we can work together fer a common goal an each earn what we really deserve in life?

– Roit. But realistically?

– Kath, doe mek fun.

– I ay mekkin fun, me wench. But this ay stuff ya can wave a magic wand at by yerself, is it?

– No. But ah'd settle fer findin someone who feels the same abaht the world as me. Is that too much tew ask? Really?

– Depends, ah spose. Ya could find someone wi exactly the same opinions as yow who turns out ter be an absolute shite. Or ya could find yerself a decent lad who juss doe bother his head wi politics. Oh, hang on; yow had one a them, an ya gid im the elbow.

– Doe start this again, Kath. I ay in the mood.

– I ay startin anythin. Ah know ya went ter visit im in hospital. How is he?

– He's in isolation. Ah cor see im.

– Isolation? He's stuck in theer all on his own, wi no one ter see? An ya juss left him loike that?

– Ah gid the nurse a present ter tek in tew im! A nice new scarf.

– A scarf? In the middle of July? In an hospital ward? He's gunna treasure that, ay he! No, that ay good enough. Bollocks tew isolation. We'm gunna see im, tomorrer.

– He's got smallpox, Kath! We cor juss barge in on im!

– Look. Ah doe care whether ya never see Billy again fer the rest a yer life. After all, iss yower life. But Jude, whatever else ya might think of im, he's one of the nicest lads on God's green earth. They doe mek many loike im.

– Ar, iss a good job.

– An he doe deserve ter be rottin away on his own. So ah'm gunna gew an see im. An ah'm gunna drag Jonah along an all, kickin an screamin if ah need tew. Yow can please yerself. Oh, an ya can top me glass up an all.

– Oh, roit. Anythin else, yer highness?

– No, that'll be all fer now, dear.

– Be careful, Kathryn. Be very, very careful.

*

Matthew walks into the kitchen on tiptoes.

– Dad?

– What d'ya want?

– Am I aroit ter gew next door ter watch the final on Satdee?

– Round Big Al's place? Ar, ah doe see why not. Doe get pesterin im, though.

– No... Mr an Mr Singh said ah could gew round theirs.

Dad puts the *Mirror* down. His face folds and creases like the newspaper.

– What d'ya wanna gew round theer fer?

– Ah think Mr Singh's invitin evryone on the street round. They'm gunnew have a party. Yow an mom can come an all.

– Fat chance.

– Dad, why doe ya loike Mr Singh?

This time Dad folds the paper up entirely, and puts it down on the kitchen table. He looks down at his hands, and speaks quietly.

– It ay that ah doe loike im. Ah'm sure he's a lovely bloke. He juss doe belong here. Thass all.

– But he bought the house, dae he?

– Matthew, yow ay really old enough tew understand. People am diffrent from one another. They've got diffrent beliefs, diffrent gods, diffrent ways a life. An thass fair enough; evryone's entitled ter live how they want. But the government am tellin all these folks they can live here, an call *this* their home. Give our place in the world – *yower* place in the world, when yam old enough – tew whoever jumps off the boat fust. Is that roit?

Matthew stays quiet. He wishes he hadn't said anything.

– Well, is it roit?

He manages to mumble an answer.

~ 112 ~

– No, Dad.

– No. So I ay gunna g'ter their bloody tay party.

Dad picks the *Mirror* up again. Matthew wrestles with whether or not to speak up again, wonders if the ceiling will come crashing down around him. In the end, he decides he has to try.

– But can ah gew, Dad?

The newspaper comes down.

– Matthew, ya can do whatever ya loike on Satdee. But… juss bear in mind what ah said, eh?

– Ah will, Dad.

And Matthew swears he'll remember it for ever and ever.

*

It's a wet Friday afternoon, Birmingham's a bustling hodgepodge of brollies and macs, and the three of them are sitting in the hospital waiting room in choking silence, trying to process the awful, gut-twisting news. Jonah's got Judy to his left, Kath to his right, and over the last couple of minutes he's ended up holding hands with both of them. Judy's still clutching a bunch of chrysanthemums she got off the market earlier, and Jonah's got a banana in his lap which he bought because they'd sold out of grapes. He doesn't know what to do with it now.

He's passed on. Three words from the nurse. Curt and direct. Meagre window-dressing on the hideous reality that Billy's gone.

Dead.

Seventeen years old, and suddenly nothing more than fuel for a furnace. No more pints of M&B for him. No more rides on Jonah's scooter, no more nights listening to Stones 45s or afternoons filling the Brummie Road End with the echo of songs and chants. His cheeky grin, his memory for pointless football trivia, his miserable scowl when Jonah managed to wind him up; everything which made Billy a human being is history. Washed away in the rain like ticket stubs after a bad result.

– Iss mar fault.

He has to say it. It's been mithering him for days. He probably won't feel any better for saying it out loud, but he can't keep it bottled up any longer.

– It was me that gid im smallpox. It musta bin.

Kath squeezes his fingers. Jonah hasn't cried since he was eight years old – the last time was when he copped a hiding off his nan for breaking one of his mom's old plates – but now there are raging floodwaters behind his eyes, dammed there, rising every minute.

– Ya wor ter know, Jonah.

– Ah shoulda towd im sooner, though. Now iss too late, ay it? Ah've gone an killed im. *Killed* im.

Judy's staring at the wall of the waiting room. She looks like she's whispering to herself, but Jonah can't hear any of the words. He tilts his head back, hoping it'll sort out the lump that's formed in his throat, and suddenly a doctor appears with a clipboard in his hand, a sombre expression on his face.

– I understand you came to see William Collier?
– Billy. Ar.
– And nurse has told you what happened?
Jonah breathes out heavily, raggedly.
– Yeah. Was it quick, doctor?
– Excuse me?
– Ah mean, did he suffer? Did he gew in his sleep?
– Oh, no. He was awake. But it was all quite painless. A quick and simple departure. He even managed to eat a bowl of semolina when it was all over.

They're so lost in their grief that it takes a few seconds for the last sentence to sink in.

– He did what, sorry?
– He ate a bowl of semolina. And some rice pudding, too.
– Am yow tekkin the piss, mush? His body ay even cold yet, an yome on abaht St Peter's fuckin dessert trolley?
– His body? I'm sorry, I think we may be at cross-purposes; we expect Mr Collier to make a full recovery, but he'll be in here for another couple of weeks yet. Didn't nurse tell you this?
– Her towd us he'd passed on!
– Yes; he's passed on to the observation ward, where he'll recuperate before being discharged.
– So the bastard ay jed? He's still breathin?
– I assure you that Mr Collier's quite alive. In fact, during his departure from the isolation ward, he was very animated indeed. I think the England soccer team won their semi-final.

Judy's on her feet, grabbing at the doctor's sleeve.

– So he doe ha smallpox no more?
– I'm afraid he never had smallpox. He actually contracted cowpox from the inoculation he was given by his doctor. We use strains of cowpox to vaccinate against smallpox, you see. You're free to see him for yourselves, if you'd like?

They don't need another invitation. They tear down the corridors, their shoes squeaking a symphony against the sterile floor, whooping and shrieking their way past startled blue-frocked nurses and glaring doctors until they reach the quiet, pastel-coloured confines of the observation ward. They spot Billy in a bed halfway down, his mousy hair rich against the white of the pillow, and trip over each other scrambling to his bedside.

He's still looking rough, but the sores on his skin are healing, and there's some colour back in his face. He looks up in alarm at their sudden arrival, stiffening at the sight of Jonah and Judy particularly. Out of breath from running, resting one arm on the frame of the bed, Jonah waves awkwardly with his free hand.

– Good ter see ya. Ya poxy bastard.

Billy shakes his head.

– Is that it? Thass the best ya can say fer yerself? Ah'm never gunna forgive yow fer puttin me in here, Jonah. Ah swear.

– Oh, come on! Ah brought ya a banana.

He tosses the fruit onto the bedspread. Billy eyes it as if it's about to sprout legs and walk.

– Brilliant. What delights have ya infected this with? Horse cholera? African dick-rot?

– Ya know, Bill, the doctor says ya never had smallpox. So really, it wor me what put ya in here at all. It was the quack what gid ya the injection.

– But I onny had the injection cos a yow! An ah've missed the World Cup! Ah'm gunna be stuck in here fer the final an all!

Kath clears her throat.

– We could allwis sort summat out, Billy.

– How? Ah'm stuck in here another fortnight. It ay loike ya can break me out.

Judy smiles.

– Doe be so sure. Jonah's got his scooter, after all. Cor be too difficult ter do a Steve McQueen over the hospital wall wi yow on the back.

Billy stares at Judy blankly for a few moments – the first time he's even made eye contact with her since she came in – and there's a long stretch of silence. Then he smirks, and pulls his arm out from under the covers, clutching a homemade blue and white scarf tight in his hand. And Judy smiles back.

– Aroit then, guys. Tell me the plan.

*

The rain drums down all through the night; heavy showers with bursts of thunder which wake Matthew up, making him clutch at his blanket until sleep comes again. Saturday dawns cool and grey, a fresh wind blowing through the streets, a woolly layer of cloud covering an island nation at the centre of the world.

Matthew can't remember a Saturday morning so quiet; except for the butcher's boy delivering the usual weekend supply of bacon and sausages, his bike decked out in all kinds of England paraphernalia – from World Cup Willie toys to Union flag bunting – and a tatter clunking by on a horse and trap, no one's venturing out into the street. Everyone's reading the newspapers, or fiddling with their televisions, making sure the signal's just right. Dad's trying to do both at the same time, munching a slice of toast in the process. Matthew thinks again about asking Dad whether he wants to come next door for the final. He decides not to; not because he's worried about Dad saying no, but because he's scared he might change his mind and say yes. During the stormy spells in his sleep last night, Matthew imagined Dad round Mr Singh's house, shouting in his face the way he did to the man from the council. He doesn't want to see that. He doesn't want anything to spoil today.

An hour before kick-off, Matthew puts on his red jumper, takes his set of bubblegum cards from his room, tucks his ball under his arm and runs out of the front door, round to Mr and Mrs Singh's. Mrs Singh opens the door for him; she's wearing bright blue loose-fitting trousers, and embroidered veils that wrap around her head and upper body. She welcomes Matthew in to the front room. He's disappointed to discover he's the only one there.

But he's not on his own for long; the Singh's daughter comes in a few minutes later. She's called Aasha, and she's just turned eight. She comes and sits near the telly with Matthew, cross-legged on the floor in her own colourful pink and blue clothes. Matthew takes out his bubblegum cards and lays them face-up on the brown carpet. Gordon Banks. George Cohen. Jack Charlton. Bobby Moore. Ray Wilson. Nobby Stiles. Alan Ball. Bobby Charlton. Martin Peters. Geoff Hurst. Roger Hunt. Aasha watches him closely, quietly.

There are a few knocks on the front door in the next half-hour, and some of the other neighbours trickle in nervously, wives carrying plates of sausage rolls and husbands with bottles of Brew XI. Mrs Singh comes round pouring cups of tea. One of the men – Mr Dawley from number 83 – whispers to his wife that he's going to nip out into the yard and check Mr Singh's shed at half-time to see if he's hiding a sword in there. He says he served with a few of these "seek" blokes in the war, and they all carried them. Mr Johnson from number 96 asks how they got their tin helmets on over those turbans they wear, and Mr Dawley says they never bothered with them. They'd charge through any crossfire or barrage with nothing but a thin strip of cloth between their skulls and the hot shrapnel. Mad bastards. Brave bastards too, mind. Then Mr Dawley looks at Matthew and Aasha with a guilty face, and pardons his French. Matthew nods. Only weak minds rely on swear words, that's what Dad says.

Then at three o'clock, Mr Singh walks in and puts the television on, and the talk stops.

It's time.

*

ENG-LAND! ENG-LAND! ENG-LAND! ENG-LAND!

It's an impasse. A stand-off between the sides. In the last year, Judy's been on four anti-Vietnam demonstrations and half a dozen picket lines, but she's never seen anything like this.

The blokes have formed a rough outward-facing semi-circle around Billy's bed; Jack and Wilf, Shemmy and Puffin George, with Jonah sheltering behind them, a heavy DER telly cradled in his arms. The matron and three nurses are standing in front of this little expeditionary force, all stern expressions and hands on hips, while Judy and Kath watch from their perch on one of the ward's vacant beds.

ENG-LAND! ENG-LAND! ENG-LAND! ENG-LAND!

Jack's leaning against the wall, a seventy-one-year-old with a dodgy hip acting more like the corporal he was half a century ago, waving a crutch at the nurses to keep them in no man's land. Wilf's seven years older than Jack – half the time he still believes it's 1917 and he's about to get gassed for the first time again – but now he's ordering Jonah to get behind his wheelchair so they can't snatch the telly out of his arms. Shemmy's banging an empty bedpan against the metal frame of Billy's bed as if he didn't just have his gallbladder removed a couple of days ago, and Puffin George is taking big gulps of breath before croaking *ENG-LAND!* at a barely audible volume from his coal-wrecked lungs. The matron – a petite, grey-haired woman called Margaret who makes up for being smaller than anyone else in the room with a steely, authoritative voice – berates them with more than a little exasperation.

– This kind of behaviour won't help any of you, you know! If you get back in your beds now, I *may* let you listen to the match on the wireless.

Jack answers her with his own NCO bark.

– Balls ter the wireless! We've got weselves a telly, an we'm watchin it! *ENG-LAND! ENG-LAND! ENG-LAND!*

The matron has the look of a woman who knows in defeat that her best chance of keeping control is to pretend this was her plan all along.

– Very well. As long as you behave yourselves, you may watch the television. But if I hear any kind of commotion in here, I shall tell the doctors immediately.

Shemmy pipes up.

– Ya can invite em in ter watch it wi us, if ya loike.

Wilf elbows him to shut up. The matron spins round haughtily and stamps out, the gaggle of nurses trailing her obediently. Jonah plonks the TV set down on a meal trolley with a groan, then claps his hands together gleefully.

– Gather round, ladies an gentlemen, gather round!

From the moment they switch on and the tube flickers into life, they can hear the Wembley crowd. Where a minute ago there were six blokes chanting *ENG-LAND*, now they can hear ninety-six thousand at it. The teams file out onto the pitch. Her Majesty strolls into the royal box with Stanley Rous and Harold Wilson. The Royal Marines band plays the national anthem, and follows it up with a quick blast of *Deutschland Uber Alles*. They huddle onto the peach blanket of Billy's bed, all squashed together, and Judy finds herself lying next to him, propping herself up by his shoulder.

There's no harm in that. Friends should always stick by each other's sides.

The match begins, and Billy takes it on himself to points out bits and bobs of information about what's going on.

– They'm playin at a really high tempo, look.

– Is that roit?

– Ar.

– Really fast an slick. Bit aggressive an all.

– Hang on; is it a football match or a Kinks song?

– Yome hopeless, yow am.

Billy smiles as he says that, and squeezes her arm gently. There's a sudden round of applause as Kath reaches into her coat and pulls out a bottle of brandy. The booze is passed round, and with a quick sip sliding down her throat, Judy relaxes into the hard mattress.

*

– STOP HIM, YOU SILLY BUGGERS!

The shout from Mr Singh startles everyone so much that half of them miss the goal. A high ball from Siegfried Held into the England box is poorly cleared by Ray Wilson, whose header comes straight to Helmut

Haller on the edge of the penalty area. Bobby Moore rushes in to make a tackle, but Haller brings the ball onto his right foot and hits a shot which bobbles under the dive of Gordon Banks and into the bottom corner of the goal. Everyone in the living room groans, while Kenneth Wolstenholme urges viewers to take solace in the fact that in the last three World Cup finals, the team which scored first lost. Mr Dawley shakes his head.

– We doe need ter know about other World Cup finals. Juss look at the bloody war. We let the Krauts tek an early lead then, an we still polished em off in the end. No need ter worry.

Mr Singh nods.

– We had a lot more firepower "up front" back then, though, didn't we?

Mr Dawley looks up in surprise at Mr Singh, and Matthew watches the two of them gaze steadily at one another for a few seconds. He doesn't know what Mr Dawley's looking for, but whatever it is, he seems to find it, because he smiles.

– Ar, yam roit theer, matey.

Six minutes later, after Wolfgang Overath brings down Bobby Moore, Moore sends a quick free-kick to the edge of the German six-yard box, and Geoff Hurst pops up unmarked to head the equaliser past Tilkowski. And Mrs Singh awkwardly puts her hands over her ears as everyone else in the room shouts loud enough to bring the house down.

*

As the half-time whistle goes, the old timers in the ward are having a singsong, buoyed by the England equaliser and a string of incredible saves by Gordon Banks. They're halfway through *It's A Long Way To Tipperary* when Judy taps Billy's arm.

– Ah still doe gerrit, ya know.

– Doe get what?

– Football.

A brandy-soaked voice chimes in from the left-hand side of the bed.

– Jude, juss think of it loike chess.

– Kath, ah doe *loike* bloody chess! Ya *know* ah doe loike chess!

Billy interrupts.

– Well, think of it loike one a yer political books, then. Loike how they describe society.

– Gew on.

– Well. The defence is the proletariat, roit? The workin class. Good, no-nonsense blokes dewin jobs that tek a bit a skill an knowhow,

~ 119 ~

but ay all that glamorous. No kid ever wants ter be a defender in the playground, but as they grow up, some folks realise iss what they'm suited tew. Theer's honesty an dignity in bein part of a decent back line.

– Okay then.

– The midfield is the beaujolais.

– Ya mean the bourgeoisie?

– Ar. Them lot. The middle classes. They'm a bit more refined in they talents; they'm shopkeepers servin up chances fer the forwards ter score. Some on em am creative an artistic; some want ter climb the ladder an be goalscorers themselves, an think they'm too good ter do any defendin. But some ay forgot they roots; they remember midfield was born out a defence, an they loike puttin a tackle in. But the main thing is, they produce goals. They doe juss *control* the means a production; they *am* the means a production.

– Roit.

– An the centre-forwards... well, they'm royalty, obviously. Doe atta do all that much in the grand scheme a things, but when they do, iss bloody important. Same way no laws get med unless the Queen signs her name on em, no matches get won unless the striker hits the net. They'm the pomp an the glory, the poster boys. Heads a state, ay they?

– I atta say, of all the things I expected when ah come here today, a Marxist analysis a football wor one.

– Maybe, Judy, juss *maybe*, theer's a lot ya doe know abaht me.

She glances at him with a puzzled expression, and he smirks back. After a few moments of thought, she clears her throat.

– But see, why do the defenders need ter toil away in anonymity fer no glory or reward? Why cor the *defence* become the means a production?

From his perch at the foot of the bed, Jonah groans wearily.

– Oh, brilliant. Look what yow've done. Yow've bloomin well started her, ay ya? Her ay gunna shurrup abaht this, now.

– Jude, how would the defence produce goals every game? Be realistic.

– Well, they can kick the ball long, cor they? Ya can have one centre-forward, one head a state, up the top a the pitch ter score. Keep the rest a the men back, and juss keep kickin it roit up the field whenever they gerrit. No need fer a midfield, no need fer any a that borin passin.

– Jude, it'd be shite ter watch that! Football ay just abaht scorin goals! People want ter be entertained!

– But ya doe win matches by how much yow entertain the crowd, do ya?

There are a few seconds of awkward silence. Jonah sighs contemplatively.

– See, this is why football ay a girl's sport. They juss doe understand it proper.

– OI!

Kath flings a pillow at Jonah's head. He ducks it, and then pops a Woodbine in his mouth. Judy takes another swig of brandy.

– Well, now ah know what ah need ter do wi me life.

– Yeah?

– Yeah. Ah'm gunna become a football manager. Break down the barriers a gender! Bring Maoist philosophy ter the pitch! POWER TO THE OPPRESSED DEFENDERS! LONG LIVE THE REVOLUTIONARY REARGUARD! CLASS WAR FROM THE BACK FOUR!

Kath's doubled up, hands laced across her belly, laughing fit to burst. Billy finds himself leaning his head over towards Judy's shoulder. The recovery ward choir finish their rendition of *Tipperary* – a song written by a Black Country man, Jack tells them, a lifelong Baggies fan – and they switch to singing another of his songs, written for Albion's 1932 cup final, as the teams re-emerge on TV:

Wembley day is near again!
Yow'll hear a mighty cheer again!
Yow bet we'll get some beer again!
Wembley day is near again!

*

As the second half begins, it starts teeming with rain at Wembley. England put more and more pressure on West Germany. At the Singhs' house, no one dares to take their eyes off the telly except for Mrs Singh, who's topping up cups of tea all around the room. Matthew's telling Aasha about the England team, about who plays for which club, about who his favourite players are, and she nods quietly, still not saying a word.

Twelve minutes from time, Hunt feeds a ball through the penalty box to Alan Ball, whose shot is tipped round the near post by Tilkowski. Ball takes the corner, Hurst controls the ball on the edge of the box, has a right-footed shot which Hottges tries to boot clear, but the German full-back misjudges, slices the ball up in the air, and it lands in front of Martin Peters. And there's that moment, that wonderful heartbeat when everyone knows he'll score. He has to score.

The ball hits the back of the net.

Peters celebrates, and with just ten minutes left on the clock, the flags are flying. The crowd chant *WE WANT THREE! WE WANT THREE!* and England do their best to oblige, but can't quite find the right shot to beat Tilkowski. With four minutes left, and the crowd roaring *Rule Britannia*, England break through on goal and Hunt squares the ball for Bobby Charlton, but running at full tilt, Charlton scuffs his shot wide.

Matthew's up on his feet by the final minute, bouncing up and down in anticipation of the final whistle. Aasha's watching him with a smile on her face, while some of the grown-ups pester him to stop blocking their view. West Germany have a free kick twenty-five yards out, and behind the five-man England wall, nearly every player on the pitch is in the penalty box.

It happens quickly at first, and then slowly, agonisingly. Emmerich strikes the ball hard and low through the goalhanging crowd, and George Cohen blocks it, but it spins loose to Held, who shoots at goal; Banks parries the ball across the six-yard box and starts scrambling across his goalline, but the goal's wide open at the far post, and Wolfgang Weber's running in, pouncing on the loose ball, side-footing it into the back of the net. A German equaliser. In the very last minute.

Afterwards, Matthew doesn't even remember running out of the house into the Singhs' back garden. It just happens in the heat of heartbreak. He's got his ball under his arm, and he bounces it on the ground once or twice, then gives it a couple of sulky kicks against the wall.

– Bloody typical, eh?

He looks up to see Mr Singh in the doorway. He doesn't answer him, but gives the ball another kick.

– So, what happens now, then? They share the cup?

– Extra time. They play fer another half an hour.

– And if no one wins in the next half an hour?

– They'll have a replay on Tuesday.

– Another match? What if no one wins that?

– They have another load of extra time. Then another replay. They juss keep playin till someone wins.

– Then I hope someone wins in the next half an hour. My digestion is not helped by all of this prevarication.

– It shoulda bin us! We deserve ter win! We'm miles better than them! Miles better!

– Perhaps. But in my experience, the world doesn't tend to care much for what people deserve. We get exactly what we're given; anything else must be worked for, and prayed for. In fact, it's a good thing we have sport. It teaches us some important lessons at precisely the age we need to learn them.

~ 122 ~

– Me dad says it builds character, bein a football supporter.
– Your father sounds like a wise man. Does he say anything else?
Matthew hesitates.
– He says… no. Nuthin.
– Go on.
– Mr Singh. D'yow keep a sword in the shed?
– Why? Do you?
– No. But ah doe come from India.
– No, Matthew, I don't keep my kirpan in the shed. I do have a very interesting watering can in there, and I think there are a few spiders too, but nothing else.
Matthew kicks the ball again.
– Ah doe loike spiders.
– Something else we have in common. Are you coming in for the extra-time? Or do you want to stay outside and practise for the day you score your goal at Wembley Stadium?
Matthew picks the ball up and tucks it under his arm.
– So we'm gunna work hard ter win the match?
– And pray, Matthew. Don't forget to pray.

*

The sun's out at Wembley, and the players cast storm-black shadows on sea-grey turf. Play surges from one end of the pitch to another through the first half of extra-time, cramped and tiring legs coaxed into titanic bursts of effort.
– We'm gunna lose this, ya know.
– Shurrup, Jonah!
– We shoulda wrapped it up in the ninety minutes. Scored a third goal. The Krauts have got a spring in they step now. They've got one hand on the trophy already. Juss watch.
None of them are singing anymore. None of them are laughing. Jonah's still smoking, but everyone else is suffering in silence and tense expectation. Every time the Germans come forward with the ball, they all gasp – even Judy – and start bellowing at the screen to tackle them, to clear it, to attack, attack, attack. And finally, England respond; Ball charges down the wing, and centres the ball for Hurst, who traps it neatly on the edge of the six-yard box, swivels and smashes a shot which ricochets off the bottom of the crossbar, bounces on the goalline and flies back out again.
– YES!
– Has he scored?

– Woss gewin on?

The referee, Gottfried Dienst, looks confused, uncertain. The England players are shouting for the goal to be given. The West Germans protest that it's hit the goalline. Dienst runs over to Tofik Bakhramov, the linesman. Shemmy groans.

– The ref's bloody Swiss, ay he? Neutral bastard ay gunna mek a decision!

– Iss aroit, iss aroit! The linesman's a Russian! He'll be on our side!

Bakhramov signals a goal for England. Jack, Wilf, Shemmy and Puffin George start chanting.

STA-LIN-GRAD, STA-LIN-GRAD, STA-LIN-GRAD!

The rest of the match is an emotional cakewalk, everyone screaming at the telly for England to get that goal which'll finish the job, and screaming in horror whenever the Germans work their way towards the England penalty box. The whistles from the crowd are urgent, pleading, as West Germany win one more corner in the final minute.

As the ball swings in, Banks comes off his line and punches it well clear to Hunt.

It's all over, I think!

The referee checks his watch and waves his arms to continue play, as Moore hoists a long ball upfield to Geoff Hurst.

And here comes Hurst, he's got... some people are on the pitch! They think it's all over!

– GEW ON, GEOFF! HIT IT! HIT IIIIIT!

They don't hear the rest of Kenneth Wolstenholme's commentary. As Hurst strikes the ball cleanly towards the top corner at the near post, the nurses come running in to quieten everyone down, but within seconds, even they're screaming and cheering fit to deafen all England.

*

The celebrations carry on for hours. Margaret, the matron, soon comes in and sets the junior nurses back to their duties, but even she stops to watch Nobby Stiles hopping and skipping around the Wembley pitch with the Jules Rimet trophy, and limits herself to a motherly frown of disapproval when she notices Kath slipping the brandy bottle under the blanket.

After another hearty singsong – Jonah teaches the old folks *Lazing On A Sunny Afternoon*, and then they finish off with *Goodnight Irene* –

~ 124 ~

they shuffle off to their beds, drawing the bright orange curtains round for privacy. Jonah and Kath leave fairly soon after, one after the other, Jonah making an excuse to hang around for an extra five minutes and not have to catch the same bus as her. He hasn't been the same around Kath since she started seeing Tommy. Whatever friendship the pair of them had seems to have hit the rocks, and although he doesn't talk much about it, Billy's not sure how long it's going to take Jonah to put all this behind him.

– Maybe he never will.

Judy looks up.

– Woss that?

– Nuthin. Ah was juss thinkin abaht Jonah.

– Roit. D'ya offen think abaht Jonah while yam in bed?

– Cheeky mare!

– Aroit, aroit! Onny a joke! Woss botherin ya abaht Jonah?

– He really had his heart set on Kath, dae he? The poor bastard. Cor be easy fer im. Seein her wi his brother, ya know.

– Maybe he's better off. Ah love Kath an evrythin, but ya know what her's loike. Changes her mood evry five minutes, her does. Her'll probly gi Tommy the elbow befower long. That might gi Jonah a chance, eh?

– An what if her doe want im? What if he loves her ter bits, an her still doe want im? What then?

– Bill...

– Jude. Ah've been dewin a lot a thinkin. Time on me hands, ya see. Yow was roit, ya know, the other month. All ah do wi me life is work, drink an watch football. An I enjoy it, course ah do; but ah need ter do more. Ay gunna be around forever, am I? Ah've gorra mek the most of evry second.

– Billy, I...

– Ah could do that on me own, obviously. Ah spose ah'd find somebody ter while away the time with, sooner or later. But honestly, if ah'm gunna mek the most of evry second a me life, ah'd rather do it wi somebody who can mek me smile. Somebody who can mek me care abaht things all around the world ah never even knew was happenin. Somebody who can knit the onny navy blue an white scarf in the Midlands.

– Billy...

– If ya still feel I ay worth it, then fair enough. Ah'll wish ya all the best an we'll move on. But ah need ya ter know exactly how ah feel. Judith Anne Fletcher, theer might come a day when ah doe wake up thinkin abaht ya, an doe fall asleep thinkin abaht ya, but it'll tek summat bloody awful ter mek that happen. Cos even when ah thought ah was dyin, ah never stopped.

~ 125 ~

– Billy. Shurrup.

Judy puts her finger to his lips. Then, slowly, she takes that finger away, and presses her own lips to Billy's. Then, after a few moments, she gets up, and draws the curtain around the bed.

*

Matthew's on the doorstep. He cuts the string, and loops it. The rainclouds have cleared, but it's still a bit chilly out, and his red jumper doesn't quite keep out the night air's bite. He pierces a hole in the gold foil, and threads the string through the hole. He's going to go home soon, but he just wants to make the most of whatever's left of today. He makes another hole in the foil, and threads the other end of the string through. He plays the image over in his mind: Bobby Moore shaking hands with the Queen and then taking the trophy off her, Mr Singh looking up at the ceiling and clapping his hands together in grateful prayer. He ties the loose ends of the string together and carefully lifts it over his head to let the gold foil disc hang round his neck. His very own winner's medal.

As the England team did their lap of honour, Mr Dawley leaned forward off the settee and told him to treasure the moment, because Matthew might never see it again in his lifetime. But how do you turn a moment into treasure? He sat and thought about it until he remembered all the cups of tea Mrs Singh had been making during the match, and all the milk she used in them. And he went into the kitchen and found some discarded foil bottle-tops, and a length of string, and came outside to make his own treasure.

The door opens behind him, and Aasha comes outside and sits staring at him quietly, smiling. She reaches over and takes the little homemade medal between her fingers. Matthew picks up one of the other bottle-tops he brought outside and the leftover string, and uses them to make another medal. He slips the string over her head and then shakes her hand to congratulate her on being part of the winning team. Then he gets up off the doorstep and hops around on the pavement with his arm in the air, just like Nobby Stiles, dancing with the make-believe trophy in his hand. And Aasha giggles, and the sound echoes off the bricks of the houses, diffusing in the cold air of another English night.

October 1967

The fight flares suddenly, like a pan fire, and spreads at the same speed. There have been scuffles on and off during the match itself – mostly just handbags on the terraces, the locals getting wound up about the Albion contingent showing up in full voice in the middle of their end, singing *THE BRUMMIE ROAD IS HERE* – but yet again, it's outside the ground after the final whistle that the real trouble starts. Over the last few months, you could set your watch by the five o'clock punch-ups which happen around the supporters' coaches in whatever dismal corner of the country they're visiting.

It's no different at the Hawthorns. The old factory down the road from the ground now has a rough skull-and-crossbones marked on the wall in dribbling white paint, and a warning for visiting fans heading out of Birmingham up the Holyhead Road into the Black Country: STAY OUT OF THE BRUMMIE ROAD END. The terraces are packed every week, and little mobs from different towns each have their favourite spec which they occupy and defend against outsiders; Tipton and Handsworth on the right side of the stand, Smethwick over the left, and West Bromwich lads in the middle. Still, some weeks, you'll see a set of away supporters saft enough to give it a try, their scarves hidden away till kick-off, when they thrust them up in the air and shout their team's name a couple of times. It's never more than a couple of times. They're kicked and mauled off the terraces before they can manage a third.

No matter where they go, it's always thirteen or fourteen-year-olds starting the aggro; spotty little herberts lurking about with their scarves on show, ready with taunts or abuse. Backing them up are the older teens, all balls and bravado. Today's the same.

Except for the eggs, that is.

The first one smashes against the side of the coach, plastering yolk and shell fragments over the cream bodywork. The second hits the ground a few yards in front of the Albion fans in a futile explosion of goo. The third egg arcs gracefully through the air and whacks right into the middle of Billy's chest, wrecking all of his new townie clobber in one messy impact. The stuff goes everywhere. His blue V-neck jumper, turned-up Levis, crombie, black Dr Marten boots; the whole lot, splattered.

– Ya fuckin little shit!

The kids are cheering the direct hit. Some of them have got different scarves tied around their arms, colours from up and down the country, showing them off as prizes they've taken from opposition fans they've battered. Half the time, the little bastards just steal the scarves off younger kids, or buy them off a market stall on an awayday and then brag to their mates that they won a fight on their tod. The Albion lot around Billy – Jonah included – are jeering, asking the other lot if they've got the balls to do anything more than chuck eggs.

Billy's careful not to wind up on the front line, always making sure there's a body or two between him and the action; in fact, the only action he usually gets is ducking the odd punch, maybe flinging one back, feeling his knuckles scrape someone's jaw or thump into their ribs. Although Jonah's a bit more cocky, always more ready to talk with his fists, he tends to hang back as well. You can't pick up a newspaper these days without seeing the words FOOTBALL HOOLIGANS in some hysterical headline, accompanied by an indignant story about the despicable crimes these sociopaths go around committing. The tabloid journalists who write the stuff have never been within ten miles of a football ground – sometimes they even recycle stories from the old mod and rocker battles to keep it sensational – but the problem is, people believe every word of it. When you've got a decent job with career prospects, the last thing you need is your gaffer scrutinising your cuts and bruises over the top of his *Daily Mail* on Monday morning. And then there are the wenches to worry about. Jonah's been seeing Iris Duckhouse for a year or so now, and for Billy, there's still Judy. Always Judy.

Shut away in her world of badges, pamphlets and Little Red Books, she doesn't have a high opinion of football fans fighting one another. Why not unite? Fight a worthwhile enemy? There's a whole ruling class just crying out for the kicking of the century. She's been bending Billy's ear about it for months, ever since she cottoned on to the rucks that are happening after matches nowadays. Billy doesn't have the heart to tell her that so much of it is just kids being kids, all bollocks and bluster, showing loyalty to the scarf round their neck the same way they'd have showed loyalty to their own fashions and music a few years back. And besides, any revolution spearheaded by fourteen-year-olds is bound to come a cropper if its objectives are any more complex than a few packets of Park Drives and some saucy pictures of Diana Rigg.

– Roit, ya little wanker. Ya want yer eggs scrambled or beaten?

Jonah's collared the Half-Dozen Kid, and he's shaking him about with his left hand, his right clenched ready to give him a clout. In the end, he doesn't manage it; there's a warning shout from behind him, and Billy turns to see a couple of delegates from the local constabulary watching from the turquoise cocoon of an Austin A40 panda car across the street. They enjoy the spectacle of a good punch-up, the plod, but they've got a nasty tendency to wade in and nick whoever's left standing at the end of it. Above the fear of getting an earful at home or being labelled a hooligan at work, no one wants to end up in a cell in some strange town's police station on a Saturday night. There's an orgy of pushing and shoving, and after a frantic few minutes, everyone ends up back on the coach none the worse for wear.

Except for Billy, who's the worse for everything he's wearing.

– Ah doe believe it. Ruined, the lot on it.

– Cheer up, ya miserable bastard. At least we dae lose this week.

– Is that it? Thass the best we can say abaht a two-hundred-mile round trip? We dae lose? Christ, iss worse than ah thought.

Even the most optimistic Albion fan – and Billy's never fitted into that category, even with a belly full of Brew XI – would struggle to put a brave face on the last twelve months. If the team carries on the way they have since summer 1966, they'll be going down faster than the *Torrey Canyon*. As it is, they only managed to avoid relegation last season with a couple of games left; they bowed out of the Fairs Cup with barely a whimper in the autumn, and suffered a record defeat in the FA Cup against Leeds United in February. Their only consolation was reaching the League Cup final for the second year running: this time playing a single match at Wembley, versus Third Division Queens Park Rangers.

The Albion tickets sold out fast, and Billy was gutted not to get one. A first trip to Wembley would have made up for a whole season of suffering, and it could be years before he'd get another chance. At half-time he was even more disappointed not to be there, with Albion already 2-0 up thanks to a couple of Chippy Clark goals. No Third Division club had ever won a major trophy before, let alone come from two goals down against top-flight opposition to do it. He wasn't at Wembley to cheer them on, but he was at least happy they were going to lift the trophy again.

Bloody QPR.

Albion spent the whole of the second half with the wagons circled around their goal, while the Rangers number ten, Rodney Marsh, ran rings round them. First, Roger Morgan pulled a goal back twenty minutes into the half, heading in a Mark Lazarus cross. Then Rodney Marsh equalised, firing in off the post with a quarter of an hour to go. With Albion on the ropes, QPR pressed home the advantage, and punished them with nine minutes left when the ball broke loose to Lazarus after a goalmouth scramble, and he shot into the empty net to win QPR the cup.

And of course, it didn't end there. Albion appointed Alan Ashman as manager in the summer, but they're still struggling in the league. The few high points in the season so far – the joy of seeing Tony Brown equalise with his hand right in front of the Cowshed at Molineux to snatch a late point, and Phil Parkes getting sent off after chasing him all round the pitch – have paled in comparison to defeats against Chelsea, Liverpool,

Arsenal, Southampton. The team just need something to fall into place for them; a missing piece of the jigsaw to turn up. But for all the fags smoked and pints drunk over the topic, no one's got a bloody clue what that could be.

It's a long coach trip back to the Black Country; a long transition through the dark window from fields back to factories. It's a relief to finally make it back to the Throstle Club outside the Hawthorns, a little beacon of light and warmth in the smoky Saturday night chill. The ground's sombre with no match being played, its hulking unlit stands huddling mournfully in the darkness.

– Oi! Humpty Dumpty! Ya comin in fer a pint?

– In this state? Ah need ter gew an get these washed, Jonah.

– Suit yerself.

– Doe yow need ter gi Iris a ring, anyway? Ya know what her gets loike. Her'll be sharpenin the knives by now. Thinkin yome off in some strip club.

– Oh, doe bloody start. One time! One soddin time down in Soho, an ya never hear the end of it! An it wor even a strip club, it was a *gentleman's* club!

– Lot a wenches in theer wi nuthin on.

– Ar, but they already had they knockers out when we got in theer, so they wor really *strippin*, was they?

– How unreasonable of Iris not ter see the vital distinction.

– Any road, yome juss lucky ya dae stick one a them matchbooks from the club in yower pocket an all. Cos Judy never found out about that one, did her?

– Ah was onny in theer cos a yow!

– Oh, mar fault again, is it? Ah musta tied ya up an dragged ya in theer, eh? Bill, yow had eyes loike beachballs as soon as ya sid that club. Yer tongue was trailin halfway down the road. Ah thought ah'd atta drug ya juss ter get ya back out again.

– Yeah, yeah. Roit, ah'm off.

– Try not ter bump intew any yampy eleven-year-olds on yer way home.

– Yeah, yeah.

– Same time, same place next week, Humpty.

Same time, same place, next week, every week. If it wasn't for the Albion, Billy knows he'd probably have lost touch with Jonah after leaving school; become just another face down the pub every now and then, worth a nod of the head across a crowded snug, a raised pint jug through a cloud of smoke, a couple of questions about how life's treating him if they met at the bar or in the bog.

But supporting the same football club; that makes all the difference. They could disagree on everything under the sun – politics, religion, music, wenches – but as long as they can have a conversation about who's going to fill that gap on the right flank now Ken Foggo's gone, and whether Jeff Astle's up to the same standard as Derek Kevan yet, they've got a reason to be mates. Even when the team's playing like shite, they carry on, every bloody week. Why? Why not just write it off, find some other way to spend their Saturday?

Billy doesn't know for sure, but he's got a feeling that for all the talk of loyalty and pride, the real reason they stick by the club through the worst of times is so they can have an excuse to be mates with all the people they wouldn't be mates with if it wasn't for football. It doesn't make sense. It doesn't have to. Sense gets left outside the turnstiles at three o'clock on a Saturday, and sometimes, the world's a better place for it.

*

– Ah think it looks lovely. Really smart.

– Well, yow wear it, then!

– I ay got the legs fer it no more, sweetheart. It'd be nice on yow, though. Honest.

– Mom, iss barely even long enough ter be a jumper, let alone a dress! Ah cor gew outside in that! Besides, theer ay nuthin wrong wi me jeans.

– An after Kath put all that effort inter mekkin it, an all? Iss a shame ter lerrit g'ter waste.

And to think some folks have the nerve to go on about a generation gap. Some bloody gap! Judy's sure her mother must have taken a knock to the head at some point over the last twenty years that's left her acting half her age. Either that or some *Doctor Who* baddie swapped their personalities. She's got nothing against looking smart, even a bit stylish every now and then, but the size of that dress! Kath's lost her marbles. She must have done.

They hear the bang of the front door closing. Judy and her mom turn as Billy shuffles in, a tired expression on his face. His clothes look odd; stiff, discoloured, and slightly smelly.

– What happened ter yow?

– Juss had some trouble at the match. Nuthin ter worry abaht.

– Have yow an Jonah bin fightin again? Woss that on yer clothes?

– Egg.

– Wheer'd it come from?

– Out of a chicken.

She puts her hands on her hips, and fixes him with a good hard stare.

– Yow *have* bin fightin again, ay ya? Evry time! Evry soddin time!

– We'm onny defendin weselves! Ya should see some a the loonies who come hangin round the coaches at full time!

– Armed with eggs? Oh, they sound loike real psychopaths, ar. What do they do if they really lose they temper? Bombard ya wi cabbages? Bludgeon ya wi celery?

– Oh, loff it up, thass roit. Ya know how much this gear cost?

Judy's mom smiles.

– It wo be the fust time we've managed ter get yer clothes clean, our Bill. If ya toss em in the basket, ah'll see tew em.

– An what am ah gunna wear?

– What abaht this? Kath med it fer Judy, but Jude thinks the hemline's a bit tew short fer her. Yow've got a nice pair a legs, though, Bill. Ah reckon yow could pull it off.

Judy bites back the giggle that's about to erupt in her chest. With an innocent smile, her mom scurries off to find some of Dad's old clothes for a red-faced Billy.

– Ya know, ya should tek a leaf out a Tommy's book. Renounce violence. Learn ter love the world.

– Oh, an start wearing all flowery shirts an technicolour trousers an all? He ay roit in the head, Jude. Ah never thought ah'd say it, but ah feel sorry fer Jonah, havin ter put up wi it. He'd think he was well blessed if ah took up this long hair an flower power business too.

– What is it abaht lads? Yome never happy unless yam dividin yerselves into opposite extremes. Long hair, cropped hair. Hippies, hooligans. Iss gorra be one thing or the other, ay it? Theer ay never a happy medium.

She watches Billy rub his head, rasping his fingers over the severely shorn hair. In the old days, a shaved head was the quickest way to get rid of lice; the standard cut in the army, the prison, the workhouse. The perpetual look of institutionalised working-class youth. No one on the outside – no one with their freedom – wanted their individuality stolen by the barber's razor. No one until now.

First the peacock mods, the lads with a bit more money in their pockets to follow fashion, started to grow their hair out and wear more exotic and colourful clothing. Then the harder mods, the townies, the lemonheads, reacted with a military dress sense; their Dr Marten boots and their turned-up Levi Sta-Prest trousers, and hair so short you could strike a match on their skull. Where the peacocks and hippies spend their time dancing at freak-outs, the townies crowd football terraces on a Saturday, losing themselves in the anonymity of the mob.

– We look smart. Them lot look scruffy. Thass the difference. Iss abaht havin some pride, ay it?

– Pride? Ya come home covered in a week's worth a groceries, an yam *proud* of it?

– Ya know what ah mean. Look, ah might onny be a machinist, but ah'm still proud a that. Some footballers these days am buyin emselves sports cars! They've got built-in record players, the whole lot! I ay got none a that – ah doe even want none a that – but ah'm proud a what ah do have.

– Billy, thass the sweetest thing ah've heard all year. In fact, ah'd kiss ya if yow wor plastered in albumen.

– Oh, come on. Gi the eggman an hug.

– Gerroff!

– Come on; spread a bit a flour on yerself, an ah bet we'd mek an half-decent cake.

– Bill, put that down. I ay jokin. Ah'll wallop yow so bloody hard.

– If yome a-gewin ter Saaaan Franciscooooo… be sure ter stick some flour in yer haaaair…

– Billy! Aaaargh! Mom, tell im!

*

Kath's the last one stuck in the office with the sun setting over the warehouses to the west, the last of the natural light draining from the windows, surrendering the office to the dim glow of the ceiling bulbs. Just what her headache needs. It's been a long day, she's managed to get behind with the invoices she was supposed to be typing, and her skull's throbbing fit to burst.

The radio's on with *Flowers In The Rain* crackling out, and she turns the volume dial down. It's always exciting when a local band makes it big on the national scene, but at the moment, The Move are a bit too much. Besides, it's all flowers and love these days. All you need is love. Be sure to wear some flowers in your hair. Love is all around. Flowerpot men, for Christ's sake! It's getting boring. And besides, Kath's got all the flowers and love she needs in her life. Thanks to Tommy Cartwright, she's got everything.

She'll be twenty next month, and already people are giving her winks and nudges, asking her when they'll be announcing the engagement. *Time's gerrin on! Ya must be eager ter start a family a yer own, eh?*

Yome gunna look gorgeous at the altar! But why rush? They're young, and having a fantastic time. There aren't the pressures there used to be, even on a Catholic girl. Every Friday and Saturday night is an adventure, either at the dancehalls with crowds of young immigrants dancing to imported ska, soul and rocksteady 45s, or in Birmingham, at the Whiskey A Go Go above Chetwyns on the corner of John Bright Street. They get all the local bands at the Whiskey – The King Bees, The Modonaires, The Moody Blues, Jugs O'Henry, Graham Bond, Denny Lane, The Spencer Davis Group – but they're starting to get proper Motown and soul artists across from America too, like Ike & Tina Turner, who Kath and Tommy saw there in the summer. On Fridays and Saturdays there are all-nighters at the club, and anyone with the energy can dance until eight o'clock the following morning.

And then there's the money she's putting aside for setting up that fashion boutique. It probably won't be for a few years yet; she'll start out local, maybe find some shop space in West Bromwich, near the Golden Mile, then branch out into Birmingham if it goes well, and from there see what the world offers. Life's a precious and wonderful thing, and every hour is important.

That's one of the few good things about working late. With the building empty, she can move around easily, go where she wants. The lights are out in Mr Barrett's office, but there's enough of a glow from the adjacent typing pool to make her way quietly into the cramped room and feel her way around. His desk's a shadowy block in the gloom, and she opens up the middle drawer, gropes behind his carelessly-stashed bottle of White Horse, and finds the petty cash box in its usual spot. It's small and dark, mahogany wood with gold trim, the key a short, stubby bit of iron that grinds in the lock. She's as quick as ever; her heart's always thundering when she does this, her fingers always slick. It's not really stealing; she always replaces the money the next time she gets paid. It's just a short-term loan, a bit of extra cover for all of the nights out, and why not? She works hard enough to deserve twice what she's on. Women are cheap labour for companies – if she's heard Judy say that once, she's heard her a hundred times – and it doesn't hurt them every so often to give a bit extra to an empty purse.

She takes twenty bob in all, which'll be enough for this weekend, and puts the petty cash box back carefully, making sure nothing's visibly disturbed. She stands up, the cash in her hand, and realises for the first time that she's made a terrible mistake.

It's the smell which gives him away. It fills the room. It always does. As soon as she breathes it, Kath feels sick. It's Old Spice, a ton of the stuff, which never quite masks the stink of booze and sweat beneath.

– Keepin busy, me wench?

Mr Barrett's in the doorway, a hulking silhouette. His words are slightly slurred, but he sounds clear, lucid. Insinuating.

– Mr Barrett. Ah was just... ah've had a quick clean around the place, an...

– Ah can see what yam dewin.

Kath's arms and legs are shaking; an odd feeling, when the office is so warm.

– Ah'll juss put this back.

– No, iss fine. Ya can keep that.

– Ah doe want tew. Please.

He walks forward, steady on his feet in the semi-darkness.

– Ah'll atta report ya ter the police, though, wo I? Thieves atta be dealt with the proper way.

– I allwis put the money back. I allwis pay it back. Please, Mr Barrett.

– Course ya do. Ya know when ter do the roit thing. Yam a good girl, ay ya?

He reaches the opposite side of the desk. Over his shoulder, Kath can see the bright light of the main office through the doorway. He stares through her.

– The thing is, if ya run away, ah'll atta ring the police. Wo be pleasant, that. Ah doe relish seein young people in trouble wi the law. Causes a reputation, it does. A stigma. Employers, friends, family. No one loikes a thief.

– I ay a thief!

– Leave plenty a fingerprints around the place, did ya?

She keeps her head down, eyes to the floor. She can feel tears on the way. She holds them back.

– We can come tew an arrangement, cor we, eh? Yow an me?

He takes a step around the desk, and Kath moves in the opposite direction.

– Now, now. Come on. Play fair.

– Ah'm leavin the money. Look, ah'll pay twice what ah took.

Kath puts the twenty bob down on the desk, but Mr Barrett carries on moving towards her, and then rushing forward suddenly with a speed she never suspected, he grabs hold of her arm tightly, painfully.

There have been times Kath's imagined what she'd do if someone ever attacked her. She pictured herself fighting like a cornered animal, a wild beast battling for its life. She never expected to be still, shivering, compliant. She never expected all of the pleading that gushes from her, the hope that the monster grabbing at her might have mercy, because people are kind, people are good, people don't hurt each other like this.

Mr Barrett puts his arms around her shoulders. She flinches.

– Come on. Iss fine. It wo be that bad, ah promise.

But it's worse. It's much, much worse.

April 1968

There's a flood of movement outside the gates, a sudden clash of uniforms and overalls, light and dark faces, the stink of sweat and diesel mixed with the oily burnt fumes of the foundry. The police are out in force, making their presence known, quick to jump in at any sign of trouble. So far there's been no trouble. So far.

But Jonah's been seething all afternoon. Three times today he's been called a scab by some prick in a turban. Three times. He shouldn't have even stood for it once, but with the plod on the prowl and the union warning them not to get into any trouble with the coloured pickets, he's got to keep his nose clean. Bide his time. Jonah's no scab; none of them are. His union – the union of the white workers at the foundry – isn't out on strike. The Indians and Pakistanis are all in the TGWU, the only union which'll accept them as members. The TGWU doesn't recognise their picket either; it's a wildcat strike. But official or not, the picket line's still outside the gates, protesting against redundancies.

The redundancies of coloured workers.

Management are cutting back on labour costs, and the Asian employees want a workshare scheme which'll keep everyone employed on reduced hours. If they get their way, a lot of good, hard-working family blokes are going to end up on a three-day week. But the bosses are offering to safeguard the jobs of white workers at the foundry, keep them in full-time employment and make sure that it's the immigrants who get laid off first. That's fine by Jonah. It's fine by a lot of the blokes at the foundry. When hard times come, you look after your own. It's only fair.

But every morning and every evening the pickets are stood outside the gates in their ill-fitting suits, overcoats, patterned jumpers, carrying their wooden placards, chanting accusations of betrayal as the white faces emerge from the foundry's brick confines. And this time, Jonah's ready. He's been pissed off all day, but he's smiling as he walks out into the sunshine with a big handwritten badge pinned to his overalls, which says I'M BACKING ENOCH.

Jonah's never had much use for politicians in the past, and until last week, the Tory MP for Wolverhampton South West was just one in a long line of bastards living a cosy life in Parliament at the common man's expense. But then on Saturday, in front of cameras at the general meeting of the West Midlands Area Conservative Group at the Midland Hotel in Birmingham, this MP delivered a speech about his constituency, about ancient Rome, about the waters of the river Tiber awash with blood.

About the barbarians at the gates. And now, whether they're interested in politics or not, the whole country knows all about Enoch Powell.

The furnaces and casting machines are still ringing loud in Jonah's head as he reaches the picket line, and he stands with a grin on his face, waiting for them to see the badge. Only none of them are paying him the slightest bit of notice. They're all focused on some white girl in blue jeans and a red cardigan who's moving down the row of blokes, talking to each of them; she's handing out what look like sandwiches wrapped up in foil, and shaking hands with the ringleaders of the strike.

And then comes the awful realisation that he knows who the girl is. Of course he bloody does. Because there are a million white girls in the Midlands, and there are probably more than a few who own blue jeans and a red cardigan, but there's only one you'll ever find doling out butties on a Pakistani picket line.

– Judy, what am ya dewin?!
– Aroit, Jonah. How's life as a braindead fascist treatin ya?
– Iss fine. How's life as a self-righteous commie treatin yow?
– Cor complain. Gerrin through a lot a cheese an onion cobs, loike.
– Ah noticed. What exactly d'ya think yam playin at?
– Playin? Johnny Cartwright, yow should know better than anyone that I ay playin. This is a fight.
– Ar. OUR fight. Not yourn.
– Wrong, Jonah. Iss evryone's fight. Evryone who wants ter put food on their table an keep a roof over their head.
– An we'm supposed ter do that on a three-day week, am we?
– Maybe not. But why is it the coloured workers bein laid off fust? Theer's blokes on this picket line who've worked this job fer years. What happened ter seniority an experience?
– Oh, so yow'd rather see white men on the dole? Done out a jobs in their own bloody country?
– Ah doe want ter see no one on the dole, Jonah. Black, white, brown, any soddin colour. Ah doe want ter see any honest folks suffer fer the mistakes of gamblers in suits.
– But sufferin's part a life, missis. Some poor bugger allwis ends up gerrin the short straw. Ah doe see why it should be me or any a mar mates.
– An thass what it boils down tew, ay it? "Ah'm aroit, Jack." God forbid ya might ever see the bigger picture.
– So woss this bigger picture, then?

– That the people who tek nine tenths of the pie fer themselves distract ya by pointin at a black face an sayin, *Look at im! He's tryin ter pinch yower slice!* An ya fall fer it, Jonah. Ya fall fer it evry time.

– Roit. So if ah start wavin a placard abaht an singin WE SHALL OVERCOME, all the problems'll juss gew away? Jesus Christ, wake up, Jude. The world ay loike that. Iss dog eat dog.

– "We must learn ter live together as brothers, or we will surely perish together as fools."

– Lovely. Try tellin it ter some a these boys. Ya know, the ones who refuse ter work next tew us juss cos we'm white.

One of the pickets – a tall lad called Hardeep who works in the casting shop – wanders over.

– Is this scab bothering you, Judy?

Jonah pushes his shoulders back and lifts his chin.

– Yow use that word abaht me again, pal, it'll be the last word ya say fer a week.

Judy steps quickly in between the pair of them as they start squaring up.

– Fellas, fellas. This ay helpin. Save it fer the real enemy.

But Jonah stares at Hardeep, and Hardeep stares at Jonah, and for all the world, it feels like they've already found their real enemy.

*

On Saturday morning, Billy's awake before sunrise. In truth, he's barely slept. This dawn is going to bring something incredible. Something revolutionary. A new world. There's a feeling of upheaval simmering in the streets, a sense that the old order can be turned upside down. All it'll take is one final push, and they'll carve their names indelibly into the pages of history. And when it happens, the entire world is going to remember the year 1968.

After all, it's not every season the Albion manage an FA Cup run like this. It's more than revolutionary; it's monumental. Three months in the making already, and now they're just one win away from Wembley. One more win! Who'd have thought it back in the autumn, back when it felt like they'd be facing relegation by now? Alan Ashman's done the greatest of jobs from the dugout, moulding the team into a formidable attacking force again, but he's been helped every step of the way by one man out on the pitch.

The missing piece of the jigsaw.

In all of the years that the club's existed, there may have been better footballers to wear the stripes of West Bromwich Albion – in the likes of Ronnie Allen and WG Richardson, there may even have been better goalscorers – but no player has ever been loved by supporters like Jeff Astle. No player has ever made a cheer echo around the ground with nothing more than a sly grin at the crowd. No player has ever scored a goal at the Birmingham Road End and marched straight over to the stand, arms outstretched, as the fans flood from the terraces to embrace him. No one until this number nine from Nottinghamshire.

Jeff Astle is the king of the Brummie Road.

He arrived just as the Brummie Road End found its voice, and they've sung his praise ever since. His face is on copies of the Sports Argus week in week out, and every day his picture finds its way onto new bedroom walls around the Black Country. Because Astle is a player with personality; a star and a showman on the pitch, but down the pub, in the shops, up the high street, side by side with those who cheer him from the terraces, he's a man like any other. Thousands strike their name onto scoresheets across England every Saturday, but only Jeff Astle can be found pacing the streets of West Bromwich as the sky darkens, his feet on the ground in an age of astronauts.

Since Astle's come into form this year, Albion have been unstoppable. Every other song on the terraces these days is about the King, but there's a new favourite which has been doing the rounds in recent weeks. It's to the tune of She'd Rather Be With Me by The Turtles, and when Billy opens the front door, he hears Jonah singing it as he saunters down the street.

– LA-LA-LA LAAAA, LA-LA-LA LAAAA, WE'M GUNNA WIN THE FA CUP!

Billy lights a fag and stands in the doorway as Jonah bounds up to the house.

– Rarin ter gew, eh, Bill?

– Course I am. Ah can smell glory in the air.

– Nah, that'll be me. I had beans fer breakfast.

– Oh, brill. Yam lucky ah've just abaht lost me sense a smell from all these curries Jude keeps tryin ter cook.

– That reminds me, ah need tew have a word wi yow abaht the little commissar.

– What?

– Yer missis. Her's excellin herself at the moment.

– Thass funny, cos lass night her was tellin me ah needed tew have a word wi yow.

– Me? What have ah done wrong? Iss her, pokin her nose wheer it doe belong!

– An as per cowin usual, iss me who gets it in both ears, ay it? Bugger me. Can we talk abaht it on the bus?

Billy grabs his jacket, pulls his arms through the sleeves, and pats the pocket quickly to check for the tight wedge of paper wrapped in its rubber band. It's better than any lucky charm. There's one more game to go. One more game, and those slips of paper in his pocket will be worth everything.

There are few possessions more precious to Billy right now than the bunch of ticket stubs in his pocket. Each one's proof of entry to a different cup tie; each one gives him a slightly better chance of a ticket for the final if Albion win today. The most valuable is the three-month-old blue slip of paper which shows he was one of the four thousand who travelled down to the third round fixture. The very first tie in the cup run; the simplest tie in the cup run. The one where they nearly came a right cropper.

On a bright and unseasonably warm January afternoon, Colchester should have become the third Division Three side in less than a year to knock Albion out of a cup competition. It was the normal routine: Billy and Jonah caught the coach down from the Throstle Club at half seven in the morning, along the M1 – a familiar trip these days – through Bedford and Cambridge, into the affluent sprawl of the Home Counties. Albion had sold out their ticket allocation, and Layer Road was packed with sixteen thousand bodies; a cosy local ground creaking at the seams with supporters crammed onto open terraces, the clustered pyramids of suburban rooftops visible over the top of the stands, and Albion's travelling contingent standing shoulder to shoulder in the Layer Road End with thousands of annoyed Essex faces.

At the pub before the match, one local told them the stand had been built back in the Forties with POW labour; if that was true, then the slightly-pissed congregation of Albion and Colchester fans crammed together immediately honoured those origins by kicking off World War Three. Scuffles broke out everywhere; the same old awkward, cramped and usually brief terrace fistfights. The only toilets in the ground were at the back of the main stand, so going for a piss meant walking round the perimeter of the pitch, past home fans spitting and shouting abuse. Some of the Brummie Roaders got up onto the Layer Road End's low roof, and with no police around to deal with them, the Albion chairman Jim Gaunt had to come out and talk them down.

But the chaos on the terraces was nothing compared to the chaos in the Albion defence. After just eight minutes, Osborne and Talbut got themselves in a tangle over a simple cross from the left and Reg Stratton tapped home to give Colchester the lead. Stratton should have had a second ten minutes later when he hit the underside of the crossbar with a thundering header, and along with all the other Baggies fans in the Layer Road End, Billy got shoved about ten yards to the left with a triumphant surge from the Colchester lot.

Finally, Albion fought back. Five minutes after disallowing an equaliser from Dick Krzywicki, the ref blew for a penalty when Duncan Forbes clattered Astle while jumping for a header. Tony Brown slammed the leveller home from the spot. Four thousand Albion fans up the Layer Road End surged down the terrace to shove the home fans ten yards to the right again.

YES, YES, YES, YES, THE ALBION ARE THE BEST!

In stoppage time, with the match heading for a replay, a Colchester free-kick into the box caused a goalmouth scramble; Albion cleared the ball off the line, but then Mickey Bullock caught the loose ball, and to groans of horror and disbelief from the Baggies fans, smashed home a Colchester winner.

Billy put his head in his hands. The United fans surged down the terrace again in victory, but even as the celebrations spread around the rickety stands of Layer Road, the referee blew to disallow the goal and signal a free-kick for the visitors.

And something clicked for Albion there and then. They stopped being a team that shuffled meekly to their fate. They became a team which shaped their own fate.

They started with the replay on the Wednesday night, attacking Colchester from kick-off, hunting for goals. John Kaye got the first after ten minutes, shooting from thirty yards out with such power that Ernie Adams in the Colchester goal couldn't keep it out. After twenty minutes, Astle headed home from a Dougie Fraser cross. He scored again a few minutes later, and Chippy Clark added a fourth with ten minutes left.

Albion were on the road to Wembley. And the Brummie Road End was following them all the way.

*

As the bus winds through Dudley Port, Jonah rambles on about the strike at his place, the nightmare of trying to look after his job, the embarrassment of Judy sticking her oar in; and when all's said and done, what's Billy going to do about it?

The best Billy can do is stay awake and look vaguely interested.

It wouldn't be so bad if he hadn't had it off Judy as well, yesterday. *Yow ay gewin ter the match wi Jonah? He's an arrogant, mouthy, reactionary little tosser!* Billy couldn't argue with that. Over the years, Jonah's tried to steal his girl, got him lost halfway up a motorway, and come perilously close to infecting him with smallpox. But in spite of that, they've got a bond.

It's called West Bromwich Albion. And even if they lose everything else they've ever had in common, that bond will remain. He's an arrogant, mouthy, reactionary little tosser, but he's also a mate.

Leaning back in his seat, Billy sighs. If only his mate and his girlfriend could leave the politics to one side and be a bit friendlier with one another, he'd be a happy man.

*

A red ticket with bold black type: The Dell, Milton Road, Northam.

The twenty-first of February, 1968.

A fourth round replay between Southampton and West Bromwich Albion.

A crowd of twenty-six thousand gathered inside a small and fierce ground, a bear-pit where the hostile atmosphere alone was enough to rip some of the First Division's best teams apart. A poor team on the road, Southampton built their reputation inside the Dell; they were imperious on home turf.

It took them just ten minutes to find a way past Albion, with Terry Paine feeding a long, high ball through to Frank Saul, who managed to knock John Osborne unconscious as he fired into the net. When he came to, Osborne got four minutes' magic sponge treatment for his head injury, and to Billy's dismay, spent the rest of the half reeling around like a bloke who'd just broken into the M&B brewery and glugged his way through a year's supply of beer. They had their faces in their hands as Albion's trainer came and crouched behind the goal to shout instructions to Ossie, after it became apparent he couldn't even see properly anymore.

And Ossie listened to the calls of the trainer, and Ossie carried on jumping for the high balls Southampton dropped into the box. And somehow, Albion dug in and found an equaliser. Hope chipped a ball into the path of Astle, who chested it down for Kaye; Kaye played it back into Astle's path, and Jeff shot home to make it 1-1. The pace of the Albion forward line caused Southampton too many problems, and when Graham Williams' cross came into the box just before the half-hour, Jimmy Gabriel headed it away from his own keeper's hands, straight to the feet of Tony Brown.

2-1 to Albion.

WE, ALL, LIVE, UP, THE BRUMMIE ROAD END!
THE BRUMMIE ROAD END!
THE BRUMMIE ROAD END!

But at half-time, Osborne was staggering off the pitch, barely able to stand up anymore. When the team came out for the second half, little Graham Williams had pulled on Osborne's long jumper, tying up the sleeves to make them fit. Ron Davies, the Southampton striker, was doubled up laughing at the sight of Williams in goal. Johnny Kaye dropped back from his usual forward position to become a centre-half, and Saints supporters in the Milton Road End kept themselves entertained flicking fag butts and throwing stones at him.

Eight minutes into the half, Hughie Fisher managed to dummy his way through the makeshift Albion back line and send a thumping shot past Williams to put Southampton level again. The Baggies goal turned into the Alamo for the rest of the match. Billy could barely watch as Graham Williams kept coming for Southampton crosses, punching and catching everything despite being six inches shorter than everyone else in the box. Somehow, they survived. Somehow, they held on.

And in injury time, Graham Lovett – just back from the terrible car crash which had kept him out for eighteen months – picked up the ball, ran deep into the Southampton half, and took a speculative shot at goal which sailed past Eric Martin's hand and came back off the post.

The rebound fell for Chippy Clark, who stroked it to Astle. With a deft flick of the King's boot, Albion were heading into the fifth round.

On the terraces, surrounded by scowling Southampton fans, they found their voices and started up a ragged tune: *NO ONE CAN STOP THE ALBION!*

*

The 74 lurches its way down the high street in the Saturday traffic, with the usual army of shoppers clogging the pavements on both sides of the road.

– Thinks her's bin med president a the Race Relations Board, her does.

– Ya say that as if iss a surprise. Ya know iss what her believes in, Jonah. Mekkin the world a better place. Gerrin a fair deal fer everyone.

~ 144 ~

– Oh, doe yow start an all, Bill. I had enough of it yesterdee. Look, ah doe want ter sound out of order or anythin, but come on. Doe ya sometimes feel, ya know…

– What?

– Doe ya juss get bloody sick of her?

– Ah get bloody sick a the pair on ya. On abaht strikes an immigration an Christ knows what. Is it so difficult tew understand that some of us juss doe care? Ah doe want ter be part a the global proletarian revolution, an ah doe want ter mek Britain bloody "great" again. Ah want ter gew down the pub. Ah want ter play some dominoes. Ah want ter play some darts. Ah want ter drink some beer. Ah want ter drink some more beer. Ah want tew have a fish supper on me way home. An most of all, above evrythin else, ah want ter watch me football on a Saturday, preferably standin up the Brummie Road End an mekkin some noise. Is it too much tew ask? Is it really so much tew ask that ah live me life without bein pestered by people wi an axe ter grind?

– Fair enough, mucka. Yower choice. But remember: theer might come a day when juss livin yer life ay an option no more.

*

A white ticket with faded type: Fratton Park, Frogmore Road, Southsea.

The ninth of March, 1968.

A fifth round tie between Portsmouth and West Bromwich Albion.

A fine, sunny day. Forty-two thousand pairs of eyes cemented on the shapely figure of Miss Pompey '68 – a petite, doe-eyed redhead – parading around the pitch before kick off. The ten-minute period she spent strolling the touchlines, being showered with hearty propositions from the stands, was the only time all afternoon that peace reigned inside the ground. The Brummie Roaders were out in force, and they'd come to take the Fratton End.

The trouble erupted in scattered bursts, and Billy was careful to stay one step ahead of it. He hadn't gone full-on flower power – he was still ready and willing to defend himself if need be – but he was getting fed up of the violence at matches, and not just because he didn't fancy seeing his new mohair suit top egged at any point in the near future. He paid to watch football, not go bareknuckle boxing.

And what an afternoon's football. Johnny Kaye had a header saved by John Milkin in the first few minutes, before Pompey started putting pressure on, and Ossie had to stop a smart Albert McCann effort. As Sammy and his boys tangled with the Fratton End mob, Billy took care not to be too enthusiastic in front of the Pompey fans surrounding him when the first goal came just before the half hour; Astle glancing Bobby Hope's free-kick into the far corner.

Four minutes later, he was as solemn as could be when Chippy Clark pounced on a low Dougie Fraser cross in the six-yard box for a second. Albion kept up the pressure till half-time, with Astle having one goal disallowed and another effort cleared off the line by George Ley. In the second half, when Osborne parried a Mike Trebilcock header straight to Ray Hiron, who nodded a goal back for Portsmouth, Billy waved his arms in the air as convincingly as he could, managing to avoid the attentions of the band of Pompey thugs elbowing their way through the crowd.

The heavy mob had spotted an Albion fan in a blue ski jacket mouthing off further down the terrace. All around him, the crowd were throwing coins, bottles and other missiles at Ossie, and while the police around the perimeter laughed, one of the coppers marched onto the pitch to give an official caution to John Talbut for bad language after being kicked by a Pompey forward.

Billy kept his eyes forward, praying no one would ask him for the time or anything else that might give away his accent; if nothing else, he'd begun to realise that what he might get off the Portsmouth fans would be nothing to what the local constabulary would dish out if he tried turning to them for help. He caught another glimpse of the Albion lad in the bright blue ski jacket, his back to the pitch, judging his best escape route from the yokels closing in on all sides. Then that head of short sandy hair tilted up, and Billy made eye contact with the cornered Albion fan.

It had to be. It just had to be.

– AROIT, BILL! WHAT AM YA WAITIN FER, MATE? GET STUCK IN!

It took five minutes, a lot of windmilling arms and a few knocks around his ribs and jaw before Billy could escape the pit of Portsmouth fans and leg it after Jonah, who was already halfway down the side of the pitch. He ran down the track beside the turf, in front of the main stand, in line with the Albion players who'd got possession of the ball and were surging upfield alongside him. He heard a cheer go up from the scattered pockets of Albion fans around the ground and looked around, confused, thinking they'd scored the crucial third goal. It took him a minute to realise they were cheering him. They'd seen him take on half of Portsmouth single-handed. They thought he'd done it on purpose.

As a patch of Baggies fans welcomed him back like a conquering hero, he kept his mouth shut and accepted the praise. Football violence was a bloody stupid idea, but it felt good to get a bit of respect from the boys. Besides, the fad was bound to pass sooner or later. After all, scrapping on the terraces often meant missing the best parts of the game, and when all was said and done, nobody showed up at matches just for a fight, did they?

*

The bus rumbles on past the Hawthorns – it feels strange not to be getting off on the Birmingham Road for once – and they're soon passing from the Black Country into Birmingham along the Holyhead Road.

– Roit, so woss wrong wi juss livin yer life in peace an quiet?

– Nuthin. But not evryone wants ter do that, do they? Some gew around hurtin folks, robbin folks. Layin claim ter things which ay theirn. Ya know the sort.

– No white people have ever done that, then.

– Course some have, but iss who's dewin it here an now thass the problem. Yow heard what Enoch Powell said: some owd biddy, last white person left on her street, an the blacks am stickin dogshit through her letterbox. How abaht that? Iss a disgrace. Absolute disgrace.

– Which woman's this, then?

– Well he couldn't name her, could he? It'd put her at risk.

– Nah, course not. We'll just atta presume he's tellin the truth. After all, if ya cor trust a politician, who can ya trust?

– Ya can keep yer sarcasm, pal. Ah wor born yesterdee. Course ah know he might be mekkin it up, but *if* iss true, what then? Is that the kind a country yow want ter live in?

– An what abaht if theer's someone who could do summat really good fer the area? Ah mean, loike, what if ya got a black fella playin fer Albion? Wouldn't ya support im?

– Have yow gone fuckin saft? A black mon playin football? In *England*?

– Pele managed it. Eusebio did an all.

– Ar, in the middle a summer. Can you imagine em come December? They'd be gewin out wrapped up loike Quinn the Eskimo! Black blokes playin fer the bloody Albion. Ya know, Bill, juss cos yer wench is a bit simple, it doe mean yow atta leave yer brain at home an all.

– It was just an example.

– It was a stupid example. Iss all well an good talkin abaht fairness an equality, but evry so offen, ya need ter use a bit a common sense, mate. Trust me.

*

A white ticket with red type: Maine Road, Moss Side, Manchester. The eighteenth of April, 1968.

A sixth round second replay between West Bromwich Albion and Liverpool.

The tie that no one expected Albion to win. Bill Shankly's team were hot favourites for the cup, and they'd already beaten Albion home and away in the league. But in the quarter-final of the FA Cup, the two teams drew 0-0. In the replay, they drew 1-1.

The fixture went to a third match, at a neutral venue.

The rain raged all day long, April storms making moats of the Moss Side streets surrounding Maine Road. It seemed as if half of the Black Country had begged the day off work or skived school. Every train to Manchester Piccadilly was crowded, the specials and the ordinaries, and when they reached Maine Road, seventeen thousand travelling Brummie Roaders were herded into different sides of the ground. Billy and Jonah ended up down the side of the enormous Kippax Stand, just outside the cover of its roof with rainwater pouring down on them, sheltering awkwardly under the brolly of a Catholic priest and devoted Manchester City fan who took pity on them. In front of them, an angry Liverpool fan spent half of the match yelling swear words at his team, then turning round each time to cross himself and say *sorry, Father*.

As the rain clattered against the umbrella, they did their best to sing along to its beat.

LA-LA-LA LAAAA, LA-LA-LA LAAAA, WE'M GUNNA WIN THE FA CUP!

Seven minutes in, Albion opened the scoring with a direct attack – what they called "route one to goal" on the telly, on *Quiz Ball* – as Ian Collard played a smart through-ball from the centre circle for Astle to chase onto, and with Chris Lawler and Ron Yeats closing in on him, Astle shot past Tommy Lawrence to give Albion the lead, beating the Flying Pig at his near post.

For the first time in nearly two hundred minutes of football, Albion had the lead over Liverpool.

But the Reds fought back, dominating midfield with a brisk passing game, and after Kaye and Talbut accidentally clashed heads in central defence, leaving Kaye with a deep cut above his eye, Albion started to buckle. Six minutes before the break, Callaghan crossed from the left flank and Tony Hateley headed an equaliser past a stranded John Osborne.

More than a few skint fans were sharing cups of Bovril at half-time, passing them round like nips of whisky. Travelling away always cost a few bob, and during a long cup run with frequent replays – especially given the shaky economy, folks watching their spending all over the country – every penny counted. For the middle of April, it was more like a winter night, and most of them were shivering in wet coats and convinced that Liverpool were only going to turn the screw more and more in the second half.

But Albion came out again and attacked right from the whistle. On the hour, Bobby Hope – fit again after a recent injury – cut inside from the right wing and played a short ball back out to Dougie Fraser who'd moved onto the flank in his place. They passed it right through Liverpool: Fraser to Collard, Collard to Astle, Astle to Lovett, Lovett to Clark. Clark beat the offside trap with his run. Clark slammed the ball into the bottom corner. Clark put Albion 2-1 up.

They carried on attacking, knowing how fragile the one-goal lead was, and Kenny Stephens had a third flagged offside minutes later. Then came the Liverpool response: Shankly's men launching wave after wave of attacks, Ossie getting battered from every angle going for crosses. But Albion held on. Somehow, they held on.

BERTIE MEE SAID TER BILL SHANKLY
HAVE YOW HEARD OF THE NORTH BANK, HIGHBURY?
SHANKS SAYS NO, I DON'T THINK SO
BUT I'VE HEARD OF THE WEST BROM AGGRO

Great granite clouds rumbled in the evening sky, and rain tore down into the dark streets; they made their way from Moss Side to Piccadilly Station without brollies, their scarves and raincoats soaked through, and finally made it onto their platform to discover a horde of red-scarved supporters opposite. They were hopelessly outnumbered.

In most places around the country, it would have meant an instant punch-up, and they'd have been on for a right kicking. But the Kopites turned and applauded them across the empty tracks, and as they waited for the packed train which would take them home, singsong Scouse accents implored Albion to go on and lift the cup.

*

In Birmingham, they change to the number 7 to take them to Villa Park. There are plenty of Blues fans on their way to the match too, but no trouble; at least, not yet.

– Ah think we'll atta agree ter disagree on the coloureds, Bill. But either way, yome wrong.

– An argument breathtakin in its erudition an maturity.

– Well, her's got ya brainwashed, ay her? This might be a bit out of order, but ah've gorra say it; doe ya think ya can maybe do a bit better than Jude? Ah mean, her ay the onny wench in the world.

– Yam absolutely roit, Jonah.

– Yeah?

– Yeah. That *is* out of order.

– Well, ah'm sorry, but ah juss cor stand the… charmin little madam.

– Thass an impressive U-turn from someone who once took her out on a date.

– Three years is time enough ter come ter yer senses.

– Ya fancied her, though, dae ya? At the time, loike. Befower her picked me.

– Oh, her picked yow, did her? Is that what happened?

– Course it is. Why?

– Nuthin. Never mind. We'm ninety minutes from Wembley, Bill; theer's better things ter talk abaht than yower moody missis.

*

Something's the matter with Kath. Judy can't work out what, but it's been going on for too long. There are times she catches her staring blankly into space, and she has to call her name two or three times before she drifts out of the trance. A few weeks ago, she asked outright if something was wrong, and Kath really lost her temper, snapping at Judy to mind her own business.

Is it Tommy? She broke up with him months ago, and for a while Judy thought it must be a hangover from that, even though she'd never seen Kath get upset about any ex-boyfriends in the past. But the weeks passed, and nothing changed, and now she's not convinced that's it at all. She's determined to get to the bottom of the mystery, but it'll just take a bit more guile. A cautious approach.

So she's invited Kath along to the new supermarket in town. It took some coaxing, and promises of all the amazing things they're selling under one roof – you can save up to thirty bob on a week's shopping! – but eventually Kath gave in. They browsed the shelves for half an hour or so, wandering in a daze around the warehouse-sized shop with its criss-crossed aisles and gaudy displays; it felt so sterile, stripped of all the familiar chitchat between wives you see in ordinary shops, and yet there was that futuristic allure to the cheap prices, the plentiful goods, the odd metal trolleys, the little conveyor belts where you put your shopping to be rung up on the cashier's till. After buying a few bits and bobs for her mom and a bottle of gin to share with Kath later – an ideal tongue-loosener if ever there was one – Judy left the store with a glum friend in tow and a healthy crop of Green Shield stamps stuck in her new buyer's book.

And now, on their way to the bus station, she seizes the initiative; gently at first, testing the water before she plunges in.

– How's things, anyway? Seems loike ages since we caught up!

Kath turns her head and glances Judy up and down; a look of contempt which sends a sudden shiver through her.

– Ah'm fine.

Judy waits for Kath to ask how she is in return, but all she gets is awkward silence. Thrown off course, she abandons the cautious approach and starts to babble.

– Thass good! Onny, ah worry sometimes that ah'm ignorin ya, what with all the pickets gewin on, an spendin time wi Billy. But if ya was upset wi me abaht all that, yow'd say so, wouldn't ya? Ah mean, ya wouldn't juss…

– Iss nuthin ter do wi yow, me wench.

Kath breathes in sharply after saying that, a short gasp which makes Judy turn and look at her again in surprise. She catches a glimpse of Kath's eyes, and she's frightened by the tired look there.

– Things have gone wrong, me wench. So wrong. Ah med a mistake, an ever since, ah've…

Kath stops as the wind carries a gust of shouting and hollering from a sidestreet, followed by telltale signs of a commotion; passers-by craning their necks to see what's happening, shopkeepers peering through windows, a couple of folks moving away from the noise with a brisk skip in their step.

Judy marches round the corner. She hears the clatter of boots as Kath tries to keep up. She's expecting a football fight. She's heard enough about them off Billy, and she's got no intention of involving herself; she just wants to see.

But she doesn't expect the sight which greets her on that street.

There's a crowd of lads up ahead, on the opposite pavement. They're jostling for position, and as a couple of them move apart, Judy spots the object of their attention: a family, a man and woman and two kids. A little cluster of dark faces, the children scared and crying, the parents trying to stay calm and protect them. The lads are pushing the dad, shouting at him. Some are wearing mohair jackets and the army boots which are fashionable now. One's got long, tangled brown hair and flared corduroy trousers; he looks like he should be in his bedroom listening to a Jefferson Airplane LP, not kicking lumps out of some West Indian family on a Black Country backstreet.

– Hey! Knock it off!

Judy's running across the street before she's even had time to stop and think, so angry that she just can't stop. They're chanting *ENOCH, ENOCH, ENOCH,* and one of them's got a fistful of the father's shirt.

– Oi! Leave em be!

The one who's grabbed the father – a slim, dark-haired lad with acne scars and a wispy moustache – turns round.

– Fuck off.

Judy opens her mouth to speak again, but before she can get a word out, the lad lets go of the West Indian man, walks over and grabs her round the throat. He pins her up against the wall, squeezing her neck, and she flails at him, trying to break his grip. He looks more amused than angry. She kicks out as dark spots start to form in front of her eyes, and then the boy punches her in the belly and slings her to the ground.

She sucks in breath. Her hands sting from grazes. Her stomach aches. A useless thought whizzes circuits through her head: *he hit me; he hit me.* The pavement's cool, scratching her cheek like Billy's chin when he's grown a shade of stubble. She spots movement above her, and looks up to see Kath crossing the street. She wants to warn her, tell her to run, but she can't get the air into her lungs, and in a heartbeat she's panicking. She sits up and watches Kath face the thugs down. They look startled, confused. The one who hit Judy steps forward with his fist clenched again, but Kath screams at him, incoherent rage from the depths of her body, spit flying from her mouth and sticking to his face.

A warning shout. Three more West Indian men are coming down the street, their shirtsleeves rolled, and the thugs are off. They don't run; they don't want to lose face, end up looking like scared kids, but they're not hanging round for a fight they'll probably lose. Judy's world is a pair of Mary Quant boots above her, then a pair of knees in diamond-patterned Wolsey tights, then Kath's face, all pale make-up, violet eyeshadow and red hair. She feels numb, and swallows awkwardly as Kath puts an arm around her shoulders.

Did she really think she could stop racialism just by confronting it? That the type of people whose minds run on bigotry like a car runs on petrol would see the error of their ways just because she was helpful enough to point it out to them? How stupid. Childish. Naïve. She can't believe it. That the tidal wave of human progress can be stopped so suddenly; by a punch, by a police baton, by a single bullet from a rifle in Memphis.

She's never felt so small.

Kath cradles her head as the Jamaican men come over and ask if everyone's okay. The mother from the family kneels down next to Judy, and the father ushers their crying kids away. The woman says she's a nurse – her name's Dolly, she works at Hallam Hospital – and after running her fingers over Judy's belly and abdomen, asks her if she can feel any sharp or acute pain. She can't. Kath's fingers are beneath her chin, gently tilting her head upwards, and Judy looks carefully at her best friend's eyes. Behind the mascara and the eyeliner, she can see there's something horribly wrong.

But then, she's gradually coming to realise that there's something horribly wrong with the whole world.

*

QUE SERA, SERA!

It wasn't easy. At times it was a nightmare, on the pitch and off it. They were herded into Villa Park's open Witton End, and even before kick-off, Birmingham fans were busy making themselves known. There were a few pre-match scuffles in the pubs, and Jonah was expecting it to get a bit more good-natured as they approached the ground, but even on the terraces the atmosphere was volatile.

WHATEVER WILL BE, WILL BE!

It all came to a head when a bunch of rough-looking bastards started punching their way through the crowd next to Billy and Jonah. One pulled out a machete, and in the moments before the police waded through the crush and grabbed hold of him, Jonah had enough time to wonder just how mental someone has to be to walk into a football ground carrying a tool like that. And then time to wonder how many more out there are just as mental. Or worse.

WE'M GEWIN TER WEM-BER-LEE!

The match was just as tense, and Blues had more than their fair share of early chances through Fred Pickering, with Ossie on top form to keep him out. But then Astle took a knock to the face, and Albion got an indirect free kick just outside the box. Bobby Hope teed it up, and Bomber went for goal; Jim Harriott parried the shot to his right, but the King was straight onto it, drilling in the rebound from eight yards out. In the second half, Kaye had one disallowed, and Talbut managed a goalline clearance to deny Blues a certain equaliser.

Then, with seconds left on the clock, Bomber charged forward into the penalty area from inside-right, and hit a low shot in off the post to book Albion's place at Wembley.

QUE SERA, SERA!

And Jonah's lost count of how many pints he's had since full-time. From Witton, they made their way into Hockley, had a couple in the Hen & Chickens up Constitution Hill, then nipped under the railway arches to Le Metro, where Dodd the Mod – doing the rounds as a doorman these days – let them in for free. And at some point in the last three-quarters of an hour, in the nicely-sauced cells of his mind, going round Kath's house started to seem like a really good idea. No; a fantastic idea. The sort of masterplan which can't possibly go wrong, because he's thought every single aspect of it through. Of course, by the time he gets on the last bus, he's struggling to remember most of the finer details of that masterplan, and even the overall objectives have started to shimmer in a haze, so he just smiles and settles for quietly humming *What A Wonderful World* instead.

He told himself he didn't really care back in the winter, when she gave Tommy the heave-ho. He even sympathised a bit with his brother. Since Jonah finally gave up on the near-deranged attentions of Iris Duckhouse, he's found himself more than a little cynical about all things romantic.

Then, before the home match against Stoke last month, he saw Kath standing outside Bradfords Bakery on the Birmingham Road, the same spot where they always used to meet up when they went to matches together a couple of years ago. He parked up the scooter with a grin on his face, and went over to chat to her. What he got was a vacant stare and terse, monosyllabic replies, and when he tried to touch her arm to get her full attention, she snapped and started using such bad language at him that passers-by were stopping to stare at them.

Unfortunately, women are nutters. It's a sad conclusion to come to, but it's the only explanation Jonah has left. It's just programmed into their heads at birth. With that in mind, he's got to tell her once and for all that he doesn't even care about her anymore. Unless she still cares about him, in which case he might consider caring about her again a little bit. Possibly. He starts humming again. Green trees and red roses.

It takes a while to weave his way across the estates from the station – the stars are always worth looking up at on a night like tonight – and when he finally totters round the corner of Kath's street, he sees a figure sitting on the doorstep next door. His vision's not at its best, but he can tell exactly who it is. Just his luck to go looking for the diamond and find a lump of rock. What a wonderful bloody world.

He strolls an unsteady path over to Judy.

– Aroit, missis?

She looks up at him, and he nearly takes a step back at the pure rotten misery on her face.

– No. No I ay aroit. Wheer's Billy?

– He's gone back to his dad's place. He wor really in a fit state, to be honest. Why, woss wrong?

– Of all the people in the world ah could discuss it with, Jonah, yome juss behind the Moors Murderer in the peckin order.

Jonah shakes his head, takes a deep breath, and reminds himself it's not their fault that they're all lunatics.

– Look, come on inside the house, at least. Yow'll catch summat nasty out here.

– Be quiet, then. Me folks am asleep.

It's warm inside the front room, with the smell of Saturday night's chicken and chips still fresh around the kitchen door. Judy sits down on the faded green settee in the middle of the room, the floorboards creaking under the carpet as the sofa's wooden legs take her weight. Jonah pauses for a few moments, and then decides to join her. It's his good turn for the day. If he can tell Billy that he managed to cheer up his dismal sow of a girlfriend tonight, he'll be right in Bill's good books. The saft bugger might even get the first round in for a change.

– Jonah, what is it that meks folks so vicious ter people they've never even met?

He glances at her, and notices for the first time that her hands are shaking.

– Depends who yam on abaht, ah spose. Ah'll wallop any bastard who tries comin up the Brummie Road wi the wrong scarf on. Nuthin personal against em, but yow've gorra protect woss yowers.

– An what if iss not they scarf? What if iss they skin?

– Doe start this now, Jude. Ah've already had it once today off Billy.

– No, Jonah. Ah'm the one who's had it today.

It's more than her hands shaking now. Her whole body's on the go, shivering as if she was in a fever. She's got a bottle of gin in a shopping bag by her feet, and Jonah opens it up just to calm her down a bit. After grabbing some glasses from the old cabinet in the corner, he pours a large measure for her and a small one for himself, and with no tonic water around the place, he empties the dregs out of a bottle of R Whites to top them up. He gives Judy her glass, and she gulps it straight down, so he refills it with another large dose.

And after another shaky sip, she tells him the story. How she was walking through town. How she tried to stop some coloured family getting started on by hooligans. How one of them attacked her. Jonah shakes his head.

– Ah doe believe it. Look, whoever these dickheads am, they ay nuthin loike me. Iss one thing standin up fer yerself, lookin after woss yowers. But hittin wenches an pickin on innocent families? Thass coward's stuff, tharris.

– Ya sure coward's stuff ay sittin on the ground feelin sorry fer yerself while yer best friend protects ya?

– Is that woss botherin ya? Jude, come on, me wench. Ya know the kind a bottle it teks ter face down a bunch a scummy bastards loike that in the fust place? Yow'd do well up the Brummie Road, yow would. We could team yow up wi the Tipton mob! Yow'd keep all the visitin nutters off our patch. Yow'd be our secret weapon.

– Wi me secret powers a lyin on the ground an cryin me eyes out?

Jonah shakes his head, and then moves off the settee to kneel in front of her.

– Look; ah doe believe the same things yow do. It all seems loike castles in the air ter me. But Judy, ah respect the fact ya believe in it so much. It teks passion ter risk yer own neck fer what ya believe, an thass what yow did. Thass worth summat, ay it? Course it is.

She looks at him, so lost. And then it happens.

It's an accident. His hand slips. He's trying to take the empty glass which she's clutching to her chest, meaning to fill it again, but she moves it away, and suddenly he can feel the gentle swell of her breast beneath his palm. And she looks at him with wide eyes, and he should take his hand away, but he doesn't. He strokes his fingers around her cotton-covered flesh, and rests his other hand above her hip, and just like that, it may as well be a dark West Bromwich street outside a cinema on a cold January night.

It should have happened back then. It didn't. It happens now instead.

Her mouth's warm, soft, her tongue bitter with gin and sweet with sugary lemon, and Jonah feels such muddled, hazy happiness as they shed thin layers of clothing, quietly, ever so quietly.

May 1968

– Jonah. Ya know what, mate? We've had our differences, an sometimes yow've wound me up a bloody treat, but when it comes down tew it, yome a decent bloke. Me best mate in the whole wide world. An ah wouldn't wish fer anyone else.

Billy has another gulp of Red Barrel. Jonah swirls his own pint around the glass. He's feeling a bit queasy, and it's got nothing to do with those three bottles of light ale on the coach or that sausage butty at the service station.

– See, friendship's all abaht loyalty. Loyalty an trust. An ah've allwis knowed ah could trust yow, Jonah. Whatever else might come between us, yow'd never do anythin ter hurt me.

– Shurrup an drink yer pint.

– No, doe get all Mister Modesty. Iss true. An whatever problems ya might have wi Judy…

– Ah doe loike her! I ay bin anywheer near her! Her's not mar type!

– Jonah, what am yow on abaht? Ah was juss gunna say that whatever problems ya might have wi her, I hope ya can accept her in the future, and get along wi her. Cos nuthin's gunna come between me an Jude. An ya know, if ya spent a bit more time wi her, ya might even see parts of her yow've never sid befower.

– Oh really?

– Ar. Politics meks strange bedfellas.

– So it does. So it bloody does.

The pub's heaving full of folks, being conveniently located just up Wembley high street, and they have to speak up to make themselves heard. It's mostly Albion in the boozer – young fans wearing blue and white plastic hats, middle-aged men in grey macs and flat caps, one coloured bloke sporting a smart suit and tie and a blue peaked schoolboy's cap – but here and there, Jonah spots a few scarves of solid blue, telltale accents carrying the melodies of the Mersey. Everton have travelled down in force. Their coaches mingled with the Albion fleet along the motorway on the journey down, little white stitches in the traffic's warp and weft, supporters trading rude gestures through the windows with all the enthusiasm they could muster. There was plenty of banter back and forth at the motorway caff, but no real aggro. Jonah's always found Scousers an easy bunch to get along with anyway, but aside from that, it's cup final day. When your only religion is football, this is as sacred as a day can be.

Their day started in the car park at the Throstle Club, where a fleet of coaches were waiting to ferry down the lucky few with valid cup final tickets, along with a bustling horde hoping to chance their way in. There were Albion fans who missed the early rounds, fair-minded Birmingham supporters who fancied a day out in London and didn't mind cheering on a fellow Midlands club for the privilege, and even some of the more free-spirited locals who drifted between Molineux, the Hawthorns and Fellows Park on Saturdays as the feeling took them. After the photographers from the local papers finished snapping, it was all aboard the coaches, and away.

Jonah and Billy have done the journey to London more times than they can count since that haphazard hitch two years ago, but it always brings back the kind of good memories which come from pitting youthful wits against the world and living to tell the tale. Jonah kept half the coach entertained with that story and plenty of others, their exploits being embellished all round the ring roads of Birmingham, down through the Warwickshire countryside, onto the motorway, off the M1 at Elstree, down the North Circular, across the junction of the Edgware Road, past Brent Reservoir and finally down Wembley Way.

They stopped in the car park off to the right of the stadium and then filed off the coach, stretching their cramped legs, an army of men admiring the twin towers in marble-eyed awe. They had to shift out of the way to allow a limousine past, heading towards the VIP parking section, and they all stood on tiptoes and craned their necks to see it stop and the doors open. A few reporters hanging around the area rushed to surround the solid block of bodyguards who emerged, and behind all those bodies, Jonah glimpsed a mop of brown hair, a hand waving at all the journalists shouting PAUL, PAUL, and CAN WE HAVE A PICTURE, MR McCARTNEY? But he was quick to push past them, making straight for the stadium.

The cup final makes ordinary supporters of even the most extraordinary people.

Of course, if there's one supporter who's far from ordinary at the best of times, it's Billy, and today he's been worse than usual. Staring out of the coach window in silence, responding to jokes and chit-chat with evasive grunts. Before they got into the pub, Jonah was hoping it'd blow over. He's spent the best part of a month trying to forget what happened in Judy's living room; that gin-drenched disaster. He hasn't spoken to her, not since that night. Not since they finished, breathless and flushed, groping for their discarded clothes with all the dignity of thieves fleeing a ransacked house to the sound of sirens. There was a hesitant and guilty kiss in the hallway, then tears from Judy, and Jonah's growing realisation through the fog of eight hours' drinking of just how shit the next day was going to feel. What he didn't realise was how bad the day after that would be. And the day after that. And again and again, every single morning, his conscience crushed within seconds of waking by the memory of those first few seconds, the feel of her body under his hands. The point when they could have stopped.

So many mornings of shame, so many chances to think. What happened that night was a mistake, a massive one; he's never going to live it down, never going to scrub the guilt from his mind completely. But he's hardly the first bloke in history to go trespassing on forbidden ground after a few pints. It's rotten, it's horrible, it's disloyal, but it happens. After all, Tommy did the same thing to him with Kath; maybe not *exactly* the same, but similar. With that in mind, there's no real need for Billy to know about it; obviously there's a chance that Judy might tell him, but he reckons if she was going to do that, he'd have already woken up to the sound of Bill putting his windows through by now. She's bound to see it's for the best if they both keep quiet. She might get some mad ideas in her head from time to time, but deep down, Judy's a sensible girl. Jonah's always liked that about her.

So he's come out today determined to put the whole sorry business behind him and actually enjoy himself. Unfortunately, Billy's got other ideas.

– D'yow ever think abaht gerrin old?

– Old?

– Ya know, loike, turnin thirty or forty or summat.

– Not if ah can help it, no.

– Ya doe think ya might look back one day on stuff loike this an think, this is what it was all abaht?

– Bein down the pub?

– Bein part a the Brummie Road End. Wi nuthin ter fret over. Nuthin ter burden ya. Juss standin on the terraces an singin ter the rafters. What if this is the best that life ever gets?

– Bloody hell, woss brought this on?

– Nuthin. Ah was juss thinkin.

– No, choosin between ketchup or brown sauce is thinkin. Yome philosserphoisin, yow am. Loike Confucius. "Life passes by loike fart in wind tunnel."

– Look, forget abaht it.

– Come on, woss wrong?

Billy squeezes a Mackeson beermat between his fingers and taps the edge against the table.

– Iss Judy. Her's late.

Jonah looks around, alarmed.

– Yow ay meetin her here, am ya?

– No, ah mean her's *late*. In a feminine sense.

– Oh. *Oh...*

– Ah mean, come on. What if her's... ya know, what if her's got a cob in the oven? Ah'm nineteen, mate. Nineteen! Ah cor be a dad!

– Jesus. Ah thought her was on the pill.

– Her musta forgot. Her's bin under a lot of stress recently, an... hang on, what d'ya mean, ya thought her was on the pill?

– Ah juss meant, ya know, her's a modern girl an all that. An they doe even atta be married ter get hold of em now, do they? Sorry. Carry on.

– Ah wish ah could carry on. Havin a kid'll be the end tew all this, wo it? We'll atta find somewheer ter live. An tie the knot, an all; ah've gorra do the roit thing by her. How much is all that gunna cost? How many years will ah spend providin fer a little babby? Five? Ten? Fifteen? Ah mean, it'll tek a couple a years fer it ter walk proper. It wo start school till 1973. By the time it finishes the juniors it'll be 1979! Nineteen seventy fuckin nine, Jonah!

Jonah sits silent. The date doesn't seem real; it belongs in some film about space travel and cities on the moon, not in a conversation down the boozer. But sooner or later, it's going to come around, and where will he be?

It's a worrying thought. But not the most worrying thought in his mind right now. Not by a long way.

*

– Matthew!

– Remember; me name ay Matthew. Iss Jeff. Jeff Astle.

– Sorry Jeff.

– Iss aroit, Ossie.

– But I'm not Ossie. I'm Aasha.

– No, today yam Ossie. The goalkeeper. Look, try an save this un.

– Why is Jeff Astle trying to score past his own goalkeeper?

Matthew stops and rubs his chin.

– Good point. Yow'll atta be Gordon West, the Everton goalie.

– What do I have to do?

– Try an stop me scorin, so Everton can win the cup. An if ah score, then Albion win. Ya ready? Here it comes! Oh. Good save. Ah tell ya what; iss best a three, ay it?

There's a shout from inside; Aasha throws the ball to Matthew, and he follows her into the house. The kitchen's rich with the smell of triangle pies. They're not really called triangle pies – the Singhs call them *sumoasers* – but ever since the first time he had one, a massive three-cornered pastry full of hot spicy potato and peas which barely fitted into his mouth, they've always been triangle pies to Matthew. They're brilliant on a cold winter day after school, especially when he's had Games last thing on a Wednesday, and he walks home with Aasha, stopping by her house before his parents get home, still aching from thumping a hard ball round a lumpy pitch in the wind and rain.

Their shoes skid on the scrubbed lino as they rush through the kitchen. Mr Singh calls again from inside the front room.

– Come quickly! They're getting ready to sing their song!

They make it through the doorway just as the band strikes up *Abide With Me*. Mr Singh's standing to attention, saluting the television. Matthew and Aasha stand next to him obediently as the players and fans on the grey screen start singing.

– Matthew! Sing the words!

– What am the words?

– I don't know. You must know them!

– Ah doe. Ah know the bit wheer they sing "aboid wi me", but thass it.

They settle for humming along uncertainly, and joining in raggedly with the "abide with me" choruses. The song finishes to a crescendo of applause, Princess Alexandra takes her seat in the royal box – with all the Everton supporters booing her for wearing a red outfit – and Matthew, Aasha and Mr Singh sit down for kick-off, all three of them squeezed onto the sofa. Mr Singh asks Matthew to point out all of the Albion players in their changed white kits. There's Ossie in goal, Doug Fraser at right back, and the captain, Graham Williams, at left back. Then the two centre-halves, John Talbut and John Kaye, and three midfielders in front of them: Graham Lovett, Bobby Hope and Tony Brown. Chippy Clark's out on the left wing – just like he's always been, ever since Matthew's very first match – and Ian Collard's on the right. And up front, Jeff Astle, whose picture clippings from the newspaper have filled the pages of Matthew's scrapbook over the last few months, until he's had to start pasting new pages in at the back just to make room for them all.

Nothing will beat what Jeff did three weeks ago. Nothing will beat the night of Matthew's birthday, when Manchester United came to the Hawthorns – European Cup semi-finalists and contenders for the league title – and Matthew was there with Dad. They don't usually go to evening matches, but Dad said it was a special treat since Matthew was a proper man now, turning ten.

Everyone wanted to see them. Too many people. Thousands and thousands allowed in, thousands and thousands more forcing their way through locked turnstiles, thousands and thousands on top of that breaking down gates to get inside. The stands were crammed with bodies, people not just jostling for space but trying to avoid getting hurt, struggling for breath when they were caught between other bodies and pressed up against crush barriers.

Matthew's heart rolled with panic and delight as Dad hoisted him up out of the crowd, and with hands beneath him supporting his body the whole way, he was passed down to the front of the Brummie Road End over thousands of heads, seeing the pitch from higher than ever before. When he reached the front, there was no space even around the little concrete wall, so a bloke took hold of him and set him down with a load of other kids sitting in dense rows on the asphalt track at pitchside.

As the players warmed up for kick-off, Jeff Astle wandered towards the goal to talk to Ossie, and taken by a sudden impulse, Matthew stood up and waved.

– Jeff! Iss me birthday! Jeff!

The tall centre-forward with the side-parting looked around in surprise, and Matthew looked him right in the eyes. Jeff didn't say anything. Nor did Matthew. Jeff smiled and winked, and then turned away to run back to the centre-circle.

The turf glistened in the floodlights' glow. In the dark recesses of the Smethwick End, little points of light flared from lit cigarettes. The far end of the pitch was a foreign kingdom which Matthew only glimpsed through a forest of players' legs, but after ten minutes, a roar from the back of the Brummie told him that Tony Dunne had misplaced a backpass to Alex Stepney, and with all the boys around him craning their necks and rising to their knees to see the sudden flurry of action, Matthew spotted Astle intercepting the backpass, turning Denis Law, and then whacking one in off the far post.

The ground was hard beneath Matthew, but he didn't care. His tenth birthday turned into the greatest night of his life. Ronnie Rees made it 2-0 after robbing the ball from Francis Burns just before half-time; then Nobby Stiles started a fight with Jeff Astle, and Matthew was right up on his feet with all the boys at the edge of the pitch, throwing jabs in the damp air and yelling for Jeff to give him a hiding; he might have won the World Cup, but no one comes to the Hawthorns and tries to lamp Jeff. No one.

ASTLE IS THE KING
ASTLE IS THE KING
THE BRUMMIE ROAD WILL SING THIS SONG

Albion kicked towards the Brummie in the second half, same as always, and with a clear view of every single attack, each moment froze in Matthew's mind:

Nobby Stiles, still seething about his own defence's performance and looking to vent his frustrations, hacking down Ronnie Rees in the area ten minutes into the half.

Bomber – with his tongue curling out the corner of his mouth in concentration, just like Matthew used to do when he drew pictures at school – stepping up to put away the penalty.

Astle getting his head to a Bobby Hope free-kick just sixty seconds later to make it four.

A war of chants surging back and forth between the Brummie Road and United fans down in the Smethwick End, as the teams hammered away at each other like prize fighters.

Doug Fraser conceding a penalty which Denis Law scored.

Bomber thundering down the wing, sending in a cross which glanced awkwardly off Astle's head, but fell right into the path of Asa Hartford to tap in at the far post.

And more than anything else, captured in the hazy light under a halo of mist and sweat, Astle coming in on that cross fifteen minutes from time. Astle launching himself into a diving header. Astle making it 6-1 to Albion, completing his hat-trick in front of the frenzied Brummie Road; then getting up off the ground, and looking right over at Matthew with a huge grin on his face. And Matthew was on his feet dancing, shouting *he's scored it for me, he's scored it for me!* and trying to run onto the pitch to celebrate with Jeff and all the players. The copper patrolling the byline, the big one all the older lads called Dixon, caught hold of him and dragged him back to the other boys, giving him an earful along the way. Normally that would have been enough to upset him for the rest of the night – he couldn't imagine much worse than getting told off by a policeman – but heading back to the rest of the boys who were cheering him, and the whole Brummie Road End behind them, layered so far back into the floodlights' glare that he couldn't even see where it all ended, nothing in the world could upset Matthew.

In the last ten minutes, United pulled a couple more back through Denis Law and Brian Kidd, but it didn't change a thing. When the ref blew the final whistle on a 6-3 victory, Dad picked his way through the elated masses bursting from the terraces onto the pitch, put an arm round Matthew's shoulders near the corner flag, and with a straight face, asked him *good birthday?*

It was the best of birthdays. It was the best of matches. As he perches on Mr Singh's sofa, kneading a cushion beneath his knuckles, he just hopes that today can live up to the promise of that night. This afternoon could go horribly wrong in more ways than one.

He's waiting for it, waiting for it, and sure enough, just as the players take their positions to kick off, there's a knock at the door. Mr Singh must see the look on his face, because he rests an arm on Matthew's shoulder.

– Everything will be fine.

– Am ya sure?

– Of course, Matthew. We hope and we pray, and our prayers are answered, isn't that so?

Matthew nods, but he reckons it's going to take more than prayers this time, as Mr Singh walks into the hallway and opens the front door.

– Just in time, sir, just in time! Come in!

– Ta. Yow've done a good job wi the place, ay ya?

Matthew takes a deep breath and holds it in, as if he's got the hiccups. He reckons that's the best way of praying. Use every muscle you've got to send a thought whizzing up into the heavens. *Everything will be fine.*

– Aroit, Matthew.

The newcomer ruffles his hair, then sits down in the beige armchair closest to the telly. Matthew lets the breath out and hopes that his prayer's been heard, somewhere.

– Aroit, Dad.

*

– Our name's on the cup this year.

– Ya said that last year. Look what happened.

– Ar, but lightnin doe strike twice!

– Jonah, when yome abaht, lightnin never stops strikin. If yow found the end a the rainbow, yow'd onny come back wi a tin a paint.

– Shurrup! Theer ay nuthin wrong wi mar predictions.

– Remember when ya said Muhammad Ali was bound ter get knocked out soon?

– He woulda bin if he hadn't got sent ter prison. Trust me, yow've heard the last a Muhammad Ali now. Proper flash in the pan.

– An how abaht last year, when ya talked me out a puttin me money on Foinavon ter win the National.

– Bloody fluke, that was! T'ay mar fault three dozen osses cor jump a soddin fence.

– Well, ah'd prefer it if ya just kept yer gob shut this aft…
– WE'M GUNNA WIN!
– Ah cor hear ya, ah cor hear ya! La la la la la la!
– ALBION FER THE CUP! ASTLE TER SCORE THE WINNER!

Billy keeps his hands pressed tight over his ears as he pegs it through the car park with Jonah chasing him, weaving through the thick clusters of folks who are milling around, singing and swapping team news, or crying out to buy spare tickets like pilgrims at a medieval market. On either side of him, there are more parked cars than he's ever seen in one place before, a ridiculous jigsaw of brightly-coloured metal, and he supposes there'll only be more and more of them in years to come. A country covered in car parks. Roads ruled by futuristic Austins and Triumphs and Morrises with all sorts of mod cons, and who knows what other ways of travel will be invented in the meantime? His kid's going to grow up in a strange and wonderful world.

His kid.

He takes his hands off his ears and stands in front of the entrance, beneath the great Wembley arches, thinking it again. His kid. When you turn the words over in your mind a few times, they don't sound so bad. It's terrifying to think about having to care for a baby, having to go out and earn the money for nappies and prams and medicines and dummies and all the rest, but what comes after that? A new person. Someone you can teach about the decent things in life; someone you can help to avoid all the mistakes you've made.

His kid.

– Come on, then! Ya gunna stand out here all afternoon?

Jonah's caught up with him, and puffs his cheeks out as he gets his breath back.

– Woss the rush?

– The rush is findin a decent spec. If we end up wi a shit view, iss yower fault.

– Jonah, juss tek a second an appreciate wheer we am. Juss soak it up. We'm at Wembley. Iss cup final day, an we'm at Wembley. It might never happen again.

– Doe talk bollocks. We've got the best cup side in the country! Gunna be plenty more cup finals fer us in the future!

– Ya never know woss round the corner, mate. Please. Juss hold yer horses fer a minute an appreciate how it feels ter be here.

They stand in silence for ten seconds – long enough for a shiver to run up and down Billy's spine – and then walk beneath the arches, into the heart of the Empire Stadium.

~ 167 ~

*

– Is anyone gunnew have a crack at goal? Never sid so many blokes scared ter shoot. Look at em, all sittin back, no one gerrin forward. Timid. No one ever won the cup by defendin.

Dad slurps his tea after that judgement, and shakes his head in disgust. Matthew watches him and decides to shake his own head too, showing he's even more disgusted at how bad the match is. It's not just defensive, it's rough too; eleven different players have needed treatment in the first half-hour with a variety of cuts, bruises and lumps. Dougie Fraser's had three stitches in his knee, Johnny Kaye's had to come off – the first man ever to be substituted at Wembley – with Dennis Clarke replacing him, and even the players who've escaped unscathed aren't covering themselves in glory. There's no joy for Astle up front against Brian Labone and Howard Kendall, while Chippy Clark's having an equally hard time with Tommy Wright.

Mr Singh clears his throat.

– Correct me if I'm mistaken, but aren't Everton a stronger team than our boys?

Matthew nods.

– Beat us twice in the league this season.

– And this Astull fellow, he's quite a good player?

– Jeff Astle's the King!

– So, surely it makes sense for both teams to be cautious of each other?

Over in the armchair, Dad snorts amusement. Mr Singh looks over with his eyebrows raised.

– Have I got that wrong?

Dad twists his head round from the screen, a half-smile on his face.

– "Our boys"?

– Sorry?

– Ya said "our boys", when ya was talkin abaht the Albion.

– Yes. Our team. West Bromwich.

– But they ay yower team, surely? Ah mean, it ay yower town, fer starters.

Matthew stares at the telly. His face is hot. All of a sudden, it seems like he can hear every single noise inside Wembley a little bit clearer.

Mr Singh chuckles.

– Of course it's my town. I don't live anywhere else.

– Ya come from somewheer else, though.

~ 168 ~

– Yes, I did. And now I'm here. This is my home.

– So ya juss swap one home fer another? Iss that easy, is it? Pack yer bags, hop on a boat, an abracadabra, yam a whole new man?

Matthew puts his hands over his mouth as Johnny Morrissey lofts a ball into the Albion penalty area. With the goal at his mercy and only Osborne to beat, Jimmy Husband shoots clean over the crossbar. Matthew closes his eyes. He wants the match to get more exciting. He wants it to get more exciting so Dad and Mr Singh will stop talking.

He doesn't want Mr Singh to end up hating Dad.

Mr Singh says something quickly to Aasha in another language – Matthew reckons it must be Punjabi, because she's taught him a few words of it in the past – and she runs off into the kitchen. Mr Singh turns back to Dad and nods his head slowly.

– It's never "that easy", as you say. When a man's fighting, he dreams of peace. When peace comes, he dreams of prosperity. If prosperity is lacking in his own land, he dreams of paradise overseas. When paradise proves to be six men sharing a house with two bedrooms, working seven days a week in a cold and rainy town to send money back for a family he never sees, naturally, he longs for his own land again.

– So really, yow'd loike ter gew back wheer ya come from, then?

– That's the dangerous thing about dreams, Mr Freeman. We remember places we've loved as perfect wonderlands they never were. West Bromwich is not a perfect wonderland either, but it has opportunities. When I had enough money to provide for them, I brought my family here, and I've worked to build a better life for us ever since. Any place where I can offer my family safety and security is my home, Mr Freeman. Now, perhaps, you understand why I'm supporting *our* boys today?

Matthew looks up at Dad for the first time all match. Dad looks back down at him, and then up at Mr Singh.

He slurps his tea and turns back to the telly.

*

0-0 after ninety minutes, and Billy's getting that ache in his back and legs from standing still too long. It's not usually this bad; in an ordinary match, you'd get chance to move around a bit more with crowd surges during exciting moments and after goals, but what exciting moments? What goals? They're in an enclosure full of Albion fans with terraces so broad you can fit two rows of people on every step. The problem with that is the people in the rear row of each tier have got a bloody awful view, and no chance of shifting position. Ninety minutes of negative football from both teams have left thousands of spines rigid and sore.

But finally, a couple of minutes into extra time, signs of life; Tony Brown gets the ball in the Albion half, and passes to Collard on the right flank. Collard plays it forward to Bobby Hope, and Hope gives it back to Bomber, who's advancing up the pitch. Bomber meets a solid wall of amber shirts on the edge of the box, but manages to shield the ball and get it back to Bobby Hope, who takes a touch and then drives a shot just over from twenty yards out.

The sun breaks through the clouds for the first time all day. Albion hassle Everton for possession in midfield, and Fraser manages to pick up a stray ball on the halfway line. He strokes it forward to Jeff Astle, who skips a sliding tackle and runs at the defence. He's got Chippy to his left with space ahead of him, but twenty-five yards from goal, he tries a shot instead. There's a groan from every throat around Billy as it goes astray, hitting Brian Labone instead.

But the rebound falls back to Astle on the edge of the box.

It falls to Astle's left foot.

Jeff Astle's never had a left foot; not in a football sense. His right foot and his forehead were forged for goalscoring; his left foot is only there to stand on. But the rebound falls right across his body, onto his weaker side, and in an instant, without a single touch to control it, Astle puts the laces of his left boot right through the ball, and it flies true, up past Gordon West's glove, and if there was a world where that ball could carry on flying, soaring into the eternal top corner of some heavenly net, then Billy would keep it there. Suspended in space. The never-ending goal.

Because when the net ripples, when the crowd goes berserk, when Jeff Astle runs towards the crowd with his arms raised in celebration; that's the moment everything changes.

*

As it happens, the sight of a bright, possibility-filled future fading away is depressingly ordinary. It's not all weeping and wailing in some halfway house or alleyway, it doesn't come with angry shouts or furious blows; it's just pastel walls and copies of the Reader's Digest arrayed on a rickety little table. A friendly nurse calling names one at a time. A urine sample in a sterile jar, in a blank little bag, sent to a laboratory.

And then the waiting; the sickly hopes and fears which fill the hours and days before you know for sure. There's anger, too; anger at how many hoops she jumped through to get prescribed those bloody pills. Anger at herself, at how she stopped taking them regularly because of all the headaches and nausea they caused. But the isolation is the worst. Finding out you're no longer alone in your own body is the most absurdly lonely feeling Judy's ever known. There's no one to talk to, but sooner or later, everyone will need to know. Mom and Dad will be the worst. And Billy, although he already knows there's a chance. But then there's Jonah. What the hell does she do about Jonah?

The new life inside her is quiet.

There's really only one person she can tell first. The one person she's always trusted, who's always been there. It has to be Kath.

But where is Kath? Judy's seen less and less of her recently; the last time she popped round was weeks ago. She went next door to knock for her earlier, but no one answered. The whole town's shut away in so many living rooms, curtains pulled to, crowded around the television set – even Judy's mom and dad are watching the action at Wembley – and Judy's left to bear the world's weight on her own.

There are options available; she knows that. It's legal to have it done now, if she can prove there's significant risk; a risk to her physical or mental health. It wouldn't be a trip to some factory after hours, the smell of raw alcohol and the scratching of a wire coathanger. There are proper clinics, proper nurses. It can be done.

But the more she thinks through that plan, the more her mind rebels against all the logic and reason she can throw at it. Through all the emotion, through all the stress and worry of the last few days, she still can't shake the feeling stirring in her body. It might be a cruel trick of biology, but there's no escaping the primal, overpowering sense that what's growing deep within her is a part of herself.

Judy curls up on her bed and tucks a hand across her stomach. She fishes an old book off her shelf – *Tom Sawyer*, one of her own childhood favourites – and starts to read aloud. Her fingers mark the page as she falls asleep.

*

The atmosphere simmers in the last twenty minutes. The fans without tickets stuck outside the stadium stormed the gates at the beginning of extra-time, and a fair few Everton fans have ended up in the Albion enclosure. Astle's goal sparks a punch-up near the back between a load of Irishmen with Everton scarves and some with Albion colours. It could be tension between Catholics and Protestants – they're at each other's throats in Belfast over civil rights at the moment, although Jonah reckons that'll all blow over soon enough – but then, it could just as easily be over football. Either way, Jonah stays well out of it today; he's got no interest in profaning cup final day with his fists. He just crosses his fingers tight and wills the seconds away.

The Everton fans sing louder and louder as Joe Royle tries a first-time shot which Ossie manages to palm down and catch on the bounce. Jonah finds his voice again, and with Billy's help, tries to rally the rest of their enclosure.

AL-BI-ON!
AL-BI-ON!

Everton have a free-kick, which Ray Wilson sends high into the box, but Ossie races off his line and snatches it just an inch from the head of Alan Ball – the man Jonah once watched taking Albion apart in a Blackpool shirt, that rainy November day he first stood up the Brummie Road – and then Ossie flings the ball straight upfield for Bomber to chase, and he picks it up on the halfway line with Lovett and Clark alongside him, the three of them driving towards the Everton goal with only one defender to challenge them; they're cheering him, roaring at him to finish it off, but he passes to Lovett, and Lovett's tired left foot sends the ball arcing high over the crossbar, into the vast space behind the Wembley goal.

Jonah slaps a palm to his forehead in disbelief, but it doesn't matter. He doesn't even realise that the ref's blown the full-time whistle until he sees the players with their arms aloft in triumph, the Everton team sitting despondently on the turf, and the rolling bellow of victory echoing all around him. He shakes his head, his mouth wide open, and tries to process what's happened.

They've won the cup.

West Bromwich Albion have won the FA Cup.

The moment every lad dreams of when he first pins his loyalty to a football team, the moment some spend a lifetime waiting for and still never see. He's here. He's seen it. It's happened. For the first time since he was a boy, pretending to be Ronnie Allen out in the school playground, it's happened. But it isn't until a pair of arms loop round his neck, and Billy hugs him, shouting incoherently and laughing like a maniac, that he knows it's all real. Tears prick his eyes, and doesn't that just sum it up? He's never once cried about having his heart broken, about losing both his parents, about anything that life's thrown at him, but eleven blokes kicking a ball around a pitch can leave him in this state. Bloody saftness, it is. Absolute saftness.

But he loves it all the same.

Everyone's waving their hats, their caps, their scarves, their programmes in the air. The band are back out on the pitch as the team climb the steps up to the royal box. Graham Williams takes the cup off Princess Alexandra, and hoists it in the air to the descending cadences of a deafening crowd.

AAASTLE!
AAASTLE!

*

Discoloured, wrinkled, shrivelled skin. Innards dried and desiccated, their chemical bonds failing and fluids becoming toxic. Mould creeping across the surface, smothering, devouring and degrading the life beneath. Kath put the peach by her window a week ago, and in the languid light, sitting on an old wooden chair, cradling her chin in her hands, she's watched it rot from the inside. Since finishing her notice at work, she's had a lot of time spare, and she's spent almost all of it here. Alone. Her parents think she's at work on her sewing machine, creating new designs, new dresses, fashions to take the world by storm, to launch her brand new business.

It just goes to show how much can be hidden behind a closed door.

It's all over, one way or another. It happened too many times, but it's over. Too many days and nights feeling nauseous and terrified, crying in a bathroom, scrubbing her hands and face in a cracked old basin and trying to avoid catching a glimpse of the human wreck in the mirror, but it'll never happen again. Not since the afternoon last month when they heard a sudden thump from that dark, dusty office, and one of the new girls rushed to the window and screamed as she saw him through the blinds, lying flat on his back on the floor, his face blue. She ran for one of the telephones to call an ambulance, but Carol Parker stopped her.

They said he used to be charming, once. But it had been a long time since anyone had seen any charm in Mr Barrett. Everyone knew what he was like. There were a lot of rumours about him. There were some jokes, whenever anyone dared. There was the rule – only ever whispered, usually to girls just starting the job – that you never went to the supply room on your own when he was on the prowl. Keep your wits about you and you'd be safe. Never comfortable, but always safe.

And in the end, all of that was what finished him, when his swollen black heart couldn't take any more sneaky glasses of whisky. That was why Carol Parker shook her head when the new girl went to dial 999. That was why he lay on the floor, struggling to breathe, surrounded by an office full of women who hated him.

They watched him die.

Even at the very end, Kath wanted to scream at him, kick him, spit on him, all of the things she swore to herself she'd do the next time he came near her, but never did, always terrified of what would happen afterwards. Terrified that all the blame would be on her. Instead, she went back to her typewriter and started drafting out her notice.

What now? What is there to look forward to? Everything fell apart with Tommy months ago, when she stopped being able to look at him, let alone share a bed with him. There's nothing keeping her here. Her suitcases are packed.

It's time.

The taxi winds up the Cradley Road through Netherton as the sky gets dark, heading towards Dudley, and the taxi slows as it approaches Primrose Bridge. The headlights burn over the brick, and through the windscreen, Kath can see wet lettering daubed in white paint on the side of the bridge; four words in block capitals spelling a single, simple statement.

ASTLE IS THE KING

The cup final was today. She forgot all about it. It's been months since she went to an Albion match; it's as if those days were another lifetime, each of them small drops in a puddle of discarded dreams.

– D'ya know how the match finished today?

– Yow a Baggies fan, me love?

– Yes.

– An ya missed the cup final! Thass a poor lookout!

– Please, juss tell me the result.

– 1-0 to Albion. Astle scored the winner in extra time. Walloped it, he did!

Strange, the things which tie you to a place. All of the time she spent planning to leave, she didn't think she'd miss that much about the Black Country. Her family? It's time she had her independence from them. Judy? They had some great times together, but they've been growing apart for years now. Jonah and Billy? Good lads, but hardly poster boys for a cosmopolitan lifestyle. She even decided against telling them all she was leaving, wanting to avoid sentimental farewells; a letter or a phone call at the end of her journey will do. But suddenly, out of nowhere, a bit of graffiti on a canal bridge tugs at her heart, and she feels the sudden urge to tell the driver to stop, turn round, take her home. Where she belongs.

She closes her eyes and shakes her head. She hears a note of concern in the driver's voice when he speaks.

– Yow aroit, me love?

Kath answers him quietly.
– Ah'm fine. Carry on.

*

Three up Oxford Street. Two in Soho. Two down Piccadilly. No; *three* down Piccadilly. It must have been three, because he got bought a pint there by some chirpy Cockney who'd had a flutter on Albion to win and Astle to score. That makes eight, but he's sure that can't be right, because he feels fine. Since the coach left Wembley and drove them down to Hyde Park Corner – where it'll pick them up again at midnight and take them home – Billy's breezed from pub to pub with all the other lads on a wave of elation, and every pint has just made him that little bit happier. With a Wimpy hamburger for tea and a gallon of beer sloshing its way through his body, his troubles have wafted away into the night.
– Iss gunna be aroit, ay it?
– What is?
– Evrythin. Ah was werritin over nuthin, wor I? Things am gunna be fine. Even if Jude is, ya know, protestin fer two these days. Ah bet ah can mek a good dad. Ah bet ah can.
– Ar. Maybe ya can.
There's a glum look on Jonah's face. While Billy's gone from misery to euphoria over the course of the day, it seems like Jonah's gone the other way completely. As they wound their way from pub to pub singing, his efforts seemed pretty half-hearted, and now wandering up Park Lane, you'd think he'd spent the day watching kittens being drowned, not Astle scoring a pearler and Graham Williams lifting the cup. There's jubilation all down the street – literally, with some Albion fans dancing through the traffic and stopping cars to serenade them with the usual hymn of *EE-AYE-ADDIO, WE'VE WON THE CUP* – but Jonah's a one-man dark cloud.
– Woss the matter?
– Nuthin.
– Fair enough.
– Look, Bill. Ya was tellin me earlier on how ah'm yer best mate, an nuthin could ever change that.
– Course!
– D'ya really mean it? Would ya still be me mate even if ah did summat really stupid? Ah mean, if ah really regretted it afterward? Would ya forgive me?
– Ar, ah doe see why not.

~ 175 ~

– Ah want ya ter remember summat. Ah've knowed ya longer than anyone. An ah'm the one who looks out fer ya. Ah'm bein honest, here. Ah've med a mistake, a massive mistake, but ah want ter mek amends.

– Come on, Jonah. What have ya done?

And he tells him. He tells him something absolutely ridiculous.

Something silly. Laughable.

Something quite detailed.

Something possible. Plausible.

Something horrible.

Before the world starts spinning, there's just enough time for Billy to grab Jonah and push him into the nearest doorway, shaking his head, telling him to admit it's a wind-up, it must be a wind-up, and then shouting, and snarling, and finally swinging his fists into the evil bastard until some of the other lads come running over to drag him away.

From there, it's all a blur.

February 2002

The King was evrythin tew us. A hero. An icon. A reminder of all the things an ordinary mon can do wi a bit a talent an a fair chance.

Evrythin.

In front a hundreds a people at St Peter's Church in Netherseal, Derbyshire, on the thirtieth a January 2002, they took evrythin, an they laid it ter rest.

*

The day after the King's funeral, ah got a phone call. From one a me old mates. Me best mate, once upon a time. It was bad news. It was the worst of news.

He's had his test results. He's in trouble. He's startin chemo straight away, an wi a bit a luck he's got a few months left in the tank, but no more than that. An thass how it is: when the world wants ter fling shit at us, it doe mess abaht.

See, no one gets ter turn the clock back. No one can change they mistakes; the best ya can ever hope is ter mek amends fer em, however difficult that is. An when yer day comes round, when yer number's up, at least ya can look back on all the years yow've walked the earth an say, ya know what? Ah gid it me best fuckin gew.

Never leave anythin unsaid. Never leave anythin undone.

*

The day after the King died, Jason Roberts scored the winnin goal against Walsall down the Smethwick End, lifted his shirt up and showed off a t-shirt underneath. A t-shirt wi a picture.

A picture a the King.

An twenty thousand folk lit up, lifted from mournin ter joy. Why? Because we knew then: Jeff Astle will never be forgot. The King a the Brummie Road may be gone, but he'll be remembered. Allwis.

Theer's talk of a memorial fer Jeff, somethin permanent at the Hawthorns, up the Brummie Road, something that'll remind people who he was, what he did. An thass exactly as it should be, but fer the rest of us, we atta settle fer summat a bit more humble.

Find yerself a place, a place ya love. A place ya belong.

Let all yer cells melt inter the ground, nourish the soil, become a part of evrythin ya love.

Let yerself tek root, deep beneath the surface, underground.

Part Two

1978 – 1979

August 1978

Underground.

Deep beneath the surface, a city unseen. Beneath concrete and clay, a hundred and twenty feet down, a web of tunnels running all the way from Hockley to Digbeth; hidden bunkers and communication lines ready for a nuclear attack. And under the shining windows of the Birmingham Shopping Centre, the flickering fluorescence of New Street Station; damp concrete caverns where escalators pass shops and boutiques, and the walls vibrate to the rhythm of the Intercity.

Matty's underground, and he's running. He's running as far and as deep as he can, his red Dr Martens squeaking on a polished floor as he tears past the shoe shop, the army recruitment office, the Ikon gallery, along to the escalators as the first shouts echo from the ramp way behind him.

The whole world's on the run. The news is a catalogue of chaos: bombings, shootings, kidnappings, hijackings. Strike action and work-to-rule, picket lines and Green Goddesses. Carnivals and race riots. Rape and murder in the towns, in the cities. British troops patrolling grey, windswept housing estates across the Irish Sea; cousins and older brothers in uniform, phoning home most nights, sending carefully-worded letters in the post. Mothers praying their boy won't be turned into column inches by some car-bomb or ambush. Every town's sent its fair share of lads over there, and a few haven't come back. You don't have to look far these days to find a man who's bled red for England.

It's been four months since Matty Freeman's twentieth birthday, and the world's a dangerous place.

Having your mates round you is the best way to deal with danger. Unfortunately, it also tends to be the best way of finding danger in the first place. A wrong word, a wrong glance. A shout, a gesture. Your clothes, your hairstyle. The colour of your skin. Even your football team, although Matty can think of a dozen better things to fight over than that. That's the problem with the unseen city, these divisions which run beneath the surface; the fact is, there are a million potential sparks which can start the fire, and it only ever takes one. Matty doesn't even know what's kicked it all off tonight; one minute they were in the Golden Eagle up Hill Street, surrounded by a happy load of skins and new mods, singing along to *Dreadlock Holiday* with pints of lager all round, and suddenly about ten nutters in soulboy bowling shirts and drainpipe jeans erupted out of nowhere, hot on the heels of Wanky Darren, who was legging it so fast his boots were a blur.

Darren was helpful enough to shout out to Matty and Trev as he ran, marking them as fair game for the soulboys, so they had to be quick on their feet. Matty managed to chin the first tosser who came running at him, but with more behind and the numbers against them, it was either peg it or get battered into next week. He grabbed Trev's sleeve, stubbed his fag out on the pub's black marble façade as he sprinted out the door, and then he was pounding concrete, racing the few hundred yards back to New Street.

Now he's down the escalator, under the shopping centre and in the station itself, with Wanky Darren way out in front, heading for the Wolverhampton platform. There are crowds of folks around – one thing you can always rely on at Birmingham New Street – but they can still hear the shouts of the soulboys behind them, coming down the escalators, the squeals of women being pushed out of the way, a few men threatening to call the police, but only making the threat once the thugs are well past them. None of them'll bother, and they're only shouting it to save face. They don't want a hiding off these knobheads. Nor does Matty, but somehow, he's the most likely to cop one.

There's no way out now except by train. If they can make it onto the next local to Rolfe Street, they've got a chance; the soulboys might climb aboard too, but at least the cramped space of the carriages will level the odds a bit. Even holding their own and jumping off at the next stop would be better than getting a thraping on some dank, shadowy platform in the bowels of New Street.

The train's at the platform – three rail-blue carriages behind a yellow-fronted locomotive, the double-arrow British Rail logo dusty on its side – and Darren wastes no time, pulling the door of the nearest carriage open and jumping straight inside. He leaves the door open, and Matty's sure his legs are going to give way before he reaches it, but a dozen more strides and he's at the platform's edge, hopping on board, coughing as his lungs burn with exertion. He turns round to look for Trev, but all he can hear are angry shouts and the clatter of boots down the staircase just obscured by the nearest pillar. Down the end of the platform the guard checks his watch, and starts ambling toward the door Matty's holding open, his whistle in his hand.

Matty grits his teeth. If Trev doesn't make it in time, he'll get off and stick by him whatever happens. Darren can please himself, the dopey bastard. Matty won't leave his mate in the shit, even if it means dropping himself in it. He tries not to think about the worst that could happen. His heart's pumping like a drum roll, and not just because of the run down here. The guard's a few feet away, raising his arm to push the carriage door shut, and Matty takes a deep breath and steps back out onto the platform.

And then the shout.

– Hang on!

Trev's on his way down the platform, and the first of the soulboys comes crashing out of the stairway behind him. Matty holds the door open as the guard reaches him, saying *all aboard now please, sir*, and Matty gives the guard a quick thumb-up and shouts *COME ON, TREV!*

He's twenty yards away, running at full tilt. The soulboys are gaining ground on him.

Fifteen yards. The guard says *come on now, mate, enough's enough*, and pushes Matty back on board the carriage.

Ten yards. The guard slams the door and blows his whistle.

Five yards. Matty slides the window in the carriage door all the way down and sticks his arms out.

As the train starts to move, Trev grabs Matty's arms, climbs up on the carriage step and comes in head-first through the window. The soulboys reach the train and try to grab Trev's flailing legs, but Darren hauls him through, and the three of them collapse in a heap inside the carriage, gasping in breaths and laughing hysterically. Darren gets up, and sticks two fingers up at the fuming soulboys out of the window.

Trev shakes his head and looks up at him.

– What was that all abaht, then?

Darren turns round.

– Ya what?

– What d'ya do ter piss that lot off?

– Oh. Juss got friendly wi some wench on the dancefloor. Proper looker, her was. Shame her's already gewin out wi some fuckin gorilla in a bowling shirt.

– If her was anythin loike yer usual sort, ah bet her wor far off bein a gorilla herself.

– Fuck off!

– We know what yome loike, Wanky.

So that's it. If it's not football, or turf, or race, it's women.

But nothing beats the feeling of a clean getaway, whether you're nine or nineteen; knowing if you get caught you'll get lamped into next week makes it all the more interesting. It's not the end of the world.

As far as Matty's concerned, it's the beginning of a new world.

*

The new season starts tomorrow, and Christopher Collier's up in his bedroom. He's got a lot of work to do.

First, he pulls out his Football '78 album and flips its glossy red cover. He tears open his first packet of stickers with all the thrill of a hunt; he's got Terry Cooper, Graeme Souness, Stewart Rennie, the Coventry City team photo, a grinning Steve Wicks, and his first Albion face, Bryan Robson. He takes his time getting them perfectly angled in the album, not a single edge over the lines. That's six down; just five hundred and nineteen left to collect.

Next, he makes sure all of his football games are handy, with Wembley and Kenny Dalglish Soccer on top of the stack in the corner, and Monopoly relegated right down the pile till Christmas. By the time that's done, the late summer sunset's pouring through his window, daubing a wide orange stripe across blue-and-white pennants, ending on a square patch of space on his wall.

That's his last job.

Right there, in the glowing gap between the blue banners and his new *Shoot* league ladder. That's the place. He picks up the poster and positions it carefully, before pressing each blu-tacked corner against the wallpaper. He's been waiting to fill this space for weeks, ever since Mom told him to take his Willie Johnston picture down. She said he shouldn't have posters of people who take drugs. He tried telling her that Willie didn't take any proper drugs – not the ones which ruin your life and turn you into a thicko; just some ordinary hay fever tablets – but her mind was made up. She heard off Dad how Willie got a red card in that League Cup match against Brighton two seasons ago for kicking the referee up the arse, and coupled with him getting sent home from the World Cup for narcotics possession, she's convinced herself that he's some kind of maniacal drug-addled psychopath, unfit for Christopher's wall. He wasn't sure he'd be able to get another poster as good, but then along came this one, just at the right time.

He stands back from the wall, and stares at Laurie Cunningham. But Laurie's eyes are fixed firmly on the ball at his feet.

There's a knock on the door, and Dad pokes his head in.

– Tea's done, owd pal. Nearly finished what yam dewin?

– Yeah.

– Bet yam lookin forward ter tomorrer, eh?

– Ah spose so.

– Bloomin heck, doe get too carried away.

– Iss juss… ya know this year?

– Mm?

Christopher takes a deep breath and then says it really quickly.

– Can we gew an stand up the Brummie Road End?

~ 186 ~

Dad drums his fingers against his leg. Then he rubs his hand over his mouth, his index finger stroking his moustache.

– I ay sure abaht that, kidda. Ya sure ya doe want ter try standin up the Smethwick End fust? It'll gi ya a feel fer what iss loike. It ay what yam used tew, ah'll tell ya that now.

– Ah've stood on the terraces fer years.

– Yow've stood up the Woodman Corner. It ay the same, bab. Ya doe get the crowds, the surges. Idiots tryin ter tek the home end.

– Iss the loudest place ter be, though, ay it? An some a them from school am gewin up this year.

– Oh, is tharrit? Crikey O'Reilly. Ya know, ah was fifteen when the Brummie Road choir fust started. Fifteen! Yome onny nine!

– Nine an half, Dad.

– Oh, pardon me. Either way, iss still young.

Christopher stays quiet and crosses his fingers; he's been through this before. It took weeks of begging before Dad even took him to a match for the first time, a few months after his seventh birthday. All the lads at school were spending their Saturday afternoons at the Hawthorns, and coming in on a Monday morning with rosettes and badges they'd bought from the club shop pinned to their coats. Dad tried to talk him out of going, telling him it'd only make him miserable. He said the club was going through hard times; ever since Don Howe took them down to the Second Division in '73 with his abysmal defensive football and left them stranded there, the team had been stuck in limbo. The old heroes of the last decade were all but gone, and no one was stepping into their boots. Not yet.

But by the winter of 1975, no one at school was bothered by Don Howe. Howe was long gone, replaced by Johnny Giles, and Albion were learning how to pass their way through the opposition, how to attack their way to victory again. And every Monday, to the ringing of the schoolbell, Christopher heard all about Joe Mayo, Mick Martin, John Wile, Len Cantello, and saw all the lads in the playground trying to be Willie Johnston. And he went home and asked Dad if he could go as well. He asked, and he asked, and he asked, and finally, along came that glorious sunny Saturday in March.

They were playing Bolton, who were right above Albion in the race for promotion. Christopher was with Dad up the Woodman Corner, beneath the wooden scoreboard, standing alongside more blokes than he'd ever seen in one place before. And in the first half, he watched Willie Johnston glide past Ritson, the Bolton right back, to put in a cross for Joey Mayo to nod in at the far post. And then in the second half, he watched Mick Martin loft a free kick over the Bolton wall into the six-yard box, where John Wile sprinted away from Paul Jones and headed the ball into the top corner, right in front of the Brummie Road End. And Christopher was torn between going wild about the goal, and looking to his right over the red railings that separated the Woodman Corner from the Brummie Road to see that huge packed terrace moving and roaring, people jumping up, climbing onto the crush barriers to celebrate, and singing loud enough to shake the foundations.

THEY CALL IM WILLIE! WILLIE!
FASTER THAN LOITNIN!
NO ONE YA SEE, IS FASTER THAN HE!

They were there again a fortnight later to see Albion take apart Carlisle United with goals from Martin, Mayo and Alistair Brown. Over the Easter weekend, they watched Ally Brown and Len Cantello score in a 3-1 win over Fulham, and Willie Johnston run rings around Nottingham Forest in a 2-0 win a couple of days later. There were only two more matches left in the season, and both were away from home. Albion were in the third promotion spot, two points ahead of Bolton, but Bolton had an extra game left to play and a greater goal average. Albion only managed a draw at Leyton Orient in their penultimate game. To get promoted, they needed to go to Oldham on the last day of the season and beat a team who'd only lost two home matches all year.

Everyone at school was bragging they'd be getting a coach up north for the game, but in the end, Christopher was the first one of them all with his place booked. Dad was even more excited about the big match than Christopher, and he insisted that it was time Christopher have a proper awayday.

And what an awayday.

On the twenty-fourth of April 1976, a hundred and twenty coaches steamed up the motorway with blue and white flags and scarves on show. Fifteen thousand Albion fans packed into Boundary Park on three sides of the ground, with Christopher, Dad and half the lads from school up the open Rochdale Road End, their blue and white scarves tied round their wrists, some even wearing the new replica Albion shirts that had gone on sale in the club shop. It seemed like every way he turned, Christopher saw someone he recognised, someone he knew, a face from school, from his street, from his estate, from the Woodman Corner.

They sang to steady their nerves, and the noise never stopped. Oldham were marking Albion out of the game, and the players looked as hemmed in on the pitch as Christopher felt down the front of the terraces. Then came the news – heard over portable radios and chattered in Chinese whispers through the stand – that Bolton were beating Charlton down at the Valley. As things stood, Bolton would be promoted to the First Division and Albion would carry on rotting in the Second.

But ten minutes into the second half, the vital chance came.

There was only one man it could fall to. The man it had to fall to. In 1966, he'd been a lad learning his trade, scoring in every round of the League Cup. Ten years on, with hair down to his collar and a moustache for all seasons, he was the lynchpin of Albion's attack. He was the bridge between the old Albion Dad used to love, and the new Albion Christopher was just starting to love. His name was Tony Brown. They called him Bomber.

And when Mick Martin played the ball out to Paddy Mulligan on the right touchline, and Mulligan floated a deep ball in towards the penalty spot, and Alistair Brown cushioned a header back to the edge of the box, Bomber was there waiting. Ready to flick the ball up with his right foot, and then put the laces of his left right through it. On the volley. Past the diving Chris Ogden, straight into the corner of the goal.

For Christopher, the world was a manic whirlwind of scarves and surging bodies, toilet roll streamers flying over his head to land on the pitch, an almighty din from thousands of throats deafening him to the point where he couldn't even hear his own voice in the roar. He imagined this was what it must be like to be capsized at sea, shipwrecked with the waves rolling all around, only these waves were human, a tide which spilled out onto the pitch in celebration while the players clung to one another triumphantly, and as the initial surge subsided and Christopher climbed up on Dad's shoulders, pumping his fists in the air, crying out with all the joy and relief he could tear from his lungs, he knew there was only going to be one place for him on a Saturday afternoon, for the rest of his life.

It may have been a couple of years ago now, but Christopher's been looking forward to this day. Ever since the final whistle blew at Boundary Park, and Christopher ran onto the pitch with fifteen thousand other fans, sprinting across muddy turf, passing a bloke on his knees in the penalty area kissing the spot Bomber had scored from, ending up in the centre circle sandwiched between Dad and an enormous man swigging from a champagne bottle with tears rolling down his face. Since Johnny Giles climbed up to the executive boxes with the rest of the team, a bright line of green and yellow shirts against a dull canvas of brown and beige overcoats, and announced that Albion were a First Division club again.

Christopher's been waiting a long time for this moment.

– Come on, Dad. Brummie Road tomorrer? Pleeeease?

Dad sighs loudly, stick his hands in his pockets, and then slowly grins.

– Ar, why not?

They catch the 74 to the ground early Saturday afternoon, and Christopher's surprised to feel his hands moist with sweat, his stomach tight as they see the towering Birmingham Road End from the top deck of the bus, rising high above the rooves of the Woodman pub and the Throstle Club, the word ALBION spelled out in white letters across the blue frontage. He shouldn't feel this nervous. He's come a long way since that first Saturday afternoon outside the gates in 1976, with his Pele lunchbox and a bottle of Cresta in a carrier bag, holding Dad's hand and wondering if the stories about football grounds were all true; if they were going to get duffed up by hooligans, pushed around by bad policemen. That never happened. It does sometimes, to some people, but not if you behave yourself, not if you're sensible. That's what Dad always says.

But the Brummie Road, the home end; that's the space the away fans want to take. That's where the police keep the strongest patrols. It's where the likes of Leeds and Manchester United show up in force, looking for blood. It's where you need to keep your feet, raise your voice and defend your territory. The place where proper blokes stand. He shouldn't feel this nervous, but he does. He wipes his hands on the blue and white scarf tied round his wrist as him and Dad get off the bus.

The matchday crowd's thick and sluggish, ambling towards the turnstile queues, a human glacier melting on a summer day; their bellies are well-stoked with beer from the Woodman, the Blue Gates, the Old House At Home. The chants are already going – AL-BI-ON! AL-BI-ON! – and here and there, above the heads of the crowd, policemen on horseback trot against the tide. Christopher keeps his eyes peeled for anyone from school he can nod to on his way in, let everyone know exactly where he's heading. If he could see some of the others, he'd feel better, but the lines of supporters heading into the ground are strangers to him. He carries on shuffling towards the Brummie Road End, seeing fans in short-sleeved shirts drinking lager by the bowling green at the back of the Throstle Club, right next to the wall where some rival fan last season painted the words CUNNINGHAM IS A BLACK CUNT.

It's almost disappointing at first, getting through the turnstiles and onto the Brummie Road itself; he feels like there should be a band playing a fanfare for him as he walks onto the terraces, but instead, there's just that smell of fag smoke mixed with the chocolate-sweet scent of Café Crème; the call of programme sellers flogging fresh copies of Albion News, the tannoy crackling out that old reggae song, The Liquidator, and blokes all around the terraces holding bottles of beer and Golden Goal scratchcards, whistling birdnoise into the air.

As the teams warm up and the stand fills, men gather in clusters and kids wander down to the fence at the front carrying milk crates to stand on. Christopher feels a warm bubble of anticipation building. They're standing just in front of the stand's central exit, right in line with the goal, giving them a clear view all the way to the Smethwick End with the noise of thousands surrounding them. The sun's shining high over the Halfords Lane Stand – fans beneath the scoreboard in the Woodman Corner are already shielding their eyes against the glare – and the pitch is perfect, the kind of pristine green turf that can only mean an August match. In the months ahead it'll be pummelled by wind, rain, frost, snow, ice and hundreds of studded boots until the surface is nothing but mud and finely-scattered sand, but right now even Wembley couldn't look any finer. And they'll need to be on top form against the cup winners. Bobby Robson wants his Ipswich side to play like Holland, bringing total football to England's shores, and Christopher saw in *Shoot* that he's even signed two Dutchmen to make it happen: Arnold Muhren and Frans Thijssen. Dad starts on about when Bobby Robson used to play for Albion, back when he was just a lad going to his first ever games, but Christopher tunes him out, clutches his programme and waits patiently for the first goal he'll see as a Brummie Roader.

It takes twenty-one seconds.

He's almost taken by surprise. Ally Brown strikes a low shot past Paul Cooper in the Ipswich goal, the keeper from Brierley Hill beaten right in front of the Brummie Road End. And as Dad grabs hold of his arm to prepare him for the surge from the back of the stand, sweeping them down the terraces towards the pitch, Christopher knows. He knows right then.

This season is going to be very, very special.

September 1978

A light teatime mist hugs the estate, the smell of boiling veg and steamy mash wafting from windows all down the street. Jonah pinches a fag between his lips, sucks through it till the tip flares in the grey haze, and then blows fog from his lungs to add to the gloom. He's taking a different route home from work, swinging by the chippy; not the normal plan for a Tuesday evening, but he's a free man these days. The divorce papers are in the post to prove it.

The road curves round the edge of the estate; a squat line of old terraced houses with a couple of tower blocks standing sentinel above the rooftops, and behind a chainlink fence over the far side of the road, the ruins of the old glassworks, all crumbling walls and weed-choked rubble. On Jonah's right, there's a goal drawn in white paint on the side of the row's last house, and a bunch of kids in hand-me-down jumpers and frayed flares are playing cuppies around it, locked together above their ball in a writhing mess of tangled legs and stabbing elbows all over the pavement and the road. It may be a fancy new ball with its black and white hexagons, but this is English football the way it's been for centuries; a street game for anyone tough enough to stick it, a free-for-all where cuts and bruises are the badge of a real player. The lads are calling each other Robson, Cantello, Cunningham, Regis, all the current Albion names – amazing what sitting third in the league after four matches can do for local pride – but really, they're learning how to fight for their own place in the world. Jonah's glad to see it. Too many kids these days get pampered and mollycoddled; he's sick to death of it.

The country's going to the dogs. If he had the money, he'd emigrate tomorrow. Follow his brother's example one more time. Set himself up somewhere new, somewhere with a decent climate where they'll reward hard work. New Zealand, maybe – not Australia, he doesn't want to end up stuck with Tommy all over again – or possibly South Africa. He knows a couple of blokes who've moved out that way, and he gets the odd postcard and letter from Durban, Cape Town, Johannesburg. They wax lyrical about the weather and the standard of living; they've even got their own servants in the house, and there's proper law and order around the neighbourhood. It sounds like paradise.

He feels an imaginary sun warming his face on the far side of the world, and smiles. There are shouts just out of sight, over by the carcass of the glassworks, the rough song of angry and unbroken voices. It's always been the same; boys'll be boys.

He takes a disinterested glance across the derelict ground as he passes, and then stops. There are four kids over the far side of the ruins – not much more than stick figures at this distance – and they've cornered a boy in a green anorak, pinned him against the wall. As he watches, one of them punches him in the belly.

Jonah winces. There's boys being boys. Then there's boys being bastards.

He finds a gap where the chainlink fence has been detached from its concrete posts, pushes through with his head bowed low, and walks towards the group.

The glassworks is a shell of a building, mostly demolished, with broken walls four or five feet high tracing out old storerooms and workshops, charred braziers and drifts of empty bottles marking the corners where the tramps hole up for the night. Jonah keeps his eyes on the little gang – still in their school uniforms, all cropped hair and cocky grins – and eventually they hear his footsteps. A couple of them turn their heads, and Jonah nods to them.

– Nuthin loike a fair fight, eh?

– Fuck off.

It's the one who's got the kid pinned against the wall with a fistful of anorak who says that. The others looked nervous and uncertain as Jonah approached, but they smirk and lift their chins as their ringleader mouths off. Little sheep, the lot of them.

– Yow need a smack ter keep that mouth in order, sunshine?

– Ya can try if ya want, mush.

– Well, if ya think ya can stick me an this fella together, why not?

For the first time, Jonah looks at the kid in the anorak, and from this angle he can see the face under the fur-lined hood; the sudden glimpse of bright eyes against black skin startles him. He can't be more than nine or ten; younger than the dickheads picking on him. It's one thing sticking up for yourself and your own kind – being proud of your country and everything – but four against one, and hardly more than a babby at that? That's not British. Never in this world.

The big brave heroes are all sizing Jonah up. Barely a day over thirteen, and they're ready to take on a grown man as if he wasn't nearly twenty years older, a foot taller and Christ knows how many stone heavier than them. He stares them out. He doesn't care how hard they think they are; Jonah's had it as rough as anyone, and no little shit's about to dish it out to him. After about half a minute, they think better of it and start backing away, saving face by spitting and running their gobs at him.

– Juss wait. Come this way again, we'll fuckin batter yow, mush.

– Ar, course ya will. Keep walkin, pal. Keep walkin.

– That guz fer yow an all, Sambo. Doe get comin round this estate.

As the mist shrouds them, they're jerking their arms out in Nazi salutes, chanting *KU KLUX KLAN* over and over. Jonah shakes his head, and turns round to the black boy in the anorak.

– Yow aroit, bab?

He nods, and juts out his chin.

– I coulda handled that myself.

– Ar, it looked loike it.

The boy looks over his shoulder uncertainly.

– They might still come after me.

– Bloody Nora, ten seconds agew ya could handle em yerself. Mek yer mind up! Wheerabahts d'ya live?

– D'you know Thompson Street?

– Oh, ah knew someone who lived up that way a while back. That used ter be a nice area, that did.

– It still is.

– If yow say so, chief. Look, come on, ah'll walk ya back theer. Woss yer name?

– Daniel.

– Ah'm Jonah.

– We got a lot in common then.

Jonah frowns. It doesn't look like it from where he's standing.

– Really? Woss that, then?

– We were both in the Bible! We nearly got ate by wild animals. God saved us.

– If ya say so. Ah doe bother wi any a that meself.

Judging by Daniel's expression, Jonah may as well have said he often turns into a llama and plays up front for Stenhousemuir.

– You don't bother with the *Bible*?

– Not juss the Bible. God, religion, the whole lot. Never bin mar thing.

Daniel goes quiet for a while, which suits Jonah fine. It takes another couple of minutes' walking – they're well across the estate now, away from the glassworks – before he pipes up again.

– How d'you do the right thing, then?

– What?

– If you don't believe in God, and you don't read the Bible? How d'you know right from wrong?

– Ah juss know. If summat's roit, iss roit. If iss wrong, iss wrong.

– But what if you're wrong? I mean, what if you're wrong about whether something's wrong?

– Friendly warnin, Danny: if ya carry on talkin shit loike this all yer life, people am gunna be queueing up ter lamp ya.

– Maybe God tells you the right thing, and you just don't know it.

– Maybe he does. It ay very loikely, but ah spose iss possible.

– So, you've never been in a situation where you did the right thing even though you didn't have to? You've never heard a voice telling you to do it?

No. It's rubbish. Jonah may have decided to get involved back at the glassworks a few minutes ago, but there were no voices telling him to do it. He just stepped in because it was right. And fair enough, he didn't know that Daniel was black before he got involved, but even if he had known, he'd still have done it. Definitely. He's almost certain he would have. Because bullying's bullying, and when it comes to stuff like that, it doesn't matter who you are, where you come from, what you look like.

– Nah, mate. Ah reckon ah'm big enough ter mek me own mind up abaht woss roit an wrong.

Daniel's house is just a few doors down from the maisonettes where Bill and Jude used to live. Not that he's seen either of them recently. The last time he even caught sight of Bill was back when the skinheads ruled the Brummie Road, when the terrace anthems were *Knees Up Mother Brown* and whatever reggae songs were doing the rounds that weekend. He hasn't spoken to him for longer still. He tried to apologise, tried to make amends. There's only so much grovelling a bloke can do. He heard that the pair of them got married – Tommy even showed his face at their wedding, not long before he left the country – but was there an invitation for good old Jonah? Was there fuck. Not that it's tricky to work out why. *Does anyone present have a reason why this couple should not be joined together in holy matrimony?* Well, the groom's a whinging little coward, and the bride's knickers tend to get a bit loose after a couple of large gins. How's that for starters?

All the same, he does wonder how much they've changed down the years. He's been through his fair share. And when it comes to change, what about this bloody street? There's not even a white face in sight. Jonah stopped feeling comfortable a while ago; he's been glancing over his shoulder every now and then, and he just wants to make sure the young 'un gets back safely and then be on his way. He knocks on the door, and a tall coloured man with closely-cut black hair opens up. He looks at Daniel, and then suspiciously at Jonah.

– Oh, aroit mate. Yer boy was havin a bit a trouble on his way home. Thought it might be a good idea ter mek sure he gets home safe.

−What kind of trouble?

The question's directed at Daniel, who looks down and kicks the toes of his shoes against the doorstep.

– Just some boys.

– What boys? What was they doing?

Now the dad looks at Jonah, who shrugs his shoulders.

– Juss kid stuff, wor it?

He looks back at Daniel, and nods.

– Alright then. Thanks for seeing him home, mate. You want a brew?

– No, no. Ah need ter gerroff.

– Fair enough. I'm Neville, by the way.

– Jonah.

– Well cheers, Jonah. Good to know there's still some decent people around.

Jonah nods.

– Oh, ar. Decent's me middle name.

*

Bill's in the middle of tidying the house up when it happens.

With Christopher staying late at school for football practise – he's got a chance of making the team as a centre-half this year, if he keeps working on his headers – and Judy putting in some overtime, he's sorting out a few odds and ends, carrying a pile of *Roy of the Rovers* comics up to Chris's room. He puts them down on top of the stack of games in the corner, and as he turns to leave the room, he sees the poster on the wall. It's been up there a few weeks now, but he's never really stopped and looked at it before. He perches on the edge of Christopher's bed and stares at Laurie Cunningham as the realisation sinks in.

Cunningham's twenty-two years old. Eight years younger than Bill.

He's just a lad. They all are. A whole generation of footballers younger than him.

When you grow up watching icons and role models, men you idolise and emulate in crowded playgrounds and empty parks throughout your childhood, it's hard to imagine a day when those men won't be running onto the pitch on Saturday afternoon anymore. It's harder still – almost impossible – to imagine the day when footballers will no longer be blokes you look up to, but strip-thin little kids who aren't a patch on the legends you used to love. No one expects that day to come, so it's a bloody surprise when it catches you all of a sudden, unforgiving and undeniable, as plain as your pot-belly and the grey hairs in your moustache.

Bill barely noticed the gradual disintegration of the team he loved. Chippy Clark went back to Queens Park Rangers the year after Albion won the cup, but at the time, Bill was busy putting food on the table for his wife and newborn baby. When Dougie Fraser transferred to Nottingham Forest in 1971, he was still working every shift he could get just to pay the rent and put a bit aside for the future. Bobby Hope's move to Birmingham City in 1972 came just after his father died; something which had been coming for a painfully long time, but still managed to surprise Bill in the worst way possible.

In the end, it took a cataclysmic departure from the club to really pull his attention away from his own life. In July 1974, Albion sold Jeff Astle. The day his transfer to Dunstable Town was confirmed, Bill drove out to Primrose Bridge in Netherton, where the words ASTLE IS THE KING were still painted on the smoky brick, just as they'd been since the night of the '68 cup final. There were cars parked all around there, blokes stood in small groups chatting quietly, others staring out over the cut with a fag in their mouth, heads bowed in doleful silence.

And of course, it never ends. One day, Christopher will see Laurie Cunningham hang up his worn old boots, and Cyrille Regis, and Bryan Robson, and the rest of his heroes. By the time that happens he'll be past posters and *Roy of the Rovers*, probably looking to find himself a nice girl to settle down with, have a lad of his own who'll worship new idols in striped shirts. It's the most natural thing in the world, Bill knows that. But why does it have to happen so bloody fast?

He gets up and wanders over to the bedroom window with that thought tracing bright images in his mind. When he looks out into the street, he's tempted to dismiss what he sees as a hallucination. There's figure standing across the road, ghostly through the white mesh of the net curtain: thinning blond hair down to his neck, long thick sideburns, a leather jacket over a light blue shirt, faded jeans. And an odd familiarity to his face.

It can't be. Why would he show up here after all these years? It must be his imagination. But Bill turns round and walks downstairs anyway, heart kicking, stomach rolling. He goes into the front room and peers out through the window in there to get a better view, pushing his face right up to the glass.

There's no one standing across the street. Nothing there at all except for the row of maisonettes opposite. He smiles to himself, relieved, shaking his head at what a saft bugger he can be sometimes.

And then the face appears suddenly from the side of the window, filling the pane, squinting through the glass from inches away, and Bill jumps in shock.

They stare at each other silently through the window for a few moments.

– Bill! Is that yow in theer?

He says nothing. He wants to duck down beneath the window and pretend he's not even here. It wouldn't solve anything, but in a pathetic, tortoise-like way, it would be satisfying to just keep the past shut outside, on the doorstep, where it belongs.

See, the past is a dangerous place. Almost everything to do with Bill's youth is locked away in a big black box in his mind, chained and padlocked so tightly that even that nosy cow Pandora would think twice about ferreting in there. He thinks of it as the Jonah Box. And the thing about the Jonah Box, the really disturbing thing is that on the outside, it's beautiful. All over the sides and the lid are wonderful scenes from Bill's teenage years, painted in vivid detail, as if they happened yesterday. It's a proper Sistine Chapel job. Images of pints down the pub, trips to away grounds, Saturday afternoons spent singing their hearts out side by side; stare at those pictures for long enough and you'll find yourself lifting that heavy lid. And then *wham*. Out will come the memories of getting let down by Jonah, getting betrayed by Jonah, the memories of the screaming rows with Judy after he found out what the pair of them had done. Scars which took years of effort to heal. Scars which never really stopped hurting.

But now the Jonah Box isn't just open. It's tapping on the window. It's too late to hide. The tortoise act won't work. He has to deal with it head-on. Bill walks into the hallway and opens the front door to his worst nightmare.

– Warrow, our Bill! Long time no see!

– Not long enough. What am ya dewin here, Jonah?

He grins awkwardly.

– In the neighbourhood, wor I?

– That ay an answer.

– It wor much of a question. What kind a thing is that tew ask yer best mate, eh?

– I ay askin me best mate. Ah'm askin yow.

– Oh, come on. Am ya gunna invite me in, at least?

– Is murder still a crime?

– Course it is.

– Ah'd better not, then.

– Come on, Bill. Doe be loike that. I ay sid ya fer... how long now? Ten years?

– Ar. The happiest decade a me life. Why spoil it now?

– Thass it? Ten years, an yow ay got nuthin more ter say than that? Ah mean, it'd be nice ter catch up a bit, at least! Find out woss changed!

– Nuthin's changed, Jonah. Thass the problem.

– Well, maybe not fer yow, but what abaht me? Yow ay gorra clue how much ah've changed. Fer all ya know, ah could be a millionaire now, livin in a mansion. Ah might be married ter Felicity Kendal!

– Jonah, mansion-dwellin millionaires doe gew moochin abaht this estate of an evenin wearin a leather jacket off the market an reekin a John Player Specials. Especially not if they'm married ter Felicity Kendal.

– Aroit, aroit. So I ay joined the jet-set juss yet. But all the same, Bill, ten years is a long time. I ay the bloke ah used ter be.

Over Jonah's shoulder, Bill spots a hunched figure trudging down the street, and his stomach knots.

– Well, thass brilliant, Jonah. Ah'm dead pleased fer ya. But it ay no use tellin me. Whatever we used tew have in common, iss in the past. An ah reckon iss best left theer.

Jonah clicks his tongue, staring Bill in the eyes. Eventually he nods.

– Fair enough then, if thass how it is. Ah shor darken yer door no more.

And Jonah turns round just as Christopher starts walking up the path to the front door, his sticker-covered bag hoisted up on his shoulder.

– Aroit theer, young un!

Christopher looks up in surprise. Bill closes his eyes and contemplates banging his head against the doorframe.

– Leave im be, Jonah. Christopher, gew on inside.

– Woss that writ on yer satchel, mate? "WBA Brummie Road End"? Yow ay a Brummie Roader, am ya?

– Yeah.

– Bloody hell! Ya must be a proper fan ter be up theer at yower age! Ah used ter gew up wi yer dad evry match. They was a proper team back in the Sixties, ya know.

– They'm a proper team now!

– Ar, ah spose ya cor knock em. Hey, them black blokes am dewin aroit, ay they? Cunningham and Regis, an the right-back?

– Brendon Batson.

– Ar, thass the one. Never thought ah'd see the day. But credit wheer it's due, eh? They never loaf abaht, allwis get stuck in. That

Cunningham's bloody dynamite wi a ball at his feet! He took to that left wing loike a dog ter water!

– D'ya still gew up the Brummie Road, mister?

– Me name's Jonah. But ya can call me Uncle Jonah if ya want.

– No, Christopher, doe call im that. He ay yer uncle.

– Nah. Ah'm more loike yer godfather, really.

– No, Jonah, yow ay that neither. Chris, doe listen tew im.

– Calm down, Bill, yam confusin the poor kid! Look at im, he's gewin cross-eyed!

– Aroit Chris, thass enough now. Inside.

Bill waits until Christopher's shuffled past him into the house, takes a quick look behind him to make sure he's not loitering within earshot, and then pulls the door to for good measure. Jonah grins.

– Nuthin in common anymore, eh? Dae tell us ya was still gewin up the Albion, did ya?

– Is it really that important? What me an me son do of a Satdee afternoon's our business.

– Aroit, fair enough. Still. Spose ah might see ya at the weekend, eh?

– Jonah, ah'm warnin ya now. Ah'm a happy mon, wi a happy family. If yow wreck that, ah'll bloody swing fer ya this time.

Jonah looks at him, and smirks.

– As if ah would.

October 1978

Change is gradual. It happens by degrees.

Sometimes there are moments of sudden watershed in history, shocking events which tear through the fabric of the status quo scattering headlines in their wake, but those moments don't come from nowhere. They're born from forces and frictions which build up over months, over years. Civil rights. Women's lib. Punk rock. Movements which flickered to life long before they made the nine o'clock news, growing slowly, quietly, incrementally.

Change always happens by degrees.

In 1978, West Bromwich has been changed by three degrees.

*

Batson, Regis, Cunningham. Three men playing for a professional club in the first division of English football, like hundreds of others. Slogging through ninety minutes every Saturday afternoon in all weather, like hundreds of others. But the sports pages and the television cameras aren't focused on the hundreds of others. They're focused on the triumphs and failures of the Three Degrees: a trio of black men, together in one football team.

Christopher doesn't understand the fuss. He loves watching them play, but when all's said and done, he loves watching every Albion player in action. It doesn't matter whether it's Cyrille Regis with his pace and strength up front, or Bryan Robson picking out passes from the centre-circle like a magician; Laurie Cunningham with guile and trickery on the wing, or Bomber thundering home another unstoppable twenty-yarder; Brendon Batson roaming forward from the right-back position, or Len Cantello stamping ruthless authority on the midfield like an English Gunter Netzer. As long as they're wearing blue and white shirts, what difference does the skin beneath the stripes make?

But if there's one thing he's learned from two months of standing up the Brummie Road End, it's that people can see exactly the same thing and still have opposite views on it. When you've heard a bloke behind you shout *WELL PLAYED, STATHAM* at exactly the same moment that someone in front shouts *GERROFF STATHAM, YOME SHIT*, you learn pretty quickly that opinions come in every shape and size. And Christopher's heard plenty of opinions on the Three Degrees. For some of the black fans braving the Hawthorns turnstiles for the first time, they're an inspiration. To most of the white fans who've been there for years, their talent deserves respect, whether it's grudging or not. But for away fans, they're targets to be abused, hated, threatened. No matter how much the Brummie Road drowns them out, the songs and chants from the visitors' section of the Smethwick End most Saturdays get inside your head and stay there.

But what happens at matches is totally different to what happens in normal life, outside football. Christopher believes that right up until one Tuesday afternoon after school, in the park. The day of the school team trials.

– Shit.

He rocks the swing, letting the rusty chains creak and sway, feeling the solid weight of his muddy boots, the laces tied together, hanging round his neck. Then he lets an even better one loose.

– Fuuuuuuuck.

Swearing feels good. He hears it all the time on the terraces – even Dad does it every now and then up the Brummie – but the one time Christopher tried it, during the Liverpool match last month when Kenny Dalglish robbed the ball off Tony Godden for a last-minute equaliser, Dad gave him a knock round the head and told him to watch it. He hasn't sworn at a match since, but here in the park, no one can stop him. And he reckons he's earned a few curses today.

He let the ball bounce.

What a stupid thing, what a *saft* fucking thing to have done. He was a cert to be centre-half in the school team this year, just like Ally Robertson in the middle of defence; he can scythe the tips off blades of grass with a sliding tackle. But he had to bottle that header, didn't he? Same as always. A long clearance from the opposition goalie, the ball spinning in a darkening sky, cold and wet, spitting rainwater off its black and white hexagons, and as it dropped down towards his face, he couldn't do it. He couldn't grit his teeth and get his forehead angled to the ball, like Dad always tells him to. A chorus of nerves screamed at him to get his head out of the way of the rock-hard missile bombing down, and he did. He shuffled forward and let the ball bounce just behind him, meaning to turn and clear it, but it was already too late for that. Charlie Bradley was right onto it for the other side, nipping in and putting it straight into the back of the net. And that was it: Funnyfarm Francis blew his whistle and had one of his psychotic episodes there and then, waving his arms about and screaming that any gutless fairy who couldn't stick their head to a long ball should just pack their kit up and go home. Christopher's trial was over and done with. Final year, final chance, fucked.

He leans his head against the chain of the swing and thinks up a really good one. The best yet.

– Sweaty bollooooooocks.

– We doe wanna know abaht yer medical problems, ta.

The voice from behind startles him. He twists the swing round, and sees Rolo with his hands in his pockets, and a few of the other lads from school.

– Ya come ter laugh at me? I ay in the mood.

He stares the whole group down. It's a motley bunch, as Mom would say. Rolo, the only lad in school who carries an emergency packet of crisps in his pocket in case he gets hungry when the tuck shop's closed. Daniel, who once brought in a figure of Jesus to play with on toy day. Asif, who's wanted to be a comedian ever since he stayed up to watch Billy Connolly on telly one night, and also thinks that being a comedian just means insulting people constantly. And worst of all, Rajinder, who's a Liverpool fan.

Rolo shakes his head.

– Nah, Chris. We got booted from the trials an all. Funnyfarm sent us packin just after yow.

Christopher looks up.

– All on ya?

Asif nods.

– Well, Rolo lasted till the end before getting cut. They must be desperate for goalies this year, man. They're even giving fat bastards a chance.

– Up yowers.

– True though, innit?

Christopher shakes his head.

– How come ya got cut? Yome the fastest kid in school! An what abaht Daniel's left foot? Iss lethal! Why'd Funnyfarm leave ya out? Am ya tellin me theer's three lads better than yow?

Rajinder looks awkwardly at Asif, and then Daniel.

– No, Chris. I'm saying there's three lads whiter than us.

At first, Christopher thinks he must have heard Rajinder wrong. He stares at him, and Raj stares back solemnly. He really means it. Christopher shakes his head, tries to explain that it must be a mistake.

– But… Funnyfarm's a teacher!

Daniel, Asif and Rajinder trade more awkward glances.

– Look, Chris, don't worry about it.

– Am ya sayin he never picked ya juss cos yow ay white? He cor do that!

– He picks the team, Chris. He can do what he wants.

Christopher shakes his head again. There must be other another reason for Funnyfarm to have cut them out of the school team. He can't think of any, but he doesn't want it to be about skin colour. It's so unfair. He doesn't want it to be that.

– We should complain.

Rolo shrugs.

– To who? Who's gunna tek the word a five kids over a teacher?

– Well, we cor juss give up. We cor let im win.

Daniel claps his hands suddenly.

– How about formin our own school team?

– We'm six short of a startin eleven, Danny. An we'd need subs too. An somewheer ter play. Ya reckon Funnyfarm'll let us use the school pitch? It wo happen.

They sit quiet and glum for a few moments. Rajinder chips in.

– Well, what about them posters down the high school?

– What posters?

– Five-a-side! They do leagues for different age groups! The season starts at half-term!

It could work. Rolo in goal, Chris in defence, Asif and Raj out wide, Daniel up front? It really could work. And best of all, there's that image in Christopher's mind of winning a trophy. Taking it into school on the last day and showing everyone. Showing Funnyfarm.

– How do we sign up?

– Submit our side and our team name by next week.

– Roit. So what do we call ourselves?

Asif grins.

– Call yourself whatever ya loike, fart-arse. We do.

– Ah meant our team name.

– How about Asif and the All Stars?

– Nah.

– Asif and his Poxy Teammates?

– No.

– Asif and the Smelly Scrotum-Pokers?

– Pack it in, Asif.

Daniel clicks his fingers.

– Maybe it should be somethin to do with the Albion. Like how they've got the Three Degrees. But there's five of us.

– The Jackson Five.

– The Famous Five?

– The Fucked-Up Five!

Rolo shouts that out of nowhere and cripples them laughing. It takes them a few minutes to get it together again.

– No, guys, it needs ter be somethin serious.

– Like what?

– Loike... the Allsorts?

Asif nods.

– Nice. What does it mean, ya knob-goblin?

– Well, iss summat me mom allwis says. "It teks all sorts." Loike, evryone's diffrent, but we all live on the same planet an stuff.

They take a minute to digest this.

– The Allsorts. That'll do.

– We could practise now!

– No. Ah cor stop out late.

Mom'll go spanner if he comes home after five again. Since that paperboy was murdered in Stourbridge last month, she's been really strict about it.

– Well, after school tomorrer? How's that?

Christopher nods. That'll do nicely.

The Allsorts will have their first training tomorrow night.

*

There are bad awaydays, and there are worse awaydays. Then there's Leeds United.

It's always trouble. It was trouble in 1971 when Jeff Astle denied Leeds the league title and their fans invaded the pitch, throwing missiles at the linesman and sending death threats to the referee. It was trouble in 1976 too, when Johnny Giles returned there with his newly-promoted Baggies side, and Leeds fans in the upper tier of the away stand started jumping down to fight the Albion support and waiting to ambush them in mobs outside the ground. A lot of Albion fans won't go back; there's just too much trouble around that cold, vicious place.

But at five past three on Saturday afternoon, Matty and Trev are inside a small pen in the corner of the ground, with a couple of hundred others who've caught the special up to Yorkshire, hemmed in on three sides by blue steel fences, with a low wall behind them looking right out onto the junction of Lowfields Road and Elland Road. There are two coppers inside the pen policing the section, and Matty calls down to them, waving his arm at the fences.

– Sorry mate, is this the football ground or the zoo?

The copper eyes him steadily from beneath his domed helmet, and answers in a monotone.

– You'll be grairtful for them fences, lad. Trust me.

~ 207 ~

The whispers have gone round that there's already been trouble in the city centre, in spite of the heavy police escort they had on their way to the ground. Some Leeds kid got battered into the traffic and run over. Elland Road's tense, angry, and the tiny away pen is getting plenty of attention from the home supporters in both adjacent stands. Matty always tells himself he's more interested in football than fighting. He's practically lived up the Brummie Road End since the mid-Sixties, and he's seen all the changes in that time, on and off the pitch; he's followed the Albion up and down the country too, whenever he's had the cash. But he's never been to Elland Road before. He's heard all the stories, and he couldn't resist the temptation. The element of risk is part and parcel of any away trip, and going to Leeds away is a matter of pride. If you can follow your club there, you can follow them anywhere.

It's only when he's inside the pen that he starts to have second thoughts.

It's almost a relief after twenty minutes when Leeds score first. It's a shit goal to concede – a Tony Currie free-kick floats into the box, and Paul Hart's mistimed header falls for Arthur Graham to volley into the bottom corner – but around the terraces, that sense of savage frustration dies down a bit. The Albion players stand with hands on their hips, questioning looks directed at one another. They started the season so well, but recent weeks have been plagued by mistakes and misfortune: three draws and a defeat in September, including that jammy equaliser from Liverpool. A convincing 3-1 win at Stamford Bridge undone by Spurs snatching a 1-0 win at the Hawthorns, Peter Taylor scoring early on the counter then Barry Daines playing a blinder in goal to preserve their lead.

The team needs some confidence, some belief. Everyone does, now and then.

– Come on, Albion! Gerrat em!

The shout from the back of the away pen gets a chorus of jeers and whistles from the Lowfields Stand, but it works. Albion spend the next twenty minutes probing the Leeds defence, working the ball out to the wings and putting crosses in. Matty's opening a new pack of fags just before half-time when the ref blows for a foul on Cunningham. It's a free-kick over on the right-hand touchline, just inside the Leeds half. Batson plays a short ball to Cantello, who chips it across field to Tony Brown, standing thirty yards from goal.

He scored his first senior goal in September 1963, a full year before Matty even set foot inside the Hawthorns. Fifteen years later, he's put away two hundred and eight in the league – the same number that Ronnie Allen scored up front in the Fifties – and all from midfield. His gift for being in the right place at the right time and his knack for unstoppable shots have put Bomber just one goal away from becoming Albion's greatest ever goalscorer.

As Cantello's pass reaches him, Bomber takes one light touch, and with the ball bobbling over the ground in front of him, puts the laces of his right boot through it. In the away pen in the far corner, at the opposite end of the ground, Matty's standing right behind the line of the shot. He sees it rocket from Bomber's foot through a crowd of white-shirted defenders – he's sure it's going to fizz just wide – but it bounces in front of the six yard line, past the glove of David Harvey, strikes the inside of the post and spins into the back of the Leeds net. It's the equaliser. It's the record.

Bomber barely celebrates. He shakes his fist once in triumph, accepts the congratulations of Bryan Robson and John Wile, and trudges back to the Albion half. And the travelling Albion fans barely celebrate either; not after they spot the flood of Leeds fans racing through the empty sections of the South Stand to start climbing the fences. The coppers manage to drag them away and restore order after five or ten minutes, but as Matty and Trev sit down on the terraces at half-time, the tension around Elland Road is back.

The second half is nothing but Leeds pressure down the far end of the pitch. Long, high balls into the penalty area, one after another. One from Byron Stevenson gets flicked on by Eddie Gray on the edge of the Albion box, and Trevor Cherry volleys it left-footed right for the corner of the goal; Matty groans and puts his hands on his head, but Tony Godden springs to his right and touches the shot wide with his fingertips. Minutes later, Brendon Batson slices a clearance with his left foot, spinning it straight to Graham, who blasts a bouncing shot up towards the top corner; a ballboy in a red tracksuit just in front of the away pen leaps to his feet to celebrate a goal, but Godden jumps up like an acrobat and pushes the ball over the bar. Matty knows there's no way Albion can hold out. There's no way they can weather this storm. They're a tiny line of Subbuteo men at the far end of the field, crowded around their own box, trying to preserve a point.

But then, ten minutes from time, they break out. Bomber swings a corner into the six yard box which Currie heads back out to the near side for a throw-in. Bomber throws it to Cantello, who works a quick one-two with Willie Johnston in the centre of the Leeds half and then strokes it out to Batson on the right. Batson plays it short to Johnston and then gets it back on the wing, twisting and turning to dummy Paul Hart, playing a low cross in to the penalty spot which Leeds don't clear, and then Cunningham pounces, laying the ball off to Cyrille Regis in the D, and Regis thunders a shot past Harvey into the corner of the net.

This time, the Leeds fans stay where they are. They turn and stare at Matty and Trev and the hundreds of other Albion fans cheering behind the fences. They stare for a long time: cold and silent as the Albion chants begin.

NICE ONE, CYRILLE
NICE ONE, SON
NICE ONE, CYRILLE
LET'S HAVE ANOTHER ONE

And with three minutes left on the clock, a long clearance from Godden falls for Laurie Cunningham after a mistake in the Leeds defence, and suddenly Cunningham's roving down the right wing with the ball at his feet, two Leeds players trying to mark him, block his route to goal, but Cunningham's running with a dancer's gait, short stuttering steps followed by long, graceful strides, the ball never more than six inches from his toe; with a sudden burst of speed he's round both players, dodging a vicious lunge, at the byline, pulling the ball back for Willie Johnston, who controls the ball with his left foot, putting it right in the path of Regis, who smashes home his second from twelve yards out. It's all over.

And now the real trouble starts.

They stick together and move fast as they leave the ground, all the travelling fans in a herd, looking for natural strength in numbers even with coppers all around them. Clearing the immediate area, marching up Elland Road with the noise of the motorway rising like a tide, Matty can't help a grin; he's ticked Leeds off the list, and no aggro. Why all the fuss?

Then Trev clears his throat.

– Ah need a piss.

Matty shakes his head.

– Hold it.

– Ah cor, mate. Ah'm bostin fer it.

– We'll be at the station in fifteen minutes.

– Fifteen minutes! Ah'll ha pissed meself by then!

– Shoulda gone back at the ground.

It's not the first time this has happened. There's barely a tree, wall or phone box between Brunton Park and the Goldstone Ground that Trev hasn't pissed on, up or in. In fact, Matty's started to wonder whether it isn't part of the fun for Trev on an awayday; he's like a dog marking territory, always eager to do something saft for the occasion. He does it everywhere. He just hasn't done it in Leeds yet.

– Come on. Theer's an alleyway up here.

– Doe do it. Ah'll fuckin leave ya behind this time, Trev.

– Just half a minute.

Hanging back until the police escort can't see him, Trev nips into the cobbled alleyway, behind a cluster of metal dustbins. Matty sighs, leans against the wall of the nearest house and looks up at the grey sky. He waits for the sound of water hitting brick, but there's nothing.

– Trev?

– Soz. Stagefright.

– Hurry up, ya knob.

Matty looks down the road to where the bulk of the Albion fans are turning the corner, heading out of sight. Finally, he hears the telltale sound of a flowing stream behind him, and a groan of satisfaction from Trev. A Vauxhall Cavalier drives past with a white and blue Leeds scarf up in the back window. A mother pushes a pram down the opposite side of the street, the white wheels clattering and catching on the uneven paving slabs. Eventually, the flow dries up in the alleyway, and he hears Trev zipping his fly.

– Cheers. Ya see wheer the others went?

– They turned roit. Less gerra move on.

They trot down the street to the traffic lights at the corner, and turn right.

There's no one there.

They run a short way down the street, to the next junction. Matty can feel his heart starting to gallop, but he keeps his expression plain. If he starts fudging it in front of Trev, he'll never hear the end of it.

– Look, the station'll be this way.

– Ya sure?

– Course ah'm sure.

They wander across the junction and up a steep hill, into a mazy housing estate. The sky's getting dark, streetlights flaring orange as they warm up, and the whole estate's a labyrinth of terraced rows funnelling cold gusts of wind off the moors. Lines of cars are parked up and down the kerbs – Cortinas, Marinas, Minis, Allegros, even the odd Datsun – but there's barely a human being in sight. It's Saturday teatime, and the place is a ghost town. Everywhere they turn, they find the same view of endless houses, tower blocks, vacant industrial estates.

– We'm lost.

– Ah noticed.

– We need directions.

– Wheer from?

Trev points.

– Playground down theer.

At the end of the street there's a play area. It's just a patch of concrete with a leaf-covered slide, and some swings wrapped around the top of their frame, and four lads on Raleigh Choppers wearing jumpers, trousers and tatty shoes – about nine or ten by the look of them – are riding round in circles. Matty wanders down with Trev lighting up next to him.

– Aroit, lads. Which way ter the station?

One of the lads has got a brown cowboy hat on that's too big for him, and he answers, eyeing them carefully from just under the brim.

– You West Brom?

– Nah, we'm the Narnia Intercity Crew. Wheer's the station, mush?

– That Bryan Robson's a good player.

– He is, ar.

– Dawn't think much o them coons, though.

Trev eyeballs the kid.

– Three-one, sunshine. They doe care what ya think. So. Station?

The Chopper Cowboy stares at them sulkily for a few moments, then points them back the way they've come.

They head back down the hill, across the junction. It's pitch-dark now, and they walk past factories and yards, endless yards of steel fences and railings, moving from one circle of streetlight to another. They're almost at the railway line when Matty realises they're being followed.

He's glanced over his shoulder once or twice as they crossed the estate, and seen some lad down the end of the street – no scarf, no football paraphernalia – walking along with his hands in his pockets. He dismissed it and carried on walking. The next time he glanced, there were two lads behind him. Getting closer.

They can see the bridge over the railway just down the road as the first chants start.

YUH-NYE-TID! YUH-NYE-TID!

– Matty.

– Ah know. Keep walkin.

There's no other way. They pick up their pace. If they turn round and face the mob, they'll get slaughtered. Matty doesn't even want to glance back and look at the numbers; there are enough voices back there to tell him they're in trouble.

YUH-NYE-TID! YUH-NYE-TID!

His stomach's heavy, his mind pounding with possibilities, but he still reckons they've got a chance. Matty's been in some difficult spots in the past, at the football and away from it, and he's learned to live by his wits; he's sure they're in with a chance.

Then they reach the bridge, pace up over the slope in its centre, and Matty sees right the way down the road. And he sees a dozen more Leeds boys ahead of them, coming their way.

LEEDS! LEEDS! LEEDS! LEEDS!

Matty and Trev stop in the middle of the bridge, boots thudding on the pavement in front of them and behind them as Leeds close the distance. Matty glances round quickly to look for another escape route, but the mob behind them are already running up the slope – there's about fifteen of the bastards, all eager to be first to the kill – and there's nothing to do now but stand and take it, punch and punch and hope for the best before they hit the ground, curl up and wait for the kicks to stop and the sirens to start.

The pack closes in, the group ahead just five or six yards away, and Trev rushes at them suddenly, without warning, sprinting forward and windmilling his arms. After a second's startled hesitation, Matty dives in to back him up. He puts all his weight behind the first punch, getting this skinhead right round the jaw, and he sees Trev break through the Leeds mob and run down the road with four of them peeling away to chase after him, but Matty's off-balance, and he gets a fist hard in the ribs, and through the pain it comes as a surprise to find himself lying on the cold, wet ground.

There are boots kicking him, and he curls up to protect his head and torso, lying foetus-like in the road. But then the kicks stop, and hands grab hold of him. They lift him up, and he opens his eyes, sees that he's being carried towards the side of the bridge, and with a panicked lurch, he realises what's going to happen. He starts kicking, struggling, screaming.

They dump him on his belly over the concrete side, knocking the wind out of him, and someone grabs his legs and pushes. He kicks out against them, but the hands hold firm, and his head and torso scrape over the bridge, and suddenly he can feel gravity tugging at him, blood rushing up his neck to his cheeks, and he's hanging right over the railway line, thirty feet of air and electric cables between him and the hard, dark sleepers below. He starts to yell, and spit drips out of his mouth and clings to his cheeks and forehead.

His life doesn't flash in front of him. It's all tangled up in there – first day at school, first football, first match, first kiss, first shag – but that's swamped by the broken-record whirling of the words *shouldn't have come here, shouldn't have come here*, and a clear picture of his mom's face, and any other time he'd be ashamed of that, but not now.

Now Matty just wishes he had another day.

There are noises up above, and he feels the hand on his right leg loosen, and he sways to the side, dropping a foot further down, closing his eyes and waiting for the drop, wondering whether he'll feel anything as he hits the rails. Something cuts painfully into his legs, all the way around, and he hears laughter up above. The laughter gets quieter, vanishing into the distance.

With a sickening lurch, he realises that there are no hands holding onto him anymore. The Leeds mob have gone. They've left him hanging off the bridge, upside down, tied tightly by his legs with a thick length of wire.

He starts shouting for help. The minutes are hours. A couple of times it feels like the wire's slipping around his legs, and in those moments everything inside him seems to give way. He's still choking on his fear when he hears running feet above, boots on the pavement, and finally, Trev's voice.

– Lads, he's here! Gi me hand!

There are more agonising seconds for Matty as Trev and two other Albion fans haul him up, getting hold of his legs and pulling hard to get him back over the side, onto the pavement, and then finally he's sitting on his arse on the concrete, his back up against the side of the bridge, breathing hard and way too fast, sucking air in and out of his lungs with heavy puffs. Trev kneels down by him.

– Yow aroit?

He doesn't answer. He doesn't trust his voice not to shake. He keeps his mouth shut and nods. Trev grins.

– Another great escape, eh?

He shivers. Trev gives him a hand getting back to his feet.

– Come on, mate. Less get back home.

The train rumbles through Sheffield, Chesterfield and Derby before slowing to a crawl as they approach Birmingham, passing endless sleepy platforms – Burton, Lichfield, Sutton Coldfield, Erdington, Gravelly Hill, Aston – and finally stopping in the deep tunnels of New Street. Coppers are prowling the station in force – Manchester United were at Villa Park today, and from the looks of the smashed windows in the shopping centre, they've had some fun on the way back – but Matty keeps his head down, same as everyone else, and the plod leave them be. As they get onto the local for Smethwick and sit down on the worn leather seats of the front carriage, sinking down and putting their feet up against the carriage wall, Trev clears his throat awkwardly.

– Sorry about earlier, man.

– Earlier?

– Wantin a piss.

Matty shakes his head.

– Cor help when ya need ter gew.

– But, ya know. Ah dae mean ter gerrus lost.

– Nah.

– An on the bridge an that… ah'd never ha left ya theer. Ya knew that, yeah?

– Course.

– Fuckin Leeds, man. Nutters.

This time, Matty doesn't bother answering, and Trev leaves it alone. That suits him fine. He's only got one thing on his mind now, with home getting closer by the second. After a day like today, there's only one person he'd ever want to see.

After waving goodbye to Trev outside Rolfe Street and walking down the quiet roads behind the station, Matty stops at the shop. The bell jingles as he opens the door, and she's there behind the counter; apron on, her long black hair tied into a plait. She looks up at the sound of the bell, and her sharp brown eyes study him behind fine-rimmed glasses.

– Matt?

– Aasha.

– What have you been doing? Look at you!

– Football.

Her mouth hangs open.

– You ended up like that playing football?

– Not playin. Watchin.

She comes out from behind the counter.

– Do you want to go to hospital? I can give you a lift; Dad'll watch the shop.

– Iss onny a few cuts.

– Your hands are shaking.

– Iss cold out.

– Look, I'm going to call Dad down.

– No, Aasha, doe bring him…

– *Papa-ji!*

– Oh, fer fuck's sake. Ya know woss gunna happen now, doe ya? He wo shut up. Ya know what he's loike.

There's an insistent tapping from the staircase behind him; the sound of a walking stick. Matty closes his eyes.

– Bloody right I won't shut up!

– Aroit, Mr Singh. How's life treatin ya?

– Better than it's treating you, I suspect. What have you done this time?

– I ay done nuthin.

– Matthew, you're a nice boy. You've always been a nice boy. But look at you! Dressing up like one of these hooligans from the television!

Matty breathes in deeply. Mr Singh's been Smethwick's leading expert on football hooliganism ever since he watched a special edition of *Panorama* about it last year.

– Ah'm a football fan. Not a hooligan. Theer is a difference. Iss juss that sometimes, yow atta defend yerself.

– Matthew. You're a bright young man, and you can go very far in life.

– Ar. Ah gew pretty far ter get ter the Job Centre on a Monday mornin.

– Of course, things are difficult for young people now. But they can always change. They can get better, if you have some patience, if you're prepared to work hard.

– Wait, lemme guess: and pray, as well?

– It's up to you whether you pray or not, Matthew. But all this running around and fighting on Saturdays? It won't help you.

– Matt, are you ready?

Aasha's dangling her car keys from her fingers. Matty nods to Mr Singh and touches his fingers to his forehead in a half-hearted salute.

– Aroit then, Mr Singh. Tek care.

– And you, Matthew. Take as much care as you can.

He follows Aasha out to the back of the shop, where her blue Austin Maxi's parked in the alley. She turns her key in the lock, climbs into the drivers' seat and leans over to pull up the lock on the passenger door. Matty gets in, the leather squeaking beneath him as he sits down, and shutting the door behind him, he turns to face her.

He won't be going to hospital. He knows that as well as she does. It's a familiar ritual with different excuses every time, but always the same result.

They're careful to check the mirrors and windows, making sure the alleyway's free from prying eyes before they kiss.

November 1978

– Mrs Collier! Mrs COLLIER!

– What is it, Alison?

– Miss, Terry's pretendin the fire hose is his willy, miss!

Jude turns round to see Terry Taylor – a spotty herbert of fourteen with a crop of short, spiky dark hair – waving the enormous red hose that's tucked in the back of his trousers and flopped out of his unzipped fly at the front to a crowd of screaming, giggling third-year girls in the middle of the hall.

– Ring the exorcist! Iss me possessed todger! Iss gorra mind of iss own! Someone grab hold of it!

– Terry.

– Becky, come an gi us an hand, eh? It needs a good hard yank ter gerrit under control!

– TERRY!

Becky Hall flushes the deepest shade of scarlet Jude's ever seen in a face, and holds her palms up to her open mouth. She couldn't make it more obvious how much she fancies Terry if she tried. They're too young. They're all just too bloody young.

– Terry, if you're struggling with feelings of sexual inadequacy, I can always make time to discuss it with you after school.

He squirms at her faux-sympathetic tone, and Jude feels a quick stab of guilt at how satisfying that reaction is.

– Nah, miss.

– In which case, could you remove all of the school property you have stuffed down your trousers now, please?

The other lads in class snigger, and Terry smirks to them as he starts reeling the hose back out of his groin.

– Put it where it belongs, Terry. Do I have your full attention, 3C? You've all opted for Drama this year. Does anyone have any experience of acting?

A few hands go up hesitantly, at a variety of diagonal angles.

– Alison, what role did you play?

– Angel a the Lord.

– Excellent. And get rid of that gum, please. Nigel?

– A Roman soldier, miss.

– Anyone have any speaking roles?

Terry slouches back from the fire hose and idly puts his arm up, tilting his head to one side at the same time.

– Terry?

– Ah was in an Easter play in the infants, miss. Ah played a singin egg.

– Right. Well, that's something we can build on. Anyone else?

Silence. Sullen stares from teenage faces. Jude fights back a yawn. She was up earlier than usual this morning, queuing at the grocer's for a couple of loaves before the bakers' strike empties the shelves, then checking in on her parents, seeing if Dad was any better. Taking 3C for Drama is insult to injury for a tired, stressed mind.

– Miss, what play am we gunna do?

– Well, that depends. I thought I'd take some suggestions from you.

She tries to keep the note of dread out of her voice. She'd considered a few potential choices for the production – *A Midsummer Night's Dream*, maybe *The Importance Of Being Earnest* – but forcing Shakespeare or Wilde onto the volatile minds of 3C seemed a recipe for Terry-induced disaster. Late last night, she decided in frustration to just give them the choice. In a wild burst of optimism, she thought it might even encourage them to involve themselves.

That optimism evaporates as she gazes at the quiet class.

Lisa Murphy puts her hand up.

– Miss, does it have ter be a play already written?

– It does help if we have a script to perform from, Lisa.

– But we could do a play of our own. Write the scenes ourselves.

Jude blinks. In the barren intellectual desert of 3C, that idea is an unexpected oasis.

– Excellent. But you'll need to decide what the play will be about.

The class start to murmur, and there are a few giggles and titters from the back as some lewd suggestions are passed along in whispers. Then Terry speaks up.

– Do one abaht the local area!

– Okay, good. Anything specific?

She hopes someone will suggest the industrial history of the region. It's something she's got plenty of books on, and she can steer them in the right direction. But Terry surprises her with his second idea of the day.

– How abaht the Albion? They'm a hundred years old next year!

A murmur of assent ripples through the class.

– Football's not a strong point of mine.

– We'll taych ya, miss! Yow can learn us how tew act, we'll learn yow abaht the Baggies!

Jude thinks carefully.

– Alright then. A play about the history of West Bromwich Albion. Does anyone know anything about the club?

Hands shoot into the air all over the room.

It's a good start. Better than she'd dared hope.

*

Bill's seen more home matches down the years than he can count. He's stood to watch games, and he's sat down to watch them. He's been in every stand and corner around the ground, seen the action from every possible angle. But over the last few months, watching matches in the same place he stood as a lad, he's come to realise something.

Nowhere feels more like home than the Brummie Road End.

Nowhere else outside of his own house offers him the same kind of comfort and familiarity. No matter how many things change over the years, it's still filled with the same faces, the same accents. Men who work the same jobs, drink in the same pubs. Men who share memories of matches stretching back for decades. Walking out onto the Brummie Road terraces at two o'clock on a Saturday afternoon is diving into everyday Black Country life. You hear about some kids these days choosing to support clubs from other cities, attaching themselves to Liverpool or Arsenal so they can cheer goals by Kenny Dalglish or Liam Brady on Match of the Day, covering their wall in posters and clippings of the fashionable clubs the newspapers and magazines devote pages and pages to, but the fact is that these kids are lost in a world where they'll never really belong. They'll never stand on the terraces surrounded by voices just like their own, kiss their hand and tap the exit sign on their way out with thousands of other blokes doing the same, no matter what the result, leaving part of themselves in this sacred place until the next time.

It's all come pouring back into his mind since Jonah's joined him and Christopher on Saturday afternoons. Over the last two months, Jonah's dodgy predictions and dreams of future glory have become as much a part of the Saturday routine as a morning fry-up, *Sports Report* after the match, Chinese for tea and Jimmy Hill rounding up the day's action before bed.

The Jonah Box is well and truly open. And today, it's in a good mood.

– Get a bit a momentum gewin, the sky's the limit fer us this year!

He makes the announcement as they shuffle towards the exit. Christopher's enthralled. He hasn't learned yet.

– D'ya reckon?

– Course. See the way we took em apart fust half? Should have had three or four.

Except they didn't get three or four. They managed one goal through a Bomber penalty after Brendon Batson got hacked down in the area running onto a Cunningham through-ball, and the packed Brummie Road End expected the floodgates to open with scarves waving and flags flying, same as they did against Coventry last month. But instead, Villa fought back. And Villa snatched an equaliser through Allan Evans. And after five wins in their last six league games, closing the gap on Everton and Liverpool at the top of the table, Albion have dropped a crucial point at home.

But listening to Jonah carry on, you'd think they were all set to do the double.

– Tek no notice of him, Chris. Jonah, stop gerrin his hopes up.

– Ah was roit abaht Wembley, wor I? Abaht Astle winnin the cup?

– Ten years agew!

– Well, iss time fer me ter be roit abaht summat else then, ay it?

They fall into silence after that, walking through the exit and down towards the gates. Mentioning the cup final in '68 brings back memories of more than just Astle's goal. As Christopher goes off to the toilet, Bill scrambles for a subject to change to. He falls back on a tried and tested option.

– Pub?

It's become another part of the routine, ever since that first afternoon they saw Jonah on the terraces before kick-off, wrapped up in his leather jacket and scarf, a bottle of Skol and a fag on the go. He parks his Cortina down Halfords Lane on matchdays, and to save them getting the bus, he always gives Bill and Chris a lift down the pub where they can sit on the wall of the car park with a pint apiece – Christopher happy with a bottle of Vimto and a packet of smoky bacon crisps – and catch up. And there's been plenty to catch up on. Jonah may not have changed into a whole new man over the last decade, but one disastrous marriage and an urge to get out and see the world have made a mark on Jonah as clear as the lines on his face and the flesh around his jaw.

He doesn't take them home when they're done chatting, though. Bill won't risk Jude seeing the strange car through the window, finding out who he spends Saturdays with these days. He'll tell her at some point; break it to her gently. But not now. Not with all the stress from her job, and her dad being ill. He's doing the compassionate thing.

– Cor do the pub today, Bill. Got company.

– "Company", eh? Anyone ah know?

~ 220 ~

– Not bloody loikely. Hang around wi many film stars, do ya?

– Ah doe need ter knock around wi film stars ter know they doe gew gallivantin up West Brom wi Johnny Cartwright of a Satdee night.

– Well, future film star, anyway.

– All set fer a career in the blueys, is her?

– Course not. Her's got class. Works in an office, an evrythin! Till her gets noticed by one a them Hollywood talent scouts, obviously.

– Obviously. Well, best a luck, mate. Remember: the path ter true love never runs smooth.

– Ah doe want true love, mucka. Bin theer, done that, got the divorce papers. A night a fun an frolics'll do me fine.

– Yow ay tempted ter gi it another gew? If ya meet the roit girl, ah mean? Settle down, start a family?

– Am yow tempted ter gi Jude the elbow an live a life a freedom? Ah mean, ya must wonder what iss loike after all this time, eh? Some other wench must catch yer eye now an then?

That tone in his voice, that note of mischief. The old Jonah, there for just a second.

– Jonah, doe start. Ah love Jude. Allwis have.

– Ah'm onny pullin yer leg.

– Well doe.

– Yome happy wi yer missis, ah'm happy wi me freedom. Thass how it is.

– Fair enough.

Bill nods, Jonah's words floating idly through his mind: *some other wench must catch yer eye now an then?* He's sure he didn't give anything away. No guilty expression, no strenuous denial. It's just Jonah being Jonah; he couldn't really know anything. And besides, it's not like Bill's really done anything wrong. Just a smile and a joke at the end of a working day; a bit of sweet talk to prove he's still got some charm left in him.

Christopher joins them, and they walk outside. Jonah turns left at the corner, heading down Halfords Lane.

– Stay out a trouble, yow pair!

– Have a good un tonight, pal.

– Bye, Uncle Jonah!

Bill winces as he hears that, but he doesn't tell Chris off. Uncle or not, Jonah's a part of his life again. A part of Chris's life, too.

They shuffle their way down the Birmingham Road with the crowd, past the van selling burgers and hot dogs, and spot a bloke with long hair and a thick moustache wearing a check shirt with sleeves rolled up to his elbows, a union badge pinned to his lapel, a stack of posters cradled in his arm.

– Free posters! Cyrille Regis! Free posters!

Christopher manages to snag one as they walk by, and it's a thick wedge. He opens up the poster; there's a book wrapped inside.

– Dad, woss this?

It's a slim book with a hard red cover, completely plain.

– Ah doe know, mate. Check inside.

Tucking the poster under his arm, Chris opens the book and traces his finger across the print on the inlay page.

– "The Manifesto a the Communist Party. K. Marx an F. Engels."

– Ah doe think thass yower sort a thing, Chris. T'ay as good as *Roy a the Rovers*.

– Should ah throw it away?

– Nah. Stick it away somewheer safe. Yer mom loikes this sort a thing. Might mek a nice Christmas present.

Wrapping his scarf tight round his neck, feeling the warmth thick in the twelve-year-old wool, Bill wanders into the night with Christopher's hand tight in his own.

December 1978

Winter creeps over the Black Country. It inches its way across the land: morning snow coating meadows where gypsy horses tug against icy tethers; braziers lit outside factories each morning, flooding light and warmth over donkey jackets and overalls; fogged-up windows grimy with layers of industrial frost. With a molten sun low in the sky, the canals freeze quickly, reflecting millions of headlights and streetlamps; soft decorations on the hardest of landscapes.

In the night, in the cold, they wait on Halfords Lane. In the early Christmas chill, they huddle outside the Hawthorns with their autograph books and World Cup memorabilia. Waiting to see those faces. Those faces which belong on television and in magazines. Those faces which belong to another world, a glamorous shore far from this concrete darkness.

Those faces here in West Bromwich, tonight.

Their training session finished, the Valencia players walk out onto the street. There's a surge to be first to get to them, the first to get the autograph of Mario Kempes or Rainer Bonhof. Football's rock stars, beamed into living rooms around the world for those few brief weeks in the summer, capturing imaginations amid streams of ticker tape; then gone so abruptly, lost from television screens, never to be seen by English eyes again.

Until the third round of the UEFA Cup.

Until Valencia were drawn against West Bromwich Albion.

In the cold night, in the Black Country winter.

*

It begins in the changing room before kick-off, the smell of old sweat, deodorant and Brylcreem clinging to the walls, bits and pieces of old kit slung into dusty, forgotten corners. They gather round, huddle above the sacred packet, and say the words together.

Chicken crisps, you give us life.
Chicken crisps, you give us sustenance.
Chicken crisps: give us victory.

All footballers have their superstitions, and the Allsorts are no different. They performed the Ritual of the Chicken Crisps for the first time last month, after Rolo's emergency bag of Smiths fell out of his pocket onto the changing room floor before a match, and Asif suddenly fell down on his knees and started worshipping it, shouting *all praise Rolo's god!* until they were clutching their bellies, paralysed with laughter.

Then, when they'd stopped laughing, they went out and hammered some team from Dudley 4-0.

They haven't stopped winning since, so the chicken crisps come out now before every single match. Christopher always grins as they do the ritual – it's just a bit of saftness, really – but it's *their* saftness. And that's what counts. That's what makes you a team.

Because they may not be the best footballers in the league – even in the nine-to-eleven age group there are more talented kids running round the school hall on Wednesday nights – but the Allsorts have managed to outdo them, playing to their strengths. Playing for the fun of it. Playing as a team. And somehow, they've worked their way up to second in the table; just Christopher, Rajinder, Daniel, Asif, Rolo and a packet of chicken crisps. They're two points off the top; two points behind Bilston Rangers.

Bilston Rangers, who are waiting out in the hall for them tonight.

Rolo puts the chicken crisps away, tucking them safely into his bag, and they walk out through the narrow corridor with its peeling plaster and dirty tiles into the hall where the wide, low indoor goals have been set up, and the Bilston lads are standing by their goal in white shirts and blue shorts, whispering to one another, glancing up as the Allsorts arrive. Christopher doesn't like the expressions on their faces. They look the same way Funnyfarm always does when he's about to make an example of someone.

It's not long before they find out why. Within sixty seconds of kick-off, one of them hacks Rajinder down just below the knee, and another backhands Asif round the jaw as he spins round, pretending it's an accident. Neither gets a booking. The referee – a grey-haired old bloke with a pot belly and thin, hairy legs – blows his whistle and shakes his head.

– Now then, lads, let's all just play fair, shall we?

We AM playin fair, Christopher wants to shout. The Allsorts haven't done anything wrong. They're here to play football, here to enjoy themselves the way they always do, but the Rangers are here to win. And within minutes of clattering Asif and Raj, they're 2-0 up; their striker, this big lad with thick black hair and braces on his teeth, gets round Christopher and places the ball in the bottom corner with his instep. As the Allsorts kick off again, their keeper starts yelling from his goal, firing them up, and they get even more vicious. When Christopher gets caught on the ball by their midfielder, he gets a sharp elbow right in his ribs, and turns to the ref with angry tears behind his eyes as the bastard scores one-on-one against Rolo.

They have to stick together. It's the only way. At half-time, Christopher calls the others over. He doesn't know what he's going to say. He wonders what John Wile or Ron Atkinson would say to the Albion players in this position. But as they huddle round in a five-man circle, he realises it doesn't matter. Albion are a different team with different players. What matters are his own teammates, and Christopher knows them better than anyone.

– New plan fer the second half, lads. They'm playin rough, we've gorra play rougher. Time ter bring out the secret weapon.

They stare at him, four puzzled faces. He turns to Rolo.

– If I hold em down, Rolo, ya reckon yow can pump out five a yer killer farts?

They collapse into sniggers. Rolo grins.

– I ay got that many stored up, Chris.

– Well, in that case we'd best have a gew at bein better than them. Cos we *am* better. It teks Allsorts, lads. It teks Allsorts.

They murmur it after him – *it teks Allsorts* – and then line up for the second half.

And the difference is there straight away; the Rangers are sitting back, confident they've done enough to win it, and they give the Allsorts space to play. They pass the ball around the Bilston boys, make them do the running, always looking for that bit of room, and it opens up beautifully as Rajinder gets the ball from Asif in the middle of the hall, sees Daniel making a run for goal, and he plays the through-ball which Daniel traps with his right foot, brings onto his left and then hammers in off the post. They're back in it.

The Rangers turn nasty again. As the minutes tick down and they drop deeper to defend their one-goal lead, they start hacking at Daniel's legs and barging into Rajinder when he tries dribbling down the wing, but this time the ref actually does something about it. With a free-kick fifteen yards from goal on the left-hand side of the hall, Asif stands over the ball, with Daniel and Rajinder goalhanging, surrounded by the whole Bilston team, and Christopher waiting in the centre of the hall, ready for a counter-attack. Asif chips the ball up, Daniel manages to shake off the two Bilston lads marking him and gets his forehead to it, but it's a weak glancing header which falls to one of the Rangers defenders, who thumps it clear up the hall.

And it comes to Christopher, on the halfway line. He can't believe they've thrown the match away after playing so well in the second half, after *deserving* to be level, and as the ball bounces in front of him, instead of passing it back across to Asif, he gets his head down, swings his right foot and absolutely leathers it.

There are plenty of reasons why it ends up where it does. For one, with his goalmouth packed full of bodies, their keeper doesn't see it coming till the last second. For another, it takes a deflection off a defender's leg on the way which probably stops it from flying just wide. But none of that matters. None of it matters to Christopher when his shot flies past the goalie's hand, and ripples the back of the net like a breeze.

He stands still for a second, his mouth open. It's only when a thick arm wraps itself around his neck and he feels Rolo jumping up and down behind him, and Asif and Rajinder and Daniel come running over screaming and cheering him that he realises it's really happened. He's snatched the equaliser with seconds left.

He tries to stay calm. He tries to shrug it off, act like it's all in a day's work, the way Roy Race would after smashing a fifty-yarder into the top corner to win the cup for Melchester.

But he's not Roy Race, and this definitely isn't Melchester.

– *GET IN YOU BEAUTYYYY! YOOOOU'RE NOT SINGIN ANYMORE!*

The Rangers glare daggers at him as they kick off again, but he just can't keep the grin off his face. As the ref blows the whistle for full-time, he feels like he's floating a foot off the ground. And of course, the best part is still to come; they've only drawn the match, but because of Christopher's goal they're still unbeaten, and they have to do it. It's become a routine, a tradition.

It's time for the Allsorts Dance.

As the Rangers team stand with their hands on their hips, shaking their heads, the Allsorts form a line in the middle of the hall, wave their arms up and down singing *WE ARE THE ALLSORTS, WE ARE THE ALLSORTS*, then spin round and then slap their arses at the Rangers, chanting *WE SPANKED YOU! WE SPANKED YOU!*

That does it. The ref blows his whistle and starts herding them back to the changing room, and parents are running over to hold back the Bilston boys who are pointing at them and yelling all kinds of abuse, but the Allsorts are laughing, laughing all the way out.

They're still laughing in the car park when Uncle Jonah pulls up in his Cortina, with Dad in the passenger seat. Normally they go back to someone's house after a match – it's always best round Rolo's, where they can get the Subbuteo out of the loft and have a cup competition – but tonight's special. There have been a few special nights for Christopher already this autumn, but this is the first one he'll be spending with his team.

The Allsorts are going to see the best players in the world.

Watching a match on a schoolnight has always been a rare treat. Most of the time he listens to evening games on his portable radio, stretching the aerial out to its full length and pushing his David Bowie cassettes out of the way to make space for the set on his bedside table. Then he rests his head on the pillow as Tony Butler's voice fills the room, telling everyone to get their prayer mats out when things are going badly, and yelling *hail Atkinson, hail Addison, hail Albion!* when they win. Sometimes Dad comes in and sits at the foot of his bed to listen if it's a really good game – he always tells Christopher it reminds him of the 1966 World Cup, seeing him in bed with the radio on, though he never says why – and they'll be there for an hour or two in near-silence, ears cocked to the speaker, sharing the commentary like a brolly on a rainy Saturday.

The UEFA Cup's different. This is the first time Albion have been in a European competition for ten years, and Christopher didn't even need to pester Dad to see the foreign teams coming to the Hawthorns. They saw Galatasaray together in September, when Christopher took a Union Jack along to wave during the match – though Dad ended up holding it when his arms got tired – and they saw Sporting Braga in October, when they went up the Smethwick End for the first time and got stuck behind some old Portuguese bloke who kept raising his arms and shouting *oooohaaaa* whenever Braga managed a shot on goal. They beat both sides comfortably home and away. But then the third round draw pitted them against Valencia.

The end of the road for Albion.

With Kempes and Bonhof at the heart of their team, and some of the most talented young players in Spain around them, Valencia are Europe's rising stars. They're the strongest team in the competition, and easily the favourites to lift the trophy in April. Even Uncle Jonah was downbeat about the first leg a fortnight ago – *it'll be all over fore they come here; they'll rip us apart at their place, they will* – and listening to the radio commentary that night, Christopher thought he was right. They were 1-0 down within a quarter of an hour when Tony Godden palmed a curling Valencia corner awkwardly into the air, and Dario Felman headed in from a yard out as the ball dropped back down. The Albion players were being pelted with oranges and tangerines by the local fans whenever they went to take throw-ins or corners; the entire Estadio Luis Casanova was screaming for a rout, and the home team settled back for a comfortable game.

And then they met Laurie Cunningham.

Laurie ran at Valencia. Laurie drove Valencia back. Laurie turned Valencia inside out. Laurie caught the attention of all Spain with his speed, his balance, his grace. Even listening on the radio, Christopher could picture him dancing down the wing, running rings around the Spanish defenders, and when he smashed home the equaliser just after half-time, Christopher jumped around his bedroom, hugging Dad and bouncing up and down until Mom came and shouted at them for making the lights flicker downstairs.

It finished 1-1 after Laurie had terrorised Valencia for another half an hour, all of the fruit from the terraces now being hurled at him alone, and not a single one coming close to him. And before he switched his light off that night, Christopher gazed up at the now-familiar poster on his wall with a warm surge of pride. Because of all the heroes treading all the football pitches in Europe, there's no one like his.

When he's got his eye on the ball and clear space ahead of him, death itself can't catch Laurie Cunningham.

– Aroit theer, mate! Iss... nah, doe tell me. Iss Daniel, ay it? Hey, how's God gerrin on? Is he wearin his Albion scarf tonight?

The first surprise of the evening is finding out that Uncle Jonah already knows Daniel and his dad; when Christopher asks him about it in the car, Jonah just says that he saved Daniel from the lion's den a while ago. Even Dad looks confused by that. But it isn't the last surprise of the evening.

Far from it.

They set off for the Hawthorns: Christopher, Dad and Asif in Jonah's lime-green Cortina and Daniel, Rajinder and Rolo in the red Allegro with Daniel's dad. Uncle Jonah switches the radio on as they head into West Bromwich, and with the car heater on the blink, they sit there shivering while some bloke sings about getting hit with a rhythm stick. As they approach the ground, they slow down to a crawl, and then stop. Jonah rubs the windscreen with a cloth and slumps back in the driver's seat.

– Bloody Nora.

The traffic's a thick clot inching through a sluggish flow of supporters, thousands of them traipsing down the Birmingham Road with the pavements already too full to walk on and the road getting more and more clogged. It takes half an hour just to crawl down Halfords Lane to a parking space, and as they lock the car doors and step out into the cutting night air, Christopher starts to wonder whether they'll get into the ground at all tonight. He can't even imagine how it would feel to have to head home and listen on the radio now, after being so close. After waiting so long.

Dad wraps his brown suede jacket tight around him and pulls on his woolly blue hat as they head for the Brummie Road gates, walking past a few Spaniards on the way who are offering a gulp from their bloated wineskins to Albion supporters. They spot Daniel and his dad with Rajinder and Rolo up by the Halfords Corner – Daniel's dad says they parked in town and walked down rather than try and drive through the crowds – and as a group, they join the nearest turnstile queue.

Rolo's shivering even in spite of his thick anorak and scarf. Christopher gives him a quick pat on the back.

– Iss aroit, mate. Iss fine.

Rolo nods and smiles weakly, but his eyes are still wide and nervous. When they were planning this trip last week, he told Christopher he went up the Brummie Road once last season and got knocked over in a surge near the front after a David Cross goal, lying face down on the terraces with his body angled downward and hundreds of blokes treading on his back. They all did their best to shift their weight as they flooded over him, steering themselves to either side, planting at least one foot on concrete rather than flesh; they pulled him to his feet again as quickly as they could, but he ended up cut and grazed, his back bruised all shades of purple and blue, shaking and crying down the front of the stand.

He's stayed up the Woodman Corner ever since.

– It'll be safe this time. Yam with us.

But looking all around them, even Christopher's not sure whether it'll be safe tonight. The queues are longer than he's ever seen before; there's no way everyone can fit inside the ground, no way at all. He crosses his fingers as they shuffle forward slowly. He keeps them crossed as they make it into the gates, through the turnstiles, into the Brummie Road End.

But he can't believe what he sees when he gets out onto the terraces.

There's still an hour to go till kick-off and the ground's full, bursting with fans, with thousands more behind them trying to get in. They push their way down towards the front, but soon it's too packed for them to move any further – too packed for Christopher to go and buy his usual bag of Smax off the snack bloke – and they settle for standing behind a crush barrier a few rows up. The air reeks of beer and Bovril, and they're engulfed in a bitter mist of fag-smoke. Blokes are pissing into empty beer bottles where they stand – you can smell it in the cold air, all the bottles that have spilled – and still the bodies keep piling into the Brummie Road.

It's freezing cold, but Christopher's already sweating in the crush, steam rising off the bodies all around him.

The boot boys up the back of the stand start drumming the soles of their Dr Martens against the metal sheeting behind them, sending a rolling wall of noise echoing through the eaves and down the terraces to the pitch. Christopher often sneaks glances up towards the back, looking to see all the older lads up there. He's fascinated by them. He's afraid of them. He imagines being up there one day in a polished pair of boots and turned-up jeans, making the noise, starting the chants, being mates with them, being one of them. Then he imagines them picking on him, taking the piss out of him, or getting hurt in one of their goal celebrations, trampled on the terraces like Rolo. He wants danger, but he wants to be safe. He wants to be someone new, but he wants to stay the same. It's easy enough to live out those choices in your head, but what about when it comes to making them for real? How do you know what's right?

He looks over at Rolo, who's pale and quiet, and when Rolo looks back, Christopher gives him the thumbs up.

At least when your mates are with you, you know exactly who you are.

With a bit of help from the grown-ups, the Allsorts manage to perch up on the crush barriers, sitting in a line, up out of the hot clamour all around as they wait for kick-off. The minutes drag by, Christopher stares at every last little thing in the stadium to take his mind off the waiting – the stick-figure silhouettes of folk in the entrances up the back of the Rainbow Stand, the pinprick orange points of lit cigarettes in the shadows, the advertising boards for Metalrax Engineering, Ledra Steel, PJ Evans Cars – and then finally, the noise slowly builds from all around the ground as *The Liquidator* crackles from the tannoy, and the players file out of the Halfords Lane Stand. There's a spontaneous ripple of applause through the Brummie Road as Mario Kempes shakes hands with John Wile and they exchange club pennants in the centre-circle. Then the applause turns to song, louder than Christopher's ever heard.

AL-BI-ON, AL-BI-ON, AL-BI-ON!

His stomach's tight with excitement – he almost feels sick with it – but he forces himself to stay calm, watch the action, wait for Albion to put Valencia to the test.

Within five minutes, they do.

Albion win a free-kick just over the halfway line over by the Halfords Lane; Derek Statham launches it long and high from the flank into the penalty area, and Ally Brown just manages to get his head to it and flick it on. There are no Albion players on hand to pounce, but as the Valencia centre-half tries to control the bouncing ball with his chest, it spins up onto his arm instead.

HANDBALL!

The sound of forty thousand throats yelling the same thought. And the referee blows his whistle. He points to the penalty spot.

Bomber stands over the ball, staring at it, his tongue curling out the corner of his mouth, refusing to make eye contact with the Valencia keeper. The entire Brummie Road End, packed in close and tight, shifts from one foot to another, anxious, tense.

Bomber runs up.

Bomber smashes it right-footed into the bottom corner.

And the second the ball hits the net, the flags are flying, the banners are waving; there's no surge, not this time, because there's just no space on the terraces, but everyone has their scarves up, and everyone's shouting and singing. Even the WPC patrolling the track in front of the stand is clapping her hands and adding her voice to the roar as Bomber runs off to celebrate with the rest of the players down by the Woodman Corner.

It's one of those nights. Christopher can feel it. It's one of those nights when the whole ground may as well be thinking with one mind, singing with one voice. A few Valencia fans are trying their best in the Smethwick Corner, with one of their supporters banging a drum to let their players know they're there, but they don't stand a chance here.

Not in the Black Country. Not tonight.

They're singing and swaying as Bryan Robson chips the ball from the left wing to the edge of the box, and Cantello brings it down from knee-height on the run, chases the ball to the byline and spins round to put in a cross. They're singing and swaying as Cabral clears the cross high into the air and it bombs straight down to the right boot of Laurie Cunningham, who traps it with a single deft flick. They're singing and swaying as Cunningham knocks an inch-perfect ball to the far post for Cyrille Regis to volley under the keeper, and Bomber runs in on the loose ball to tap in.

They're booing and whistling as the linesman flags Bomber offside.

They're booing and whistling again in the second half when the other linesman flags Statham offside as he turns in a rebound after Bomber's shot hits the post. But minutes later, they're chanting Cyrille Regis's name as he gets his head to a square ball from Cunningham.

They're chanting his name as it drifts past a watching defender and stranded goalie. They're chanting his name as it hits the post and rebounds back for the keeper to snatch.

And they're holding their breath as Valencia get a free-kick up the Brummie Road End, on the left-hand side. They're holding their breath as Mario Kempes stands over it. They're holding their breath as they face the possibility that Valencia could still snatch a draw, could still force the game to a penalty shoot-out. They're holding their breath as Kempes hammers a furious, curling left-footed shot at goal, and Tony Godden springs seven or eight feet to his right from a standing position and parries it out to safety.

ONE TONY GODDEN!
THEER'S ONLY ONE TONY GODDEN!
ONE TONY GOOOODDEN!

They're singing a hymn ten minutes from time. They're singing a hymn they once sang as a joke during Albion's first-ever Sunday match a few years ago. They're singing a hymn as Cunningham picks up the ball on the right and runs at Angel Castellanos. They're singing a hymn as Cunningham skips past the full-back's tired lunge and reaches the byline. They're singing a hymn as he puts a low cross right into the middle of the box, and Bomber volleys it first-time across goal into the bottom left-hand corner.

They're singing a hymn.

THE LORD'S MY SHEPHERD, AH'LL NOT WANT;
HE MEKS ME DOWN TEW LIE
IN PASTURES GREEN; HE LEADETH ME
THE QUIET WATERS BY

When the referee blows for full-time, the howl of triumph around the Hawthorns bewilders a few Valencia players, who stare around them in disbelief. They don't understand how they've lost here tonight. They've been beaten by a team with strength – the strength of Bryan Robson to keep Bonhof shackled all match, the strength of Laurie Cunningham to beat frozen Spanish full-backs in a harsh Midland night – but they've also been beaten by a team with belief; the kind of belief which comes from having forty thousand people united in support of you.

Christopher will never forget that sound. He walks out of the Brummie Road End with his ears ringing, knowing he'll still hear that noise when he's lying in bed, and at school tomorrow, and knowing that it's worth it. Now he knows what a good team needs to succeed. He looks at the rest of the Allsorts, chattering away nineteen to the dozen as they shuffle their way through the thick crowd back towards the car, and he smiles.

The quarter-finals aren't until March, but if Albion carry on playing like this, then surely the trophy's theirs. Surely.

*

Christmas is cold, wet, barren. It's *Mary's Boy Child* on the radio every five minutes. It's Margot Fonteyn appealing on behalf of the Samaritans. It's Angela Rippon in a plain white blouse reporting protests against the Shah in Iran. It's a few brave souls caroling on doorsteps, and pissed-up crowds having rowdy singsongs down the pub. It's a sleepless night spent remembering old mistakes. It's a good belt of whisky in a mug of morning coffee. It's John Wayne killing Red Indians by the dozen. It's Noel Edmonds introducing Boney M and Showaddywaddy on *Top of the Pops*. It's dry turkey, hard sprouts, thick lumpy gravy. It's the queen addressing the people of the United Kingdom and the Commonwealth. It's Frank Spencer learning to fly. It's Eric and Ernie on ITV.

It's an endless crawl of loneliness.

It's a three o'clock kick-off at Old Trafford on the thirtieth of December. It's thousands of boots tramping through snowy Salford streets with the bus drivers on strike. It's mud on the pitch and thugs in the stands. It's the Stretford End booing Albion players for setting foot on Manchester United's turf. It's the Stretford End booing three Albion players for setting foot on Manchester United's turf with black skin.

It's snow by the corner flags and frost on the crush barriers. It's Brian Greenhoff opening the scoring after twenty minutes with a right-footed volley past Tony Godden into the top corner.

It's 1-0 to Manchester United.

It's a United attack breaking down after a misplaced McIlroy pass. It's Len Cantello playing a one-two with Ally Robertson. It's Cantello twisting and turning, assessing his options, and stroking a pass out left to Derek Statham. It's Statham setting off up the wing, playing it infield to Ally Brown, getting it back, knocking it to Laurie Cunningham in space, who hugs the touchline with nothing but green grass ahead of him. It's the United fans making monkey noises at Cunningham. It's Cunningham sliding a pass along the edge of the area; it's Bryan Robson stepping over the ball with a quick feint; it's Bomber running in and hooking a left-foot shot round the leg of McQueen, past Gary Bailey and into the bottom corner.

~ 233 ~

It's 1-1.

It's Cunningham chipping a ball into the centre-circle sixty seconds later, where a United head nods it straight to Bryan Robson. It's Robson skipping a challenge and finding Cunningham again. It's Cunningham driving infield from the left wing, running at the red shirts ahead of him. It's Steve Coppell sticking a leg in, but Cunningham keeping his feet; it's David McCreery lunging in, but Cunningham sidestepping him like a dancer. It's Laurie Cunningham twenty-five yards from goal with Greenhoff and Thomas shoulder-to-shoulder in his path, both stooped forward, eyes cemented on the ball at his feet, waiting for the dummy, waiting for the trickery.

It's Laurie Cunningham slipping a simple pass between the two hypnotised defenders for Cyrille Regis to trap. It's Regis backheeling the ball into the middle of the box. It's Len Cantello running in and blasting it into the roof of the net.

It's 2-1 to Albion.

It's fresh snow whirling in the air. It's a United free-kick by the corner flag, played high into the area by Stewart Houston. It's Gordon McQueen unmarked just outside the six-yard box, heading a close-range equaliser past Godden.

It's the third goal in three minutes. It's 2-2.

It's Bryan Robson getting caught in possession after a stray pass from Batson leaves him off-balance. It's Sammy McIlroy dummying his way into the box and scoring. It's just over half an hour of the match gone, and it's 3-2 to United.

It's nearly half-time. It's Batson taking a throw-in midway through the United half, on the right touchline. It's Robson knocking a left-footed ball infield to Statham near the centre circle. It's Statham lifting a high ball to the edge of the box, Cantello flicking it on, McCreery trying to volley it clear but slicing his left foot through thin air, and Robson poking the loose ball into the six-yard box. And it's Bomber pouncing, prodding a shot under Gary Bailey, turning away with fists clenched in triumph as the ball trickles over the line.

It's half-time. It's 3-3.

It's hot Bovril and lukewarm pies held by numb fingers. It's coppers stamping their feet by the fences to get their blood flowing. It's Gary Bailey walking down to take his place in goal at the Scoreboard End for the second half, gesturing to the frozen fans that he's lost count of the score.

It's a dark sky over Manchester and dark shadows on the pitch. It's Albion controlling the game, moving the ball around swiftly, passing with precision on turf that's pocked and furrowed. It's Cunningham

~ 234 ~

breaking up the wing, darting through gaps and riding wild tackles. It's Cyrille Regis hammering a first-time shot for the top corner, and Gary Bailey sailing through the air to snatch the ball with both hands just before it crosses the line.

It's Tony Godden launching a long left-footed kick downfield which bounces in the centre circle. It's Regis heading the ball on for Cunningham to chase. It's Houston and Buchan trying desperately to hack Cunningham down as he runs through on goal. It's Cunningham keeping his feet and slamming the ball low past Bailey into the bottom corner.

It's 4-3 to Albion.

It's a throw-in from McIlroy to Coppell in the Albion half. It's Coppell turning near the corner flag, trying to beat Bomber, but Bomber sticking a foot in and nudging it clear to Cunningham. It's Cunningham bursting forward down the right with the ball bobbling at his feet, never out of his control for a single second, coaxed along by his boots even as he looks up to pick out a pass, and he finds Ally Brown making a diagonal run towards the corner, tracked by Brian Greenhoff. It's Ally Brown selling Greenhoff a dummy with a sudden twist, turning towards goal in one movement, leaving his marker stranded.

It's Ally Brown touching a simple ball between Greenhoff and Houston into the wide-open space of the penalty area.

It's McQueen spotting the danger too late as Cyrille Regis sprints past him into the box.

It's Regis beating Gary Bailey to the ball just outside the six-yard box, and thumping a first-time shot into the back of the net. It's 5-3 to Albion. It's Regis wheeling away with his arms stretched out above him, delight on his face. It's Bomber grabbing him in a triumphant embrace; it's more black and white players in blue and white stripes joining them; it's one team, together, achieving what no one believed they ever could.

It's West Bromwich Albion playing like champions.

It's a local coach speeding down a long motorway, full of happy fans lost in booze and fag-smoke, and one man lost in thought. It's a man who's always thought for himself, and always had strong opinions. It's a man who believes in things he can see, and who's seen something which goes against things he's believed for years.

Jonah sips a bottle of beer and stares out of the window, another rotten Christmas behind him, and plenty on his mind.

*

Matty's nearly ready when Dad calls him. He's been skinning up on the sleeve of *Give 'Em Enough Rope*, with the record playing on his turntable – only quietly, just loud enough so he can tap his foot along to *English Civil War* – but when he hears the shout, he stops and listens carefully.

– Can ya come down fer a minute, Matthew?

Matty doesn't answer; he finishes rolling the joint quickly and tucks it in the breast pocket of his Brutus shirt. He was going to open up his bedroom window for a crafty smoke, but with Dad prowling, it's best saved for later. He puts his skins in a drawer, sticks the rest of the pot back in the bottom of his wardrobe, takes the Clash off, and opens his bedroom door. Dad's down the bottom of the stairs.

– What is it?

– It wo tek long. Come on down.

– Cor ya tell me here?

– No.

Matty shakes his head and trudges down the stairs. He follows Dad into the front room, where the little gas fire's turned up to full and there's a glass of scotch by the armchair; Dad sits down and has a sip of it. Matty looks at the clock on the mantelpiece over the fire.

– Ah'm in a bit of a rush.

– Ar, ah know. Got yer party. Well, theer ay no easy way ter say this, so ah'll spit it out.

Matty holds his breath and waits for some mundane pearl of wisdom. But he doesn't expect what comes next.

– Ah know abaht ya. What yam up tew.

So he knows about the pot. Matty shrugs his shoulders; he's old enough now that he shouldn't have to be playing hide and seek over it anyway.

– Mar life, mar choice.

– Course it is. An yow'll probly know how ah feel abaht it an all.

– Yower life, yower choice.

– But ah've gorra think abaht the family as a whole. Matthew, whatever else ya might think abaht me, ah've allwis put this family fust.

Matty stays quiet. Distant alarm bells are ringing in his mind at the direction the conversation's taking, but he still doesn't realise what's coming until Dad polishes off his whisky and looks him in the eye.

– Ah never thought ah'd say this, but Jesus, we need ter set it straight. Ya doe atta gew sneakin abaht no more, actin loike yam embarrassed ter be seen. If ya reckon her's the roit wench fer yow, Matthew, then thass good enough fer me.

Matty's stomach turns. It's ten times worse than the pot. It's a hundred times worse.

– I ay sayin ah'd be happy abaht it. Christ almighty, yer nan'd turn in her grave. An ah wouldn't be puttin up no special decorations, or eatin any a that dodgy food, or worshippin no cows or elephants or nuthin, but, ya know. Ah wouldn't stand in yer way. Ah wouldn't tell ya ter sling yer hook or nuthin loike that. Ah'd never do that, whatever ya choose ter do. Family's family.

It's got to be a trick. He's trying to draw Matty out, get him to admit it so he can humiliate him, give him the bollocking of a lifetime. Matty thinks about laughing it off, denying everything, turning round and walking out, but the expression on Dad's face stops him. He looks tired, and his eyes glisten in the firelight. Matty speaks before he's even finished thinking it through.

– Her is special, dad. Honest.

– Special's good, Matthew. Ya cor gew wrong wi special. Now, off ya go. Ah've said me bit. Enjoy yer New Year.

Matty's whistling to himself as he walks next door, where the Singhs have got a disco record playing. Some of Aasha's old schoolmates in fancy dress – it's either *Grease* or *Happy Days*; hard to tell the difference – are congregating in the hallway with glasses of vodka and orange. He asks them where he can find Aasha, and they point him to the kitchen.

She's mixing drinks at the table with her back to him. Through the door to the living room, Matty can see Mr Singh standing over the turntable, waving a record sleeve and insisting it's time to take this rubbish off and put some Tom Jones on. Matty sneaks up behind Aasha and puts his arms round her waist. She shrieks – a short, sharp sound – and after spinning round, puts her hands over her mouth and checks that no one's heard her over the music.

– Matt, what are you doing? Not in here, please!

– Theer's no better place. Ya wo believe the good news.

– Whatever it is, it can't be that good. You know how things are.

– Not anymore! Thass what ah need ter tell ya. Theer's nuthin ter worry abaht! Evrythin's gunna be fine! From now on, things am gunna be diffrent. Iss time ter be open. Let evryone know abaht us.

– Matt, we've talked about this. You know what people would say.

– No, iss fine! Ah spoke ter me dad befower comin round tonight! He's okay wi it, love!

She sighs and looks down at the floor.

– And what about my dad?

Matty shakes his head.

– What d'ya mean? Yower dad loves me. He allwis has.

– He loves you as the boy from next door, Matt. Not as a son-in-law. Never that.

He stares at her. It's a joke. It must be. He looks in her eyes, bright through those glasses, and with a clench of his stomach, he realises she's not winding him up.

– How come?

– It's complicated.

– Uncomplicate it. Ah'm a decent fella. Woss wrong wi me?

– We have different ways of doing these things. People from outside our faith…

– Iss cos ah'm a white bloke? Thass it?

– It's not about colour, Matt. It's about culture. Tradition.

– Roit. That time-honoured tradition of not lerrin any white faces in the family tree.

– Matt, it's got nothing to do with that. It's just that my father still has his beliefs, and they're very strong.

– Oh, an mine doe? Fuckin hell, Aasha, ya know what mar dad's loike when he gets gewin! He meks Enoch Powell look loike Bob Dylan! But even he's prepared tew accept ya intew our family. Think abaht that.

– Would he accept you raising his grandchildren as Sikhs? That's what my father would want.

– Why is it up to me old man what me kids'd grow up as? Actually, come ter think of it, why is it up ter *yower* old man?

– Okay, so what do you suggest? I leave my whole family behind, Matt? I elope with you, and we live on some new estate where people treat us like dirt because of who we are?

– Wouldn't atta be loike that. Look at Trev; his mom's white, his dad's black. Grew up in one a the roughest parts a town. It dae hurt im a bit.

– Have you ever really asked him about what it was like?

Matty runs a hand through his hair and shakes his head.

– This is bollocks. Absolute bollocks.

– Matt, please try and understand.

– Ah do understand. Believe me. I understand that yow've allwis enjoyed bein wi me, and ah've allwis enjoyed bein wi yow. Ah know that next ter that, religion an culture's nuthin.

– That's really nice, Matt. Really punk rock.

– True though, ay it?

~ 238 ~

– Maybe for you. Not for the rest of the world. And not for me.

She walks over to the sink. She turns the tap on and starts washing her hands, her back to him. He kicks one of his boots idly against the leg of the table.

– Well, if thass really what ya think. But ya know what? People allwis have a choice what they do. Fer instance, ah've got the choice ter fuck off out of here roit now.

– Where are you going?

– Ter get pissed.

She switches the tap off and turns round.

– Matt, don't be an idiot.

– Ah could gi yow the same advice, missis.

He turns round before she can answer and storms off down the hall, past the *Grease* girls and through the front door. He stands outside for about half a minute, waiting to see if she comes out after him.

She doesn't.

He wraps his Harrington tight round him and walks away, down to the end of the street. He hoists himself up onto the wall by the pub and fishes round in his pocket for the joint. He pulls it out and sparks it up.

He sits there until the cold gets too much, until the snow starts to fall. Then he heads home, past the lights and music of the Singhs' party, and sees in the year 1979 alone.

January 1979

The snow falls and falls, and New Year's Day dawns to the sharp crunch of wellingtons on cold, white pitches.

Groundsmen, managers, chairmen: they argue until they're warm from their own words, the fog of their breath forming a hazy pall around their heads. They huddle together in thick jackets and sheepskin coats to talk about damage to the pitch, the potential for injuries, the loss of income, the cost of reprinting programmes. But only one man can decide. One man has the power. When all's said and done, it's the referee who chooses whether the match is played out on a wrecked field or left to the busy imaginations of the pools panel.

One by one, the referees make their decisions. One by one, all over England, they telephone Lancaster Gate to notify the Football Association that the afternoon's fixture will not be taking place due to adverse conditions, and must be postponed to a later date.

Except at the Hawthorns.

At the Hawthorns, where the pitch is a solid rink of frozen mud with a half-inch coating of snow, the day's game is kicking off at three o'clock, as scheduled. At the Hawthorns, where the surface is so slippery that the referee nearly loses his footing as soon as he walks out to inspect it, Albion will play Bristol City.

Because Ron Atkinson insists that the pitch is fine. He tells the referee that professional footballers can run around on the surface without any trouble at all, and he'll send his players out to prove it.

And Ron Atkinson sends the Albion team out wearing specially-designed American astroturf boots which grip the ice as if it's asphalt. They warm up for half an hour, sprinting across the treacherous ground without a single slip. The referee watches them, and makes his decision.

And a bank holiday crowd of thirty-five thousand comes by car and by foot, beating a slow, cautious path to a snowbound stadium.

*

Five wins in a row, three months unbeaten, two points off the top of the table with a game in hand. Over the holiday, Christopher's stared at the league ladder on his wall for so long he could see it in his sleep: the full colour background of Pat Jennings saving an Ian Bowyer shot; the ninety-two team names printed on little card tabs; the progress tracker at the bottom where he's traced out the lofty peaks of Albion's position through the weeks. As usual, he got bored of updating the Third and Fourth

Divisions in the autumn, and he gave up on the Second Division last month after Wrexham dropped off the chart and got sucked up the hoover, but still, every single Saturday night Christopher takes the *Sports Argus* up to his room and carefully updates the First Division from the back page, without fail.

Liverpool, Everton, West Brom. Those three tabs at the top, in that order. And he's waiting for the day he can move the blue West Brom tab up to second, then first. Just the thought of it's enough to wake him up early the morning of every home game, shivering with the excitement in his bones.

Because he has to be there. He has to. Every single match feels like something special now, something he'd regret for years if he missed it. He has to see them. He has to see this team every step of the way to glory.

So today he was up before Mom and Dad, watching telly and reading some of his new *Shoot* annual before Grandstand. When they finally came down, Mom made some beans on toast looking a bit pale – Dad said she was ill, although she'd seemed fine when Christopher went to bed last night; in fact, she'd been singing along to a Crosby, Stills & Nash record with a massive glass of brandy – and then Dad asked him casually, quietly, if he was bothered about the match today. He said with public transport not running, they'd have to find a different way to get to the ground, and the game might not even be on when they got there. They'd already heard David Coleman read out the list of postponements so far – *Nottingham Forest, Middlesbrough, Birmingham City, Queens Park Rangers, more on the way so keep watching* – and they'd been hanging on to hear about the Albion match, but the clock ticked away and still no announcement came from the Hawthorns.

And Dad's voice was full of persuasion and regret when he asked Christopher whether they ought to give it a miss this time. It was a tone he often used in the run-up to Christmas and birthdays; the one which said *I'm on your side, mate, but we can't have everything our way.* So Christopher pulled the expression he always used in response. The furrowed brow and tight lips. A slow nod of the head, before looking solemnly down at the floor. The expression which said he understood completely; there was no choice, so he'd be brave about it, and with a bit of luck he might just get over the disappointment by 1987.

And sure enough, ten minutes later, glancing anxiously over his shoulder to check that Mom wasn't within earshot, Dad circled his finger round the telephone dial and asked Uncle Jonah in an urgent whisper whether they could get a lift to the match today (and then explained in a slightly less urgent whisper that no, he wasn't off his bloody rocker at all).

A lift off Uncle Jonah. It seemed like such a good idea.

When they get to Groves Court, they find Jonah standing by his Cortina with the bonnet up and the engine silent.

– Brilliant idea, this, Bill. Juss what ah wanted ter be dewin on New Year's Day.

– Woss wrong wi it?

– Iss the battery. Bloody thing. Allwis loike this in the winter.

– Ya tried jump-startin her?

– Look round ya, Bill. Ah cor jump-start her without another car. An most folks have got more sense than ter be dickin abaht on the roads today.

– No chance of us itch-oikin then, ah spose?

– As much chance as Peter Knowles poppin round fer tea an scones wi the Antichrist.

– Well, small mercies, eh?

– Look, iss gunna need a push. Christopher, theer's a blanket in the garage, mate, could ya gew an fetch it? We'll be needin it. Here; tek the key an lock up after ya.

Christopher catches the small metal key Uncle Jonah tosses to him and runs round the corner of the block to the garages. Pulling the door open to a strong smell of paint and turps, he peers awkwardly into the gloom. There's a dartboard on the far wall, next to a glossy poster of a woman with no top on, her boobs out on show – he stares at that with his mouth open for a few seconds, until he imagines what Mom would say if she saw him, and turns away with his face hot – and then he spots a tartan blanket spread over a bulky mound in the far corner. He picks it up to see about a dozen jerry cans stacked beneath. The top one's got four words scrawled on the side in big black capitals: THE MOSS EVANS CONTINGENCY. Curious, Christopher picks one up, quickly unscrews the top and sticks his nose above it. He gags at the thick stink of petrol and fiddles with the cap to screw it back on.

Putting the can down and snatching the blanket, he turns to leave the garage, but stops as something catches his eye. On the shelf next to the stack of cans, there's a black and white photograph. He picks it up, and he's surprised to see Mom and Dad on there in old Sixties clothes, Dad clean-shaven, Mom with shiny straight hair, smiling at the camera. Then he notices the photograph's been folded in half, and turns it over to look at the other side: there's another lad there with blond hair a bit like his own, hands shoved in the pockets of his parka. Uncle Jonah. Standing next to him is a girl with long hair, wearing a short skirt, sticking her tongue out.

~ 243 ~

This side of the photo's smudged with fingerprints all around the corners and the edges, forming a blurry border around Jonah and the girl.

Christopher puts the picture down. He wasn't prying. Not really. Not in a bad way. He was just looking; that's all. He closes up the garage quickly and runs back out to find Uncle Jonah behind the wheel and Dad waiting at the back of the car with his hands on the boot. Jonah turns the handle to wind down his window, and Christopher hands the blanket it to him through the window.

– Cheers, big fella! Now, am ya aroit ter gi yer dad an hand back theer?

Christopher nods and walks round to the boot where Dad's shaking his head.

– Ah doe believe ah'm dewin this. All so we can gew an see a game which might be called off anyway. Ah want me bloody head lookin at, ah do.

Christopher stays quiet. He's starting to feel guilty about dragging Dad out today, but still. It'll be worth it.

– Gew on then! Push!

Jonah's voice startles him, and he strains hard against the icy green metal of the Cortina. At first it won't budge, but then Dad puts his weight into it too, and Christopher feels the wheels turning, the bulky machine starting to roll along. He hears the engine splutter as Jonah tries the ignition.

– Keep gewin, lads, keep gewin!

They push and push, Dad grunting with the effort, and Christopher can feel sweat prickling at him beneath his coat. And they push harder, straining their muscles, and finally Jonah shouts in triumph as the engine responds to the ignition and starts to hum.

And just as the Cortina springs to life in front of them, Christopher and Dad push the car over a broad patch of ice, planting their own feet on it a second later, only for their legs to shoot out from under them. Christopher scrapes his knees and arms as he falls, and Dad hits the ground hard next to him as the Cortina chugs away. Dad groans, and shouts loud enough to scatter the pigeons strutting around the adventure playground.

– AH WANT ME BLOODY HEAD LOOKIN AT!

It's freezing inside the car. The heater still doesn't work, and from the passenger seat, Dad points out something even more concerning.

– Jonah.

– Yeah?

– Is that a hole?

~ 244 ~

– Sorry, wheer?

– Down theer. A hole. Jonah, theer's a bloody hole in this car.

Christopher leans round and sticks his head between the two front seats, above the handbrake. He can just about see it; a fist-sized chunk missing from the bodywork down in the driver's footwell, clear daylight shining through beneath the pedals.

– Oh, that. Ar. Ah'm gerrin that looked at soon.

– No wonder iss so cold! Iss loike gerrin a lift off Fred Flintstone, this!

– Why d'ya think ah bring a blanket wi me?

Uncle Jonah takes a hand off the steering wheel to gesture at the tartan blanket from the garage spread across his legs. Dad shakes his head.

– Oh, brilliant! As long as yome aroit, then! Me and me son onny juss dived headfust inter the ice an snow on yower bastard behalf!

– An whose bloody idea was it ter gew ter the match in the fust place? Christ alive, yow'll drive me spare, Bill. Honest. Anybody'd think yow've never sid an hole befower.

They freeze all the way to the ground, where the gates are open for business, and a huge crowd's shuffling through the snow to see the First Division's only remaining fixture. But in spite of the packed rows of well-wrapped punters – jumpers, scarves, gloves, overcoats, woolly hats – it's no warmer on the terraces.

They stand and they shiver. They stare at a frost-white pitch with freshly-cleared green lines and an orange ball in the referee's hands. They blow on their hands and they stamp their feet. They nurse flasks of tea, soup, Bovril. Some of the older lads pogo up and down like punk rockers in the middle of the crowd. But nothing warms them. Not today. Just before kick-off, Christopher looks up into the roof of the Brummie Road, the great lattice of girders which hold up the huge steel canopy above their heads and sees a pigeon perched with its wings tucked, head down, absolutely still. He wonders if it's frozen to death. He wonders if anything can survive this weather.

Bristol City can't.

It's obvious right from kick-off. For the Albion players in their astroturf boots, it's like playing at Wembley in May, but the City players struggle to even keep their balance, slipping and sliding like kids on the rink down Silver Blades. They open the scoring after eleven minutes; Bryan Robson slips nimbly past three red-shirted players and blasts a right-footed shot from the edge of the area which John Shaw can only parry aside, straight into the path of Ally Brown, who side-foots home from the corner of the six-yard box.

OHHHH, ALLY ALLY
ALLY, ALLY, ALLY, ALLY, ALLY BROWN

Albion press for a second goal, but as Christopher looks up into the roof ten minutes later to check on the frozen pigeon – it's gone, flown to some warmer place for the day, maybe even for the year – the Robins break away on the counter, and Brendon Batson ends up using his hands to block a Tom Ritchie header on the goalline.

The referee blows. Penalty to Bristol City.

The crowd jeers and whistles. The players gather on the edge of the box. Ritchie steps up to take the penalty, and as he runs up, Ally Brown scoops up a handful of snow, presses it firmly, and lobs it at the ball.

Ritchie hits the post.

Christopher's doubled up laughing as the ref turns round to find the culprit, and Ally Brown's looking at everyone stood around him in mock-confusion. The Brummie Road's almighty cheer turns to a disgruntled boo as the referee blows his whistle and orders a retake.

Peter Cormack takes the second penalty and makes it 1-1.

ATTACK! ATTACK! ATTACK, ATTACK, ATTACK!

The team hear the Brummie Road. The team respond. The second half's only just started – the floodlights flicker in the gloom and take an age to warm up to their full glow – and Christopher's in the toilet as Albion win their first corner of the half. The walls all around him reverberate with the applause and boot-stamped approval of the terraces above, along with a muffled chant of COME ON YOU BAGGIES, and Christopher looks up at the ceiling as a hush of anticipation descends.

Then the earthquake begins.

It's John Wile who scores, crashing a header into the back of the net from Bomber's corner, but Christopher doesn't find that out until later. Right now, he's lost in a dusty haze of piss-soaked plaster cascading from the ceiling and the walls, zipping his trousers up and staggering towards the door, the sledgehammer-thumping of thousands of feet right above his head like explosions. As flakes of paint and plaster tumble around him, the toilet turns into a strange snowglobe, terrifying and exhilarating; and if there's one thing Christopher will remember from this day, it's the moment when he sees all the power and passion of the Brummie Road surround him and shake him to life, until he stumbles out of the toilet, rests his back against the wooden shed wall of the club shop, and slowly realises that he's pissed all over his shoes.

Back up on the terraces, no one seems to notice the smell – there are blokes out there letting off some rank farts which earn more grumbles – but either way, Christopher's not bothered by the time the third goal goes in, eight minutes from time. After Batson, Robson, Bomber and Cantello pass their way through the Robins defence, Ally Brown smashes his second into the bottom corner right in front of them, and the two points are theirs.

They're level with Liverpool. For the first time since August, they're neck and neck with the leaders. The whispers, the murmurs, the shouts, the chants, the songs: the whole Brummie Road is saying the same thing. Albion can do it. This is the year. They can really do it. And they stamp, they celebrate, they sing, sending hot clouds of breath rolling through the cold air like phantoms in the floodlights.

It's a brisk walk back out to the car, a familiar feeling of unity surging through the crowd – the kind of happiness and harmony which only really comes with a good performance and result – and Uncle Jonah lifts his arms in the air and laughs.

– Ah know what yome gunna say, Bill, but honestly. This season, iss ours. Nuthin can stop us now. Mark mar words. Nuthin!

– Jonah, I ay sure what worries me more; the fact yow've gone an said that, or the fact that I agree wi ya.

Uncle Jonah laughs and whacks Dad on the back so hard that Dad starts coughing, and the pair of them talk about Chippy Clark and Graham Williams and Bobby Hope all the way down Halfords Lane.

As they reach the Cortina, the blizzard starts, blown in on a northerly wind; flakes whirl a frantic dance in the darkness, catching the rich beam of headlights along the Birmingham Road briefly before settling on the ground, a thick new crust underfoot.

The snow falls and falls, and in its soft white curtain, anything seems possible.

*

The radio's on and the baby's crying. She slides two well-chewed fingernails under the ring of a can of Mackesons and pulls the tab up with a fizz. It's what they told her to do.

They told her a lot of things while she was expecting. They told her to stay in regular contact with the father, in spite of their "difficult situation". They told her to always wear bright colours, to be cheerful, to forget about her heavy figure. They told her to stick with cigarettes for the stress, but no more than five a day in case it affected her breathing during labour. They told her to eat pilchards and drink half a pint of stout every evening when her iron levels sank during the third trimester. They told her she shouldn't breastfeed if she could afford formula. They told her to take tablets preventing lactation. They told her to listen to the radio whenever she was worried, to take her mind off things.

The radio's switched on now, as loud as it'll go.

She sips at her stout as the commentary begins from Carrow Road, a crackling voice describing a bare rock-hard pitch, a low sun in the sky and long shadows on the ground. It's soothing to hear the names buzzing from the speaker in quick succession as the team pass the ball around: Statham, Robertson, Wile, Tony Brown, Alistair Brown. There's order in hearing those same names each week, order amongst all the chaos. No matter how many strikes are on, no matter what madness she sees in Iran and Uganda and Cambodia on the nine o'clock news, no matter how few hours' sleep she gets as Emma wakes up crying in the night again, those names are the same each and every Saturday. A few years ago they were Irish names – Ray Treacy, Paddy Mulligan, Johnny Giles, Mick Martin – and even in the most troubled of times, the radio often mentioned the tricolour being waved from the Brummie Road terraces alongside so many Union Jacks. It sounded incredible.

It sounded like home.

She yawns, and opens a box of Farley's rusks. She picks up a fork and starts to mash a couple up with some milk. This is the routine. It's best to have one, especially when you're missing a lot of sleep, and you're prone to forgetting things. Something else they told her.

Excitement from the radio: Phil Hoadley mistimes a defensive header and the ball bounces into empty space in the box; Cyrille Regis darts in, controls the ball and lashes a low shot past a stranded Kevin Keelan into the bottom corner. She clenches her fist around the dripping fork and waves it in the air, sending drops of milk flying around the kitchen.

– YES!

She smiles for the first time in days. From the speaker, the faint melody of *THEER'S ONNY ONE CYRILLE REGIS* echoes beneath the commentator. In the front room, Emma cries louder; she goes back to mashing the rusk, a little faster now.

The radio and the newspapers have been a lifeline, a vital connection to this team during her years away. She was nursing a queasy belly and a five-month bump last April, scoffing tinned mandarin oranges and drinking evaporated milk during the FA Cup semi-final when Albion were outfought by Ipswich and lost 3-1. She even managed to catch the beginning of this season in the maternity ward through a radio cassette player just next to the ashtray on her bedside table. The notes clipped to her bed described her as an "elderly first-time mother"; she saw them one day and told the nurse it was a mistake, that she was only thirty, but the nurse just patted her shoulder and said that was quite old for a first baby, but she shouldn't worry – worrying's bad for baby – she should listen to her radio and be nice and calm.

So she listened to Ally Brown's opening goal as the woman in the next delivery suite screamed her way through labour. She listened to Bomber's winning goal as the nurse slapped the woman round the face and told her to stop disturbing the other mothers.

She stayed calm, like they told her to.

She walks into the front room, leaving the kitchen door open to hear the play surge from end to end, Regis running the Norwich defence ragged. Emma's sitting up in her cot, eyes closed, wailing fit to burst. She looks so small, so hopelessly frail; the midwife says there's a chance she might need growth hormones, but it's always best to wait, never rush these things. Above all, don't *worry*. Everything will be absolutely fine.

She picks Emma up, cradling her and singing to her until she quietens down, staring up at the old crucifix on the wall, dark against the yellowing paper around it. Then she carries the soft bundle in her arms into the kitchen and uses a lukewarm teaspoon to feed her the soggy rusk. It's tricky to tell how much Emma actually eats, because more of it seems to end up decorating her face and bib. After cleaning her up, she carries Emma back to her cot, gurgling and stringing together meaningless vowels and consonants; a happy language all of her own.

There's a small pile of terry nappies which need washing, and she makes a start on them as the second half begins. That's part of the routine, too. One Norwich striker called Justin Fashanu – a seventeen-year-old making his debut in place of Martin Chivers – keeps causing problems for Wile and Robertson, and she gripes at the defence under her breath. The commentator says this Fashanu lad'll have a long, bright career ahead of him if he carries on like this, but for now, Albion just have to concentrate on keeping him in check.

But five minutes into the half, as she's in the middle of the laundry, Brendon Batson leaves the pitch to change his boots, switching to those special astroturf studs which grip the frozen pitch. While he's off the field, Norwich attack the wide-open space on Albion's right flank; Canaries left-back Ian Davies puts a cross in from that side and World Cup veteran Martin Peters loops a header into the top corner to make it 1-1.

She swears, and then wanders across the room to finish off the tin of Mackesons she opened earlier. She throws the empty in the bin, but doesn't open a second. She's seen booze wreck people. She's seen a lot of things wreck people. She won't go down that road. She's determined not to go down that road.

The commentator wonders whether it's time yet for Albion to bring on their new star man, the player who's smashed the British record transfer fee – David Mills, signed from Middlesbrough last Sunday for an incredible £516,000 – but instead they fight on with their starting eleven. Cantello's chasing the Norwich players down and sticking in hard tackles all over the shop, and Regis sends one shot dipping from twenty-five yards to hit the crossbar, but the score stays 1-1, and Albion have to settle for the point. And as she switches the radio off, one last chant from the travelling fans in the South Stand buzzes through the speaker: *WEST BROM, WEST BROM, TOP OF THE LEAGUE!*

Emma's finally asleep, wrapped up warm and lying face-up; the midwife says it's not healthy for her to sleep that way – there's a risk of her airways closing – but Emma always screams the house down lying on her front. She watches her daughter sleep for a little while, then pulls a pack of Benson & Hedges from her handbag and opens the front door to sit out on the step. Her ma's getting on now, but she can still sniff out lingering traces of fag-smoke inside the house, and the years haven't dimmed her enthusiasm for long, hypocritical lectures.

Some things just don't change. This street never does; it's still a grimy but proud little community under that layer of snow packed down hard and grey by winter boots. There may be more cars parked outside houses these days, not quite so many kids running around in hand-me-downs, but the mornings are still so many feet trudging along the road to the factory, the nights still faint traces of conversations from the other houses carrying through paper-thin walls. Every now and then she hears the old couple next door. She hasn't seen them. In all honesty, she doesn't know what she'd say.

She blows smoke out into the air and whistles an old tune. She takes another long drag on the cigarette, then whistles another line of melody. From next door, from the old couple's house, she hears the faint sound of singing. She turns her head to listen, and realises after a few moments that it's the same song she's whistling; one she once recorded in a booth as a giggling teenager with an old friend. It's Dusty Springfield. *I Only Want To Be With You.*

She sucks on the fag. Her lungs fill with warmth, her mind rich with a sudden nicotine flow which shocks her brain cells awake. The door opens to her right, she hears a voice humming Dusty loudly, clearly, and a young boy – around nine or ten, a blue and white scarf tight round his neck – walks out onto the street and blinks in the daylight. A woman wrapped up in a suede coat follows him out, still humming, fiddling with her keys as she pulls the door to.

– Bye, Mom! Dad! Ta-ra!

The boy puts his hands in his pockets and looks up at her as she finishes her fag. She smiles at him, and then nods her head to the woman on the next doorstep.

– Alright, me wench?

The woman glances across at her quickly.

– Hello, love.

And the woman stops. She turns round again slowly, as if she's expecting some mirage which might melt away under her gaze, fade into the winter air.

– Kath?

– How are ya? Hey, good to see that curly hair again! Was bound to come into fashion sooner or later!

– Oh, Kath. Jesus.

– Bin a long time, eh?

She's startled when Jude steps forward and throws her arms round her neck.

– Bloody hell. Christ alive. Kath.

February 1979

– Jesus, look at ya! How many have yow had?

– Couple.

– Roit. An when yow'd finished that couple, how many more did ya have?

– Couple.

– Brilliant. God almighty, ah'd get more sense out a Kath's little babby than this.

The angrier she gets, the more she slips back into her old voice, all the *yows* and *cors* and *shors* which drifted away during years of teaching. Bill grins, even though he knows it'll land him in worse trouble. Right now, he doesn't care. He's just glad to be home, glad to be in one piece.

Glad to be away from Anfield.

– Look, ah'm sorry. Ah got a bit carried away. Iss bin a bad day.

As it happens, "bad day" is the mother of all understatements, but she doesn't need to know what happened this afternoon. Things are bad enough already, without her finding out exactly what they've been through since they left home this morning.

– Oh, a bad day! So ya lost a football match, an thass a perfectly good reason ter get legless in front a yer ten-year-old son?

– Sorry ah cor set a more shinin example. Next time ah'll let im do summat more wholesome wi his Satdee. Loike knittin a jumper an watchin Delia Smith on the telly.

– Well, at least Delia Smith doe gew around gerrin drunk an mekkin an exhibition of herself at football matches!

– Fer the record, ah was sober at the match. More's the pity.

Bill tries to focus on her eyes, but gives up after a few blurry seconds and looks down at the arm of the sofa instead. There's no winning this row. There's no winning a lot of them – there are times when life with Jude just feels like a series of uneasy truces – but tonight, Bill's in an arguing mood. Normally he'd let it all go, avoid rocking the boat, but he's had a few pints, and he really has had a bad day. A bloody awful day.

And all because it had seemed like a good idea to go to Anfield.

Nineteen days without a match. Nineteen days of freezing cold weather, postponed fixtures piling up like so many mountains of rubbish. A full nineteen days with Albion sitting at the top of the First Division. And finally, today, for the first time in nearly three weeks, they could play a match. Play *the* match. The one everyone's been waiting for.

Liverpool away.

A chance to beat the title favourites – Bob Paisley's conquering giants – and put clear daylight between themselves and the rest of the league. Prove themselves the best. Prove that Albion deserve to be England's champions this year.

But they hadn't reckoned with Kenny Dalglish, and they hadn't reckoned with the mood on Merseyside. Bill's used to aggro; he's seen some hostile atmospheres on away trips in his time, seen it in all sorts of places, but nothing like today. Liverpool haven't played a league match since Boxing Day. The lights have been out and the streets have been cold. For a fortnight, the city's dead lay unburied, fresh bodies stored in a derelict factory in Speke, the cemetery gates locked and picketed. The mood around the whole place was foul and ugly from the minute they arrived, and it was all aimed at Albion.

Their coach stopped half a mile from the ground, and from there they ran a gauntlet: hassled for tickets on all sides; arms, shoulders, necks grabbed by teenagers wanting to hear their accents, wanting to know where they were from, who they were here to support. Hate and abuse yelled at them as they stood packed into the back of the Anfield Road End. Hate and abuse yelled at the team, at the Three Degrees, even as Dalglish gave Liverpool a first-half lead, even as he played in David Fairclough to double that lead just after half-time. Jeers and boos as Ally Brown headed in from a corner with twenty minutes left. Jeers and boos as Laurie Cunningham fluffed the chance for a late equaliser.

But that was nothing compared to the walk back out to the coaches in the darkness after full-time. It was nothing compared to the mobs roaming Stanley Park with darts and knives, attacking any stray Albion fans they could catch, young and old. It was nothing compared to the bricks smashing through the windows of the coach as they drove away from the ground.

A bloody awful day.

It was a cold and miserable ride back, even after Christopher stopped crying and Jonah finished rambling to everyone around him about the days when Anfield used to be the safest place in the country to visit (turning to Bill every so often to say *ay that roit?* and waiting for Bill to nod his agreement). So when the coach dropped them off outside the Throstle Club, they headed to the pub quietly, still shivering and shaking. Jonah was driving home, so he made a point of sticking to just three pints and a short, but Bill poured a whole lot more down his throat. He deserved it. He needed it.

And in the back of his mind, he knew it'd lead to this when he got home, but when push came to shove, he didn't really care. At the end of the day, there were worse things in the world than Judy in a strop. Far worse.

He rubs the arm of the sofa as she glares at him. He remembers the day they picked it out five years ago; he didn't like it that much from the beginning, and he said so, but in the end he caved into Jude's insistence that what the front room desperately needed was a nice bright shade of avocado. So he bought it, and nearly did his back in getting it in here, getting it just how she wanted it.

And on that day, it really did look good. Everything looked good. That day he wouldn't have believed it could get so worn and frayed, its colour so faded, its fabric coarsened by the simple strain of everyday life. He wouldn't have believed it could happen so quickly.

– It ay even abaht settin an example, Bill. Iss abaht havin a bit a responsibility. What if somethin had happened ter ya? What would Chris ha done?

– Oh, leave the poor lad out of it. He's a bright kid, he's got his head screwed on. An besides, if anything had gone really wrong, Jonah woulda looked after im.

The quiet that descends on the room is sudden and heavy. He sees her expression shift from surprise, to disbelief, to fury, and wonders what he's said wrong.

Then he realises.

He was going to tell her at some point. He really was. He was going to have a proper conversation about it – break it gently, listen to her point of view – but now it's too late. It's not his fault, though. He's had a lot on his mind.

– So thass it. Ah knew ya was up to summat. Sneakin around. Little phone calls here an theer. Ah never thought it'd be him, though. Him.

– Now, Jude. Calm down.

– Normal husbands have affairs, ya know. If they start to feel the years rushin past em, they sniff out some impressionable slip of a girl, book a hotel room an have at it. I even thought that might be what ya was up tew, but no, that'd be too simple fer yow, wouldn't it? It had ter be Jonah. Football, pubs, an Jonah. Seventeen all over again.

– Come on. Theer ay no need fer this.

– An lettin our son around im. *Our* son, Bill.

That emphasis. Daring him to contradict her. He can't believe she's playing that trick. Bill struggles to keep his voice level.

– Look. He meets us fer matches abaht once a fortnight. Thass all.

– Fer how long?

– A few months.

– A few months!

– An he ay loike he used ter be, neither. Ya know, iss possible fer a person ter change.

– Course it is. But we ay talkin abaht a person. We'm talkin abaht Jonah.

– Ah'm tellin ya, he's diffrent. Ya know what ya said abaht Kath bein a whole new woman, gerrin married, becomin a mother? Well, iss the same wi Jonah.

– Become a mother now, has he?

– He was married fer five years. He's calmed down a lot. Ah'm tellin ya. He ay the same.

– He's stopped manipulatin folks, then? Stopped tekkin advantage a people when they'm vulnerable?

– Well, he teks responsibility fer his own mistakes, at least.

Bill's losing his temper, and he can sense the minefield he's blundering through now. One wrong step. Just one wrong step, and it'd be the worst explosion of all. The type which could finish them both.

– Woss that sposed ter mean?

– Nuthin.

– If theer's summat ya want ter say, Bill…

– No, not this. Not again. Not now.

They collapse into a long silence. His head's starting to ache from the beer, and crawling into bed seems like a better idea than ever. But he sits on the sofa instead, with his wife.

They sit side by side, with nothing left to say.

*

Jonah's making plans.

It started with two telephone calls this morning. The first was short, loud and incoherent. The second was longer, quieter and apologetic.

It seems the last ten years haven't changed Judy all that much.

Having first demanded that Jonah stay away from her son – and if possible, her husband as well – during a screeching thirty-second-long fit, she then hung up on him before he could attempt a word in his defence. He stood with the phone to his ear and his mouth open for a few seconds, before slowly putting the receiver down, rubbing his head in disbelief, and deciding to get on with his day. He managed to get all the way back into the living room, sit down in front of Pebble Mill On Sunday and make a start on the crossword before the bloody phone started up again.

This time she was calmer; her voice was a bit strained, but her tone was polite. And Jonah listened quietly as she apologised, then he pointed out as patiently as he could that her son was a good lad, her husband was a good dad, and if she could find it in her heart to not lock them both inside the house every Saturday afternoon, he'd always appreciate the company up the Brummie Road or down the pub. That went for her, too. Bygones being bygones, and all that.

A short and awkward silence. She thanked him, and said she'd think about it.

A longer and awkwarder silence. Then she asked him if he knew that Kath was back in town.

He told her he didn't know. He didn't know that at all.

She's staying at her mom's house. She's got a babby, six months old; her name's Emma, an adorable little thing. She's come back to get away from her husband – some bloke she married while she was living down in London; bit of a bastard, apparently – and she's likely to be here for a while. She's in a fair state; it's understandable with everything she's been through, with the lack of sleep, with all the pressure of looking after a little one – blokes don't appreciate how tough being a mother is – but another friendly face might be just what she needs to perk her up. Just a thought.

He thanked her for letting him know. He wished her all the best. He said goodbye and he put the phone down.

He made a cup of tea. He paced around the flat for an hour, kicking a balled-up pair of socks from one room to another, mumbling to himself. Turning things over in his mind. He lost track of the time. It was only when he glanced at his watch and saw the numbers 13:17 glowing faintly on the display that he realised he was late.

It's become a routine, going down the boozer on a Sunday afternoon. If he's honest, it was already a routine even when he did it by himself, but for the last few weeks – since he ran into a familiar face down there and got chatting on a regular basis – it's been something to look forward to without fail. An hour and a half in a warm lounge, a couple of pints, a chance to hear a different point of view on things.

Today it's a chance to get some advice.

– So who's this bird, then?

– Wench ah used ter know years back. Good-lookin, loike. Her was allwis a bit out a me league, ter be honest.

– How far out yer league?

– Bayern Munich versus Dudley Town.

– They got some decent players, Dudley. Me cousin had trials with em last year.

– Oh, yer cousin? Mar mistake; they'm poachin some real world-class talent nowadays. They'll be ready ter tek on Muller an Rummenigge wi one a yower kin on board, will they?

– Hope springs eternal, mate.

– Ah should bloody well hope so. Ah've got abaht ten years' worth of hope in the bank.

– Long time, ten years. Folks change, Jonah. Specially growin up. I bet she's a different bird these days.

– Ya reckon?

– Course. I bet she weighs twenty stone an looks like Bob Monkhouse.

– Shurrup.

– And she's just waitin for you to sweep her off her feet with a forklift truck.

– Shurrup. Yow ay helpin.

– Start by helpin yerself, pal. Stop worryin. Get yerself round there, say hello to her. Catch up on old times. Don't push her, don't rush things. Just give her a helping hand for a while, see how the land lies, make yer move when the time's right.

It makes sense. They're not dopey teenagers anymore. He's got a wiser head on his shoulders. And if the worst comes to the worst, it's just another photograph to go in the bin.

– Ar, ah spose iss the best way.

– That's the spirit. No use going with the flow; sometimes you've gotta fight for what you want.

– Loike a salmon!

– Yeah. Wait... ya what?

– Salmon! They swim upstream ter reproduce. They gew against the current!

– Right. Not sure if I'd compare meself to a fish, mate, but whatever works for you. As long as ya don't smell like a salmon, you're laughing.

– Nah, I've got some proper aftershave. Posh stuff. Off Walsall market, loike. By the time ah'm done wi it they'll be able to smell me in Africa.

– Talkin about Africa, d'you read that leaflet I gave ya?

– Ah flicked through it.

– And?

– Yeah, it's interesting.

Actually, Jonah tried his best to ignore the leaflet at first. He's not that interested in apartheid. You always get long-haired hippie types and student wankers bleating about it, saying there are blacks in South Africa getting tortured and murdered by the government, by the police; he's never really paid much attention in it all, and deep down he's always reckoned the buggers must have done something to deserve it. After all, he's got mates out there; he hears about it straight from the horse's mouth.

But after he sat down and read the leaflet – a black and red strip of paper with a grainy photo of two coppers dragging this coloured bloke unconscious down the street, and the word **SOWETO** covered in coils of barbed wire at the top – he started to wonder what the hell's actually going on down there. It's one thing wanting a bit of law and order on the streets, but some of the photos in the leaflet turned his stomach. They were just ordinary people, living their lives. Ordinary people, with a government who hated them.

– Anyway, best be getting a move on. Don't want the missis on the rampage.

– Aroit, Neville. Tek care, mucka. Say hello to Daniel fer me.

– Will do! See ya later, Jonah. And... well, ya know. Best of British, mate.

*

The Saturday streets are all movement: the last of the shoppers bustling home in the dusk while supporters flood away from the match, and in the middle of it all, Matty's ready. They're all ready.

They're waiting near the station.

Trev's with him, and all of his new mates, all the blokes Trev's got to know over the last few months; since that night in Leeds last October. He says they're a good bunch; hard, but fair. Trev's been meeting up with them on awaydays all winter, coming back with plenty of stories and a few cuts and bruises, but Matty wasn't interested in all that stuff. Not until today.

Today's a special occasion.

Things have been looking up for him recently. He's found some work, even if it's only helping with repair jobs at an auto place, and he can afford to get to a few more matches, get a few more pints in on a Friday and Saturday. He can afford to go out on the pull, and he has. He doesn't know what Aasha thinks about that, and he doesn't care. When all's said and done, she's only got herself to blame.

All the same, he can't stop thinking about it. He goes out of his way to avoid her, and her mom and dad, which is a tricky thing to do when they live next door to you. But with a bit more money in his pocket he can find a place of his own. Just somewhere simple, a little flat or bedsit, rent not too steep, conditions not too shabby. Sometimes he catches himself wondering whether she'd make that move with him. There are people who'd hate them for it, course there would be – there probably always will be, because every race and religion in the world churns out their share of hate-filled tossers – but then he remembers that night at the party, the moment he realised exactly what the problem is.

It's not about culture, it's not about tradition. That's the biggest cop-out he's ever heard. It's about fear. Fear of the unknown. She'll never face that fear. It's a stupid attitude to have, and Matty's sick of it. Why spend your life being scared of the world? Why not get out there and take it on face to face, show a bit of fight? He never used to think of himself as a fighter, but you've got to defend yourself in this world. You've got to.

He's not running anymore. These days, Matty's standing up for himself.

Today, he's waiting by the station. He's waiting for Leeds.

They came down on the ordinaries from Yorkshire, changing at New Street for Smethwick. On a freezing cold February afternoon, they were marching around in short-sleeved shirts and vests, hands in pockets, heads high. Looking for trouble. Asking for it.

Matty joined the rest of the lads down the Birmid Club on Great Arthur Street, and they walked to the ground from there, stopping for pints at the Cock Inn, the Waggon and the Old House At Home en route. The match was shit – the highlight was Bomber scoring a volley from outside the box to give Albion the lead – but it doesn't even matter that Leeds came from behind to win 2-1. It wouldn't matter whatever the result was. Trev's told him that the dickheads who hung him off that bridge last autumn are part of the mob in town today. That might be true, but he's not too bothered whether they are or not.

He's got scores to settle and a place to settle them.

He waits, and he waits, and eventually the sirens begin in the distance as the fists fly, underground.

March 1979

In the shadow of the tower blocks, in a concrete cradle, they play for their country.

Ninety-eight thousand people come to the Marakana; two of them never leave. One Red Star supporter is hit by a stray firework and dies of his injuries; one rival Partizan fan who's come specially to see an English club play in his hometown is recognised by Red Star ultras and beaten to death on the terraces. The stadium's a packed colosseum with darkness in its deepest corners, red banners rippling in the breeze, and hopeful faces clamouring at the fences to swap whatever trinkets they can for the fashionable Western jeans of the few travelling fans.

The noise boils over the Albion players even before kick-off: patriotic anthems ringing from the tannoy, constant songs and chants from the crowd, foreign slogans howled through loudhailers and yelled in chorus by thousands of harsh Yugoslavian voices. But the players concentrate on their job. Their legs are chopped and hacked. Their feet and ankles catch the rake of studs at every turn. Through it all, they attack. In the pale rays of the Belgrade sunset, in the cold electric light, they attack. But they can't beat Aleksandar Stojanovic in the Red Star goal. Laurie Cunningham dances through midfield with the ball at his feet, but he can't find the net. Tony Brown shoots from eighteen yards out, but Stojanovic's gloves deny him the crucial goal.

And with four minutes left, Dusan Savic curls a free-kick from outside the box, bending it away from Tony Godden into the bottom corner of the Albion goal. And for the remaining minutes Albion cling on, weathering more Red Star attacks, desperate to keep the scoreline at 1-0. Desperate for the chance to put things right in the second leg.

Desperate for one more chance, at the Hawthorns.

*

The school play's awful, but Kath doesn't care. She's just glad for a few hours away.

Leaving Emma with her ma for the night is an almighty relief which smothers the vague feeling of guilt in her mind. It's a chance to flush away the stress. To feel normal again. Or at least, as normal as it's possible to feel sitting next to Jonah in a school hall while several dozen fourteen-year-olds bluster and panic their way through a century of West Bromwich Albion history.

She was planning to make her excuses to Jude and spend the night at home, until Jonah asked her if she wanted a lift down in his car – he's been really helpful these last few weeks, always popping round with a few fresh groceries and even a couple of toys for Emma – so they came along together, a blanket spread over their legs in his Cortina because the heater's on the blink. And since he didn't mention the small, fiercely-scrubbed vomit stain on the shoulder of her bow blouse, she didn't mention what looked worryingly like a hole in his car floor hastily plugged with a bath sponge.

– Ah've allwis loved the theatre, ya know. Ever since ah sid Dick Whittington down the Plaza one Christmas when ah was eight. Ah remember comin out the place an wantin ter be an actor meself.

– What stopped you?

– Well, the next day ah fancied bein a footballer instead, an by Monday mornin ah wanted ter be an astronaut. Thass me problem, see. Forever changin me mind.

– Haven't you ever decided you wanted something and stuck to yer guns? Really persevered with it?

– Course I have.

– And how did it go?

He gives her a strange glance; a half-smile which flickers across his mouth and disappears.

– Well, iss a work in progress, ay it?

He's an odd one, Jonah; he always has been. But it's still good to see him. Happier times seem a lot closer with old faces around.

Inside the hall, waiting for the play to begin, they chat about the days when she used to meet him down by Bradfords Bakery, when they used to stand up the Brummie Road, arm-in-arm to stay together during surges, him always telling her jokes at half-time, making her laugh until she was doubled up over a crush barrier. She's surprised by how nervous she is; she was staring in the mirror before she left the house, trying to work out how much she'd changed since those old days, how much having Emma's changed her. She ends up babbling to him about the current Albion team – she's only seen bits and pieces of them on Match of the Day, but the way they find space on the pitch and shift formation during games is a world away from what she used to watch on the terraces all those years ago – and in a way, she's sorry when the thick black curtains in front of the stage are drawn, and she has to sit quietly and watch the play.

The scenes come thick and fast, a helter-skelter of terrified faces, breathless dialogue and awkward ad-libs. It lasts for an hour, though as far as Kath's concerned, the kids do an admirable job of making it feel like a full hundred years.

There are flat caps too big for teenage heads, baggy Victorian football shorts with all the haphazard hallmarks of Jude's sewing machine, while crashing cymbals and off-key trumpeting from the school band herald two nineteenth-century cup wins. Flashing lights and bass-drum artillery create the trenches where young Albion forward Harold Bache loses his life in 1916, and where Tommy Magee signs a contract to become the first building block of the side which wins the 1920 league title.

Moustaches drop off moist lips in the middle of dialogue, and during the 1931 FA Cup final, WG Richardson manages to fluff the winning goal by inadvertently slicing the tatty old football out into the third row of the audience. But the show plods on, and after becoming FA Cup winners five times, League Cup winners once and champions of England once, three black boys and eight white boys walk onto the stage wearing modern Albion shirts and promise there'll be even better things to come for the club in the future.

They promise there'll be better times ahead for West Bromwich, for all the Black Country. Even in tough times, work conquers all. And if there's one strength that West Bromwich can always boast, one thing which has been embodied by the town's football club for the last century, it's old-fashioned hard graft.

The cast bow to a standing ovation – it seems the kindest response in the circumstances – and there's a sudden, frantic rush to grab coats and bags when Jude comes out onto the stage to ask if anyone's got any questions about the issues which have been raised in the play. Jude smiles awkwardly as several dozen parents hurry unceremoniously towards the exit.

– Well, thank you for coming! I hope we'll see you all at our next production!

By the time she reaches the end of the sentence, the hall's empty except for Jonah and Kath. Jude waves to them from the stage.

– Hi guys! What did you think?

Jonah coughs slightly.

– In all honesty, iss the best play ah've ever sid abaht the Albion.

Kath nods.

– Definitely. The very best.

– Oh, I'm glad you've had a good time! The kids are absolutely bubbling back there. It's all for their benefit, you know, but half the time I end up learning as much as them.

Jonah pulls his jacket on and wanders forward to the stage.

– Have they converted ya then, missis?

– Converted me?

– Ar. Am ya gunna be comin up the Brummie Road wi me an Bill an young Chris of a Satdee now?

– Well, obviously I know a lot more about the club now. And I suppose I can see how important it is to the town, but... Jonah, surely you wouldn't want me around bothering you?

– It wouldn't be no bother! An Kath, yow'll come an all, wo ya? Old times, an all that?

Old times. Always so wonderful, and always so beyond reach.

– I can't really spend too much time away from Emma.

– Oh. Thass fair enough.

She picks up her handbag, and feels the impulse race through her. Just once. It wouldn't hurt, would it?

– Well. If me ma can have her for the evening then I'm sure she can manage an afternoon... actually, yeah, why not?

The delight on Jonah's face is so sudden and clear, it's heartbreaking.

– We'll get summat sorted out, then! Hey, juss wait till the old gang's back together up the Brummie Road; if that doe get the team back on course fer the title, nuthin will!

For the whole journey home, Jonah chatters about how much the Hawthorns has changed since she was last there – how much everything's changed, all around town – and she rests her head against the chilly glass of the passenger window and lets his words wash over her until they pull up outside her house. She takes a deep breath. She's ready to go back in there. She's ready to be a proper mother. If she's not ready now, she never will be.

– Ta for a good night, Jonah. I really needed it. Honestly.

Jonah nods, but stays silent. She turns to get out of the car, and as her fingers touch the door handle, he speaks.

– Ya know, ah missed ya.

– You missed me?

– While ya was away. When ya did a vanishin act on us.

She looks at the glovebox in front of her, the round air vent to the left of it, her reflection in the wing mirror. Tired eyes stare back at her.

– I'm sorry.

– We never knew what'd happened ter ya, missis.

– A lot happened to me.

He drums his fingers on the steering wheel.

– So, did dewin a runner sort things out?

– It didn't hurt. Look, Jonah, I'm tired.

~ 264 ~

– Fair enough. Ah dae mean tew upset ya. Juss… ya know.

She turns and looks at him. He tries a grin, but it looks awkward, insincere.

– Night, Jonah. Thanks again.

– Ar. Ah'll see ya soon. The Brummie Road. Doe forget.

He waits in the car with the engine running as she pulls out her door key and lets herself into the house, and she hears him pull away as she closes the door behind her. Her ma's sitting in the front room, a pile of knitting in front of her. She doesn't look up, so Kath doesn't disturb her. Instead, she walks up the stairs, into the dark bedroom where Emma's lying asleep in her cot. She lets her eyes adjust to the gloom and watches her daughter breathe softly, gently, quietly.

Kath's got some big decisions to make. She's known that for a while now. She didn't even know where to start. But it's amazing how an evening out can clear your mind.

Her daughter needs a good future. She needs someone she can rely on. And Kath's determined to make that happen. She'll do whatever it takes.

*

The gym echoes with the squeaking of black trainers on a scuffed floor, lads huffing and puffing after the ball, shouting to teammates, every movement tense, every expression fierce, every single one of them concentrating on the game. On winning.

But the Allsorts aren't winning. It's their final match of the season, and they need two points from it – nothing else will do, not with Bilston Rangers a point ahead of them at the top of the table – but they can't do it. They're 2-0 down going into the second half, and it's all going wrong.

Christopher's trying to keep his patience, but he has to bite back a shout every time Daniel spoons a chance, or Rajinder gets forced off the ball, or Asif misplaces a pass, or Rolo lets a shot squirm under him. The worst of it is that he knows he's making as many mistakes as the rest of them. They're not playing as a team anymore. They haven't been for a while.

The Ritual of the Chicken Crisps has gone now. All the fun's gone. Christopher's stopped looking forward to matches, stopped picturing the high school gym in his mind with eager impatience during boring Maths and History lessons on a Wednesday afternoon. They've given up their playground kickabouts at dinnertime, too – Rajinder prefers sitting in the cloakroom sketching pictures of Luke Skywalker and C-3PO, while Rolo's off playing British Bulldog half the time – and Christopher was just praying they could be good enough to make it over the finish line, to lift the trophy, to have something to show for all the time, all the effort.

If they could just keep it together for one more match. Bilston have been dropping points themselves, and they could still lose their last game. Grind out one more win against a team from Black Lake, and the Allsorts would still have a chance at the league title. But it's slipping away from them with every second, and when Christopher gets the ball on the halfway line with three minutes left, he goes for it. He did it once before, back at Christmas, and now the pressure's on, now everything depends on it, he's sure he can do it again.

He takes a touch to control it, lets the ball roll forward in front of him, gets his head down and whacks his laces right through it, sends it spinning through the air, seeing the trophy in his hands, seeing the look on Funnyfarm's face when he brings it into school and holds it high above his head in the playground with everyone cheering all around him.

And the ball sails high up into the air, over the low crossbar, and hits the gym wall up near the ceiling with a dull thud before bouncing back down. The others turn and stare at him, and he stares back at them. He doesn't care. At least he tried. At least he put the effort in. It's more than they've done.

He's still sulking about it a minute later when Daniel gets the ball with his back to goal, and a Black Lake defender starts hassling him, trying to get his foot round to the ball. The defender leans forward to mumble something, and without a single word, Daniel turns round and punches him. Out of nowhere. Right in the face.

The defender drops to the ground holding a bloody nose. Suddenly all of his teammates are running over to try and clobber Daniel, and all hell breaks loose. Christopher runs over and manages to grab one of them, getting a fistful of his sleeve, and he gets a clout round the ear which rattles his whole skull, but he keeps his grip on the shirt until he hears the fabric tear. Asif's struggling with this blond-haired kid who's yelling in his face, and Rolo's hiding behind his goal, scared to get involved, not wanting to get into big trouble, and the knackered old referee's blowing his whistle, and Daniel's running back to the changing room before the ref's even had chance to properly send him off.

They play the last thirty seconds of the season with four players, standing in a line in front of their own goal, trying to keep the score at 2-0, keep a bit of dignity. When the whistle goes, Christopher closes his eyes and tries to swallow the lump in his throat.

The Allsorts have thrown away the league title.

The changing room's chilly, the lightbulb dimming and flickering above their heads as they traipse in there. Daniel's sitting on one of the benches with his head resting against the wall, staring up at the ceiling. Rolo takes his chicken crisps out of his bag and pulls the packet open. He takes one out, crunches it in his mouth, then offers the pack round to the rest of them. They all shake their heads.

Christopher turns to Daniel.

– So?

– So.

– What was all that abaht?

– It's nothing.

– Ya punched someone in the face over nuthin? Ya got sent off fer nuthin?

– Guess so.

– Well, it was a great time ter do it. Perfect time. Proper masterstroke.

– You really want to know what happened? You want to know what he called me?

Daniel's kicking his heels loudly against the bench now, and Christopher hesitates, not sure what to say now.

– If iss summat really bad, ya coulda towd the ref…

– "Ref, I've just been called a filthy nigger." Anything about that in the rules of the game? Anyone ever get sent off for it?

– Ya still shoulda said summat.

– Why?

– Because!

– What difference would it make? What would it change?

– Fuckin hell, Danny, ah doe know.

– Nothing. The answer's nothing.

– No. No, that ay roit. It ay.

– I had to do something. No one else will, Chris. No one else ever does.

Christopher looks around the changing room with his hands on his head, and that lump right back in his throat. Everyone's avoiding his gaze. Rajinder's pulled a notebook from his bag and he's busy drawing some new picture of life in outer space, as Rolo tilts his head back to up-end the last of the chicken crisps into his mouth, and Asif whistles that new Village People song. And he realises with another jolt of misery that they're embarrassed. They already know. They worked it all out a long time before him.

There's no happy ending; no perfect dreamworld where everyone lives in harmony and everything's fair and square. There never will be.

Losing's a part of life. You can kick at it, scream at it, rage at it until your strength's all gone, but it'll still be there. Sometimes, you just can't win.

The sun's a low and distant light over the car park as the Allsorts go their separate ways.

*

In the shadow of the tower blocks, in a concrete cradle, they play for glory.

Forty thousand people come to the Hawthorns, from all over the Black Country, from all over Birmingham. The ground's a turbulent plateau with wind blustering through its open spaces, Union flags rippling in the breeze, and hopeful faces clamouring at the raised rows of seats between the Halfords Lane and Smethwick End to swap scarves with the few travelling fans.

The noise cascades over the Red Star players even before kick-off: reggae songs ringing from the tannoy, constant songs and chants from the crowd, incomprehensible English phrases in tough, mangled accents being hollered from the steep, dark terrace behind their goal.

And Albion concentrate on their job. They've put the same titanic effort into all seven matches they've played in the last three weeks. Eleven men have travelled the length and breadth of a continent playing football. They've spent all of their waking hours on the road or on battered, muddy spring pitches. They've been knocked out of the FA Cup, and they've fallen adrift in the race for the league title. But the UEFA Cup is still in their grasp. So they attack. In the fume-clogged Midland air, in the warm shimmering light, they attack. They force the Red Star defence onto the back foot. And in front of the Brummie Road, Batson lofts a high ball into the penalty area, Bomber heads it on, and Cyrille Regis swivels to smash a right-footed volley past Stojanovic into the top corner. It's 1-1 on aggregate, and Albion are on home soil again with the Brummie right behind them.

They attack.

They throw everything in their arsenal at Stojanovic, trying to finish the tie in ninety minutes, trying to spare their tormented legs the pain of extra-time. But no shots or headers can beat the Red Star keeper; no corners or free kicks can force a mistake in their defence. And minutes from time, Slavoljub Muslin drives through midfield on the counter. He feeds a pass through to Milos Sestic; Sestic outpaces Bryan Robson, sprinting through on goal, and Ally Robertson runs in to intercept him, to put in a sliding tackle. No centre-half in the country is a better ball-winner than Ally Robertson, but this time, he doesn't get the ball. This time the

~ 268 ~

ball ricochets under Robertson's outstretched leg and rolls through towards goal.

Sestic leaps Robertson's challenge and sprints in.

Tony Godden races off his line to try and claim the loose ball.

Sestic reaches it first and hammers it over Godden, right into the roof of the net. Godden kneels in the muddy goalmouth with his head on the ground. He knows. Everyone knows. There's no coming back from this. It's all over.

The clock on the Woodman Corner scoreboard ticks round past 9.15, and the final whistle pierces the windy night.

Red Star Belgrade have knocked West Bromwich Albion out of the 1979 UEFA Cup.

April 1979

The three women in the centre circle smile for the cameras. They're a long way from home, but Helen, Sheila and Valerie know showbusiness; they know it's the same routine in the Black Country as it is in Philadelphia. And if they're even the slightest bit fazed to be standing in the middle of a football pitch wearing West Bromwich Albion shirts, they don't show it.

When they lift their microphones, the Three Degrees – the original Three Degrees, the women whose songs have raced up the charts for years now – fill the Hawthorns with song. They've coped with the strange environment well so far, but even from the distance he's standing at, Jonah can see their surprise when the Brummie Road starts singing along with them, and the echoes of twelve thousand Black Country voices bellowing in about nine different keys echo back to them.

WHEN WILL AH SEE YOOOOOW AGAIN?

Football and music. Both have changed since those days when the home ends first formed, but somehow the spirit's stayed the same. You stand on the terraces to support your team. You support your team by opening your mouth and letting them hear your voice. You sing, and no matter how serious or silly the words are, no matter how old or new the tune is, your singing lifts the players on the pitch: it urges them to run those few yards further, to jump those few inches higher, to keep the tackles hard, the passes quick, the shots powerful. As soon as you join that chorus from the home end, you become a part of your team's performance; a part of the goals they score, the points they win, the trophies they lift. And even when they've had triumph snatched away from them, your support picks them up and sends them onto the next challenge with their heads held high.

It's the culture of the Kop choir. It's the culture of the Brummie Road. Today, it sweeps right through the stadium.

By the time the Three Degrees finish singing, every man, woman and child inside the Hawthorns is making noise. Every side and corner of the ground has come to life. The feeling's there in all four stands, in the seats and on the terraces: today, they can't lose. The support is just too good. Jonah looks over to Kath, and she's clapping her hands, chanting along as if it's 1965 all over again, as if the last fourteen years of their lives haven't passed by in an aimless blur. To his left, Bill, and Chris are enjoying themselves too, taking it in turns to yell *COME ON YOU*

BAGGIES, and even Jude's laughing at the sight of Ron Atkinson courting cameramen, always making sure he's in frame when they photograph the Three Degrees.

They've been through so much, all of them – Jonah could list his own life's struggles like a catalogue of wasted chances, and he can barely begin to guess the problems which have plagued Bill, Jude and Kath down the years – but still, in spite of it all, they're together again. They're in the place which has always mattered the most.

They're watching Everton chase shadows.

The Toffees are a strong team – still title contenders despite having dropped into third place behind Albion, with both teams trailing Liverpool by four points – relying on a strong back line of Barton, Todd, Ross and Jones to keep the goals out, and Bob Latchford and Andy King to bang them in at the other end. But today, Latchford doesn't get a sniff; he's penned in, with the Brummie Road singing *BOBBY LATCHFORD, BOBBY LATCHFORD, CYRILLE WANTS YER ENGLAND SHIRT!* Today, the Everton defence are stretched down the flanks and in the centre, George Wood being tested in goal over and over again. Albion chase the ball down in midfield with fierce tackles, attacking, attacking, always attacking, and they know they can't lose, they know it as well as everyone else in the ground. There's a crescendo from the crowd every time Albion drive forward – that anticipation of a breakthrough, of that crucial goal – and the whole ground is ready to erupt.

But they're kept waiting for eighty-three minutes; they're kept singing and shouting and gasping as Wood somehow keeps a clean sheet in the Everton goal. They're kept waiting.

And finally it comes: seven minutes from time, Bryan Robson wins the ball from Colin Todd and feeds it to Ally Brown, who puts away his sixteenth league goal of the season.

It's a sign. Jonah's convinced it is.

Today's the day.

– So.

– So?

– Ya cor tell me ya dae enjoy that. Bein up theer again. Seein th'Albion gerrin the job done!

– Oh, it's just what I've been waitin for, that.

– Bet ya cor wait ter get some sausage in ya, an all.

– What?

– Wouldn't be a Satdee if we dae g'ter the hot dog van. No, no, put yer money away, me wench. Ah'm buyin. Yow've got a babby ter worry abaht.

– Thanks, Jonah.

– No worries. Aroit, missis! Can I have one jumbo wi onions an mustard, an one… ya want ketchup on yowers, Kath? Ar, one wi ketchup, please. An can ya do us a favour an mek sure iss slightly cooked this time, please? Ya know, juss tickle it round the fryer a bit befower ya bung it in the bun?

– Oi. Less a that. We've bin approved by the council, ya cheeky prick.

– Oh, sorry. It ay evry day ya come across a mobile eatery which lives up ter the exactin standards a Sandwell Council.

– D'yow want these bloody hot dogs or not?

Jonah nods and winks at Kath. She smiles, and although it's been ten years and more since he last saw that sight, and there are lines and wrinkles around it which were never there before, it's a beautiful thing to see.

He takes the hot dogs off the wench in the van – she even tells him not to bother coming back, the miserable cow – and they walk down Halfords Lane, biting through half-stale bread and bright red sausage.

– Funny how things work out.

– Is it?

– Well, ya think abaht all the decisions yow've med in yer life, an yow atta wonder. How much could it ha changed wi a few different choices, eh?

– What if someone took the right to choose away from ya?

– Sorry, ah doe follow.

– Don't worry about it. Long time ago.

– Fair enough. See, the thing is, ah've bin thinkin abaht the future.

– Wow. D'you see yerself gettin that hole in the car fixed?

– Come on, bab, ah'm bein serious. Ah've really thought a lot abaht me future, the last couple a months. An… well, ya know. Yowers, an all.

– My future?

– An little Emma. Ah mean, doe ya think her should have a bit a stability in her life? Good role models, an all that business?

– Course she should.

– An… well, ah'm not sure what yer plans am…

– I might be going away.

Jonah nearly chokes on a mouthful of bread.

– Gewin away? Gewin wheer? Not back ter that arsehole in London?

– No. I don't know. I haven't really made my mind up. Honestly, I try not to think about the future too much, Jonah. Or the past.

– Is it really that bad?

– Which? The past, or the future?

– Either! Bloody hell, if ya cor look back an ya cor look forward, yow'll be walkin round wi yer eyes closed! Come on, it ay that bad, surely?

– Jonah, days like today are the best thing about life. They always have been. Just enjoy each moment as it comes.

– Thass fair enough, but what abaht tomorrer? An the next day? An the next? Ah doe know how ya can live loike that, Kath. Ah really doe.

– Nor do I, if I'm honest. Still. Here I am.

She swallows the last of her hot dog, and he watches her lick traces of ketchup from her fingers as they get to the car.

– Here yow am. So, is it back to the littlun now, or can ya spare another hour or two enjoyin the moments?

– What've you got in mind?

– We can allwis gew sightseein.

– Sightseeing? Are there any sights round here to see?

– Hark at yow, Mrs Fancy Pants! Theer might not be no Big Ben or Buckingham Palace, but theer's sights ter see evrywheer, me wench. Might do ya some good ter have a look round. Come on. Hop in.

She sits quietly in the passenger seat as Jonah takes the Cortina for miles and miles, in aimless circles all around the Black Country. They drive down busy dual carriageways and desolate backstreets, over canals and railway lines. They see terraces and tower blocks, churches and temples, factories and Job Centres. They give way to lorries hauling goods from across Britain and Europe, and disturb a group of Indian kids on one estate playing cricket in the road with a milk crate and a tennis ball. They see all the old folks doddering into the Lucky Seven Social Club in Wednesbury, and the cooling towers of Ocker Hill power station cold and quiet, the plant finally closed after seventy-five years. They see the steel spires of Tipton Gasworks, shut down four years ago by the discovery of North Sea natural gas, and the mills and chimneys of Round Oak Steelworks up Brierley Hill, towering over the Dudley cut, awaiting a fresh set of redundancies.

Every so often, Jonah points out somewhere they used to go as youngsters, something that's changed in the years she was away, but the rest of the time, they sit quietly. They sit and stare at a landscape which

~ 274 ~

never stops changing, where the most reliable constant in people's lives is the local football club.

Two points in the bag. A title race still alive. The prospect of steady work and wages in the weeks and months ahead. The promise of someone to spend those weeks and months with. So many simple hopes fill Jonah's car like sunlight on a bright spring evening.

May 1979

In the corner of the Smethwick End, the Forest fans go berserk. In front of the Halfords Lane Stand, Brian Clough clenches his fist victoriously. Up the Brummie Road, Bill closes his eyes. It shouldn't hurt this much, but it does.

The match is all but meaningless; Liverpool took the league title with a record points tally last Tuesday, beating Villa 3-0 at Anfield. The only consolation left for Albion is to finish as runners-up, to find whatever triumph lies in the shadow of Bob Paisley's titans. But third-place Nottingham Forest, League Cup winners and European Cup finalists, have come to the Hawthorns tonight for the last game of the season, trailing Albion by a point. And Albion have thrown everything at them through Regis, Robson and Brown; Bomber, Cantello and Trewick. And Peter Shilton's jumped and dived, punched and parried, caught and cradled every effort on the Forest goal. And just as thirty thousand Albion fans prepare to settle for the goalless draw, a point which'll see them confirm that second-place finish, Trevor Francis storms up the pitch on the break with ten minutes left and repays a little of the million pounds Forest paid for him in February with a thundering shot past Tony Godden into the net.

Bomber bangs the ball down in the centre circle for the restart with a face full of anger, full of frustration. There isn't enough time left for Albion to respond. When the ref blows for full-time, Forest celebrate a 1-0 win. They've pushed Albion down to third place with minutes of the season remaining.

Bill looks down to his left and sees Christopher with his face in his hands. He puts his hand on Chris's shoulder and rubs it consolingly. After a while, Christopher looks up, his face wet and miserable.

– This is it, ay it? This is the end.

– Blimey, mate, thass a dismal outlook. We'll just atta do better next year, wo we?

– But what if next year's no better?

– Then the year after. Thass football, Chris.

Things always get better sooner or later. Bill's always clung onto that, whether he's been watching Don Howe take the Albion down or struggling to make ends meet at home. That hope of good news round the corner's always seen him through.

But there's talk in the pubs and on the terraces, rumours of change. Rumours that Laurie Cunningham impressed watchful eyes in Valencia last winter, that the likes of Barcelona and Real Madrid are keen to sign him. Rumours that Len Cantello wants to move back to the North West.

Rumours that Bomber's nearly ready to retire. News round the ground these days is no better than it is at home, no more enjoyable than yet another row with Jude over something totally insignificant.

– Ah bet Jonah's glad he's missed this un. T'ay bin the best end ter the season, has it? It'll be fine, though. Honest. Ah tell ya what; as soon as David Mills finds his feet, they'll atta build a new trophy cabinet to hold all the silverware.

And if there's a nasty feeling in the back of Bill's mind – a feeling that actually, settling for third-best might be part and parcel of life for a lot of people, that this is as good as it'll ever get; that the bright future he once hoped for may never come, and instead he'll make do with crushed hopes from now until his last breath – he pushes it away. Because deep down, he still wants to believe that there's better to come.

He desperately wants to believe it.

*

Jonah finds out the result down the pub. He's only nipped in for a swift half – a bit of Dutch courage – and asked if anyone knew the final score while he was there. He should have guessed from the glum faces. Bloody Trevor Francis.

He's carrying a bunch of flowers, a spring bouquet of pink, blue and yellow things which stink to high heaven. The landlord makes him sit out back on an empty keg after half the blokes in the boozer start sneezing, and then after a couple of minutes sipping at his mild, he ends up jogging round the car park with a bee after him. He leaves the pub swearing to himself. This had better be worth it.

It's now or never.

The drive across town's a daydream. He feels like he should be riding his old scooter again, all polished chrome and mirrors and flag on the back – he sold the bugger years ago, put the money towards the Cortina – but it feels like that kind of night. As if years of his life have traced a course to this.

He gets the words straight in his mind, murmuring them to himself as he crawls through the Friday night traffic. Nothing pushy, nothing over-the-top – he's not climbing up her balcony or jumping out of a plane with a box of Milk Tray – just a few sentences about how well they've always got on together, how he's always felt a spark there. How he's a pretty reliable bloke, and she can always depend on him; little Emma can, too.

It's going to go really well. He can feel it.

*

The sun goes down over the rooftops, painting chimney-shadows over slate and brick, burning red patterns through the net curtains. Kath stares out of the window. She's not sorry to be leaving – her mind's made up about that – but she's glad to see one last, beautiful sight of the place where she grew up.

This time, she's not coming back.

When all's said and done, she has to do what's best for Emma. To think she spent months agonising over that bundle of life in the cot, terrified that something was wrong with her daughter. All the time, it was her who was wrong. She realised that a fortnight ago, the day she went to pick Emma up for feeding time, and her daughter looked up at her with bright blue eyes and gurgled one quick syllable twice: *ma ma*. Kath thought she'd misheard at first. Then Emma said it again, loud and insistent. It wasn't an accident. Kath picked her up and repeated it back to her, *mama*, over and over until Emma said it again; then she hugged the warm body tight to her breast, tears in her eyes for the best of reasons.

She knew for certain, then. Emma deserves a real mother. The kind of mother Kath can never be.

Emma deserves better than the fear and doubt which shadow Kath with every step. She deserves better than a mother who spends her life running from one trap to another, forever letting other people control her. Better than someone so lost in her own problems that she didn't even want to look at her own baby the day it was born.

The worst thing that could possibly happen to her daughter is to become like her.

Her mind's been tied in knots for months, but she's finally unpicked all of those knots, let everything come unravelled inside her head. She hasn't slept in days now, but she feels calm. Just like they told her to be. And she knows it's for the best if she goes away.

It's for the best if she goes away for good.

She's timed everything perfectly. Her ma's home at ten, so Emma won't be alone for too long. She's spent the whole evening with her, singing songs. She's fed her and made sure she's clean, and even tried teaching her to say her own name.

Finally, after watching the sunset through the window, she kisses Emma goodbye.

She walks up to the bathroom, humming to herself. She avoids looking at the mirror; two days ago she was washing her face in here, and she caught a glimpse in the glass of Mr Barrett standing behind her, smiling and whispering. She ended up crying in the bathtub, counting the tiles on the wall until it all went away. She's not letting that happen again.

She reaches up to the sliding doors of the cabinet and takes down her ma's sleeping pills. She heads back downstairs, still humming, and grabs the bottle of whisky sitting on the kitchen table, next to the short note she wrote earlier. She doesn't even recognise the wild scrawl on the paper – it's frenzied, manic, barely legible – but it'll have to do.

When she finally lies down, it's with a smile on her face. The sun's long gone, and the darkness is soothing. She closes her eyes and drifts away to the memory of music, dancing her way through long, carefree nights.

*

Jonah's stomach's a stormy sea as he turns the corner into the street, but he takes a deep breath and tells his nerves to behave. He parks the Cortina up outside the house, pulls the handbrake and turns the key in the ignition. He spends a good minute or two checking how he looks in the rear view mirror, until he realises that a woman who's known him since 1965 isn't likely to be judging him on the state of his hair tonight. He's just dithering. He tells himself to grow a pair.

After grabbing the flowers off the back seat and wincing again at the stink of them, he walks up and knocks the front door of the house. There's no answer.

He can hear Emma crying inside. He knocks again, hard enough to make his knuckles sting, and waits for a few heartbeats before walking over to the window, cupping his hand against the glass and peering into the darkness.

At first he can't see anything.

Then he can see Emma.

Then he can see Kath.

Then he can see the whisky.

He shakes his head and looks down at the ground. He shouldn't be podging his nose into her business. He never knew things were that bad with her, though. Drunk with a little babby to look after? If nothing else, he needs to have a word about that.

He looks in the window again.

Then he sees the pills.

A few seconds of disbelief, mixed with crawling horror.

Then Jonah's in a daydream again, this time with blood pounding in his ears as he hammers his fist against the window and starts hollering. He tries the door, kicking, swearing; across the street, one of the neighbours opens her front door and tells him to mind the bloody racket, so he spins round and runs across the road shouting, waving his bunch of flowers at her, telling her to dial 999. She screams and slams the door on him.

He bellows at an empty street for someone to call an ambulance, and fiddles with his car keys to open up the Cortina, dropping the flowers on the pavement. He scrambles round inside for something to break the window, and gets his foot trapped in the hole in the floor as he's grabbing his tyre iron off the back seat.

A jolt of pain as he pulls his foot free. He runs back to the window, trampling the flowers on the ground. He lifts the tyre iron to smash the window.

He prays to something he's never believed in that there's still time. He knows in his heart that there isn't.

April 2002

Football isn't a matter of life and death. It's more impotent than that.

It wasn't always so sterile. Once, there was a level playing field. Once, there was fair competition. There were always big clubs and small clubs, packed Kops in the cities and bare embankments in the towns, but gate money was split evenly, television windfalls shared in proportion. In those days, merit could triumph. In those days, worth wasn't defined by wealth.

But those in power brought changes. They said they wanted greater competition, but they wanted a monopoly. They made the richest so rich that they could never be challenged. They made the poorest fight tooth and claw just to survive. Then came the gamblers. Then came the debts.

We're coming to the end of the ninety minutes now, and Albion have failed to make the breakthrough they desperately need. If you're just joining us, it's goalless here at Valley Parade, as Clement plays the ball to Jordao.

They bulldozed terraces for seats. They sent ticket prices soaring. They filled a galaxy with satellite signals of Bergkamp, Cantona, Ginola. They bought trophies like trinkets. They sold history as if it was theirs to auction. Football's coming home? It never left. It just changed owners.

What an incredible journey it's been for Albion over the last few weeks! They trailed Wolves by eleven points this time last month, but they've caught them, they've overtaken them; the Baggies are in the driving seat for promotion now, but they have to win here in Bradford today. They need a goal.

It took me a long time to understand football. But I learnt, over time. I learnt how football holds a mirror up to the world, how it reflects the society we live in.

I learnt that clubs are at the heart of communities.

I learnt that when clubs suffer, communities suffer. And vice versa.

I've got the radio on, and I'm listening to the match; not in suffering, but in hope.

We're sixty seconds into stoppage time here in West Yorkshire, and as it stands, Wolves will have the advantage in the promotion race. Albion can't break Bradford down. Johnson has the ball on the halfway line; there might be time for one more attack.

Someday, the last traces of magic and wonder will be scrubbed out of football like mud off a dirty kit. Someday, it'll all become some predictable charade, league places decided by hard cash, with no room left for the glorious underdogs.

But not today.

Derek McInnes sends it long across field, and that's a fantastic ball for Bob Taylor on the left-hand side of the box. Taylor takes a touch, and… OH, HE'S BROUGHT DOWN! ANDY MYERS HAS BROUGHT TAYLOR DOWN IN THE AREA! IT MUST BE! YES! A PENALTY TO ALBION IN THE NINETY-THIRD MINUTE!

A penalty. Please, anything but a bloody penalty.

It's some terrible, twisted, cosmic joke. Eleven penalties this season, and Albion have missed eight of them. I can't listen. I open the door and go out into the yard, then realise I can't bear not hearing it. I need to know. Even if we miss it, even if we throw our chance of promotion away, I need to know.

That the course of an entire season can end up hinging on one single moment. That the course of an entire life can, too. That fortune can be so horribly against us. It's difficult to accept, but then, the truth often is.

Neil Clement hands the ball to Igor Balis. Could this be the moment? It's his first penalty for the club, and it couldn't be more important. How does Balis feel right now? His nerves… he must be shaking. He's got to settle himself, compose himself, take everything

~ 284 ~

else off his mind. **What happens in the next few moments could decide the future of West Bromwich Albion.**

Once, I was married to a man who was married to football. He lived for it. It was his escape from the world around him, and he used that escape at every opportunity.

I'm not married to that man anymore.

But last month, I had a phone call to tell me that he's ill. That he may not have long left. And although I hadn't thought about him in a long time, I'm thinking about him now.

I want that goal. I want it for him. I want something for him to live for, even if it's just a little longer. Because no one should ever feel like there's no reason left for them to be alive.

I learnt that a long time ago, too.

Igor Balis against Alan Combe. Igor Balis...

Part Three

1991 – 1994

January 1991

– He's scored.

This is how it ends. This is the tragic, humiliating demise which has been coming for so long. There's no fire, no floods, no forests reduced to ash; no irradiated earth glowing in the sickly light of a dying star. Just a crowd of fourteen thousand huddled in the rain, watching in dismay as two wretched centre-halves in blue and white stripes are tormented by an estate agent from Gibraltar.

– Ya fuckin load a shit. Set of arseholes! Absolute twat of a goal.

The estate agent's name is Tim Buzaglo. He's wearing a red shirt, white shorts and red socks streaked with mud and soaked through with cold winter drizzle. It's the first week of January. Albion are sixteenth in the Second Division, and the third round draw for this year's FA Cup has gifted them a home tie against Woking FC from the Vauxhall-Opel League, nearly a hundred places below them on English football's lengthy ladder. It's the kind of match which crops up at this time every year: professionals versus amateurs, giants against underdogs, an embodiment of grand Victorian ideals which have somehow persisted into an age of silicon and microchips. Most of these match-ups are a walk in the park for the favourites. But the reporters and television cameras are always there, just in case.

Just in case there's someone like Tim Buzaglo.

– Ya useless shithouse tossers. Run! RUN, ya fuckin weebles!

The rain slashes down onto the front rows of the Brummie Road End, clattering against advertising boards for the MEB and Sandwell Council, soaking folks watching through the green fencing at pitchside. There are gale-force winds blowing across the country today, bringing down trees and power lines, stripping tiles off rooves, but the damage happening here is different.

Bill's halfway up the terrace – in his favourite spot – sheltered by the roof, but feeling numb, and not just from the wind. He felt fine in the first half when Colin West put Albion 1-0 up, nodding a far-post header past Tim Read from a corner down the Smethwick End. If anything, he was disappointed it was just a one-goal lead. After all, it was only Woking.

– Oh, come on. Tackle im! Christ's bollocks, TACKLE IM!

But fears flow around the terraces like a strange current, sweeping along rows up and down the stands. Albion have been in dodgy form, with just two wins in eleven matches, and a vital derby triumph against Wolves snatched away last week by a stoppage-time equaliser from Rob

Hindmarch. They're on the ropes. Down in the dugout, Brian Talbot's nine lives are nearly up. The confidence and swagger Talbot brought to the team two long years ago has gone along with all the promising young players – Carlton Palmer, Chris Whyte, David Burrows – the board have sold to plug a widening financial hole.

Albion are on a slow, grinding, downhill path. They're in trouble.

That trouble finally woke up and starting prowling the pitch thirteen minutes into the second half. The floodlights glared down as Woking's Mark Biggins picked up a loose ball on the halfway line and played a short pass infield to Dereck Brown. Warm light bathed the quagmire surface as Brown knocked a first-time through-ball between Graham Roberts and Gary Strodder for the number ten Tim Buzaglo, who sprinted onto it and calmly placed a side-footed shot just inside the post from eighteen yards out.

The red shirts legged it for the corner of the Smethwick End, for the thousands of fans who'd travelled up from Surrey. They celebrated their equaliser like a winning goal at Wembley. Eleven men due back in offices or on shop floors come Monday morning were going toe-to-toe with professionals, and they had nothing to fear. Nothing at all.

AL-BI-ON, AL-BI-ON, AL-BI-ON!

The Brummie Road tried to get behind the team when Bernard McNally sent a long-range shot over the crossbar just after the restart, but Woking kept possession, kept looking for the gaps in the Albion defence. Groans started to greet every misplaced pass from the home team, every aimless high ball forward which only found a red shirt. And five minutes after their first goal, Tim Read drop-kicked a long ball up to the centre-circle, Dereck Brown headed it on, and Buzaglo outpaced Bradley, Roberts and Strodder to get through on goal again, beating Mel Rees who rushed headlong out of goal, then headed straight into an empty net to put Woking 2-1 up.

WORRA LOAD A RUBBISH! WORRA LOAD A RUBBISH!

For ten minutes, the atmosphere seethed. For ten minutes, Albion players treated the ball like the hottest of potatoes, conceding corners and throw-ins at every turn, ducking out of challenges, losing possession with every other pass. And it was during those ten minutes that Bill first noticed the bloke in front of him – a man wearing a denim jacket and jeans, with tangled brown hair in a mullet down to his shoulders – cursing an endless stream of inventive bile at the pitch.

– Stop twattin abaht, ya knobshafts! Clear it! CLEAR IT!

He had his own style, his own fashion sense, but ultimately, the bloke was no different to anyone else up the Brummie Road. Regardless of age, sex, race, politics, dress, music, or any other thing which could possibly set people apart from each other, everyone standing on the terraces on a Saturday afternoon is there out of loyalty to the club. That loyalty's usually lifelong, and it's usually enough to create unity in spite of other differences.

But the bloke in front of Bill had seen enough. And everyone around Bill had seen enough. And Bill had seen enough. After so much support, so much devotion for so little reward, the mood up the Brummie Road had turned as sour as a week-old pint of mild.

– WHAT WAS THAT, BANNISTER? WHAT THE FUCKIN HELL WAS THAT? AH'VE PUT MORE EFFORT INTEW HAVIN A SHIT!

Darren Bradley lost the ball to Adie Cowler in midfield, and Woking attacked again. They stroked the ball with confidence and skill across the harrowed turf: Cowler passing to Biggins, Biggins letting the ball run through his legs to Shane Wye on the right flank, Wye playing it back into Biggins' path as he steamed upfield. Graham Harbey put in a sliding tackle, but Biggins took a touch to dodge the challenge, and the entire Albion left was wide open in front of him. He took his time, picked out a cross to Adie Cowler by the penalty spot, and three Albion defenders stood dumbly and watched as Cowler took a touch to control it, then laid it off to Buzaglo, completely unmarked at the far post.

Buzaglo fired a low, left-footed shot past Mel Rees into the bottom corner to complete his hat-trick and give Woking a 3-1 lead.

This is how it ends. This is the tragic, humiliating demise which has been coming for so long.

– He's scored. Ya fuckin load a shit. Set of arseholes! Absolute twat of a goal.

The Almighty Mullet isn't the only one unhappy. As Albion trudge back to their position for kick-off, Bill watches five blokes climb over the low wall at the front of the Halfords Lane Stand and march onto the pitch. They get a cheer from the rest of the ground as they bear down on the players, waving their arms, making a few polite enquiries as to what the defence is fucking well playing at. As Graham Roberts calms them down, and a line of orange-jacketed stewards escort them back off the field, the Brummie Road turns its attention to the man in the dugout.

TALBOT OUT! TALBOT OUT! TALBOT OUT! TALBOT OUT!

Bill tells himself it can't get any worse, at least it can't get any worse, but he should know better. Things can always get worse. By the time Woking bring on substitute Terry Worsfold with four minutes left, a line of coppers in fluorescent jackets have replaced the stewards at the front of the stand, and over their domed black helmets he sees Shane Wye curl a cross into the box from the Woking right, and Worsfold glance a header into the top corner to put Woking 4-1 up. The pitchside photographers are off like whippets down the track, converging on the goal celebration with flashes blinking brightly.

The anger. The humiliation. When football fans lose their patience, a home end can match any revolution on earth for blind rage. The jeers and whistles sweep around the ground as Albion win a free-kick a few minutes from time. Tony Ford gets the ball down the right wing and puts in a cross which Woking centre-half Pratt can't quite clear, and Darren Bradley pounces to tuck away a consolation and make it 4-2.

Incredibly, that's what tips them all over the edge.

For the first time in Bill's life, the Brummie Road boos an Albion goal. All of the frustration and fury at the team's performance, the manager's decisions and the board's complacency becomes a hollow boom echoing around the stand, reverberating through the corrugated metal above and the reinforced concrete below. And down the Smethwick End, to cap the absurdity, the Woking fans cheer Bradley, giving him a standing ovation while all four sides of the Hawthorns wax livid at the chairman and directors.

SACK THE BOARD, SACK THE BOARD, SACK THE BOARD!

They stay in the stands till full-time. There are kids sat down on the terraces crying their eyes out, and the chants of *TALBOT OUT* and *SACK THE BOARD* keep on sporadically as the clock ticks down. Everyone's waiting for the whistle.

The rain's stopped, and they're waiting for the storm to begin.

When that metallic shriek finally calls an end to the embarrassment, fans climb the walls and fences and start walking out onto the field, slowly, deliberately. The Woking players glance nervously towards police and stewards – over the last decade, the nine o'clock news has given them good cause to be scared of pitch invasions – and the first supporter on, a bloke in a leather jacket with a pony-tail, walks straight up to Tim Buzaglo.

He looks the Woking striker in the eye, and holds out his hand. Buzaglo nods and shakes it.

Soon they're all at it; all the Albion fans, all the Woking players, shaking hands in the centre of the pitch and patting each other on the back. Because this non-league team have done something today that Albion forgot how to do a long time ago. They've come to the Hawthorns and they've played real football. They've earned their victory.

And after waving to the Woking supporters in the Smethwick End, Tim Buzaglo walks the length of the pitch to the Brummie Road End. The whole way, he's surrounded by at least two dozen Albion fans in denim, leather, shellsuits, replica shirts, a surreal guard of honour. When he reaches the byline, he looks up into the depths of the stand behind the goal and holds his hands out above his head. He applauds the Brummie Road.

Bill applauds back. Everyone does. The Albion fans around Buzaglo hoist him up onto their shoulders as a hero. He may have scored a hat-trick against them; he may have inflicted the most painful defeat on the club that any of them have ever seen. But if there's one thing the Brummie Road can appreciate, it's an honest bloke with a bit of talent and a passion for hard work. A Jeff Astle. A Tony Brown. A Cyrille Regis. A Tim Buzaglo.

The estate agent from Gibraltar takes a bewildered but happy look at the cheering horde around him, and raises a clenched fist in appreciation as the home end voices its loud verdict on the afternoon's events.

SIGN HIM UP, SIGN HIM UP, SIGN HIM UP!

It carries on outside the ground, beneath starlight and streetlight.

Bill wanders out of the gates into a surge of mayhem. He sees departing Woking supporters' coaches up Halfords Lane given a standing ovation by Albion fans. He sees supporters trying to kick in the doors of the executive entrance to the ground. He sees mounted police charging blokes chanting *TALBOT OUT*. Thirty-six years, eight months and four days since he first set foot inside the Hawthorns, and this is what it's come to.

He doesn't join in the protests. He's too miserable to be angry. He walks to the bus stop – the one he first went to nearly thirty years ago; the one which changed his young life, once upon a time – and sits down with a few other blokes who look as pig-sick as him.

There's a dog squatting by the shelter, no collar or leash, no owner in sight. It's a little Staffy, fur ragged and lank in the orange light from the streetlamps, staring blankly into space – the look of a creature stuck in some desperate trauma – and shitting a viscous pool of rank brown sludge onto the pavement. Everyone else at the stop is giving the mutt a wide berth, but Bill covers his nose and mouth and stoops to pat it gingerly on the head.

– Iss aroit, pal. Ah know how ya feel.

He never believed it could happen. Not to Albion. He never believed the club would sell its best players one by one, spend years trading diamonds for dross. He never believed they'd sleepwalk into relegation from the First Division by 1986. He never believed they'd settle so quickly into mediocrity in the Second Division, struggling for survival most years. He never believed there'd come a time when even Second Division survival started to look unlikely.

But there is one thing he's learnt over the last decade: when you're on a downhill slope which is gradual enough, you don't see the bottom coming until it's far too late. Bill found that out the hard way.

He gets back to his flat. He switches the light on. He puts the telly on and has a can of lager during Challenge Anneka. He has another during 'Allo 'Allo. He has three during The Paul Daniels Magic Show. He sits back in the armchair and spends about ten minutes in a daydream; he's at the bus stop again, and a car breaks down a few yards away. The door opens, and a woman climbs out in a long, slinky dress. It's Debbie McGee. She says she's sorry to bother him, but her car's knackered, and she needs somewhere to stay tonight. She's had enough of being sawn in half, and just wants an ordinary bloke to take care of her. Bill tells her she's in luck; it just so happens there's no one in the world more ordinary than him.

Then that little dog from the bus stop wanders over. It squats down, looks up at them with its tongue hanging out, moist-eyed and panting, and promptly squirts a thick lake of diarrhoea onto the pavement by Debbie's feet. She cups her hand over her mouth and looks at Bill in disgust, then does a runner off down the street. He legs it after her, telling her it's not his bloody dog, it's some stray, asking her to come back, to give him another chance, but she's gone; vanished into the drizzle and traffic lights of an ethereal Smethwick.

He gets up and makes some beans on toast. He has another can of lager, and halfway through Bergerac, he decides to walk into the hall, pick up the phone and dial Jude's number.

It takes ten seconds of ringing before it's picked up at the other end, and a man's voice answers.

It takes a heartbeat to slam the phone back down.

*

Chris Collier rests his elbow on the bar. He props his jaw against an upturned palm, and jabs a shaky finger at the newspaper headline in front of him.

– He's bit off more than he can chew, that Saddam.

– Ya reckon?

– Course. Ah mean, wheer can he gew from here? Peaked too soon, he has. Trying ter tek over the Middle East? Thass top-flight stuff. He shoulda started smaller. Ah mean, if yam gewin inter football management, ya doe start off by managin Liverpool, do ya?

– Bob Paisley did.

– Well, theer's allwis an exception.

– An Joe Fagan.

– Or two.

– An Kenny Dalglish.

– Okay, maybe Iraq's diffrent ter Liverpool. Although whichever way ya look at it, iss a load a blokes wi moustaches livin in a barren wasteland. But ya know, most managers lookin ter start a career'll gew somewheer loike Scarborough, or Maidstone United. An thass what Saddam shoulda done.

– Managed Maidstone United?

– Or whatever the evil dictator equivalent is. Start out simple. Get yerself a Leyland DAF Cup under the belt. Be satisfied wi what yow've got. Know what ah mean?

– Ter be honest, I ay gorra fuckin clue, mush.

Chris downs the last of his pint, cold bubbles surging over his tongue.

– Iss the illusory dividends of ambition.

– Come again?

– Ah'm sayin that someone who aims too high can get more than they bargained fer.

– Roit. Ya want that fillin up?

– Ar. Carlin Black Label, please.

The landlord eyes the spare wodge of twenties in Chris's wallet as he opens it up.

– Yow ended up wi plenty ter bargain fer, by the looks.

– But what good's it done me? Thass the question. Am I a better person fer it? Would a better person be sat in here on tod, tipping lager down they neck?

– Ah doe know, pal. Bit of advice, though, eh? Plenty a folks round here gewin through hard times.

– Oh, ya doe atta tell me. Born an raised here, ah was.

– So ya should know better than ter get cocky wi it. Keep it ter yerself.

– Come on, mate. Ah've got me head screwed on. Sort of.

Chris hands over one of his crisp purple twenties and has a sip of Black Label. As the landlord delves in the till for change, he decides to push the boat out. After all, it's a celebration.

– Can ya gimme a packet a scampi fries an all please, mucka?

He's had a good few months working construction down south – only short-term, but shitloads of overtime, enough to give him a nice thick pocket of readies – and on his first night back in the Black Country, he reckons he's earned a party.

Admittedly, it's a bit of an underwhelming party. During months of sleeping on a tatty, piss-stained sofa – all the while thinking himself lucky he wasn't kipping in the back of a Transit like a lot of the blokes on the site – he got himself through by imagining that he'd get back home with a bit of money to spend, see some old faces from school, from the neighbourhood; the prodigal son getting the rounds in, earning himself a warm welcome from someone, somehow.

With that in mind, he can't help but feel a bit gutted that his grand homecoming's actually a lone stool at the bar with a miserable landlord and a picture of Saddam Hussein for company.

So as the night wears on, and the jukebox gets louder, and Chris works his way through half a dozen more pints of lager, he sets about making new friends. It's always been one of his talents, and it's amazing what chipping in a round'll do for your popularity. Soon, the guys and girls sipping drinks off one of his twenties want to know all about him. He covers the basic ground. He's a bright spark just waiting for the world to catch light for him. Family? Nah. Not to speak of, and certainly not to speak to. Not anymore.

He tells a few jokes and a few tall tales. He has them crying with laughter when he gets up and raps along to *Ice Ice Baby* on the jukebox. He ignores the dickheads in the corner giving him the evil eye; some pillock with short, gelled black hair and a stud in his ear, another wearing ripped jeans and a black puffa jacket. And when the hunger hits his belly, he's around his ninth pint. More or less. There comes a point when counting them's more effort than it's worth. Like father like son, as Mom'd say; but which father? There's the question. There, ladies and gents, is the Countdown conundrum for today. And yesterday. And the last three or four years of his life.

How exactly did two brown-haired parents go about producing his blond bonce? Why did his old man – Bill Collier, the bloke he'd been raised to think was his dad – break down after too many pints one night during the divorce, and tearfully tell Chris that he'd always love him as a son, no matter what the truth was?

They're serious questions; ones which plague Chris when he's sober, but tend to retreat somewhere into the fog after a few pints, ready to launch another assault come morning. Not that Chris is bothered about the morning. Right now, the future doesn't extend any further than the amount of time it'll take to buy and eat a kebab, then stumble to bed.

He waves goodbye to all his new mates – he tries to thank them by name, but gets stuck after the first two, so decides to call it quits there – and pulls his brand new parka on before heading out into an unusually blurry night.

He could measure out his life in blurry nights. He had his first one after leaving school. He had another the evening that Dad – he still feels angry thinking that word – let slip about the family tree's rotten roots. He had one on a hot summer night in July 1989 after hearing the news about a car crash in Madrid; after hearing that the emergency services had pulled the lifeless body of thirty-three-year-old Laurie Cunningham from the wreckage.

Someone so clever and gifted, gone so abruptly, so unfairly. A career blighted by injury, years spent wandering unhappily from one club to another, dogged by racial abuse in any number of languages, brought to such a sudden and savage end. At Albion, he'd taken on the whole world and won. But the world had its revenge on Laurie. Long, cruel, brutal revenge.

It can happen to anyone. Anyone can get blown off course, have everything promising in their life snatched away. The only thing worse than seeing it happen to your childhood hero is having it happen to you too.

– Oh, thass a neat little header from Regis fer Cunningham! An if he keeps his head, he'll score!

Chris puts his right foot through an empty Irn-Bru can on the pavement, then lurches to one side and steadies himself on a lamppost.

– OH, WORRA GOAL! CUNNINGHAM'S SHOT LEAVES BAILEY STRANDED!

He hiccups, and stops to shovel some of the hot kebab he bought from the takeaway into his mouth with greasy fingers. Then he stumbles on, re-enacting some of his other favourite Laurie moments, weaving his way down the road with the empty can rattling off his foot every few yards. When he makes it to his usual shortcut – the bridge down to the canal towpath – he gives the can one final kick into the road, and turns onto the cut. He wanders into the dark, so lost in his one-man show that he doesn't realise the danger until it's too late.

He gets hit from behind. Knocked down, face-first. The towpath's just a dirt track, but it takes the skin off his arms and forehead, his food a mess all over the grass verge. He's on the ground, and the punches and kicks come quickly. He rolls over and catches a glimpse of the two knobs from the pub; the lad with a stud in his ear and the one in the puffa jacket. He wonders what the hard-knocks up the Brummie Road ten years ago would have made of a bloke wearing an earring, and nearly laughs, but Stud gives him another kick, then tells Puffa to go through Chris's pockets.

That wakes Chris up, and he tries to grab Puffa's hands, lash out at him, but Stud kicks him in the balls, and Chris groans and rubs his head against the ground while Puffa pulls his wallet out. Two hundred quid in there. He feels sick, and not just from the state of his bollocks. They're going to have it. They're going to have the fucking lot.

Stud opens up the wallet up and has a look inside. Then he walks over to the edge of the cut, tips it upside down, and lets all the notes flutter out into the water. He chucks the empty wallet onto Chris's face and spits on the ground.

– Twat. Try flashin yer cash around now.

Puffa gives him another kick, and Chris shrieks at the pain spiking its way up his spine. Then Puffa and Stud wander off, laughing to themselves, singing *Ice Ice Baby* in stupid voices. Chris lies on the ground till he's sure they're gone. Then he crawls over to the edge of the towpath and leans his head over the side. He reaches out and fumbles for the notes resting on the water, so many soaked portraits of Shakespeare and the Queen floating away from his grasp.

He feels sick again. Sick with the pain. Sick with the booze. Sick with the humiliation; the realisation that people in his own town would rather take him down a peg or two than just rob him.

Sick with disgust at what he's let himself become.

*

The man walks into the gloom. He can just about make out the path by the moonlight reflected in the water of the canal, an eerie brightness spreading from dark sky and water. He takes note of the image in his mind, tries to pick out the details, store them away for later, for inspiration. He does that without thinking; it's been second nature to him for years now.

He's hung back until those two wankers made themselves scarce. He heads down the towpath and spots Chris kneeling by the edge of the canal, fishing around in the water for God only knows what.

– You okay, mate?

Chris looks up, and scrambles back from the cut. The poor bastard looks terrified.

– Who's there?

He wanders forward.

– An old mate.

Chris squints at him.

– Rajinder? That yow?

– Second time lucky.

– Second time?

– I'll put that blanking you gave me ten minutes ago down to the withdrawal symptoms of the fiendish kebab addict. Oh, I see you made the most of that meal. Did you actually eat any of it before lobbing it across the towpath?

– Raj. What am yow on abaht?

– Fuck's sake, Chris, do you ever bother to look at who's serving you in a takeaway? Or are we all just menial kebab-wallas to you?

– That was *yow* behind the counter?

– No, Chris, my dad was working the counter. I cooked your food. But thanks for proving my point. Look, come on. Get up off yer arse.

He holds his hand out, and Chris grabs hold of it, climbing unsteadily on his feet.

– Well, what am dewin down here at this time a night?

– I'm not sure you fully comprehend the irony of that question, mate.

– Ah was on me way home! This is me shortcut!

– Brilliant idea. What did you do to piss those goons off?

– Hang on. Ya sid them pair come after me?

– Yep. They were hanging round at the bus stop outside my dad's place. As soon as you walked out, they started following you.

– Well, ta fer the help, mate!

– Oh, what would I have done, Chris? I'm not Frank Bruno. And in case you didn't know, Friday night happens to be Chuck The Paki In The Cut night round here.

– The gesture woulda bin appreciated. One fer all, all fer one. The old Allsorts spirit.

– The Allsorts! Shit, that's a blast from the past.

– Gone but never forgot. Ya see any a the others these days?

– The others?

– Yeah, ya know. Asif. Dan. Rolo.

Raj snorts.

– Seen Asif a while back. He's hardcore now, man.

– He's a porn star?

He smiles at the astounded and entirely serious expression on Chris's face.

– Nah. Religion. Last time I seen him, he had a proper go at me for wearing Nike trainers. He kept on that Nike are controlled by the Jews, that all their profits go straight to Israel. I think he only got started with it to piss his parents off, but then he just carried on, got more involved.

– Shit.

– It's his family you should feel sorry for. His mom and dad are gutted. His little brother's alright, though. Bilal. Tidy footballer himself, so I hear.

– What about Dan?

– He went hardcore the other way. West Midlands Police.

– Jesus!

– Yep. Doing alright at it, too. I hear they're gonna make him Head Torturer in the new Serious Crimes Squad.

– Rolo?

– No idea. Last time I seen him, he was about two stone bigger and trying to outrun a pissed-off Rottweiler down the park.

– What abaht yerself? Uni?

– Nah.

– How come?

Raj shrugs his shoulders. His arguments with his parents are his own business. He's got his own ambitions, and it just so happens they don't revolve around getting the highest exam results and trotting off to study Medicine at uni like a good little boy.

– Hey, we should get the gang together again.

– For what? It was a long time ago, Chris.

– Thass exactly why we should do it! Iss bin too long. Way too long. Hey, ah bet we could even have a kickabout or two while we'm at it.

– You'd never get Asif along.

– Ah could bloody well try.

– You want some advice, Chris? Get yourself home. Get some sleep.

Chris nods, a dejected expression on his face. He turns away to trudge home, and Raj sighs.

– Hey, Chris!

– Yeah?

Raj waves his arms up and down quickly, and starts singing a song.

– WE ARE THE ALLSORTS! WE ARE THE ALLSORTS!

Chris laughs out loud, doubling up, and then turns round to slap his arse in time to the song.

– WE SPANKED YOU! WE SPANKED YOU!
They walk off, chuckling into the night.

May 1993

The ground rumbles with the tremors.

Their seats shake beneath them, vibrations rattling through brick and metal and plastic. The first stars of the evening glisten in a navy-blue sky, and to their left, the rhythmic chant from the Brummie Road End thuds through them along with the earthquake from thousands of boots and trainers pounding against the terraces.

BOING BOING, Baggies Baggies, BOING BOING, Baggies Baggies

They jump in unison, up and down, up and down. They pump their arms in the air as they do it, like pilled-up ravers. Women and men; tattooed blokes with beer bellies, teenagers with bucket hats and curtained hair, kids down the front in replica shirts and Influence overcoats; the whole of the Brummie Road is boinging. The Woodman Corner's at it too, and even the Rainbow and the Halfords Lane join in at times.

They've been doing it since last autumn, every single match, home and away. There's barely a terrace left in the Third Division which hasn't had a legion of Albion fans boinging on it. And when the Brummie Road starts boinging, the sheer force of it rattles through the ground.

Baggies Baggies, BOING BOING, Baggies Baggies, BOING BOING

They've come so far in the last six months. For that matter, they've come a long way over the last two years. Since losing to Woking, since sacking Brian Talbot; since appointing Bobby Gould to the hotseat, since being relegated from the Second Division on a miserable afternoon at Twerton Park; since sinking to the club's worst-ever finishing position last May, since they invaded the pitch at Shrewsbury Town carrying a coffin to protest against Gould's disastrous reign. They've come a very long way.

Last summer, the club appointed Ossie Ardiles as manager. With a diamond formation, a new hero up front and a kamikaze attacking philosophy which means they're as likely to lose 5-1 as win 4-0, good times at the Hawthorns are well and truly back.

BOING BOING, Baggies Baggies, BOING BOING, Baggies Baggies

They never signed Tim Buzaglo; there was no need for the estate agent from Gibraltar in the end. Not once they found the miner's son from County Durham. He signed for £300,000 off Bristol City eighteen months ago, and set about making a name for himself. He's had tips off Ronnie Allen. He's had tips off Jeff Astle. He's got a timeless instinct for being in the right place at the right time, and when the ball breaks loose in the box, you can bet your week's wages it'll be his boot to it first, sending it crashing into the net.

He's scored thirty-seven times this season.

Robert Taylor has made that name for himself. These days, they call him Super Bob.

Baggies Baggies, BOING BOING, Baggies Baggies, BOING BOING

Tonight, they're praying for Super Bob to score. Tonight, they need two goals. Albion missed out on automatic promotion, settling for fourth place and a chance of going up through the play-offs. And on Sunday, in torrential rain at the Vetch Field in Swansea, they nearly threw their chance away after conceding twice to the Welsh side. But they fought back; they snatched a goal of their own. They kept hope alive for the second leg.

They're on home turf, and the Brummie Road is boinging.

*

These days, Freeman's doing his best to live up to his name. That's what he's always done, one way or another, but there's nothing like a spell in nick to teach you what being a free man really means. How important it is. When you're a kid, when you're some saft herbert with nothing but empty space between your ears, you talk all kinds of shite about freedom. You believe some of it, too. Freedom to go out on a Friday and Saturday? Freedom to have a few pints, a few fags, smoke a spliff? Freedom to throw a few punches on the terraces, in a railway station? It's nothing compared to being able to move freely, speak freely. To eat what you want, go where you want, see who you want, leave the lights on long after dark. Prison was a struggle – twelve dark months trapped, physically and mentally – but it taught him a few lessons.

He's on the straight and narrow. Got a wife now, a babby on the way, and his own window-cleaning business finding its feet after a tough start. He'd have laughed his arse off at that fifteen years ago, with his cropped hair and Clash albums; the idea that settling down and toeing the line is freedom. But fifteen years is a long time.

All the same, it can feel like no time at all when you suddenly hear a voice from the past.

It happened a fortnight ago, just after the season finished. He was just settling down in front of Eldorado with a plate of sausage and chips when Suze walked in and said there was someone on the phone for him. Some woman called Asher.

Saying he hadn't thought about her at all over the years would be a lie. But somehow, she receded gradually in his mind, became a distant memory, like an old injury which sometimes aches for a little while on a cold day.

Still, that phone felt bloody heavy in his hand.

He was polite in an awkward, cautious way. So was she. When she didn't tell him her reason for calling straight away, he filled the clumsy silence by asking how her family was; whether she was coping alright with the career and her kids. He already knew that much about her. She asked if his business was doing alright, pulling through the recession okay, and when the baby was due. She obviously knew that much about him.

Finally, she cut to the chase. It was her dad. He was getting older, his health starting to suffer. Wheelchair-bound these days. He didn't even leave the house much; he retired years ago, their family sold the shop – it was owned by a big company now, a horrible place – but he still went out for special occasions, every now and then.

Freeman told her to go on.

He'd never been to the Hawthorns. Twenty-five years now since they all watched the cup final together, and in all that time he kept an eye on the team's results – he'd never have admitted it, but he cared about it because it mattered so much to young Matthew – and he wanted to go along now. He'd heard about the play-offs. He wanted to see for himself. He might not get another chance.

Freeman closed his eyes and shook his head.

He told her to leave it with him.

He's managed to get them a place in the disabled section, down the corner between the Halfords Lane and the Brummie Road, where a line of wheelchairs are parked behind a low wall. His old man's come along too – Dad insisted on being there – and he also insists on sitting next to Mr Singh, so they can chat about the match.

Aasha looks good, dressed in jeans and a woolly blue jumper, wearing contact lenses in place of her old specs her face and her bearing mature, maternal. She's bought her dad a brand new Albion shirt from the club shop, all thick and thin barcode-stripes – it's the fashion these days – and the Sandwell Council logo on the front. She helps him pull it on over his own sweater, spending half a minute puzzling out how to get his turban through the collar with no small help from Freeman and his old man, the pair of them stretching the collar out until it fits. Dad shakes his head and raises an eyebrow.

– Ya cor tek im anywheer, can ya? Oi, Parama, this is the last time ah gew dressin yow up.

– Bob, if things ever get so bad that I need someone to dress me, I promise you'll be the last person in the world I ask.

– Oh, hark at im! Yow hear that, Matthew? I ay good enough ter be his butler, now!

– A good butler would be able to make a decent cup of bloody tea now and then, Bob.

Freeman looks over at Aasha, and they share a smile. Everything's the same, and yet nothing's the same. It's just one of those jokes time tends to play on you.

At least the match build-up's barely changed down the years. *The Liquidator* plays over the tannoy as the teams run out to warm up. The noise around the ground builds by degrees as they close in on kick-off, swelling into an incoherent bellow of tension and anticipation by the time the ref blows his whistle.

It could be 1978 or 1966 all over again.

Albion attack the Brummie Road End in the first half. They weather an early spell of Swansea pressure – that relieved, derisory *AAAAAH!* echoing round the Smethwick End every time the Welsh side miss a chance – and after ten minutes, Ian Hamilton picks up a loose ball on the left flank and chips it infield with his right foot; Kevin Donovan cushions a first-time header into the path of Bob Taylor, and Super Bob runs into the box, squaring the ball hard and low for Andy Hunt to slide in and knock the ball into the bottom corner.

The Brummie Road surges in the sunset, the goal-roar louder than anything Freeman's heard in a long, long time. Mr Singh raises his arms in silent triumph, and Dad bangs a metal walking stick on the ground. Aasha's got her hands over her ears, but Freeman reaches up and takes hold of them gently, pulling them away.

– Trust me. Yow'll get used to it.

They're all square on aggregate, but they need a winning goal. They spend ten minutes hunting for it, trying to finish the job while they've got the momentum; Super Bob manages to get onto a through-ball after a mistake by the Swansea defence, and he tries to wrong-foot the keeper, place the ball just inside the near post, but Roger Freestone gets down quickly and tips it wide.

And as the Swansea defence argue among themselves, Kevin Donovan wanders over to the corner flag just a couple of yards in front of them, and plays a short ball to an unmarked Ian Hamilton, who takes a touch, then curls a shot in from an acute angle right into the far corner.

The joy. The relief. The noise. Darren Bradley walks into the goal with his arms outstretched, grabs hold of the net and hangs onto it, grinning up at the ecstatic melee in the Brummie Road.

As Mr Singh lifts a clenched fist again, and his dad bangs his stick against the wall in front, Freeman looks up at the home end. The supporters up there have started boinging again, and he can see the entire stand moving up and down with their weight. The lights up in the roof flicker with each jump. It's not long before chimes over the tannoy herald an announcement from the club:

Supporters in the Birmingham Road End: please refrain from boinging, as you are in danger of causing fatal structural damage to the stand.

There are a few subdued seconds as that message sinks in.

Then a colossal cheer rippling up the terraces – as loud as if Albion had scored a third goal – and in unison, the Brummie Road starts an even louder and more determined boing, the lights flickering and structure shaking all over again.

BOING BOING, BAGGIES BAGGIES, BOING BOING

They keep attacking, through the first half, into the second. They score from a Darren Bradley header after Bernard McNally floats a cross into the area, but the linesman flags for an imaginary offside which has Mr Singh loudly threatening to chase after the blind bugger in his wheelchair.

They've only got a one-goal cushion on aggregate. If Swansea score, it'll be extra time and penalties to come. And Albion keep them at bay without any trouble until Micky Mellon, already on a yellow, goes in with a high boot on Russell Coughlin, studs showing, straight into the knee.

The ref pulls out the second yellow, then the red.

Albion have to see out another half an hour with ten men.

BOING BOING, BAGGIES BAGGIES, BOING BOING

Freeman's supported the team through far worse than this. Most of the folks in the ground tonight have seen them through thick and thin. Some were carrying the coffin for Bobby Gould last year. Some were here on Boxing Day in fog so thick you couldn't see past the halfway line from the Brummie Road, relying on the muffled cheers from the Smethwick to let them know Albion had managed a 2-0 win. Some travelled down to Exeter in January, thousands packed onto an unroofed terrace with a salty wind filling their lungs, boinging while the Devon side went 2-0 up – their fans singing *YOU'RE NOT FAMOUS ANYMORE* – and still boinging when Albion came back to win 3-2.

They've been through far worse. They can do it.

BOING BOING, BAGGIES BAGGIES, BOING BOING

They stay tight at the back. They play the ball out along the floor when they're in possession. They try and counter-attack. They get through one-on-one with Freestone in the Swansea goal twice, and he stops them both times: once denying Andy Hunt, once Darren Bradley. For six minutes, Paul Raven has to leave the pitch for attention to a head wound, and Albion struggle on with just nine men. Swansea miss chance after chance until Raven comes back on, and it's just starting to feel like they might come undone, like they could fall at the very last hurdle.

And then Colin West – Swansea's ex-Albion striker – stamps on Ian Hamilton's leg after a tackle, and earns himself a straight red card. It's ten versus ten, and chants of *CHEERIO, CHEERIO, CHEERIO* follow a sick-looking West all the way down the Halfords Lane tunnel.

BOING BOING, BAGGIES BAGGIES, BOING BOING

They chant until the end. They cheer until the end. Dad and Mr Singh are both pumping their arms up and down in the air, shouting *BOING BOING* as loud as they can but still being drowned out by the Brummie Road. Aasha can't sit still, and she's shouting *CLEAR IT! CLEAR THE BALL!* even when the ball's nowhere near the Albion goal. And Freeman's just trying to enjoy every moment, right through the dying minutes, trying to imprint all of this in his memory, because this is what freedom's all about. This is what you miss. The excitement, the tension, the expectation; he savours it all until the final whistle, when all hell breaks loose.

Fans pour onto the pitch from every stand. Tannoy announcements asking supporters to stay on the terraces go gloriously unheeded. Freeman stays where he is, behind his dad, next to Mr Singh and Aasha. He watches with a smile as fans mob the players, stripping their shirts and shorts off them, leaving them pegging it into the dressing room in their boots and boxers.

WEMBERLEE! WEMBERLEE!

WE'RE THE FAMOUS WEST BROMWICH ALBION AND WE'RE
GOING TO
WEMBERLEE! WEMBERLEE!

They stay as long as they can, watching all of the joy and the chaos, watching Bob Taylor get hoisted onto the shoulders of the crowd in front of the Brummie Road, and half a dozen coppers having to retrieve him from the celebrations so he can get back to the dressing room.

SUPER, SUPER BOB
SUPER, SUPER BOB
SUPER, SUPER BOB
SUPER BOBBY TAYLOR

When they finally make their way out, to the popping of fireworks in the streets outside, Freeman asks Mr Singh if it lived up to his expectations. Those brown eyes glance up at him, amused, somehow making him feel seven years old all over again.

– My expectations never mattered, Matthew. What actually happened; that's the important thing. And what happened was something to be very proud of.

Aasha rolls her eyes.

– That means he had a really good night, Matt. And he wants to thank you for it.

He looks at Aasha, and she mouths her own *thank you* silently. He nods.

It's never easy, going back to things which have caused you pain in the past. There are so many mistakes, so many missed chances, so many might-have-beens there to taunt you. It's never easy, but it's worth doing.

Because when all's said and done, there's freedom in being able to let go, too.

*

They're all together at the gymnasium, queuing up for the changing room, kit bags in their hands. The whole place stinks of sweat under a thin mask of cheap deodorant, walls stained by shower gel and soap lobbed at teammates' heads, the usual dressing room stuff.

That's not what the Allsorts are about. It never has been. They wait their turn, and then they treat the changing room like Buckingham Palace. Big Wayne – the bloke they used to call Rolo, once upon a time – unzips his Slazenger bag and pulls out a packet of No Frills chicken crisps, shaking them. The others shake their heads and grin. It's a nice reminder of the old days, but there won't be a ritual. They're past all that.

They don't need a ritual to be a team anymore.

Dan takes his coat off and waits for the others to notice the t-shirt he's got on underneath. Chris spots it first. He squints to read the small print, and that gets the others going too; Raj leaning round the corner of the pegs, Big Wayne peering over the top of his crisps, even young Bilal – still a bit of an outsider, here in place of his brother – glancing over.

ME?

WHEN I WAS BORN, I WAS BLACK
WHEN I GREW UP, I WAS BLACK
WHEN I'M SICK, I'M BLACK
WHEN I CATCH THE SUN, I'M BLACK
WHEN I'M COLD, I'M BLACK
WHEN I DIE, I'LL BE BLACK

YOU?

WHEN YOU'RE BORN, YOU'RE PINK
WHEN YOU GROW UP, YOU'RE WHITE
WHEN YOU'RE SICK, YOU'RE GREEN
WHEN YOU CATCH THE SUN, YOU'RE RED
WHEN YOU'RE COLD, YOU'RE BLUE
WHEN YOU DIE, YOU'LL BE PURPLE

*AND **YOU** CALL **ME** COLOURED?!*

It gets them laughing. He knew it would. As soon as Raj got in touch with him, Dan knew this would work.

The Allsorts have got unfinished business.

It's no walk in the park, their local five-a-side league. There are lads who take this seriously, who make even the most vicious of the schoolboys fifteen years ago look like choirboys. Still, there are more black and Asian faces in the teams now, and you don't often get the looks, the snide comments or the hissed abuse. Sometimes Dan feels like it's still there, but just hidden better nowadays. Maybe that's progress. Maybe.

He's never lost his faith – he had his own baby boy, Laurence, baptised just last month, and invited Chris to be godfather – but there are dark times, moments when he wonders if God's finally given up on humanity as a bad job. There are times Dan wouldn't blame Him for giving up, but then, forgiveness is divine. That's what he always tells himself when things weigh on him, at home, at work. When he gets tired of the everyday headache of policing, when he gets fed up of feeling like some kind of racial ambassador, put in a uniform to appease guilty consciences, not to be an actual copper. Forgiveness is divine. And above all, if you can go to sleep every night having made a bit of difference, having made tomorrow's world a slightly better place for your son to grow up in, then it's worth all the stress and more.

– Come on, fellas. Five games unbeaten! Less mek it six tonight!

Chris claps his hands together, doing his Mr Motivator business, puffing breaths in and out and jogging up and down on the spot in his shirt and shorts. They keep their expressions as serious and focused as they can until he turns away, and then they grin and roll their eyes at each other, same as always. He never changes, Chris.

No, that's not true. He does change. They all do; everyone changes somehow, through the years. Big Wayne with his exercise programmes, starting to get himself in shape; Raj finally getting himself off to university in the autumn, studying for an art degree; Chris meeting Alison, laying off the booze, making plans for the future. But still, there are some things which stay the same, for better and for worse. Chris has never got over thinking of himself as some kind of captain, a heroic leader. A man who hasn't even spoken to his own parents in years, and he still reckons he's got it all sussed. He's a good bloke and he's a mate, but that doesn't stop him being a dopey bastard sometimes. But then, everyone's like that to one extent or another. Forgiveness is divine.

There's a shout from outside, telling them the match ahead of theirs is into stoppage time, telling them they're nearly on. They gather by the door. Big Wayne straps his gloves on. Bilal looks up at the ceiling and whispers a prayer for his brother. Raj whistles the Star Wars theme. Chris stretches his legs out, getting his groin and hamstring muscles ready for what's coming. Dan puts his hand over his chest, feels his heart beating there, and remembers that he's blessed, today, always.

The Allsorts are prepared. They're going to play. They're going to fight. They're going to do it today, next week, next month, next year.

They're going to do it until they win, and after that too. Because some things are worth more than winning.

*

It's a cool Sunday in late May. It's alarm clocks set early, breakfast curdling in nervous bellies. It's superstitions obsessively observed. It's photographs before setting out, scarves and shirts on, boinging for the camera. It's the big day.

It's a decade of decline leading to one spring afternoon. It's a club on its knees trying to stand up again. It's a town mauled by problems beyond its control, finding something to pin its hopes on.

It's an armada of cars heading down the motorway. It's horns beeping and scarves fluttering from windows. It's BOING BOING, GOING TO WEMBLEY stickers plastered on rear bumpers. It's supporters' coaches rocking from side to side at seventy miles an hour as fans party inside. It's Everton in '68 all over again. It's Oldham in '76 all over again. It's forty-two thousand West Bromwich Albion fans descending on the capital city, painting the roads blue and white on the way.

It's the 1993 Barclays League Division Two Play-off Final.

It's the home of English football. It's a crumbling old stadium with abysmal facilities. It's delirium in spite of Wembley's decay, twenty-three years since Albion's last visit fuelling excitement and anticipation. It's a legion of Baggies taking over every pub in the area, crowding round to cheer the team coach as it drives up Wembley Way, and chanting *WHO ARE YA?* when the Port Vale coach pulls up after it.

It's the same walk beneath the twin towers and through the turnstiles that it was in 1968. It's ten thousand Port Vale fans gathered at one end of the stadium, surrounded by empty seats, their tickets left unsold. It's Albion fans filling every other space inside Wembley, faces painted, replica shirts on, flags waving, boinging with all the life and passion in them.

It's nerves and fear. It's tension and stress. It's Kevin Donovan missing a string of first-half chances. It's Port Vale working the ball around well, filled with the confidence of two league wins over Albion this season. It's fags being chain-smoked. It's feet tapping, twitching, waiting for the breakthrough.

It's goalless at half-time.

It's cat-and-mouse free-kicks and corners. It's confident goalkeeping by Tony Lange and Paul Musselwhite. It's a chance with half an hour remaining: Andy Porter losing the ball for Port Vale, and Ian Hamilton picking it up. It's Ian Hamilton launching a spectacular ball upfield for Bob Taylor, and Super Bob in a race against Vale centre-half Peter Swan. It's Peter Swan desperately hacking Taylor down as he loses the race. It's the referee walking over and reaching into his pocket. It's the Albion fans chanting *OFF, OFF, OFF, OFF, OFF.*

It's a red card for Peter Swan.

It's Peter Billing on to plug the gap in the Vale defence. It's one-way traffic in spite of the substitution. It's Kevin Donovan putting a cross in from the Albion left with twenty minutes to go, chipping the ball in for Gary Strodder six yards from goal. It's Strodder hitting the post with his header, and Musselwhite punching the rebound out to the edge of the box. It's Super Bob picking the ball up on the right flank, playing it back to the eighteen-yard line for Nicky Reid. It's Nicky Reid floating it first-time, right-footed towards the six-yard box.

It's Andy Hunt heading the ball straight into the top corner which Jeff Astle scored in a quarter of a century ago.

It's pandemonium around Wembley. It's flags, banners, scarves, inflatables in the air. It's boinging on old seats and terraces. It's sprained ankles and even the odd broken bone as people fling themselves into the celebrations. It's a deafening rendition of The Lord's My Shepherd from tens of thousands of throats.

It's the feeling of a long nightmare finally coming to an end.

It's Vale hunting for an equaliser in the last ten minutes. It's a stretched defence, a stretched midfield. It's a counter-attack surging upfield through Kevin Donovan. It's Donovan passing to Nicky Reid on the edge of the area. It's Nicky Reid smashing the ball over Musselwhite into the open goal, putting Albion 2-0 up, turning to his teammates with arms raised.

It's certainty. It's relief. It's chants of *WE ARE GOING UP*. It's heads bobbing up and down all through the stands, forty-two thousand Albion fans boinging from the pitchside fences right up to the terraces' dark summit.

It's not over.

It's Reid bombing up the right flank again in stoppage time. It's Reid's cross finding Super Bob's chest, and Super Bob falling into a fifty-fifty tangle with Neil Aspin. It's the ball breaking free for Kevin Donovan.

It's Donovan slamming home the third Albion goal from point-blank range. It's Donovan running over to the fans. It's Donovan kneeling down, flexing his bicep, tongue stuck out, a smile plastered across his face.

It's full-time.

It's the team walking up the steps to the royal box. It's Darren Bradley – whose goal against Woking was booed by the Brummie Road two and a half years ago – leading them up there. It's Darren Bradley lifting the trophy. It's a measure of pride and self-respect for a town starved of both for too long.

It's more boinging. It's clenched fists and wild embraces. It's champagne and tears.

He drove down to Wembley alone, and he leaves alone. He braves the London traffic for a quick tour of some old sights, places he saw in days long gone – back when he was a young man with a mind full of ignorance and a mouth to match – filled with bitter thoughts on a sweet evening. Filled with memories of a woman he once tried to rescue, and couldn't.

He drives back up the motorway in the lingering daylight, trying to recapture the elation he felt inside the stadium, trying to shake the sadness which has replaced it. Nothing does the trick. He wishes she could have been there. He wishes she could have seen it.

He doesn't think about it so often these days – it's been a long time, and he can't change what happened – but the letter which dropped onto the mat during the week has had him moping all over again. It's not like he hasn't tried to move on with his life; for a while, he got through girlfriends at the same rate Albion were getting through managers (though unlike Albion, he was never quite desperate enough to climb into bed with Ron Saunders). But with every single one, it always went back to square one sooner or later. There came a point when he decided that square one was probably as good a home as any, and just stopped rolling the dice.

The letter's waiting for him when he gets home, when he slings his car keys onto the table, when he takes his scarf off and hangs it over the back of the armchair. There are a lot of questions in it. Some he knows the answers to. Some, he doesn't. He's going to reply, but he doesn't know where to begin, so he's been putting it off. But it's time he wrote something. She deserves that much, at least.

Jonah sits down, picks up a pen and a blank pad of paper he bought from the 99p shop yesterday. He scribbles his address at the top, and the date. Then he looks again at the letter he's replying to. The apologies for contacting him out of the blue; the moans and gripes about living with a father who's a total wanker; the hesitant questions about her mother, about her life, how well Jonah knew her. The awkward, juvenile signature down the bottom.

Yours sincerely, Emma Riordan.

He stares up at the ceiling for a few moments, then touches the nib of the pen against the pad and writes: *Dear Emma.*

It's a start.

April 1994

The light barely breaks through the gloom. Thousands up the Brummie Road End stare down the pitch at the far goal, at the bare ground beyond. The old terraces curve round from the Rainbow Stand, past the corner flag, and then end abruptly in a jagged concrete lip behind a temporary construction fence: everything past that is just piles of earth and sand, bricks and bulldozers. What used to be the Smethwick End. It was used for the last time on New Year's Day, in a 1-1 draw against Luton. Then it was torn down.

After today, the Brummie Road will be gone too.

This is the future: a wrecking ball crashing into every home end in England, while grand designs and blueprints for all-seater stands are mapped out in boardrooms. Because the terraces are deathtraps; hazardous and sometimes lawless places where people can suffer serious injuries, and even lose their lives. And yet more often than not, they're full on Saturdays, even during the poorest of seasons, even when seats in more expensive parts of the ground are empty. Because in spite of the discomfort and the occasional danger, people love to stand and sing for their team. In spite of the risks, terrace culture is a vital part of football.

By August, it'll all be gone. But today, for one last time, the Brummie Road is having some old-fashioned fun.

It starts with Super Bob getting the ball over on the right flank, putting in a cross for Andy Hunt to knock down, and Kevin Donovan tapping in from a few yards out. A handful of workers on the Smethwick End site cheer the goal, waving their hard hats in the air just like blokes once waved their flat caps on the same rough embankment.

THE LORD'S MY SHEPHERD, AH'LL NOT WANT
HE MEKS ME DOWN TEW LIE
IN PASTURES GREEN; HE LEADETH ME
THE QUIET WATERS BY
THE WEST BROM! THE WEST BROM!

They go through all of the old favourites as Albion scrap to keep Grimsby out, to snatch the 1-0 win, to make sure they get the three points which could be crucial for survival. There's plenty of boinging – although Jonah's sure that fad'll wear itself out sooner or later – and songs from every decade of the Brummie Road, some recycled to include new names. They devote a few minutes to the Holte End, who sing and shout about things they know fuck all about. They devote a few more to Steve Bull,

~ 315 ~

and his penchant for scrap metal collecting. They even find time to make a few cheerfully wild allegations about Karren Brady's bedroom habits. It'd be a normal Saturday up the Brummie Road, if not for the fact that it's the last ever Saturday up the Brummie Road.

When the final whistle goes, everyone stays put. Some carry on singing, as if the sound alone will keep football from its path of self-destruction. Some stand and look all around them, trying to memorise every detail, keep it safe in their minds. There are stewards and coppers coming onto the terraces and posing for photos with fans. Some blokes have managed to smuggle in hammers and chisels, and they knock lumps of concrete off the terraces for people to take home with them. One man climbs up onto the Woodman Corner scoreboard and manages to make off with the painted throstle perched on top.

Everyone wants the Brummie Road to survive somehow. After years of Saturday afternoons, after days and nights spent here with mates, with sons or dads, with wives or girlfriends; after so much blood shed defending these terraces, after so many songs roared to turn matches on their head, to coax the team to so many victories, they don't want to give up. They want it to live on. And as Jonah turns to leave – with the stand slowly emptying out, blokes finally accepting the inevitable – a familiar voice up by the exit starts singing once again. He looks up and spots Bill there, his arms stretched out above his head.

ASTLE IS THE KING
ASTLE IS THE KING
THE BRUMMIE ROAD WILL SONG THIS SONG
ASTLE IS THE KING

He rushes up the terraces to shout after him, to catch up – it's been ages now, years since he last had a proper chat with Bill, what with him getting so reclusive, holing himself up in that little flat – but by the time he reaches the exit, and looks around, Bill's gone.

He kisses his hand and taps the exit sign for the last time.

*

Jonah makes good time out of the gates, onto the Birmingham Road. He doesn't want to be late. They could have picked any time, any place to meet, but it had to be here. He wanted her to come to the match, but she said it would only get her down. For today, she wants to leave the past where it belongs, and think about the future.

He said that was fine. Whatever she needed.

~ 316 ~

He meets her up by the petrol station, twirling his car keys in his fingers. He wasn't sure what to expect, but he likes what he sees. She looks nervous, but she smiles when she spots him walking over.

He takes a deep breath, and smiles back.

– Aroit, missis. Long time no see.

April 2002

– Am yow ready?

John knocks on the bathroom door, rattling the wood. He gets like this before a match, especially an important one. I spit toothpaste into the washbasin and shout back.

– I'll be out in a minute.
– Well, gerra move on, eh? They'll be here soon.

I look in the mirror before leaving the bathroom. It's become a habit, a routine over the last eight years; just a few seconds to build my confidence, a few words whispered to remind myself how far I've come to be here now. It's been a hard journey. It's been a struggle. But it's been worth it.
A horn beeps outside.

– Roit, come on! Get yer arse in gear, missis!

I open the door, and he's practically hopping from one foot to another, eager to be out the house and on the way. He's off down the stairs like a little kid. I follow him at my own speed, making every moment one to remember.
The car's parked on the kerb, Gary in the driver's seat, waving through the window. The passenger door opens, and Emma gets out. She rushes round the car to the pavement, and puts her arms around my neck.

– Hi, Mum!

John opens the car door and whistles.

– Come on then, Kath. When yam ready.

*

I needed help.
I needed so much help. But for a long time, I didn't get it. Even after John made it into the house that Friday night and called an ambulance; even after I was taken to hospital, kept under observation, given a psychiatric assessment, the problems didn't end.

They'd only just begun.

Too many doctors treated medication as a holy grail; a non-stop, ever-changing cocktail of pills which dulled my senses but left the rot behind them untouched. And as I lost custody of my daughter, and lost control of my life, my mind got worse and worse.

I lost years to illness, years when even my closest friends thought the person they'd known was gone for good. Even John gave up hope in that time. But these illnesses can be cured, like any other. It takes patience. It takes time. You can find yourself opening doors you wanted to keep shut forever. But if you work hard, and you concentrate on making small steps, taking each day as it comes, things can get better.

I'll never get back Emma's childhood. I'll never get back any of the time I could have spent living my life. But even though the past's passed me by, these days, I have a future.

And on days like today, that's enough.

*

It's a long drive through heavy traffic into town. West Bromwich has come to life over the last eight days. Since last Saturday, when Igor Balis lashed home a penalty to give us three points at Bradford – keeping us ahead of Wolves going into the final match – the whole town's been in a fever. Beat Crystal Palace today, and Albion will be a Premier League club. Lose, and Wolves could still snatch it from our grasp.

– We'm gunna be fine, guys. Doe fret. Ah can sense it. Come fower o'clock we'll be loffin. Loffin!

– If you say so, love.

– Ah do. Easy win all the way. An Big Dave'll put that gobby Clinton Morrison intew orbit, ah tell ya.

The pubs are full and the high street's chaos. It's not just the promise of the Premier League after all these years in the doldrums; people are proud of this team, the side that Gary Megson's built on a tiny budget. They're a team the fans can relate to. The local boys like Darren Moore – Big Dave – born and raised in Handsworth, with a mother who works at Sandwell Hospital, caring for West Bromwich folk every day. The foreign players like Igor Balis, who moved here from Slovakia and lives in town, on the Wigmore estate, with ordinary Albion fans for neighbours. The old faces like Bob Taylor, still poaching goals ten years after he first signed, still earning the Super Bob chants from the Brummie Road most Saturdays.

– Hey, when we get promoted, ah bet we'll be expanding the stadium, addin plenty more seats. Em, Gaz, yow pair'd best get ter work mekkin a new baby Baggie!

– John!

– Calm down, Kathryn. Juss gi'in em a bit of encouragement.

People on their way to the match are surrounded by family and friends. It's the same on any matchday, but with a game like this one, it's even more important to watch it with people you love, to share every moment with them. I'm lucky to have the family I've got. Life with John isn't perfect, but it's enjoyable, and I know I can rely on him. Seeing Emma is the highlight of any week, even though she's spending loads of time with Gary; they're typical newlyweds, never wanting to leave each other's sight. He'll be off to Afghanistan soon, and Emma says she's not worried – it's a short operation, and the army have got everything under control; he'll be safe as houses out there – but I can see the trace of dark circles around her eyes, the beginnings of anxiety and doubt. I've told her that if she ever wants to chat about it, she can tell me.

We can't always get rid of these burdens, but we never have to suffer them alone.

– Theer they am. Oh, bloody hell, woss he wearin?

– It's a cowboy hat.

– Ah can see iss a cowin cowboy hat! Why's he gorrit on?

– I might be wrong, but I think he was wearing it the day I first met you.

Bill looks gaunt and frail. He doffs his tattered old blue cowboy hat to John as we walk up to him; beneath it, his hair's completely gone. He shakes hands with John.

– Aroit, Jonah!

– How bin ya, mucka?

– Cor complain. Hey, look at me; ah'm match-fit nowadays! If iss still 0-0 after an hour, Megson's gunna bring me on as a sub!

– Well, at least tek the hat off befower ya gew on.

– Ya loike it? Jude dug it out a few weeks agew, gid it me fer me birthday. Still got the old rosette on it, an evrythin. Amazed iss survived this bloody long.

– Ar, well. Built things ter last back then, they did.

We head down to Dartmouth Square, to the place which used to be Broadhead's cake shop when we were kids. These days it's a Pizza Hut. Given the choice of crying over that or filling our bellies, we go for the fourteen-inch vegetarian bonanza. Sometimes that's the way; you just have to accept change and make the best of it. But sometimes you can make a stand and protect things worth preserving. The trick is knowing which battles to pick.

Jude's the expert on that, and she meets us inside the restaurant; she's a curly head of greying hair these days, busying herself with local politics, finally trying to change the world through the unlikely medium of Sandwell Council. John gives her a hug, and I plant a quick kiss on her head. Then she grabs hold of Bill's hand and gives it a squeeze. She's got a new husband now, a new life, but all the same, she won't give up forty years of friendship. Not when Bill needs someone. He spent so long ploughing a miserable furrow when they split up, so long blaming himself for everything, believing that he'd never done anything but hurt the people around him.

It may be late in the day, but Jude and Chris have picked him up and set him right. It's been awkward, but somehow, just for now, they've made themselves into a family again.

– So. Woss in store fer us, Jonah? Promotion today? Premier League title next year?

– We wo win the title next year, mate. Atta wait until at least 2004 fer that. But we'll show that Premier League, ah tell ya. We mighta spent sixteen years away, but ya wouldn't think we'd bin gone a minute. We'll be loike a duck ter water up theer.

– A dog ter water.

– Ya what?

– A dog ter water. Thass what yow allwis say, Jonah. We'll tek tew it loike a dog ter water.

– No, Bill. Iss a duck ter water. Iss definitely a duck. An by the way, mate; yam welcome ter call me John.

We chat about old times for a while, until Chris shows up with Alison and some of his old football mates. John shakes hands with one of them – the policeman, Dan – and asks how big Neville's getting on these days. While they're catching up, Jude tells the story of how she first woke up in hospital the day Chris was born, after an emergency Caesarean, and the first thing she saw was Bill dancing round the ward with baby Chris in his arms, singing For Once In My Life.

Chris smiles, embarrassment flushing through his face as Alison pinches his cheek and laughs. It's not been easy for him either, or for Bill and Jude. It broke their hearts, all those years he spent avoiding them, refusing to speak to them. He finally made his peace with Bill a couple of months ago, and Jude soon after.

Then he came to see John one day in March.

There was a lot for them to say to each other, but like typical blokes, they managed to avoid saying most of it. In fact, they spent more time talking about the match at Bramall Lane and how much they hated that bastard in the Sheffield United dugout than sorting out who they really are. Maybe it suits them that way; I've never really understood men, and I doubt I will any time soon. But if nothing else, I suppose it's inspiring that two people can overcome all obstacles and forge a new relationship purely through the common human bond of despising Neil Warnock.

Before he left, I asked Chris what he'd said to Bill when he last saw him. Chris told me that when he was a lad, he used to sit in his bedroom and listen to Albion playing UEFA Cup matches on the radio. And Bill used to come in and perch on the end of his bed, listening to them with him, sharing every second, celebrating every goal by dancing round the room with him. And when all's said and done, nights like that are what made him Chris's father.

Nothing else matters.

*

The Hawthorns is full to the rafters. The gates are still covered in scarves tied to the railings in memory of Jeff Astle, the King, who should have been here to see the club he loved on their big day, but instead lost his life to his sport. The terraces are long gone, but every seat in the ground is taken, every ticket sold.

There may come a day when the Birmingham Road End is nothing but a quiet shell of what it used to be. There may come a day when football supporters in every single stand of every stadium sit meekly in the glare of the television cameras, being seen and not heard. But today is not that day. Today is the 21st of April, 2002.

Today, the Brummie Road is alive.

Scarves and shirts from so many decades are on show, turning the stands a rich blue and white. The flags and banners are out too, waving in every row, and balloons are batted from one hand to another, drifting aimlessly through the air. Generations rub shoulders. Those of us who watched the cup-winning team of the Sixties, those who grew up with the Three Degrees, the youngsters who've never known anything but years of

~ 323 ~

struggle in this place. We're all here, every single one of us standing with arms around each other's shoulders, bouncing up and down as if the seats all around us were never invented.

BOING BOING! BOING BOING! BOING BOING!

The sun comes out in time for kick-off, and nerves squeeze at stomachs as Wolves take an early lead up at Hillsborough. Palace show some fight in the opening minutes, testing Russell Hoult in goal, but Albion keep working hard, keep sending balls into the box. We need a breakthrough to keep the dream alive. We need a breakthrough, and it finally comes after a quarter of an hour with a foul on Andy Johnson in the Palace half.

The free-kick's floated in to Big Dave at the far post; he heads it back across goal, and Riihilahti tries to head it clear for Palace, but he only sends it back over to Big Dave, who side-foots it through the keeper's legs from six yards out.

And Big Dave runs along the edge of the pitch, facing the Smethwick End, two huge arms pumping up and down, letting loose a wordless roar of triumph that they'd surely hear all across West Bromwich if it wasn't drowned out by our own roar.

We lose all of our composure, all of our self-consciousness. It's primal delight. We scream from depths we didn't know we had. We throw our arms around each other. We clench fists and shake them in the air, a gesture older than football, older than the Black Country, older than England.

BOING BOING! BOING BOING! BOING BOING!

Early in the second half, Hayden Mullins fouls Adam Chambers just outside the Palace box, and Neil Clement steps up for the free-kick. He puts his left foot through it, and it sails through a crowd of players, bounces awkwardly in the six-yard box, and Kolinko in the Palace goal spills the catch at the feet of Bob Taylor.

Super Bob plants it into the net without a second glance.

He runs straight over to the Brummie Road with his arms outstretched, because he knows. Just like Ronnie and Jeff and Cyrille and Laurie and Bomber, Super Bob knows what it means. And the whole stadium is noise on top of noise, yelling to bring the heavens down.

THE LORD'S MY SHEPHERD, AH'LL NOT WANT
HE MEKS ME DOWN TEW LIE

IN PASTURES GREEN; HE LEADETH ME
THE QUIET WATERS BY
THE WEST BROM! THE WEST BROM!

We sing and we chant and we watch the minutes tick down, wondering what catastrophe could possibly snatch this away from us; if the world would be cruel enough to end before we achieve what we've dreamed of for so long.

But it doesn't. The final whistle goes, and thousands pour from the stands onto the pitch in the sunshine, Palace fans in the Smethwick End applauding graciously, Albion fans kissing the turf and crying their eyes out as they realise that after so many years of misery, there's still hope in the world.

People change so much over the course of a lifetime. They change their accent, they change their clothes. They change their hairstyle, they change their car. They change partners, they change politics. But once they've found a football club that they love, it stays with them, no matter what the world throws at them. They stick with it until the day they die – their empty place in the stand mourned by everyone around them – and some young supporter fills the spot they left, learning exactly what makes their club special, learning what makes their community something to be proud of, sharing the joy of a matchday with people who matter to them.

And the weeks fly by, from one Saturday to another, and life goes on, like it does.

Acknowledgements

The opening lines of Brummie Road were written in early 2011, and in the four years since then, countless people have looked over various drafts and sections of the manuscript. Each and every one of them is due a pint from me at some point (give me a shout if you're ever in the vicinity of The Wellington, folks) but special thanks go to Tom Coley and Matt Wesolowski, who were ever-present with their feedback, editing and encouragement from start to finish.

A number of books were invaluable in researching distant games and forgotten facts. Simon Wright's *West Brom's Greatest Games* is a superb read covering a lot of the matches which feature in Brummie Road, and a whole lot more which I couldn't squeeze in. Dave Bowler's *Attack Attack* is a great overview of the 1978-79 season, and the excellent *Samba in the Smethwick End* – co-authored by Dave Bowler and Jas Bains – provides crucial background on race relations in the Black Country during the 1960s and 1970s, and the astonishing social impact of Albion's Three Degrees on that landscape. Tony Matthews' *Albion: A Complete Record* is the holy book of all facts and figures for the club and its players from the Victorian era to the present day, and Simon Wright's *Cult Heroes*, though mainly focusing on Albion legends of the past, also provides some excellent anecdotes from supporters about past matches. Lastly, whenever I felt my enthusiasm flagging for the bygone days of football in general, *Got, Not Got* by Derek Hammond and Gary Silke – a terrific, funny and nostalgic look at the golden era of football culture – got me racing for the laptop all .over again.

Where books alone couldn't fill the gaps in my research, I'd like to thank Dave Bowler and Laurie Rampling for the assistance they provided. I'm also grateful for further bits and bobs of advice and support via Twitter from Chris Lepkowski, Simon Wright and Claire Astle.

However, the biggest thanks of all must go to Alan Cottrell – one of the founder members of the Brummie Road choir in 1964 – whose memories, anecdotes and information about the early days of the choir rescued the novel from the scrapheap early in its development. Though the characters in the book are entirely fictional, many of the scrapes and escapades Billy and Jonah go through in the 1960s – including Billy's bout of "smallpox" and their ill-fated hitchhiking trip to London – are loosely based on the actual experiences of Alan and his brother following Albion during the same period. A lot of fans have shared stories with me through the years, but Alan's have always been the very best.

It goes without saying that following the input of all of these learned folks, the blame for any remaining anachronisms, inaccuracies or general inadequacies in the novel should be laid squarely at my door.

*

Jeff Astle – known to Albion fans simply as "the King" – died on the 19th of January 2002, aged 59. For several years, he'd been suffering from degenerative brain disease which gradually left him unable to recognise even members of his own family. In November 2002, a coroner's inquest ruled that the front of Jeff's brain had suffered major trauma similar to that often experienced by boxers, and that the most likely cause of this trauma was the repeated heading of heavy leather footballs in the 1960s and 70s. The coroner delivered a verdict of death by industrial injury, a landmark ruling. Jeff Astle was an ordinary man on a modest income who was ultimately killed by his job; in this case, that job just happened to be football.

In the aftermath of the inquest, the Football Association announced that they would conduct a ten-year study into the potential link between heading footballs and degenerative brain disease, in conjunction with the Professional Footballers' Association. However, this research was never concluded, and no findings ever published. After consulting with neuropathologist Dr Willie Stewart in 2014, and giving him permission to re-examine Jeff's brain – which had been donated for medical research – Jeff's family discovered that the disease which killed him has a name: Chronic Traumatic Encephalopathy (CTE). It's been linked with the deaths of numerous NFL players in the United States – usually caused by multiple concussions or low-level repeated brain trauma – but Jeff Astle is the first British professional footballer proven to have died from the disease, simply by heading a football as a young man.

While Jeff may have been the first, it's highly unlikely that he'll be the last.

At the time of writing, Jeff Astle's family are engaged in a campaign to bring about a positive change for past, present and future footballers. There are other former players in the UK now living with dementia whose families require support. There are clear risks – both immediate and long-term – surrounding head injury in sport, and yet little is done to promote awareness of these risks either among sportsmen or the public. Independent scientific research into brain injury has the potential to increase our understanding of diseases such as CTE, and should therefore be backed by sporting bodies in the common interest of all sportsmen at risk of concussion or brain trauma.

Football failed Jeff Astle. It's now failing others. The sport as a whole needs to confront the issue of head injuries, and do all it reasonably can to minimise the risk of brain trauma, provide robust support for former players living with dementia, and educate people about concussion at all levels of the game.

Visit http://justiceforjeff.co.uk/ to find out more about the Justice For Jeff campaign, and support the ongoing legacy of a man who was, in every way, the King.

Ian Richards, December 2014

Printed in Great Britain
by Amazon